Sweetest Hallelujah

# The Sweetest Hallelujah

ELAINE HUSSEY

Published in Great Britain 2013
Harlequin MIRA, Eton House, 18-24 Paradise Road,
Richmond, Surrey, TW9 1SR



ISBN 978 1 848 45250 3

59-0813

Harlequin MIRA's policy is to use papers that are natural, renewable and recyclable products and made from wood grown in sustainable forests. The logging and manufacturing processes conform to the legal environmental regulations of the country of origin.

Printed and bound by
CPI Group (UK) Ltd, Croydon, CR0 4YY

**Elaine Hussey** is a highly acclaimed and award-winning novelist who has written under the names Peggy Webb and Anna Michaels. She was born and bred in the south and is from Mississippi, where *The Sweetest Hallelujah* is set.

In memory of my parents, Clarence and Marie Hussey,
who gave me everything.

# One

THE DAY BILLIE'S LIFE changed, she was already knee deep in trouble.

She'd been playing with Lucy after her mama had said not to. Lucy's little brother, Peanut, had something that was catching, but Billie wasn't the kind of scaredy-cat who would stop seeing her best friend just because grown-ups said so.

To make sure her mama didn't know, Billie told Peanut if he opened his trap about her being over there, she'd make him sorry he was ever born. He believed her, too. Around Shakerag, the other kids knew that if they messed with Billie she'd beat the snot out of them.

Calling out, "Bye, Lucy," she set out for home. But the only way there was past dead Alice's tree.

Billie hadn't even been born when they found the body of eleven-year-old Alice Watkins up in the woods behind Gum Pond cut into six pieces. Still, she knew the stories. Everybody in Shakerag did. Somebody with a heart black as sin had snatched Alice from Tiny Jim's juke joint right out from under her daddy's nose. Then he'd done his dirty deeds and got clean away.

Alice was still hanging around like some avenging angel.

She'd warn you when something bad was about to happen. You'd hear the harmonica in Tiny Jim's Blues and Barbecue all over town, the sound so mournful you'd feel defeated. The smell coming from his barbecue pits got so strong you'd close your curtains and stuff towels under the door to keep the scent from driving you crazy. And if you were caught out in the street like Billie, at the mercy of winds that suddenly shook the trees and rattled the trash cans in the alley, you'd feel as if you were made of glass. One look from a stranger could crack you in two.

Billie started running. Everybody knew the boogie man got bad little girls first.

She ran as hard as she could past Tiny Jim's juke joint and barbecue place where Alice's arms had the longest reach. The moaning notes of the harmonica poured so loud out the door she put her hands over her ears. It wasn't any great surprise that when something awful was afoot, blues swarmed around his place like clouds of angry locusts. Tiny Jim was dead Alice's daddy.

Billie pumped her long skinny legs into double time. With the blues breathing down her neck, she rounded the street corner so fast she nearly tripped on a crack. She flailed her arms to regain her balance, but something even worse was up ahead—Alice moaning in the cedar tree by A.M. Strange Library. When she took up residence in a tree, the birds hushed singing. They'd leave nests shaded from the sun and safe from predators to perch on power lines where anything in the air could swoop down and carry them off. Even the squirrels gave up their high-wire acts when Alice was near.

It was a wonder Alice would even come to the library, dead or not. Mean old Miz Rupert laid down so many rules, you might as well stick your fingers out so the librarian could slap them as you walked through the door. She even acted like she owned the books. Billie only went when her mama made her.

Billie sped past the library toward the neighborhood park. Struck by a bright idea, she veered through the entrance so fast she fell and tore the right leg of her homemade shorts. Now she'd have genuine evidence she'd been playing in Carver Park like she'd said she would. Her mama would think she'd fallen right through the sliding board. It was rickety as all get out. Everybody fell through if they didn't mind their p's and q's.

Billie stomped around in the sand pile till she got enough sand on her shoes to look convincing, and then she flew out of the park and up the steep hill past the Mt. Zion Baptist church.

When she cut down Maple Street, Billie did a victory jig. Home was safe. A house painted robin's egg blue. Though she liked the color of Lucy's house best, yellow like sunshine, she was proud of where she lived. It was the only house on the block that didn't need painting. *A neglected house ain't nothin' but a sign of pure dee laziness,* her grandmother always said.

Everybody called her grandmother Queen, including Billie. She ruled the roost. If you walked into Queen's house, you'd answer to her, no matter who you were. She was probably waiting behind the door now to ask Billie a gazillion questions. She'd want to know about every minute Billie hadn't been under her watchful eye.

Lollygagging, Billie waved at Miz Quana Belle Smith watering petunias on her front porch next door.

"How's yo sweet little mama doing, chile?" the old woman called.

"Fine, thank you, Miz Quana Belle."

Billie couldn't put off going inside any longer. If she stayed in the yard, Miz Quana Belle would keep her the rest of the afternoon asking foolish questions. Waving once more, Billie skipped up the steps and eased open the door.

The house smelled like lye soap and fried chicken. As if Billie needed further evidence that Queen was in the kitchen bent over an iron skillet with a dishpan of soapy water nearby, she heard *Ma Perkins* on the Philco radio giving her silly advice. Queen never missed an episode.

As far as Billie was concerned, the only good thing about *Ma Perkins* was that she might cover up the sound of a little girl who didn't like rules, sneaking down the hall.

"Is that you, Billie?" Queen hollered.

"Yes, ma'am." Queen would whip you if you didn't mind your manners. And talking polite topped her manners list.

"Has you been playing with Lucy?"

Billie could hear her grandmother shuffling around in the kitchen. She crossed her fingers behind her back. Everybody knows if you tell a lie that way it won't count. "No, ma'am."

House shoes scuffed on worn linoleum, and then Queen herself appeared in the kitchen doorway carrying with her the scent of sugar and grease. She was tall, voluminous and black as a stovepipe. Her eyebrows looked like two gray woolly worms above her dark eyes, and her grizzled hair stuck out every which way. You'd be scared to death of her if you didn't know how she'd read the Bible to you every night, then sing you to sleep.

Billie tried not to squirm while her grandmother looked her up and down. "How you done tore them shorts?"

"In the park."

"Mmm-hmm," Queen mumbled. "That Peanut's got spinal meningitis. If I catches you over there I'll whup you good. You hear?"

"Yes, ma'am. I hear."

"All right, then." Queen wiped her hands on a big bibbed apron. "Be quiet, now. Yo mama's sleepin'."

When Queen went back into the kitchen, she left behind

the scent of supper—fried chicken, boiled okra and fried apple pies, Billie's favorites except for the okra, which tasted like slime. She grabbed the paper off the hall table, then tiptoed to her room. Now was her chance to read the comic strips before Mama and Queen separated the paper into a gazillion sections. *Beetle Bailey* was her favorite, but she liked *Dennis the Menace,* too. He wasn't scared to try any adventure.

She plopped onto the homemade quilt on top of her bed. Queen had let Billie pick her own design, and she'd picked Wedding Ring. Someday she planned on marrying and having four kids. And you could bet your bottom dollar they'd have a daddy in the house, not some long-distance daddy you'd never seen and only heard about when the other kids in the neighborhood yelled things like *prison brat* and *yo daddy ain't nothin but a jailbird.* That was the main reason Billie had earned her quick-fisted reputation. She didn't know if her daddy was in prison or not, and Queen and Mama wouldn't tell her. Either way, she wasn't about to let anybody say dirty rotten things about him.

Billie perched on the bed among her treasures—a shoe box with a blue rhinestone earring she'd found on the ground near Glenwood Cemetery at the south end of Shakerag, half a robin's egg shell fallen from a tree where Alice had been seen, a red bird's feather Billie might glue on her summer straw hat, and two smooth white rocks she'd found along Gum Pond—another place her mama had told her not to go.

She thought the rocks had been dropped by angels. They were close to the place where Alice had been murdered. Everybody said angels kept watch over children who wandered up that way. Billie knew it was true. She'd caught glimpses of their golden crowns and heard the flutter of their great white wings.

She put the angel rocks in her lap, and then she opened the

paper to the comic section. When she did, the scent of barbecue seeped under the windowsill, drifted along the floor and swirled up her legs. Billie's stomach lurched. It was one thing to have barbecue and blues in your house when there was a pile of ribs on the table and somebody in the corner with a blues harp in his mouth. But it was something else when Queen was making fried chicken, and there wasn't a rib or a harmonica in sight.

Lucy had said her mama was cooking chit'lins the night Peanut smelled dead Alice's barbecue. And look what happened to him.

Billie's hand shook as she tore a page off the newspaper. She was cramming it under the windowsill when she spotted the date: July 23, 1955. Last week's paper.

Queen probably had this week's edition in the kitchen with the recipes whacked out. As Billie hurried in that direction, trying to outrun the bad thing that wanted in, she heard voices from behind her mama's closed bedroom door.

"Betty Jewel, you can't keep that newspaper hid forever." Queen sounded like she was on her high horse.

Billie's mama said something in reply, but she couldn't hear what it was.

"When you gone tell Billie?"

*Tell her what?* she wanted to know. Billie tiptoed to the door and put her ear to the keyhole.

"I can't, Mama. Not yet. I want to get it all settled first."

"I been prayin' for a miracle, baby."

"Oh, Mama. There are no miracles for this kind of cancer. You might as well accept the truth. I'm dying."

The words ripped into Billie like bullets. If she had been Lucy she'd have screamed. But what good would it do? Her lips trembling, she kept her ear pressed against the keyhole, but Mama and Queen had quit talking. There was the sound of shuffling and the bedsprings groaning. Queen was probably helping her mama up. Billie slid away from the door, but she wasn't fast enough.

"Billie?" Her mama was suddenly there, her color drained so low she looked like a white woman. Queen towered behind her. "Honey, what's wrong?"

Her mama stood there like she expected some kind of answer, but Billie couldn't get past the news of death long enough to think up an excuse for being outside her door. That didn't stop the woman who could spot bad intentions a mile away and see a lie even before you told it.

"Oh, Lord. Billie, what are you doing out here in the hall?"

Billie couldn't see a thing the Lord had to do with it. He didn't take folks with little kids who wanted to grow up with a mama. He took people who were too old to get in their flower beds in the spring and plant their Canadians. Like Queen.

"I'm on the way to the kitchen to get something to eat."

"Supper will be ready in a minute. There's no use ruining your appetite."

"You're mean and I hate you!"

Her mama looked at her like Billie had split her heart in two, but she didn't care. Why would her mama die and leave her? She wanted to smash everything in sight.

"Young lady, if you speaks to yo mama like that again, I'm gone get my switch and wear you out."

Queen was older than God. She had a peacemaker for her heart and rheumatiz in both hips, but you could bet she'd fight tigers before she'd allow any sass from the likes of little kids like Billie. If she didn't mind her p's and q's, Queen was going to catch on that she'd been listening at keyholes again.

"I'm sorry, Queen."

"I ain't the one needs no apologizin' to. You better tell yo mama you sorry fore I skins you alive."

"Wait a minute, Mama. Something else is going on here."

When her mama squatted down, Billie hid inside herself where she buried the knowledge that was still screaming through her like a tornado. Outside she became a smooth, clear lake, not a ripple on the surface.

"I'm sorry, Mama. Can I go outside now?" The dark circles under her mama's eyes scared her. Up close Billie could see her trembling hands and her hair falling out in patches. Her mama looked like something awful had grabbed a hold and was eating her piece by piece while Billie had been off paying no attention. "Please?"

"Billie, were you listening at the keyhole?"

There was no use denying it. Queen might be the one with the switch, but Mama was the one with the bulldog attitude. She never let anything go.

"You're not dying!"

"Oh, baby." Her mama folded her close, and Billie held on. Maybe if she held on long enough, she could transfer her strength to her mama. "I've been meaning to tell you. I just didn't know how."

"The doctors can give you medicine." Her voice was muffled against her mama's shoulder. "They can make you well."

"They've tried, Billie. There's nothing else the doctors can do."

"No! It's not true!" Billie tore herself away and raced past them to the rusty bus parked in a roofless shed under a black jack oak in her backyard. She climbed the ladder attached to the side, then sat in the green plastic lawn chair on top of the bus. She was in her own place now, high up in the sky. The fading rays of sun felt comforting, like God's eyes peering down through the oak leaves. Alice wouldn't dare show up in a tree already occupied by God.

Billie gazed upward where she imagined the Holy Face

would be. "You gotta make my mama well." Did God listen to little girls who eavesdropped at keyholes and told lies? "If you make my mama well, I promise to be good." She made a sign over her chest. "Cross my heart and hope to die."

Quick as she said it, Billie wished she hadn't. What if God reached down and snatched her off the bus? She'd never get to see Queen and her mama again.

Billie didn't want to be an orphan. Orphans didn't have mamas to plait their hair in cornrows and make sure they wore clean socks and remind them to say their prayers at night. Maybe God was punishing Billie for not minding her mama.

"I promise I won't go to Lucy's again when Queen tells me not to. And I won't tear my shorts and tell lies about hating my mama."

Tasting the salt from her own tears, Billie swiped at her face with the sleeve of her T-shirt. "I know I'm not a good little girl, God. But please, don't take my mama."

If God heard her, He'd send a sign. That's what He did in the Bible. Maybe it would be a rainbow. Billie looked up through the limbs of the oak tree, waiting.

# Two

LOVING SOMEBODY WAS THE most dangerous thing Cassie knew. When you lose them, they take so much, it's a wonder you don't become invisible. She'd always prided herself on being in control, and yet here she was in a psychologist's office trying to keep herself from coming unraveled.

"Cassie, when the jackass is in the ditch," he said, "don't ask how he got there—just get him out."

It took her a while to digest this piece of advice. For one thing, she had a hard time thinking of herself as a jackass. For another, she was in a ditch that had no way out. She couldn't change being a widow because Coach Joe Malone was dead. No amount of wishing would bring him back.

"Get out of the ditch, Cassie."

The no-nonsense advice was typical of Sean O'Hanlon. That's one of the reasons Cassie had chosen him, that plus the fact that he was a hometown man with a Purple Heart displayed on his bookshelves. Sean had served at Guadalcanal. You could trust a man who had risked his life to save others.

"I can't see that I'm in a ditch, Sean. I'm just feeling a little blue. And even that makes me feel guilty."

"Why?"

"I'll never have to worry about my future the way poor old Eleanor Cleveland did when her husband went off the bridge."

Cassie was the only heir to the fortune her daddy had made farming a thousand acres of cotton. Still, Joe's death had consigned her to spend the rest of her life alone in a house that rattled with regret.

"That's no reason to feel guilty," Sean said. "What else is bothering you?"

"I could never have the one thing I wanted most. Joe's child."

She pictured the Empty Room, meant to hold a crib and bookshelves stuffed with teddy bears and dolls and books about Winnie the Pooh.

Sean waited, a kind man whose mere presence opened up a floodgate.

"After Joe's death, people kept telling me, *You're lucky to have such a full social life.* If I have to plan one more charity event or sit through another book club discussion on *As I Lay Dying,* I'm going to run down the street naked, screaming."

"What do you want to do, Cassie?

"I want to discuss *Lady Chatterly's Lover.* I want to write something besides wedding and obituaries at *The Bugle.* I want to march down the streets knocking on doors and telling anybody who will listen that women can do more than put Faultless Starch in their husband's shirts."

Maybe she was born out of her time, and that, as much as loss, was the reason her sister-in-law, Fay Dean, had caught her standing in her closet last week with Joe's sweatshirt stuffed in her mouth, crying.

Waiting for Sean to speak, Cassie smoothed a wrinkle from her slacks. Her pants were barely socially acceptable, a small defiance that suited her right down to the bone.

Sean reached for a doughnut from the edge of his desk then passed the box to her.

"What's wrong with me, Sean?"

"Nothing. It's perfectly normal for widows to feel pain and loss acutely around the first anniversary of a husband's death."

"Joe was too young to die. It was his birthday. I was planning a party for him."

She'd been in her flower garden gathering roses for the centerpiece when all of a sudden she'd heard a harmonica, haunting as the mixture of poverty and violence and hope in Shakerag. Her heart had separated from the rest of her body and landed at her feet among the scattered rose petals, bleeding.

Common sense told her that on a still summer day it was possible for the music in Tiny Jim's Blues and Barbecue to reach her prestigious Highland Circle neighborhood, separated from Shakerag only by Glenwood Cemetery and a block of modest houses that belonged to middle-income whites. But Cassie not only knew the legend of Alice Watkins, she'd been there eleven years ago when it was born. She'd been filling in for the crime reporter at *The Bugle* that day and had used her press pass to gain access to the parents, Tiny Jim and Merry Lynn Watkins.

For two weeks, the murder had been the talk of the town, and then the case was closed. In 1944 with a world war raging and a town strictly divided by a caste system, Alice Watkins was just another little colored girl who'd disappeared. The only thing left of her was Cassie's story, "Avenging Angel," which had spawned a legend. Her yearning could still be heard in the blue notes that haunted a town.

A year ago, standing in her garden with the soulful sound of a harmonica ripping her heart out and turning her blood to an elegiac river, Cassie had known the source of her foreboding was Alice, stripped of justice and restless for vengeance, predicting a disaster too terrible for even a sometime crime reporter to imagine. By the time Joe's best friend, Ben, had arrived to tell her Joe had died of a heart attack while he pulled a catfish from Moon Lake, Cassie had already let go of the idea of a birthday celebration and was standing among the fallen rose petals, paralyzed with pain.

Funny how you sometimes know a thing before it happens, how you can be going about the ordinary business of living when suddenly you feel electrocuted, shocked with the certainty that your world has just tilted sideways and you are about to fall over the edge.

Cassie was feeling that way now. The faint strains of a blues harp crept under the windowsills, overtaking her with a truth that was both heartbreaking and inevitable. There was no escaping the past. It was stitched to the future as surely as the thick rubber soles were attached to her black-and-white saddle oxfords.

"Cassie, before I see you again, think about finding a project that will fully engage your interest and your energy."

"Thanks, Sean."

"When you see Fay Dean, tell her I said hello."

Feeling the emptiness of her womb and the loss of her husband like a severed limb, Cassie left Sean's office. Her car was parked under a chinaberry tree out front, baking nonetheless in the blistering heat. The summer was turning out to be a scorcher, with the temperature hovering around ninety degrees.

Before she stepped off the porch, she checked to see if anybody was watching. Old Mr. Hanneford was walking his dog, an ugly shepherd that had lost most of his hair when Mrs. Hanneford dropped dead in front of the dog house last year. In spite of the fact that Mr. Hanneford was half blind and hard of hearing to boot, Cassie ducked back onto the front porch and stood behind Sean's potted hibiscus till the old man was out of sight, not because she cared who saw her but because she didn't want some busybody spreading gossip that would mortify her dear father-in-law, Mike, who believed if you had problems, you solved them yourself.

As soon as she was back in her car—a red Ford Coupe convertible she'd helped Joe pick out last year only two weeks before he died—she felt unplugged, as if somebody had jerked her life's cord out of its socket and left it lying on the floor for anybody who took a notion to come along and step on. She was glad she'd agreed to meet Fay Dean at TKE Drugstore's soda fountain for ice cream.

As Cassie drove through the dusk toward the heart of downtown Tupelo, the soulful music followed her, the blues notes whispering of love lost and lives wasted, of yearning and hatred, of a gathering storm roaring toward a town unsuspecting and unprepared.

She parked near the courthouse one block north of TKE Drugstore on the corner of Main and Green, then breathed in the beauty of a place she loved. Magnolia trees with trunks as impressive as river barges surrounded the domed building, and a towering monument honoring the Civil War dead stood in the southwest corner of the lawn. On the east side, the town's shoe-shine boy, known only as Tater, sat on one of the park benches, waiting to earn a few nickels from the lawyers who argued best in shiny shoes.

Cassie got out of her car to wait. The courthouse was a convenient place to meet Fay Dean, who had become a lawyer in spite of Mike's protests that a woman's rightful place was in the home and the town's gender bias that a woman was too tender and not intelligent enough.

Fay Dean proved them all wrong. She had carved out a

niche for herself when she successfully defended Cassie's gardener, Bobo "Chit'lin" Hankins, pro bono, for helping himself to a corn patch that didn't belong to him.

In Shakerag, they called Fay Dean Superman in a skirt. In the courthouse, her male colleagues called her names even Cassie wouldn't want to repeat.

Vivid as a lightbulb, Fay Dean descended the courthouse steps, carrying herself with the supreme confidence of a woman who knew everything worth knowing. At the sight of her, Cassie's unease faded into something manageable, angels whispering in her ear.

"I need chocolate." Fay Dean was the kind of woman who skirted greetings and got right down to the nitty-gritty. "A triple dip."

"Why?"

"Substitute for sex."

"I don't think it's a substitute, Fay Dean. Just supposed to make you feel good or something."

"How'd it go with Sean?"

"I sat there blabbering, and he essentially told me to find a project."

"Same thing I've been saying. What do you think?"

"He could be right. I need to get my mind on something besides the inane chatter at the Altar Guild."

"I told you Sean would help you." Fay Dean linked arms with Cassie. "He's asked me out."

"He'd be a great match for you. Did you say yes?"

"You know me. I'm a disaster with relationships."

"Fay Dean, what am I going to do with you?"

"Feed me."

Heads turned as they walked under the streetlights, and Cassie knew they weren't looking at her. She was an ordinary-looking woman who blended in except for her hair. But Fay

Dean had that certain *something* her brother Joe had. When you first saw her, you'd think she was just another dark-haired woman wearing a tad too much lipstick. But she had a way of smiling that lit her whole face. And then you'd think she was the most beautiful creature you've ever laid eyes on.

Cassie had known her since second grade when Fay Dean was the new girl in school. She had the ugliest haircut anybody ever saw. Mike Malone was the new postmaster in Tupelo and had cut it because his wife had died in a hit-and-run accident, and he was experimenting with ways to save money as well as struggling with raising a headstrong daughter and a too-handsome son.

Cassie had been the only second grader who hadn't laughed at Fay Dean's chopped-off hair. When you're seven, that's how easy it is to become best friends.

When you're thirty-eight, it's as easy as taking one look at somebody and knowing what they need without ever saying a word.

A cool blast of air hit them when they walked into the drugstore. Cassie breathed in the familiar smells of French vanilla and rich dark chocolate. She loved this place, the embossed tin ceiling, sixteen feet high, antique ceiling fans hanging down on sturdy brass poles. It was one of the oldest buildings in town. Thankfully, the owner had an eye for keeping the best parts of the past intact. The brass foot railing around the serving counter in the drugstore was original. So were the floors, uneven oak boards that always smelled of the oil rubbed in to keep them from turning brittle.

She and Fay Dean found two empty stools at the soda fountain and placed their orders, cherry Coke for Cassie, chocolate soda for Fay Dean.

"How did Glen Tubb's fundraiser go last night, Cassie?"

"The men talked politics while his wife herded the women into her rose garden to talk about women's issues."

"The way you're gritting your teeth, do I even want to know the women's issues Myrtle discussed?"

"Mamie Eisenhower's bangs."

"That's not surprising. Not many women in this town know much about politics, or even care."

"I know. I guess I ought to be ashamed of myself."

"Why? What did you do?"

"I told them that I don't care if Mamie wears bangs or shaves her head—I want to know what this country can to do to support last year's Supreme Court ruling that struck down racial segregation."

"They'll keep fighting it," Fay Dean said. "Fools!"

"I'd write an article if I could find a way to sneak it past Ben."

Not only was he Cassie's next-door neighbor and Joe's best friend, but he was her editor.

"You know Ben only indulges your opinions because of your friendship."

"Hush up. Maybe it's because of my brain."

The man on Cassie's right got up and left a rumpled copy of *The Bugle* behind. Cassie thumped the photographs on the front page, candidates running for state senator. "Just look at that. All men. You ought to run, Fay Dean. You'd be a better senator than the lot of them."

"I'd be laughed out of town. It's bad enough that I had the audacity to hang out my shingle and practice law."

"That makes me so mad I could spit nails." Cassie shook the paper as if it were the whole town and she was trying to shake some sense into it.

"I believe you occasionally do. In *The Bugle*." Heads always turned when Fay Dean laughed. The sound was as full as the brass section of an orchestra.

"Ben tries to keep a leash on me. Do you know what he wants me to do now? The *classifieds*."

"Is Goober Johnson retiring?"

"Thank the Lord, yes." Intent on showing Fay Dean exactly how insignificant her new job at *The Bugle* would be, Cassie snapped the paper open to the classifieds. An ad buried between Refrigerator for Sale and Free Puppies ripped into her like shrapnel.

"They're renaming the baseball field after Joe tomorrow. If we're not there, Daddy will have a stroke. Do you want me to pick you up?"

Staring at the ad, Cassie was thinking about love, how it can be the arms that catch you when you fall or the hands that open wide to set you free.

"Cassie? What's wrong?"

Cassie couldn't speak, could hardly breathe. The little ad had settled into her heart like tea leaves, and she knew she'd never be able to remove the stain.

*Desperate. Nowhere to turn. Dying woman seeks mother for her child. Loving heart required. Call Vinewood 2-8640.*

One look at the newspaper, and Fay Dean read Cassie as if she were a story she planned to use as counsel for the defense.

"Come on." She grabbed Cassie's hand.

"Where are we going?"

"To do something I should have made you do years ago."

# Three

BILLIE LOOKED UP THROUGH the oak leaves to see if God was hurrying up with some answers. But it wasn't God's voice she heard: it was Queen's.

"Billie? Where you at, chile? I got supper."

She leaned over the edge of the roof to see Queen standing by the bus with a plate covered by a blue-striped dish towel.

"I'm not hungry."

"I'm gone leave it here, just in case."

Queen set the plate on an old tool bench leaning against the side of the backyard shed, then lumbered back to the house. The screen door popped behind her, and the smell of fried food drew Billie down the ladder. She gnawed off a hunk of chicken leg, then balanced the plate and climbed back to the top of her daddy's old touring bus.

She'd bet if her daddy was here, he'd find a way to make Mama well. She'd bet he knew famous doctors. Her daddy was famous himself. Or used to be. Saint Hughes was a blues great. Ranked right up there with King Oliver and Louis Armstrong. They said the Saint with his silver horn could sway an audience like a preacher at a Baptist tent revival.

Queen and Mama didn't tell Billie hardly anything about

her daddy. What didn't come from the kids taunting her in the neighborhood came from Lucy. She'd got the information by hiding under her front porch and eavesdropping on Lucy's mama, Sudie Jenkins, and dead Alice's mama, Merry Lynn Watkins. Both of them were Mama's friends, and you could bet they knew the truth.

When Billie was little she never thought about not having a daddy. She thought normal was a household of nothing but women. It was after she got to noticing that other little girls had daddies to lift them up so they could see things like parades and stars and birds' eggs in a high-up nest in a magnolia tree that she started asking about her own daddy.

Mama would never talk about him, and Queen followed suit. She thought Mama's every word got handed down on Mt. Sinai from the Lord God Himself. If Queen knew Billie was even thinking such mean thoughts about religion, she'd make her memorize the Ten Commandments word for word. And she'd know if Billie got it wrong, too. Queen knew the Good Book from cover to cover. Mostly, she knew about spare the rod and spoil the child. She kept a willow switch behind the kitchen door.

What Queen didn't know was how a girl of six needed to understand why her daddy didn't tuck her in at night and how a girl of ten needed to know her roots.

The first time Billie had ever asked about her daddy, Queen said, "Don't go worrying yo mama 'bout such stuff," and Mama just said, "He's gone."

"Dead?"

"No, just not here."

"How come?"

"Just let it alone, Billie."

But she hadn't. When she got old enough—eight and a

half—she and Lucy started spying, sneaking around at Sunday dinners and church potluck suppers listening at keyholes.

What Billie didn't overhear, she made up. She pictured him as a darker version of Roy Rogers, only without the white hat and Trigger. She figured she got her height from her daddy. Her mama was only five five, and that's if she stretched her neck. Another thing was Billie's skin. She freckled in summer, so Saint Hughes had to be light-skinned. Mama was dark, considering her French daddy, and Queen was blacker than the ace of spades.

Billie also liked to think it was her daddy who picked out her name. She imagined him thinking about all the stars he'd performed with, then choosing the most beautiful, most talented of all, the great jazz singer, Billie Holiday.

Once when Billie had asked Lucy's mama about the Saint, she'd said, "He dropped from the American jazz scene," then went back to feeding her husband's Sunday shirt through the washing machine wringer. Billie liked to think of her daddy traveling around Europe playing his silver trumpet.

Celebrities don't have time for ordinary lives. Why, some of them hardly know their kids. Billie didn't know any of them personally, but she kept up by reading *Modern Screen* magazine in Curl Up 'n Dye, the beauty shop where Lucy's mama did the shampoos and swept up the fallen hair.

Billie used to hope her daddy would send a birthday card, but she got over it last year. You can't just spend your time crying over spilled milk. Queen said that all the time.

The only thing her mama ever shared about her daddy was this bus. It had been on Billie's fifth birthday.

"Back when I was singing with the Saint and his band, we used to travel in this bus," her mama said. Then they all piled in, Mama at the wheel, Billie riding shotgun and Queen with a big basket of fried chicken. They drove to the

Tombigbee River where they swam till their arms got too tired to lift. Afterward, they spread the picnic on Queen's quilt called Around the World, and ate till Queen said they would all grow feathers and start clucking if they didn't pack up and go home.

When the bus wore out, her mama was going to get rid of it, but Billie had a conniption fit, and Betty Jewel built a shed out behind the house so the bus wouldn't be an eyesore. She called it her potting shed and Queen called it her henhouse. Billie made her leave the roof off the front end on account of the clever rooftop patio her daddy had devised on the bus. He had built the ladder with his own hands and added a shiny brass railing around the top.

Though the railing would never shine again, Billie kept it polished. It was the least she could do.

Billie ate till every last piece of Queen's fried chicken was gone, then she set in to eating fried pies. A curtain of darkness dropped around her, but Billie wasn't scared. She wasn't scared of anything except her mama dying.

She was probably in the house right this very minute asking the Good Lord to make her well again. Billie would like to know what was good about Somebody who'd let her mama die. If He was in charge of things, how come nice people got cancer while folks like Miz Quana Belle's daddy lived to do their meanness till they got so old they didn't have teeth? He drank hard liquor and robbed gas stations. How come God didn't strike him down?

Billie couldn't ask Queen about such stuff or she'd get the business end of her willow switch.

There was nobody she could ask. Except maybe her daddy. If she ever found him.

Billie just knew the Saint would come back and live with them and pay a fancy doctor to make her mama well and they would all be a family, especially when she proved that she wouldn't be a bit of trouble. She could cook, and she'd learn to do his laundry.

She could even polish his silver trumpet. And maybe, if she was really a good girl and didn't tell lies, he'd let her play it. Maybe he'd buy her a silver trumpet, then they'd sit under a sky hole-punched with a billion stars and send a blues duet up to a moon so awesome it felt like God watching. It felt like being on top of the world.

Betty Jewel would never have let her daughter find out the truth from listening at keyholes, but now that it had happened she didn't have to pretend anymore that she was going to live. Somehow that was a relief to her. She was so tired. She was tired of pretending everything was going to be all right, tired of getting out of bed in the morning, tired of trying to live up to everybody's expectations.

*You're not dying!*

That was Billie's expectation, and it was so fierce Betty Jewel worried that when she actually did die her daughter was going to do something crazy, such as run away from home. Nobody knew whether Saint was still in prison or God knows where, but Billie might find out about his family up in Chicago, everyone of them crazy as Betsy bugs and that sister of his—that Jezzie—mean as a yard dog.

Drawing her crocheted shawl about her, Betty Jewel walked to the window. The old bus looked like a hulking animal, something extinct, a dinosaur. When her eyes adjusted, she could make out the slight figure of her daughter perched on top, a little brown sparrow getting ready to fly.

"Baby?" She turned from the window to see Queen standing in the doorway, her face shrunken as a dried-up apple.

Betty Jewel's cancer had sucked the regal and the jovial right out of her.

"Did she eat, Mama?"

"She done got that plate I took out. But she settin' up there like she don' never inten' to come down."

"Don't worry. Billie's got a head full of sense."

Queen stood in the doorway till she couldn't bear the view any longer. And who could blame her? The disease had eaten away so much of Betty Jewel she looked like a one-dimensional cardboard copy of her former self.

Her old house slippers dragging on the linoleum, Queen shuffled off singing, her way of trying to make bad things good. Always she picked a spiritual or one of the gospels. She'd belt them out, too, though it had been twenty years since she'd had the voice for the soaring solos she used to perform in church. Tonight she was singing, "Somebody's Knockin' at Yo Door."

Death, that's who was knocking. Still, Queen's expectations were softer and easier to bear than Billie's. *Lord, chile, I ain't seein' no way I can carry on without you. You gone have to hang on a mite longer.*

Queen was eighty, the age where death could come without warning. She was at least twenty years older than you'd expect Betty Jewel's mama to be. But she'd been the last of Queen's twelve children and the only one to survive. Since they'd found out the cancer was too far gone, Queen had told Betty Jewel the only reason she was still living was so she could help take care of Billie awhile longer.

*Till you finds somebody, honey. You gotta find somebody to raise that chile. Saint ain't fittin'.*

Betty Jewel shivered so hard her teeth knocked together. *Ain't fittin'* wouldn't begin to describe the reasons she'd sell her soul to the devil before she'd let Saint Hughes get his hands on Billie.

Saint and his devil ways got into her head as bad as they had the day she'd flown off the handle and taken out that pitiful newspaper ad. Lord, what had she been thinking?

*Desperate. Nowhere to turn.*

She was desperate, all right, but she'd chop off both her legs before she'd put her child in the hands of strangers. What she needed was some of Queen's divine intervention. But miracles were hard to come by in Shakerag.

"Please, God..."

Her head was pounding, so heavy with despair and secrets she didn't know if she could ever lift it again. Or was the pounding at the door?

Before Betty Jewel could get out of her chair, Merry Lynn and Sudie barged in, Merry Lynn leading the way, waving *The Bugle* like it was a red flag and she was searching for the bull.

"Betty Jewel, what is this?" Sudie cried.

"My, God. You're trying to give Billie away like a stray cat!" Merry Lynn flung the newspaper onto the couch and sank down beside it. The aroma of barbecue that always clung to her almost overpowered her Evening in Paris perfume. "Are you out of your mind?"

Betty Jewel had asked herself the same thing a million times. In the light of Merry Lynn's rage and Sudie's look that said *We're going to have a come-to-Jesus talk,* Betty Jewel's reasons for the ad drained of all plausibility—Queen losing her health, Sudie's husband, Wayne, losing his job and Sudie sitting on Betty Jewel's front porch, crying a river of fear, and Saint... Lord Jesus, the idea of Saint's sorry ass in charge of Billie was enough to drive anybody crazy.

"Not yet, Merry Lynn. I think the cancer likes to get beauty before brains."

"That's not funny, missy!"

"Both of you just hush up. There's no need for any of this." Sudie's quiet voice reminded Betty Jewel of the hymn, "There is a Balm in Gilead." In her white blouse that always smelled of starch and sunshine, she might be one of God's earth angels, a placid, plain woman put down in Shakerag to keep volatile, broken-to-pieces Merry Lynn from self-destructing and to ease the storm-tossed mind of a dying woman who didn't know where to turn. "God forbid Betty Jewel's name is called, but if it is, I'll help Queen raise Billie like she was one of my own."

"What makes you think you'd be better than me? Good God, Sudie, you've got seven kids already."

Betty Jewel wrapped her hand around the harmonica in her pocket and held on. Two years ago this kind of sparring would have had all three of them laughing so hard they'd have to hold on to each other for support. Today she couldn't unearth normal if she got a spade and dug all the way to China.

"I can count, Merry Lynn," Sudie said. "And if Queen hears you taking the Lord's name in vain, she'll whip your sassy butt with a willow switch."

"Queen knows I don't have any truck with the Almighty. If He's watching over His children, why was my Alice murdered? How come somebody took her off to the woods and did those unspeakable things, those..." Merry Lynn covered her face with her hands, a mother whose sorrow was so deep she'd mired in it years ago and never found her way out.

"If you start bawling in front of Betty Jewel in her condition, *I'm* gonna be the one whipping your tail."

"What condition?" In one of those mercurial changes she was famous for, Merry Lynn wiped her tears and turned her fierce attention to Sudie.

Betty Jewel held on to the harmonica. It was time for a come-to-Jesus meeting of her own.

"I'm dying, Merry Lynn." Betty Jewel lifted her chin a notch and dared her to deny it. "And it's high time you face it." She didn't miss the way Sudie put on her mask of denial. "You, too, Sudie."

"There's going to be a miracle." When it came to faith, Sudie was just one notch below Queen.

"Lord knows, Queen's prayed hard enough. But if my mama can't call down a miracle, nobody can."

"Shut up! Both of you just shut up!" Merry Lynn sprang off the couch, lean and wild and fierce, a black alley cat with claws bared. "You're not going to die. I can't stand any more dying!"

Making soothing noises the way you would to a baby screaming with nightmares, Sudie put her arms around Merry Lynn. "Of course, she's not going to die. She's going to get better, that's all. We'll find a doctor up in Memphis."

If they'd just let Betty Jewel talk about it. If they'd just quit denying the truth that had been staring them in the face since Christmas. She was so weak she'd had to quit her cleaning job at the Holiday Inn, and her blue dress didn't touch her anywhere now except the shoulders. She looked like a willow twig wearing a pillowcase.

And cold. Lord, she was cold all the time. While Sudie waged a battle to save Merry Lynn's sanity, Betty Jewel sank into a rocking chair, pulled Queen's hand-knit afghan over her knees and listened to her mama in the kitchen taking refuge in the old hymns—"Rock of Ages" and "I'll Fly Away."

Betty Jewel wished she could fly away. She'd fly backward to a time when she had it all—her health, her future. Love.

Thinking about what might have been hurt so bad she turned her focus elsewhere. The clock. She could hear the too-loud ticking of the big mahogany clock Queen kept on top of the TV.

And the sound of Merry Lynn's sobs. She was crying quietly now, saying, "I can't stand it," over and over.

"It's all right. I'm taking you home." Sudie herded Merry Lynn toward the door. "Betty Jewel, you rest up, then you call in a retraction to that stupid ad. And if you don't, I will. If anybody has to take Billie, it's gonna be me. You hear me now?"

"Loud and clear, Boss."

In spite of the fact that plain, petite Sudie looked as if she wouldn't say boo to a cat, she'd always been the leader in their circle. The three B's, they'd called themselves—brains, Betty Jewel; beauty, Merry Lynn and boss, Sudie. They let themselves out, and Betty Jewel thought she ought to get up and check on Billie, but she didn't have the strength to walk to the window. Snatches of her mama's song floated down the hall. Queen was singing "Dwelling in Beulah Land" now, an old hymn that promised the downtrodden some blessed relief.

What relief was there when your meager savings were running out and the only income you had was from the three people in Shakerag who could afford piano lessons and the pies your ancient mama sold at Tiny Jim's?

Betty Jewel leaned her head back, drifting on the melody to a better time, a sweeter place.

Suddenly the phone rang, jerking Betty Jewel upright.

Queen hollered from down the hall. "You want me to get that, baby?"

"I'll get it, Mama." The afghan slid to the floor, but Betty Jewel didn't stop to pick it up for fear she'd miss the caller. The phone was perched on a faux maple telephone table by the couch. She was so out of breath when she got there she could barely speak.

"Betty Jewel?"

"Oh, my god."

"Betty Jewel, is that you?"

She should tell him, *No.* She should jerk the phone jack out of the wall, then sit back down in her rocking chair and pretend that Saint Hughes was not on the other end of the line, his voice as seductive as dark honey drizzled over yeast-rising bread.

But he was there waiting, and suddenly she was faced with a new horror. He wanted something from her, and he wouldn't give up. He'd keep calling and calling, and maybe get Billie. And then… She couldn't let her mind go there.

"What do you want?" She didn't dare say his name, didn't dare chance that Queen would hear.

"I want to talk, that's all. Just talk."

Betty Jewel's worst nightmare was coming true. The Saint was trying to weasel back into her life, and she was plunged into a new kind of hell. In the kitchen Queen was singing "Amazing Grace," but all Betty Jewel could think about was taking a gun and blowing Saint to Kingdom Come.

"I have nothing to say to you."

"Well, I got plenty to say to you. You still my wife."

"Are you insane? You were so drunk the day I left it took you two weeks to notice I was gone."

"It's all gonna be different now."

"Are you out of prison? Lord have mercy, tell me they didn't let your low-down hide out of jail."

"Got out last week. I can't wait to be with you."

"I'd rather eat cow shit. Where are you?"

"Memphis." It was too close, only a hundred miles away. Betty Jewel thought she might faint. "I'm fixing to make a comeback. I'm putting together another band, found some great guys on Beale Street. I want you to sing the lead."

"I'm not ever singing with you again. You hear me? Not ever."

"Aw, Betty Jewel. Don't be like that."

She heard the oven door slam shut, knew the pies Queen was making for Tiny Jim were cooking, knew her mama would be washing the dough off her hands and would soon be coming to the den to stretch out on the flowered chintz couch and watch Milton Berle on Texaco Star Theater.

"Can you hold on a minute?" Betty Jewel eased the door shut. When she picked up the receiver, her hands were trembling so hard she nearly dropped it. "You stay away from here. I mean it."

"We were good together, sugah."

In more ways than one. Her legs wouldn't hold her up anymore, and she sank onto the arm of the old couch. "Don't you *sugar* me. You couldn't pay me enough money to sing with you."

"You and me, we got a little girl. What's she like?"

Betty Jewel bit her lip so hard she brought blood. If she screamed, Queen would come running. And Billie. Tiny Jim would have told Saint about Billie. Musicians stick together. "Don't you ever call here again. You hear me? If you dare show your face around here, I'll have you arrested. I'll say you're trying to sell me cocaine."

"You wouldn't do that."

She heard Queen's slow shuffle in the hall. "I swear on a stack of Bibles." Betty Jewel hoped God was not listening. She hoped Queen was not. She'd wash her mouth out with soap, and her a dying woman. "If the cops don't get you, I'll shoot you myself."

She slammed the receiver down and made it back to the rocking chair, but all she could think of was Saint coming to get Billie and Sudie trying to fend him off.

"Pies'll be ready in twenny minnits." The old couch springs groaned under Queen's weight. "Lord, my feets is killin' me."

Years ago when Betty Jewel left Shakerag, who would have believed it would all turn out this way—Queen getting ready to bury her only living child, Billie searching for the truth through keyholes, the Saint resurrected from the awful past, and her sitting in a maple rocking chair with cancer cells eating her alive.

But then what twenty-year-old ever imagines herself dying right at the height of middle age—or any age, for that matter—when all she had on her mind was a man who was fixing to set the world on fire? That was the Saint. Lord, that man was the most dazzling person she'd ever laid eyes on, him all dressed in white up on that stage at Blind Willie Jefferson's juke joint in the Delta, the lights turning him red and blue and green. Like Christmas tree lights. Like one of those chameleons you'd never guess from one minute to the next what color he was going to turn.

Saint Hughes. With his silver tongue and his silver trumpet. When he put that horn to his lips and commenced playing, she'd swear the angels wept. And when he started in on her with his glib talk, there was nothing she wouldn't do for him, including throw away her college education and her blossoming singing career and say *I do* to whatever he asked.

The wedding dress he bought her was white silk. The real thing, he'd said. It wasn't till years later she'd learned it was cheap imitation.

Her ring came from a Cracker Jack box. By the time she'd met him, the once-great jazz legend was already on the skids.

"Someday I'll get you a ring with diamonds big as golf balls," he'd said, and Lord help her, she'd believed him.

She'd believed everything he told her back in those days, including that he was going to reclaim his fame and be rich. It wasn't riches she cared about, though, but the dazzling future he promised.

"I'm going to buy an antebellum house bigger than any high-and-mighty cotton plantation. Miz Queen can sit on a blue velvet cushion and drink tea from a china cup and brag to all her friends that a white woman is gonna be scrubbing her floors one of these days."

Back then, Queen had believed in Saint Hughes, too, but that hadn't kept her from crying her eyes out when Betty Jewel married him. Still, she stood in the doorway and waved as her only surviving child climbed into the old school bus the Saint had painted black with his name in foot-high red lettering on the side. Betty Jewel had thought she was on the way to fame and fortune.

"Baby, I'm gonna take you on a ride you'll never forget," the Saint promised. He'd made many promises, but that was the only one he ever kept.

Betty Jewel closed her eyes and could still see Queen standing by the front porch swing, wearing a yellow voile dress calling out, "Ya'll be pa'tic'lar now, you hear?"

It was the only advice Queen had offered when Betty Jewel left Shakerag, and it wasn't till years later that she wished her mama had offered more. How to stretch two dollars over two weeks without having oatmeal three times a day. How to conjure up a dream when the only hope she had was the Saint, and the only hope he had was the bottle.

Then, later, the cocaine. Demons clawed at that man's back, demons she'd never even seen till the jobs got scarce and the music started going sour.

"Someday we're gonna live on easy street, baby."

It was uneasy street she remembered. That and the long journey that finally brought her back home.

Now she was on another journey, only this time the road she was traveling was fixing to peter out. Already she could glimpse the end. She'd praise the Lord if she was all by herself, but she's not…

She looked over to see Queen staring at her.

"What're you thinking, Mama?"

"I'm just tryin to remember that recipe for molasses cookies. I'd make some if I had me some good black-strop molasses and half the sense God give a billy goat."

Need makes liars of us all.

Still, she smiled at her mama's white lie. And that was a good thing. It was hard these days to find something to smile about, any little thing to take her mind off the future.

For Betty Jewel time had become a pink damask rose, the petals dropping one by one, the fragrance fading till the sweet rich smell of living was only memory. Sometimes an urgency ripped through her like a tornado, and she'd go to the bathroom and stuff a rag in her mouth so Billie and Queen wouldn't hear her scream.

She eased out of her chair and walked over to the window. It was too dark to see the bus, let alone a stick-figure child sitting on the rooftop.

"Maybe I ought to go out there and get her, Mama."

"Leave her be, chile. She's gotta mourn."

Betty Jewel left the window, went to the chest freezer in the kitchen and got this week's *Bugle* from its hiding place under the frozen peas. The last sentence leaped out at her. *Loving heart required.*

There was no way on God's green earth she'd let her child live with somebody who didn't love her. If Queen went before Betty Jewel—God forbid—and Sudie couldn't take Billie, she wasn't going to die. Period. And she'd fight anybody who told her different.

She slid the paper under the peas, then went back to sit down in the rocking chair. Queen was snoring with her mouth wide open. The sound of the clock on the TV came to Betty Jewel, magnified, and she shut her ears to the loud ticktock of time. Her breath sawed through her lungs, and she reached into her pocket for pain pills.

"Lord, if you're going to send me a miracle, you'd better hurry."

# Four

THE EMPTY ROOM YAWNED before Cassie, a graveyard filled with ghosts. There, underneath the window facing the east, was the spot where Joe had put the crib.

"The first thing I want our baby to see is the morning sun." He'd slipped his arms around Cassie and kissed her behind the ear where he knew it tickled and would make her giggle. "The second thing is my beautiful wife."

She'd lost their first child that night, lying in their bed in a puddle of blood while Joe cried.

She'd been farther along with the second pregnancy, almost three months. Convinced they were having a boy, Joe had bought a tiny catcher's mitt to put on the new walnut bookcase opposite the crib. Baseball, his first love. Then he'd added a harmonica. Music, his second love.

Afterward, they'd toasted each other with Pinot Grigio, sitting on the patio surrounded by the fragrance from Cassie's Gertrude Jekyll roses. He pulled a blues harp from his pocket and serenaded her with the Jerome Kern ballad he'd sung for her at their wedding—"All the Things You Are."

"You give me roses," he said. "I give you music."

The next day while he was on a road trip with his baseball team, she painted a pink rose on his B-flat blues harp. She never got a chance to give it to him. By the time he returned, she was in the hospital fighting a losing battle to save their baby.

When she got home, the harmonica with the rose was gone. She never knew what happened to it.

The baby crib, the bookshelves, the miniature baseball mitt and every other hopeful item they'd purchased were up in the attic, consigned to gather dust after her third failed pregnancy. Was that when her relationship with Joe started gathering dust?

Startled, Cassie wondered where in the world that thought had come from.

"Cassie? Did you hear me?" Fay Dean, who had dragged her straight from the soda fountain to the Empty Room, was standing with her hands on her hips and a take-no-prisoners look in her eyes.

"I was just remembering."

"Stop looking back. We're going to fill this room with everything you love. By the time we finish, it will be your favorite retreat."

"I don't know where to start."

"I do. Follow me." Fay Dean whizzed past, marched into the living room and grabbed a rocking chair that Mike had given them as a wedding gift. It had belonged to Joe's mother.

"Wait a minute. I like the chair where it is."

"You're going to like it better where I put it."

Fay Dean sailed out, a ship under full steam, leaving Cassie searching the bookshelves for the photographs she loved best: the one of Joe sitting in the boat on Moon Lake, a harmonica in his hand and his fishing pole in the water; Fay Dean and Cassie, arms linked, Fay Dean in her mortar board when she'd graduated from Vanderbilt School of Law and Cassie in her favorite pink hat, never mind that her mother always said pink clashed with her red hair; Cassie's famous mother, Gwendolyn, and her beloved daddy, John, the year they'd gone to Paris to hear Gwendolyn sing at the opera. It had been the best year of Cassie's childhood. Normally, she and her daddy were left behind while her mother trekked the world.

All these years later—her mother and daddy both long gone—she still remembered wondering why she wasn't good enough to go with her mother. If she'd had children, Cassie would never have left them behind.

As she carried the photos into the Empty Room that no longer qualified for its title, she wondered what her child would have looked like. She'd wanted a girl with Joe's easy smile.

"Cassie? What's wrong?"

"She would have been ten years old." The last baby Cassie had miscarried had been a little girl. "I wonder if she'd have been a tomboy or if she'd enjoy sitting on the bed with me reading poetry."

"Don't do this to yourself."

"After I lost her, I dreamed she was standing in a field of Queen Anne's Lace on Mike's farm, and I was doing a watercolor of her."

"Cassie, if you want to talk about this, I'll listen, but I really think you ought to focus on something else. Maybe you ought to take up painting again."

"Maybe Sean was right about making another appointment to see him." Cassie looked at the pictures in her hand. "I don't know where to put these."

"Leave it to me."

"Don't I always, Napoleon the Second?"

"Yeah, well, without me, you'd never get across the Rubicon."

"As I recall, neither did Napoleon."

Fay Dean had already swept from the room, a woman on a mission.

Cassie set the rocking chair in motion, and Joe stared at her from the picture frame, his smile both comforting and heartbreaking. Had their marriage really been made of stars and fairy dust, or had goblins crept through the cracks?

"I'm going out," Joe would say, and Cassie would look up from her supper, too weary thinking about the forever-closed nursery door to ask why.

*He loves music,* she'd tell herself after he was gone and she was trying to get up enough interest to brush the *moo goo gai pan* out of her teeth. *All blues musicians are like that,* she'd say after she finally found enough energy to crawl into bed. *They go wherever they can find the gut-bucket blues, racial divides as wide as the ocean vanishing in the commonality of music.* Joe had even gone to the Delta once, the cradle of the blues, seeking the old songs, the laments invented in cotton fields by a people with a hoe and no hope.

Later, after she'd climbed out of her depression enough to bury herself with work at *The Bugle,* she'd glance out the window, hoping to glimpse a gibbous moon, that lopsided miracle in the night sky that never failed to lift her spirits. She'd see a blanket of stars and suddenly feel as if somebody had thrown a sack over her head.

Fighting that same smothering sensation, Cassie jumped up and raced to the attic. She wouldn't look at the baby stuff, didn't trust herself. She wouldn't even look at her dusty art-supply kit and her easel, but went straight to the corner where the dressmaker's dummies stood. Grabbing one under each arm, she struggled across the floor. The fold-down ladder presented another problem. Even banishing ghosts of the past didn't seem worth a broken neck.

"Cassie? What the hell?" Fay Dean stood at the bottom of the ladder, craning her neck.

"Thank God." Cassie poked the male dummy down the staircase. "Here. Take Tarzan."

"What are you doing up there?"

"I'm coming down with Jane."

"That explains everything."

Jane bumped down the stairs behind her, and Cassie hoped she didn't lose body parts in the process. Finally, both of them stood at the bottom, Cassie triumphant and the dummy intact.

"Fay Dean, do you remember when I used to sew?"

"Back in the Dark Ages, I believe."

"Keep it up, and I won't be giving you a hand-tailored suit for Christmas."

"If I recall, you don't tailor."

"What's to keep me from learning?"

Fay Dean pumped her fist in the air. "Now, that's what I'm talking about. Soon you'll have so many projects, you won't have time to think of what you've lost."

They dragged the dummies into the room where the white wicker bookcase from Cassie's sunroom now sat along the west wall holding her favorite photographs. She placed Tarzan in the rocking chair, and Fay Dean stood Jane by the bookcase.

"They look natural, don't they?" Fay Dean said.

"They look naked." Cassie went to the hall closet and came back with one of her gardening hats for Jane and one of Joe's baseball caps for Tarzan. Her husband's scent clung to the hat, and he whispered through her mind like a song with lyrics she was struggling to remember.

"Cassie? What is it?"

"Nothing. I was trying to figure out how to get the sewing machine down from the attic."

"Daddy will do it," Fay Dean said. "Let's have something to drink. A celebration."

They kicked off their shoes, linked arms and went into the kitchen where the moon was shining through the window and anything at all could happen.

Suddenly they heard a knocking at the back door.

"Anybody home?" It was Ben, carrying a bottle of Pinot Grigio. "I saw Fay Dean's car in your driveway and thought we might all enjoy a drink."

The bottle in Ben's hand reminded Cassie of Joe, of how they'd celebrated every major milestone with that same type of wine, and how, in a heartbeat, events you think of as triumphant can turn into regret that follows you everywhere, no matter how you try to hide.

Cassie took down three glasses instead of two. They drank their wine while Fay Dean regaled them with stories from the courtroom and Ben chatted about doings at *The Bugle*. If anybody noticed how quiet Cassie was, they didn't say.

Afterward, Ben toted the heavy cabinet-style sewing machine from the attic and moved it around the room four times before Fay Dean was satisfied that it was just right.

When they both left, Cassie sat in the rocking chair staring at the sewing machine. Would her little lost girl have loved pink ruffles on her dresses or yellow ribbon?

# Five

In Betty Jewel's dreams, her daughter was a young woman dressed in a real linen suit with dyed-to-match pumps. She was eating at a restaurant where waiters served sweet tea in crystal glasses and sliced sirloin on china plates.

Betty Jewel jerked awake. Her afghan was on the floor, and the only light in the room came from the pattern on the TV screen. Across the room, Queen had turned sideways, one foot hanging off the couch, an arm flung over her eyes as if she couldn't bear to view her dreams.

Was she dreaming about the years she'd spent cooking other people's meals at the Jefferson Davis Hotel, the extra job she'd taken scrubbing other folks' toilets so she could send her only child to college?

Scooping up the afghan, Betty Jewel covered her mama, then tiptoed down the hall to Billie's room. It took a while before her eyes adjusted enough to see the small lump under the covers. Her daughter had finally come down off that old bus. Betty Jewel said, *Thank you, God,* or maybe she just thought it.

She stood awhile in the doorway, listening to the sound of Billie's breathing. Then she slid across the room as silent as a moonbeam and folded her daughter to her, all fragile bones and sharp angles, the beauty as yet unformed in her freckled face. Betty Jewel was thinking of dark rivers that swallow you whole. She was thinking of deep waters that rush by while you fall down dead in a drifting boat. She didn't want to let go this child of hers. She wanted to hold on to her until they were both very old, and then lie down together in a cool spring meadow and open up like springboks whose brown fur unfurls along the backbone when they die to reveal white as pure as a newborn.

Billie stirred, her voice a sleepy question mark. "Mama?"

"I'm here, baby." Her daughter curled against her, warm and smelling of sweat and summer and little girl dreams.

There was another scent in the room, too. Barbecue. Since Christmas it had taken over Queen's house, seeping into cupboards and behind closet doors and into the dug well behind the house. Every drink they made with the well water had a slight tang of barbecue, even their morning coffee. If Queen noticed, she kept it to herself, and thank God, Billie was too young.

With clouds gathering right over her head and a killing storm on her coattail, Betty Jewel drew a deep breath. If she didn't get off the bed now, she might never be able to. Easing up, she tucked the sheet around Billie's coltish legs. She was going to be tall. Like her daddy.

Betty Jewel closed her daughter's door and went straight to the bedroom she'd once shared with her husband. Since the cancer, she'd become a creature of the night, navigating silently through the dark.

The moon laid down a pale yellow path from the window to the doorway. But it was no hopeful yellow brick road leading to a fix-all wizard. It was an aching road, every step she took uncertain.

As she followed the sliver of moonlight to turn on a bedside lamp, her room gave off the odor of barbecue mixed with cherries. Since she'd been sick, the only thing that tasted right was Maraschino cherries. Empty jars tattooed her bedside table, the top of her dresser and even the windowsill. She gathered all the empty jars and tossed them in the garbage can.

For three weeks, Betty Jewel had been systematically cleaning house, filling cardboard boxes with dresses and shoes, hats and purses, labeling them for Merry Lynn and Sudie and the church charity closet. She'd packed her jewelry for Billie in a cigar box covered with blue velvet—the Cracker Jack wedding ring, the fake pearls and ear studs, the bracelet with charms from each state she'd traveled with Saint and his band.

But it was not costume jewelry that urged her on tonight. Rummaging in her chest of drawers, she brought out a pair of brown socks. At first glance, they looked like every other pair of socks in the drawer, folded double and placed at the bottom of the stack.

Betty Jewel wadded them into her fist, then sat at her skirted dressing table and pulled them apart. A path of moonlight gleamed off the mirror and illuminated the piece of jewelry that tumbled out of the sock.

She'd found it last week. Merry Lynn had picked up Queen to deliver her pies to Tiny Jim's, and Billie had been on top of the bus playing house with her doll.

In her cleaning frenzy, Betty Jewel had been going through Saint's stuff, too. He might never get out of prison, was what she'd been thinking. The law didn't take a kindly view to possession of drugs. And even if he got out, she'd never see him again. Not if she could help it. Any chances that he'd reformed were remote, and even if he had, she'd never been able to trust him, so why start now? One minute he was Prince Charming and the next, the devil himself.

She could sell his good white suit and his silver trumpet and get some much-needed cash to pay her doctor's bills. She'd laid his suit on the bed. It was out of style, but the dry-cleaning bag had kept the shoulders from turning yellow. Tiny Jim could probably help her find somebody to buy it. Nobody in Shakerag was picky about hand-me-downs, especially musicians. If they tried to live by their music, scraping by was all they knew.

She put Saint's good shirt and tie with the suit, then emptied his socks and underwear drawers into a paper sack. The church would get those.

His trumpet would bring her the most money. She might even get enough for the sale to pay off her doctors and have some left over for her funeral. She got his trumpet case out of the closet, then went into the kitchen for a rag to wipe off eleven years of accumulated dust.

Saint had taken better care of his trumpet than he had his wife. A good polishing was probably all it needed.

Betty Jewel snapped open the case, picked up Saint's silver horn. And out tumbled the necklace.

Heart-shaped.

Rose gold.

And inside, the frames meant to hold photographs were empty.

Betty Jewel had cried then, and she was pressing her hand over her mouth, hard, to keep from crying now.

"From my heart to yours," Saint had said when he'd given it to her. "From the one who loves you best."

The locket was the only real piece of jewelry he'd ever given her. But more than that, it had been a symbol of hope. They'd just finished their first big gig together in Chicago. The fans loved them, the money was good and the future was a shining road they'd travel. Together.

"As soon as we get a chance, we'll have our pictures made for the locket. You and me, baby. Forever."

Drugs sucker punched that chance and then dealt their future a knockout blow. The locket had vanished along with Betty Jewel's dreams. He'd probably meant to pawn it, him with his drug-addled brain, then had stuffed it down in his trumpet case and forgotten about it.

She had been first to come back home. By the time he'd followed, pleading with Queen to take him in, begging Betty Jewel to give him a second chance, she already had a cleaning job and was supplementing it by teaching voice and piano. The extra income was precious little. Few people in Shakerag could afford formal music lessons. In her neighborhood, if you wanted to learn music you picked up a blues harp and tried to find the songs in your soul.

The necklace in her hand tore her in half. She ought to sell it. They could use the money. But parting with it was like letting go of every dream she'd ever had. It was a shining little symbol of hope, one whose loss she'd mourned through the years. And now it was back, a locket that would be a nice keepsake for Billie. She idolized the Saint and would be thrilled to know he'd bought it. Betty Jewel wanted Billie to have something wonderful to hold on to after she was gone. On the other hand, she hated the idea that Billie would treasure the necklace because it came from Saint.

Betty Jewel leaned her head on her dressing table, too sick and tired to know what to do.

Facing your own end didn't make you a bit wiser than if you thought you had all the time in the world. Betty Jewel dropped the necklace into the bottom of the sock, folded it over twice, then put it at the bottom of the dresser drawer.

Beyond the curtains, the sky was taking on a pink glow. Betty Jewel climbed into her bed, clothes and all. She felt like a woman entangled in a giant ball of yarn. Pull the wrong thread and everything around you unraveled. If she could sleep for a few hours, she might wake up clearheaded enough to know what do.

When Billie woke up, God hadn't given her any answers. She was still in her yellow shorts, which meant time saved if she could sneak out of the house without her mama or Queen seeing. They'd have a holy conniption fit about her wearing yesterday's clothes. Queen always said, *If you ain't got pride, you ain't got nothin'...*

Billie didn't want wise sayings. What she wanted was breathing room. She followed breakfast smells to the kitchen, then reached under the covered platter on the table and grabbed a buttermilk biscuit.

Roy Rogers and Dale Evans sang "Happy Trails to You" from the Philco radio, which Billie took as a good sign. A glance out the window proved her right. Queen was out in the backyard hanging clothes on the line strung between the oak tree and a scraggly apple tree that was too sorry to bear fruit, so Billie didn't have to waste time saying grace. If Queen caught her in the kitchen, she'd make her say grace, even though the biscuit was in her pocket.

The hall was empty, too. Billie made a beeline for the front door. As she passed the den, she heard her mama on the phone speaking real low like people did when they were telling secrets. She might as well speak up. Billie knew she had cancer.

But you could bet your britches she wasn't planning on sitting around the house waiting for her mama to die. Being ten didn't mean being stupid. When you needed help, you asked for it.

Careful not to let the screen door slam, Billie skipped down the steps and raced off. Just her luck, old Miz Quana Belle was out in the yard weeding her Canadians. She perked up, suspicious, her voice following like a cloud of buzzing bees.

"Chile, where you goin' in them tore-up shorts? Does yo mama know?"

When Billie got to be a grown-up, she was going to let little kids have secrets of their own. She was going to mind her own business. And she was going to find a way to be the boss without having a single willow switch in her house.

As Billie outran the buzzing cloud of questions, she glanced over her shoulder every now and then to see if Alice was out and about. But there were no signs. She guessed even the dead had to rest sometimes. All that tree climbing and floating on top of church steeples and materializing under windowsills had to be hard. Billie felt sorry for her.

She hoped her mama didn't end up haunting the blue house on Maple Street when she died. She hoped Betty Jewel went straight to Heaven. Billie didn't know if it had streets of gold like Queen said, but she'd bet its park had a better swing set than the one in Shakerag. And she'd double-dog dare anybody to tell her the library in Heaven would be run by somebody mean as old Miz Rupert. Billie pictured somebody in a flowing white robe with a crown of stars on her head showing Mama to a roomful of books that still had all the pages inside.

Of course, if her mission succeeded, her mama wouldn't die.

When Billie came in sight of Tiny Jim's Blues and Barbecue, her steps slowed. The juke joint was shut tight, the front door locked, the shades down. Night was when it came alive, neon flashing, patrons jiving, music and laughter and smoke swirling as thick as molasses.

This was a place for grown-ups. Billie wasn't supposed to be here unless she was with Queen or Mama. But she'd lost count of all the things she'd done that she shouldn't. Lied to her mama. Put a bullfrog she'd caught in Gum Pond in old Miz Rupert's chair. Kept her eyes open when the preacher prayed, though Queen had told her closed eyes showed respect to Brother Joshua Gibson and God the Father Almighty, and open eyes could send you *to hell a poppin.* Last year Billie had even sent a letter to the North Pole telling Santa she hated him for not bringing her a bicycle.

She marched past the front door of the honky-tonk toward the alley that led around to the little house where Tiny Jim and Merry Lynn lived. Though she told everybody she wasn't scared of anything, that was a lie. Billie was afraid of getting cut into six pieces and nuclear bombs that could turn everybody to dust with the push of a button and cottonmouth moccasins and the wrath of Queen. But her biggest fear was being left motherless.

She decided to strike up a bargain with God before she entered the alley. "God, if you'll keep Queen from finding out I'm here, I promise to shut my eyes during the preacher's long-winded prayers. I bet you get tired of listening to them, too, don't you? Your friend, Billie."

At the last minute, she remembered to say, *Amen,* and then she entered the alley. This time of morning while most folks were in their houses eating molasses and biscuits, the alley was creepy. There was no telling what was waiting to grab her. Just in case God got busy with a more important prayer, like one from President Eisenhower, Billie balled up her fist. It never hurt to be ready to fight.

Something screeched, and she flattened herself against the brick wall. Was it a haint? Or was it a dangerous stranger, come to snatch another little girl away from Tiny Jim's? Billie didn't want to end up floating in Gum Pond in a cotton sack.

By the time a gray cat streaked by with its ribs poking through matted-up fur, Billie was shaking with relief. That was another thing. If she could be in charge of things, she'd make it against the law to starve animals and let them run loose all over Shakerag scaring little girls, even if they weren't supposed to be in the alley in the first place.

Humming "Lead On, O King Eternal" to show anybody listening she wasn't scared, she walked past the garbage cans. One of the lids was off. She hoped the cat had done it and not somebody up to no good. Just in case, she picked up speed. When she got through the alley, she had to bend over and catch her breath.

The scent of barbecue was strong out back. Tiny Jim's pits were smoking, and Billie could smell the meat slow-cooking on the coals. When he took it out of the pits, it would be so tender it would fall off the bone. You could cut it with a fork.

A curl of pork-scented smoke followed her all the way to Tiny Jim's front door. It had once been green but was now blackened from constant companionship with smoke pits. Billie lifted her hand and knocked.

Anybody else seeing the gigantic man who opened the door would have turned tail and run. But she knew him as the man who sent his gold Chevrolet Bel Air to pick up Queen and her pies, the man who passed the collection plate on Sunday, the man who showed up at your door at Christmas with a smoked ham, even if you hadn't told a soul you had nothing to eat for supper but a strip of fried fatback.

"Good mornin', Billie." Tiny Jim peered back down the alley behind her, looking for Queen and Mama, she guessed. He opened the door wider. "Come inside. You just in time for breakfast."

Queen always said, *Be polite. Just because folks is offerin' you food don' mean they got it to give.* Her stomach rumbled, and on the spot she decided to part company with *polite.* Besides, the cold biscuit in her pocket didn't compare to the mouth-watering smells inside this house.

He led her to a kitchen where the linoleum didn't have cracks. The curtains had lace on the bottom and looked brand-new. There was a cloth on the table, too, as white as Tiny Jim's big teeth.

"Do you like bacon or sausage?" She nodded and he piled both on her plate, then added two hot biscuits. "I bet you like butter and jelly on your biscuits, a growin' girl like you."

"Yes, sir."

"You got manners. I like that." He spread a big cloth napkin and tucked it into the neck of his shirt. "I done said grace. Go ahead and help you'self."

He was the kind of grown-up who didn't make up foolish conversations at the table, just sat there and let you enjoy your food in peace. Billie started to ask, *Where's Miz Merry Lynn,* then she heard her. A low moaning coming from down the hall.

"Is Miz Merry Lynn coming to eat?"

"After a while. I keep her a plate warmin' in the oven for when she's ready."

The moaning down the hall turned to a high-pitched keening. It sounded like Miz Quana Belle's hound dog last year after her pups got toted off to new homes.

"Mr. Tiny Jim, do you know how to find my daddy?"

He took the napkin from under his chin, folded it into a square and pressed it between hands as big as Virginia hams before he laid it on the table. Then he sat real quiet, looking at her. It wasn't the kind of stare that made Billie squirm, just a sad kind of look that made her wish she could say something respectful about dead Alice. Queen always said, *Speak kinely of the dead.*

"Mr. Tiny Jim, I'll bet your little girl was nice." He nodded. "I'll bet you'd never take her off and cut her in six pieces."

"You oughtn' be thinkin' such things." He pushed his chair back, reached over and lifted Billie onto his lap. "I wish you was my little girl."

Billie pictured her life as Tiny Jim's little girl. She'd have bacon and sausage every morning. She could go to the juke joint when she pleased because her new daddy would be watching her like a hawk. She'd have her own room with new curtains that had pink lace on the bottom and shiny linoleum floors that didn't have cracks.

But it would be Alice's old room, and she might have to sleep with the dead girl's cold breath whispering in her ear, her floating head perched on the lamp shade, her chopped-off legs standing in the door so Billie couldn't get past without screaming for help.

Tiny Jim turned his sad eyes down the hall where the sounds coming from Merry Lynn reminded Billie of a starving cat.

"Thank you just the same, Mr. Tiny Jim, but I've got a real daddy."

"Saint could put the mojo on that horn of his."

"Will you help me find him?"

"Billie, he was a great jazzman and a good friend, but I done reckon he'd be no 'count as a daddy."

"Why not?"

"He had problems."

"What kind?"

"Big ones. The kind little girls not s'pose to worry they purty heads over." He kissed her on the top of her head. "Now, you run on home befo' yo mama and Miz Queen catches you."

"I gotta find my daddy. He'll know how to make Mama well."

"I don't reckon the Saint nor nobody else can do that, sugah. Yo mama's in a bad way."

"I won't let her die!"

Tiny Jim just sat in his chair a long time, shaking his head and watching her with eyes as mournful-looking as a red-bone hound dog. Billie believed he was a nice man, but that didn't mean he was going to put her in his Bel Air and drive off across state lines looking for the Saint.

"You won't tell I was here?"

He winked. "I reckon a little mouse done eat them sausage and biscuits."

She thanked him for breakfast, then went back outside where the alley and the barbecue pits and the garbage cans looked the same. The cracks in the caked dirt path and the oak trees and sagging light lines sprinkled with black birds hadn't changed. The sun was coming up just like it always had, and nothing about the way folks stirred from their houses and headed off to work said this day was any different from the rest.

Only Billie knew. Sometimes you could be going along thinking you'd enter fifth grade in the fall and walk home with your best friend every day to find cookies your mama had left on the kitchen table. Then a conversation heard through a keyhole could change everything. Suddenly you'd be on an unfamiliar path without a map, without a clue where you were headed or how you were going to get there. And nobody cared that you were walking home by yourself in a sun already so hot you could fry an egg on your front porch steps. Nobody noticed that when you passed by A.M. Strange

Library, sorrow dripped from dead Alice's cedar tree and trapped you if you didn't know how to run.

Billie ran home so fast the sun couldn't even catch her shadow.

# Six

The first thing Cassie did when she woke up was put on her white pique robe with the pink piping, then step outside to get the paper. She wanted to see if that haunting little ad she'd seen in the classifieds of *The Bugle* was also in the *Sentinel.* It was a daily and four times as thick as the weekly newspaper. Still, Cassie had never tried to get a job there. Joe had always believed it was because Cassie was first and foremost a housewife who had only taken a part-time job to have a *little something extra to keep her busy.* Letting him think that had been easier than explaining how she could get by with expressing her unpopular opinions in *The Bugle* because Ben wasn't about to fire her. In small Southern towns, big connections kept crusading women with radical opinions safe—as long as they were all talk and no action.

Cassie had beat the mailman. She stood in her front yard beneath a catalpa tree, shading her eyes for him. The hot air was so sharp it looked like stars. The canopy of the catalpa tree had grown so thick nothing could get through, not even heartache. A cardinal swooped from its branches and zoomed right past her head, so close its wings hummed like a harmonica riff. It was the kind of day where anything could happen. Time could rewind, her womb could bring forth a child, or Joe might come around the corner saying, *Surprise, it was all a mistake.*

"Morning, Cassie." The mailman waved the *Sentinel* at her, then trotted across the lawn. With his short, stumpy legs, wide face and toothy grin, J. D. Cotton looked like a friendly troll. "I brought you some fresh tomatoes. My garden's just run over with them."

"You're spoiling me, J.D."

"Pretty woman like you deserves it. No offense meant."

"None taken." You might as well take offense at the Easter Bunny. As long as J.D. was on the route, housewives in Tupelo could expect fresh tomatoes and okra in their mailboxes in the summertime. Kids could expect letters from the North Pole at Christmas. Cassie took the heavy sack from him. "It looks like it's going to rain. Wait here and let me get Joe's rain slicker for you."

"I'd be much obliged."

Cassie hurried inside, set her tomatoes on the kitchen cabinet, tossed the *Sentinel* on the table, then rummaged in the hall closet for Joe's raincoat. There was no use hanging on to it.

Still, when she handed the yellow slicker to J.D., her heart broke in two.

"I'll get the coat back to you, Cassie."

"Keep it, J.D. I should have gone through Joe's things months ago."

J.D. waved as he left to continue his route, and Cassie hurried into the house.

It was today's dedication ceremony that had Cassie on edge. She had better things to do than stand in front of a crowd and make an empty speech about how much renaming the baseball field meant to her. She couldn't hug a baseball field.

She brewed Maxwell House coffee, then sat down at her

kitchen table with a cup while she scanned the *Sentinel* for signs of the woman who wanted to give away her child. Seeing none, she called Ben at home.

"Who placed that Dying Woman ad in *The Bugle,* Ben?"

"Woman up in Shakerag. Goober said it was somebody calling herself Betty Jewel Hughes. Name sounded familiar because her husband used to be a famous bluesman."

"I want to do the story."

"This is the wrong time for a white woman to be poking around Shakerag."

"All the more reason, Ben. Somebody has to speak out for these people."

"They're sitting on top of a powder keg up there just waiting to blow wide open. Can't let you do it, Cassie. It's too dangerous."

"A dying woman and a little girl about to become an orphan? Come on, Ben. That's a story, and we need to tell it."

"It's none of our business. Go to the baseball field today and enjoy the ceremony."

"Just be Joe's widow. Is that what you're saying?"

"If you go to Shakerag and stir things up, there's no telling what will happen."

"I'm not going to stir things up, Ben. I'm going to help save a little girl."

Ben's sigh was audible. If she could see his expression, she knew it would be long-suffering. Though he blustered and tried to keep his best friend's wife safe, Ben was proud of Cassie's spunk. Whatever she did, he would support her.

"Dammit, Cassie."

"Thank you, Ben."

"For what? If you go up there, you're fired."

"I know."

"I'm not kidding this time."

"Bye, Ben. I'll see you at *The Bugle* this afternoon."

"I'll be at the dedication, Cass."

*The dedication.* One more reminder that Joe was gone.

If Cassie had her way, she'd wear slacks and a T-shirt to the dedication of the baseball field. Fashion meant nothing to her; comfort, everything. But there was her father-in-law to think about, dear, old-fashioned Mike Malone, who would be mortified if she showed up looking anything less than a proper lady, as befitted his son's widow.

She put on a yellow linen sundress with a white bolero and matching pumps, even *gloves,* for Pete's sake. A glance at the clock told her she was a full fifteen minutes early. She wished she could break herself of obsessive punctuality. She was so anxious that nobody be inconvenienced waiting for her, she always ending up wasting a lot of time waiting for *them.* And now that she was all dressed up, she couldn't run out to her garden and pull a few weeds or start any little thing that entailed getting dirty.

Deciding to brave her former Empty Room, Cassie turned the doorknob. Her rocking chair beckoned—nothing to fear there—so she sat down to watch for her sister-in-law. The sight of her favorite pictures made her smile, but she couldn't say she felt the sort of favorite-retreat contentment Fay Dean had predicted.

At the sound of tires, she looked out the window and saw Fay Dean coming up the walk with Mike. Cassie hurried to the door and kissed her father-in-law's cheek.

"Mike, what a lovely surprise."

"I wanted to come by early and see if there was anything you needed me to do."

"That's sweet of you, but I think I have everything under control."

"*Pshaw.* You need some help taking care of Joe's house. Where are those insurance papers?"

"I've already paid the house insurance, Mike."

"I've told you, I'll take care of all that, hon. No need for you to try to do a man's job."

"Daddy, Cassie's not senile. The only thing she needs is an occasional shoulder to cry on."

"Well, she for damned sure doesn't need a psychiatrist. One of my mailmen saw her coming out of O'Hanlon's office and asked if she'd gone mental."

"For God's sake, Daddy. Who gives a shit?"

Mike stormed off to the front porch, and Cassie said, "Leave Mike alone, Fay Dean. He means well."

"I swear to God, Daddy's going to drive us both crazy."

"I don't know about you, but it wouldn't take much to push me around the bend." That brought a laugh from Fay Dean, which was exactly what Cassie intended. Though she waded knee deep into every controversial cause, she tried to avoid personal conflict.

*You never say what you're thinking,* Joe had told her that awful summer she'd lost her third baby, the summer it felt as if he had vanished to the moon and she was left behind trying to see into outer space. *Yell, scream, cry… Just, for God's sake, don't shut yourself off from me.*

"Are you ready?" Fay Dean linked arms, and Cassie pushed the uncomfortable memory from her mind. "Let's get this over with."

They climbed into Mike's steady Chevrolet sedan, and as they drove the few blocks to the baseball field, Cassie found herself struggling to recall the exact shape of Joe's jaw, the way his dark hair had felt against her cheek, the way he'd pull his harmonica from his pocket and start playing so his music came through the door before he did. Even the smell of Joe's old baseball jacket could no longer bring her husband clearly to mind.

Blistering in the sun beside Mike and Fay Dean, Cassie was thinking how love can waylay you when you least expect it. She was thinking how one minute you can have your future mapped out and the next you're arguing over whose fault it is you can't carry a baby full term.

And if the sound of a blues harp happened to float by on the breeze, as it was doing now, you might actually believe it was a sign. Was it Joe, telling her he'd always loved her, even during those hard months after they'd lost the third baby and drifted apart?

Last night she'd gone outside to stand under the stars. Venus had shone down on her, a heavenly reminder of the grace that had enabled her and Joe to get past their hurt and come back together.

Shored up by memories, she went onto the baseball field where the mayor would call Joe a hero.

Leaving her gloves and bolero in the car and clutching Joe's posthumous award under her arm, Cassie entered *The Bugle*'s offices on the corner of Spring and Court streets. They were in a venerable building in the center of town with twelve-foot tall windows and ivy climbing the redbrick walls.

Joe used to say she could live at *The Bugle,* and it was true. She loved the clatter of the presses and the smell of ink. Cassie settled Joe's plaque on the corner of her desk and her coffee cup on a ceramic trivet painted with rainbows. Give Your Soul a Bubble Bath, it proclaimed.

Searching her phone book for the number, Cassie dialed Betty Jewel Hughes.

"Hello." The woman at the other end of the line spoke

with dark, honeyed tones that made you want to sit outside in the sunshine and listen to the universe.

It turned out the woman was not Betty Jewel, but her mother, Queen Dupree. Her daughter, she said, wouldn't be home till late that afternoon. Though Queen sounded both ancient and anxious, she finally agreed for Cassie to come to Maple Street.

Cassie glanced at her calendar. "I'll be there today at five."

A dying woman doesn't have any time to lose.

# Seven

SITTING IN THE PASSENGER side of Sudie's old car, Betty Jewel wondered if it was possible that miracles are not prayers answered but the answer to prayers you didn't even know you should pray. Maybe she should have left off praying for a cure for cancer and the freedom for her daughter to walk into the Lyric theater downtown and sit anywhere she pleased. Maybe she should have been praying that her life would be ordinary. Wake up, cook breakfast, plant your collard greens and watch your child grow up. The things millions of women took for granted.

She had been on the front porch swing, wrapped in one of her mama's quilts and sick from her soles to her scalp, when Sudie's ten-year-old Studebaker with most of the black paint missing had chugged to a stop in front of her house. Out stepped Merry Lynn wearing a pink hibiscus-print swimsuit—Esther Williams, except colored. Sudie came around the car, her sprigged-green-print skirt swinging as she walked, and her bosom, large for a woman her size, supported by enough black latex to cover a barge.

"Grab your suit, Betty Jewel," Sudie had said. "We're going to the old swimming hole."

"I can barely walk, let alone swim."

"Sudie took the day off, and don't you dare try to say no." Merry Lynn marched onto the front porch with Sudie where the two of them made a packsaddle of their crossed arms and joined hands. "Hop on."

"I can walk."

"Not today, you don't," Sudie said. "Get on, Betty Jewel."

"I'm not doing a thing till you promise I won't hear any talk of finding a cure in Memphis."

"I promise and so does Merry Lynn, though I can tell by that stubborn look she won't say so. Now, get your butt in gear and get on this packsaddle before I put it in gear for you."

She climbed aboard her not-too-steady seat and they hauled her off to the car, thankfully before she toppled off and added broken bones to her list of troubles. Merry Lynn raced back into the house, then returned with a quilt and her blue swimsuit, the one Betty had bought in Memphis the year she'd married the Saint.

"I'm not wearing that. I don't have any meat on my bones."

"If you don't want to wear it, we'll all swim naked. How's that, missy?" Merry Lynn fanned herself with a church fan she'd pulled out of her straw handbag. "Start the car, Sudie. I'm melting."

"Well, roll down the windows."

"It won't help till you get moving."

By the time Sudie had turned the car and headed out of Shakerag, Betty Jewel knew this outing was exactly what she needed.

Surrounded by the hum of tires and the scent of pulled pork Tiny Jim had sent for their picnic lunch, she waited for her first sign of the river. It came to her as the scent of childhood, water so cool and deep it smelled green.

Around the bend, the Tombigbee meandered through ancient blackjack oaks and tall pines, cutting a path that created sloping grassy banks and carved sharp knolls into the red-clay hills.

"Remember that summer I said I was quitting college to marry Wayne?" Sudie found their old haunt, a paradise canopied by spreading tree branches and hidden by a bank of wild privet and honeysuckle. She parked under the deep shade.

"I said you were crazy." Merry Lynn reached for the quilt Queen had made and the towels she'd brought.

"And I said you should follow your heart." Advice Betty Jewel would take back if she'd understood how we color another person with our own heart's desires. What we see is not the truth, clear and unvarnished, but a fantasy built of imagination and stardust.

"Forget that heavy stuff and let's go have some fun," Merry Lynn said. "Get the picnic basket, Sudie."

As they lolled on the quilt, eating pork barbecue, they were reeled backward to a place where the dreams of yesterday might still come true. Betty Jewel could almost believe she'd turned back time.

Afterward, they stretched out on the quilt, side by side, and called out the objects they found in the clouds. Merry Lynn found two angels and Sudie found a frog. When Betty Jewel found a heart, she thought of the locket and felt a pinch of pain that stole her breath.

"Let's go in the water." Sudie stood up and peeled off her skirt. "Merry Lynn brought inner tubes. It'll be like old times."

"You two go on. I don't have the strength to struggle into latex."

A look passed between her friends, and they both started stripping.

"Betty Jewel," Sudie said, "if you don't want to see me

down on all fours buck-naked, you'd better peel off that dress before I do it for you. I don't have all day."

She thought about the cancer that steals all your dignity, and friends who give it back.

"Why the heck not?" She tried to stand up and found herself lifted by Sudie and Merry Lynn. They unbuttoned her dress and folded it onto the quilt, then led her into the shallows and helped her into a black rubber innertube, the kind they'd used as river rafts when they were children.

With the cool green water lapping over her, Betty Jewel leaned back and closed her eyes. For a blissful hour she vanished into the realm of childhood where boundaries between what was real and what was imagined vanished, where things lost might be found, and anything at all was possible, even a future.

When Sudie's car chugged to a stop on Maple Street, Queen was waiting on the front porch with four yellow plastic glasses of iced tea.

"Did ya'll have fun, baby?"

"We took her skinny-dipping, Miss Queen." Merry Lynn plopped on the porch steps with her tea.

"I ain't never done that, but now I wisht I had."

Sudie sat in a rocking chair, leaving the seat on the swing to Betty Jewel. "I can't stay long. I gotta get home and fix supper for Wayne and the kids."

True to her word, Sudie herded Merry Lynn into the car and drove off ten minutes later, both of them waving out the window, calling goodbye, and Betty Jewel was so grateful for friends who pick you up when you fall that she could do nothing but wave.

"Where's Billie?"

"I give her a dime an' she done gone to the movin'-pichure show. Gone see that Tarzan swingin' on a rope."

"Lord, Mama, she can't walk home by herself." Ever since Alice's murder, only the foolish let their little girls walk home in the dark.

"I ain't dum. Tiny Jim gone pick her up." Queen studied Betty Jewel over the rim of her plastic iced-tea glass. "That newspaper lady's a comin'."

"What newspaper lady, Mama?"

"Said her name was Bessie. Miss Bessie Malone."

Betty Jewel felt like a dying star spinning through the sky, leaving burning bits of herself behind. "Not Cassie. Tell me it wasn't Joe Malone's wife." Queen just sat there with her lips pursed. "You know I can't talk to her."

"Maybe it's bes' is what I been thinkin'."

"No, Mama. I can't talk to her."

"Lies'll eat you up inside," Queen said.

Betty Jewel turned her face from her mama, then wished she hadn't. Wisps of Alice spun slowly around the yard, phantom legs floating over the grass that needed mowing and arms spread like the broken wings of a little brown bird. But the thing that made Betty Jewel turn away was Alice's eyes, deep as Gum Pond and clear as mirrors. Look too long into Alice's eyes and you'd see yourself; you'd see your past bound to your future, the sight so disturbing it could paralyze you.

"What time is Cassie coming?"

"'Bout five."

Betty Jewel thought of her options. Hide. Not answer the door. Bar the door and not let her in.

Or let her in and tell the truth.

She'd rather walk into the darkness of her own death than face Cassie with the truth.

# Eight

By the time she left *The Bugle,* Cassie's yellow linen sundress was a wrinkled mess. As if that weren't enough, it was blistering hot in the car. She rolled down her windows, and the first thing she noticed as she drove into Shakerag was the abrupt change from paved streets to dirt roads. Sinking into a pothole big enough to swallow a beagle, her tires spun. As she stomped on the gas, dust swirled through her open windows and settled over everything inside, including Cassie.

Saying an unladylike word that would have given her father-in-law a heart attack, she bumped her way down the gutted road. No wonder unrest was brewing. If she had to travel on roads like this every day, she'd be mad, too. Add to that the mean wages and scarcity of jobs for people who lived in places like Shakerag, and Cassie had to wonder if Ben was right. Was she stepping into a boiling cauldron?

She forged forward, pulled by her own stubborn will and the smell of barbecue that made her mouth water and gave her the shivers all at the same time. There was no escaping the scent of roasting pork on the north side of town. Except on rare occasions, Tiny Jim kept his smoke pits going around the clock.

His blue neon sign was flashing, and, as she drove by, Cassie caught the strains of a soul-searing harmonica. Real this time, not the stuff of myth and magic. The musician could be anybody from a blues legend to some teenage kid with a gut-punched feeling and a harp in his pocket.

The harmonica walked all over Cassie's heart. It was Joe's second love. That's one of the things she missed most: the sound of blues at unexpected moments. She could be in the tub or putting a casserole in the oven or arranging roses she'd picked, when all of a sudden the blues would pull her heart right out of her chest.

*Joe,* she'd say, and he'd come around the corner, blues harp in his mouth, eyes shining with devilment or laughter or sometimes unshed tears. It was his love of stomp-your-heart-flat music that drew him to Shakerag.

Cassie had begged to go with him, but he'd said, *Women don't go to places like that. Besides, Daddy would disown me if I took my wife to a Negro juke joint.*

"I've already been there when I interviewed Tiny Jim, and nothing bad happened to me. Even when I drank a glass of sweet tea from their cup."

"For God's sake, Cassie. Be serious. Exposing beautiful white women to randy young coloreds is causing race riots."

"No, the riots are caused by ignorant, hysterical women and hot-tempered men who settle differences with guns and lynching ropes. You're not ignorant and I'm not foolish. Please, Joe."

She finally wore him down on his birthday. To avoid unnecessary talk, they took care that nobody in their neighborhood knew where Cassie was going, and, aside from a few raised eyebrows in the juke joint, nothing happened. In their society, white was not merely a color but a privilege, one Joe took for granted and Cassie agonized over.

That evening, he'd driven home with one hand so he could hold his harp to his mouth with the other. The only sound in the car was an old Delta blues song whose words Cassie didn't know until Joe alternately played and sang.

That was the only time he ever took her, and she'd finally stopped asking to go. She couldn't remember when. Or why. Or even if she'd ever wondered.

The lyrics Joe had sung on that otherwise silent car trip home suddenly played through Cassie's mind. *Ain't no use cryin', baby. The world done stomped us flat. Ain't no use cryin', baby. Your tears won't change all that.*

Li'l Rosie had composed that particular blues song. Cassie remembered because she'd asked Joe. She'd wanted to know who knew her so well she'd written lyrics especially for Cassie.

Or had the lyrics been for Joe? Had he been trying to tell her something, but she had looked the other way, shut her ears and walked around him?

Maple Street came into view, but as far as Cassie could see, there was only one maple tree on the entire street. The neighborhood was made up of one wooden saltbox house after the other, mostly unpainted, with a scattering of them featuring washed-out and peeling paint. The rest of the view came to Cassie in snatches—skimpy yards, many of them overgrown with Johnson grass and honeysuckle that will strangle anything in sight if it's not cut back, old tires stacked under tired-looking oak trees, sagging porches with swings on rusty chains.

Still, they were homes for somebody, raggedy havens where men with grease under their fingernails and women with detergent-cracked hands could lie together on a squeaky bed frame and forget the world outside. The houses sat back from the street on long, narrow lots. Cassie leaned down so she could peer at the numbers tattooed over the front doors.

The frame house she was looking for was painted a pastel blue faded the color of an old chambray shirt, blue gingham curtains at the windows, navy blue shutters, the one on the left side of the small wooden porch pulled loose at the top and hanging crooked. Several scrawny petunias and a few caladiums pushed their way through weeds that were trying to take over the flower beds. The gardener in Cassie wanted to grab a spade and set to work. The reporter saw the dying gardens as a metaphor for their owner.

On the porch an empty swing with a beautiful patchwork quilt thrown over the back swayed as if it had just been vacated.

When she stepped out of her car, an old woman weeding caladiums next door glared at her with such outright hostility, Cassie had to look behind herself to make sure she wasn't trailing trouble like a blood-stained shawl. She waved and smiled, but the woman stomped inside her house and slammed the door.

What kind of reception would be waiting inside this Shakerag house? When the front door opened, Cassie startled like a cat with its tail in a washing machine wringer.

Miss Queen stood poised behind the screen door. It could be no other, for she looked much the way she had when Cassie had seen her at Tiny Jim's, pounding out the blues on his old upright. It had been so long ago she couldn't remember. Ten years? Fifteen? Miss Queen's face was a map of years, her dress sprigged voile from a vanished era. She had dressed for Cassie. Suddenly she was glad she was wearing her yellow linen dress instead of her usual garb of slacks and a blouse. It seemed more respectful somehow.

"Good afternoon. I'm Cassie Malone from *The Bugle.*"

Miss Queen unlatched the screen door, but not before she'd put a gnarled hand to the white lace collar at her throat. When

Miss Queen stepped onto the front porch, Cassie thought of the Titanic—a ship capable of taking care of thousands of families, a ship that nothing could fell save an iceberg.

"Pleased to meet you, ma'am. I'm Queen. Queen Dupree."

Cassie climbed the steps onto the porch, and the old wooden floorboards creaked. Through the screen door drifted the mingled smells of lemon furniture polish and freshly baked pies overlaid with the strong fragrance of barbecue. The legend at work or proximity to Tiny Jim's? Either way, the scent gave Cassie the shivers.

"I remember you from Tiny Jim's." Cassie offered her hand to Miss Queen. "You and your daughter used to play piano there."

"Yessum." Queen peered closely at Cassie, squinting in the way of the nearsighted, but she didn't take her hand. Cassie felt foolish. Coloreds didn't shake hands with whites, not in this ancient, dignified woman's world. "I seen you there some years back."

In the way of old people comfortable with who they are and not about to put on airs to impress anybody, Queen didn't try to hide the fact that she was studying Cassie. Did she pass muster? She wished she'd taken the time to go home and put on a dress without wrinkles. For Pete's sake, she hadn't even bothered to comb her hair. She must look as if she had on a Halloween wig.

"I came to see your daughter."

"Yessum. Do come in, Miss Cassie. She's waitin' on you."

Queen led her down a hallway filled with pictures. The centerpiece was Jesus praying in the Garden of Gethsemane. In the place of honor on his right was the photograph of a little girl with cheekbones slashed high, eyes too big for her thin face and lips compressed tightly together as if she were daring the photographer to make her smile. Something about her eyes made it hard to look away. The arresting shade of green? The frank stare?

Other photographs chronicled her life from laughing babyhood to gap-toothed schoolgirl. Betty Jewel's daughter, Cassie guessed. Who would take her picture in her cap and gown? Her wedding gown? The pink quilted robe she'd wear home from the hospital when she had her first baby?

Cassie hoped her story would make a difference. Shouldering the awesome responsibility, she followed Queen into a sunlit room where a gaunt woman sat in a rocking chair, staring out the window. Though it was so hot in the house Cassie was beginning to sweat, the woman was wearing a shawl.

"Betty Jewel, honey, look who's done come to see us. That newspaper lady."

Betty Jewel's shoulder blades stuck up through the crocheted shawl like the wings of a skinny-legged bird. The flesh had disappeared from her bones, leaving behind too much skin. But when she saw Cassie, she lifted her chin. It was pride Cassie saw.

"Hello, Cassie. Please do sit down."

There would be no *yessums* and *Miss Cassie this* or *Miss Cassie that* from Betty Jewel Hughes. Dying strips you of all pretense, carves you down to the essentials.

Betty Jewel's voice, rich with melodious cadences, was mannerly, but her eyes said *keep out.* Her posture said *don't mess with me.*

Cassie sat in a straight-backed chair closest to the oscillating fan. Words weren't enough here. She needed to take action. She needed to lasso a couple of guardian angels and say, *Look, do something.*

"I'm gone leave you two young'uns by yoself so's you can talk."

The old woman slipped from the room, leaving Cassie with

her purse in her lap, wondering why she felt Betty Jewel's hostility like a cattle prod. She had to know the consequences of Cassie being here, the gossip she'd endure from the Highland Circle crowd, as well as the suspicions and tongue-waggings of Betty Jewel's neighbors.

"May I call you Betty Jewel?"

"Suit yourself."

If Cassie's maid or her gardener spoke to her like that, she'd fire them on the spot. But in Betty Jewel's home, Cassie was the outsider. Nothing insulated her in this shack in Shakerag, neither wealth and position nor the color of her skin. It looked as if she had finally let her crusading zeal get her into a situation she might not escape from unscathed.

She tried to melt her unbending hostess with a smile. "I don't mean to be nosey. I'm here to help you."

"I don't need your help, and I certainly don't need you poking into my private business."

"Look, I'm no do-gooder who just barges in. Your mother invited me." Cassie felt her temper rising, and it showed. At the rate she was going, she'd be back on the street before her hubcaps got stolen from a flashy car that obviously didn't belong in this neighborhood any more than she did.

"Mama shouldn't have told you to come here. She may sound like some shuffling, obsequious old mammy, but she's a proud African queen. And so am I."

The naked expression on Betty Jewel's face made it painful to look at her. Cassie catalogued the facts. A woman that well spoken had probably attended one of the Negro colleges down in Jackson or the Delta. No doubt Queen had sacrificed to make sure her daughter had a better chance in life. And now Queen's daughter was making the ultimate sacrifice to ensure her child's future.

Giving up a daughter in order to save her was a choice of biblical proportions.

Reining in her temper, Cassie held out her hands, palms up. "Look, I'm out of my element here, and you must be feeling as uncomfortable as I. Can we please just start over?"

Betty Jewel bowed her head and stayed that way for a long time. Was she pulling herself together? Regretting her rudeness? Wondering if she'd insulted the wrong person?

Negroes were being lynched for less. With racial violence flaring all over the South, had Cassie jeopardized the safety of this family simply by being here?

"I'm sorry." She stood up to leave. "I didn't mean to make things harder for you."

"No, wait." Betty Jewel's eyes were wet with unshed tears. "All I can say in my defense is that cancer has made manners seem superfluous."

"I'm so sorry. I can't say I know what you're going through, because I don't. But I lost my husband a year ago, so I can certainly understand pain."

"You and Joe never had children, did you?"

Her familiarity with Cassie's life was startling until she remembered all those evenings Joe had spent at Tiny Jim's. Though Joe would never spread his personal life among strangers, he was a well-known public personality. And in a town as small as Tupelo, the gossip grapevine flourished.

"No, we had no children."

The conversation reminded her all too vividly of the many ways she and Joe had found to blame each other for their childless state. Joe was dead. She wanted him to remain perfect, but a thick blue fog clouded the room, seeding discontent and making sanctifying the dead impossible. If you weren't careful, you could get lost in that kind of fog and never find your way home. Searching for something solid to hang on to, Cassie spied the piano.

"Tell me about yourself. You play, don't you?"

"I'm dying. What else is there to know?"

There was no barb in the remark, only soul-searing truth. Cassie took a notepad and pencil from her purse. "Please understand that I'm only here to write a story that might help you find a home for your child."

Inscrutable, Betty Jewel slipped a pill out of her pocket, then washed it down with a sip from the yellow plastic glass on the table beside her. "Does it make women like you feel good to help women like me?"

Cassie felt as if she'd been slapped. She had better things to do than seesaw between rage and pity with Betty Jewel, even if the woman was desperate.

"You don't even know me. If you did, that's the last remark in the world you'd make. I consider us the same."

"You mean equals? Like I can walk through the front door of your white house and go into your white bathroom without you going in there after me and scrubbing it down with Dutch Boy?"

Anger and admiration warred in Cassie. She thought of Bobo, her gardener, and Savannah, her maid. Had she ever invited them to sit down at her table and enjoy a glass of iced tea? Cassie was beginning to feel like a hypocrite until she remembered how she inquired about their children, went to their homes with soup when one of them got sick.

"Yes," she said. "Exactly like that."

Betty Jewel fell silent, her steady stare saying that when you're dying your life is reduced to the essentials. Eat, sleep, breathe. Tell the truth. The dying don't have time for lies.

"I'm sorry, Cassie. I've been rude and arrogant, and I've misjudged you."

"Thank you. Now will you please give me something I can put into a story?"

"There's not going to be a story. That ad was a mistake, and I don't intend to compound it with a news spread I have to hide from Billie."

Cassie started to ask, *Why am I here?* Then she remembered it was Queen who'd invited her, not Betty Jewel. Folding her notebook, she put it back into her purse.

"I'm disappointed, naturally, but I didn't come just for a story. I have lots of connections. Maybe I can help you that way. First, though, I'd like to meet Billie."

A fierceness came over Betty Jewel that made Cassie think of a mama eagle protecting her young from snakes. "No. She's going through enough pain without me adding to it with drama."

The screen door banged open, followed by stealthy footsteps in the hall. Then a bony-kneed, big-eyed child drifted by. Billie. Full of contradictions. Defiant and tragic. Fearless and scared. Forced by her mother's fatal illness to grow up overnight, she wore an expression that clearly said she'd rather remain a child because growing up was such a tragedy.

The look that passed between mother and daughter was almost beyond enduring. In the face of such devotion, there are things you can't do. You can't ask *How long before you die?* and *Will you give your daughter up before or after?* You can't snap pictures for *The Bugle,* though a photo would be more compelling than that heart-wrenching, hopeful little ad. You can't think of your empty bed and the empty crib in your attic and the long string of empty years ahead. You can't think of anything except a little girl who has turned her stare to you, a little girl with eyes so green they remind you of deep rivers and lost love and the unbearable beauty of the human spirit.

With one last, big-eyed stare, Billie slid past the door and out of sight. Cassie was left feeling as if her bones had been rearranged.

It took a while for them to settle back into place, and when they did, she was filled with an unexpected resolve.

"Betty Jewel, what you're doing is one of the bravest things I know. I want to be personally involved. I want to help you."

"Joe always said the biggest thing about you was your heart."

It was the kind of generous compliment Joe used to pass around. But Cassie found it shocking coming from this woman's mouth.

"You knew him personally?"

"From Tiny Jim's."

"Of course." Cassie pictured her husband in the juke joint, mellow with blues and beer, easygoing and approachable, talking about his wife to strangers as if the very telling could make her more real to him. On those long, lonely nights after the last miscarriage when she'd sometimes felt as if Joe were drifting away, as if she might meet him coming around a dark corner and not even know him, had he felt the same way?

"Cassie, I didn't mean to upset you."

"No. It's okay. Everybody in town knew and loved Joe."

A coughing spell bent Betty Jewel in two, and when she turned away Cassie saw patches of her scalp where radiation had stolen her hair. She wanted to cover her vulnerable baldness with a silk scarf, and at the same time she wanted to take a picture and spread it in on the front page under a caption titled Hero.

"Can I get you anything? Water?"

"No. I'm all right."

Cassie gathered her purse. "I should go. If there's anything I can do to help you, please let me know. Here are the numbers where you can reach me. Day or night."

As she handed over the card, another fit of coughing bent Betty Jewel double. With her face covered by her hands and her head bowed, she looked like somebody praying. And maybe she was. Maybe Cassie was, too, though she was sitting there with her eyes wide open.

Should she call Miss Queen? Phone for an ambulance?

Still bent, Betty Jewel reached into her pocket for a bottle of pills and out tumbled a harmonica.

B-flat.

Silver with a pink rose painted on the side.

The pink rose Cassie had painted.

A keening built inside her, and she pressed her hand over her mouth to hold it back.

When Betty Jewel lifted her head, Cassie found herself looking at a woman for whom everything had been stripped away, everything except love.

From somewhere in the house, a tea kettle whistled and a shaky soprano sang a hymn Cassie remembered from childhood. *Rescue the perishing. Care for the dying.*

Long ago when Cassie had played church piano, she would read the verses at the same time she read the music. Not many people can do that. It's a gift. Like knowing things before they happens.

Here is what Cassie knew: the harmonica had set events in motion that were beyond her control. She didn't know the particulars yet, only that her fate was somehow tangled up with this woman.

"Is that Joe's?"

"I didn't mean for it to come to this."

*Lord God,* Cassie was going to die on the spot. Betty Jewel hadn't denied it. She hadn't laughed off Cassie's question and offered some simple explanation. *I found this at Tiny Jim's juke joint.*

Now the woman was scaring her, but Cassie had never been one to back down from the hard things. Smile and carry on. Did her husband die without warning, leaving her to wish she'd held on to him longer the morning before he went to Moon Lake, held on and said *I love you,* instead of waving to him from the door and saying *I'll see you tonight.* Save your tears for private. In public, smile and carry on.

There would be no smiling and carrying on today.

"Come to what?" Cassie struggled to keep her voice low. Somewhere in the house was a dignified old woman who deserved better than a quarrel in her living room.

"What?" Betty Jewel's silence ripped through Cassie, as damning as the worst nightmare she could imagine. "For God's sake! Tell me."

"Something happened a long time ago, before Billie was born, something with consequences that reached far beyond what I'd ever dreamed."

Betty Jewel's voice sounded like distant music, a smoky blues song that could haunt a person forever. Cassie fought to hold back terror so fierce it would consume her.

"I never meant to hurt you, and I certainly never meant for it to come to this."

"You and Joe?" The question tore from Cassie's gut, deep where the fearsome truth dwells. "Tell me this is not what I think it is."

"I'm sorry, Cassie." If Cassie could go deaf on the spot, she would. "Joe is Billie's father."

Look for disaster long enough and you're sure to find it.

# Nine

Lord God, Cassie was sitting there looking as though somebody had poked a hole in her heart and drained out all her blood. Betty Jewel regretted telling her flat-out that Joe was Billie's father.

"Cassie?"

She jerked as if she'd been electrocuted, then bolted. Betty Jewel struggled from her chair, calling after her. "I didn't mean to hurt you. I'm sorry."

But she was already out the door, tearing off in her fancy red car. Betty Jewel hung on to the door frame, whispering, "I'm sorry." Now she was the bloodless one. She slid down the door frame and rested on the floor, still apologizing to the woman who was no longer there.

Queen came out of the kitchen with soapy water glistening on her hands. She looked so normal that for a moment Betty Jewel could pretend none of this had happened. She could pretend she'd decided to simply make sure Sudie would help Queen raise Billie and not mess around trying to fix the past.

"You done tole her?"

"Oh, God, Mama."

Queen bent down and tried to help her up, but Betty

Jewel pushed her arm away. "Don't. No sense in you falling down, too."

"It's gone be all right, baby. I been prayin' 'bout this."

Queen didn't merely pray: she battered the gates of Heaven with her petitions till God got so weary He'd say, *All right, Miss Queen, have it your way.*

Betty Jewel tried hard to conjure up her mama's faith, but she couldn't. She couldn't think of anything except how she'd destroyed another woman's life. Not once, but twice.

Not only that, but she'd probably destroyed her daughter.

"Where's Billie?"

Queen patted her hand. "She didn' hear nothin'. She done gone outside to that ole bus."

"Thank you, Jesus."

"Amen."

The prospect of her daughter spending another night on top of the bus paled in comparison to the tragedy of finding out the man she idolized was not her daddy.

"Mama, do you think Billie's ever going to accept this cancer?"

"Give her time."

"I don't have time."

When Queen put her hand on Betty Jewel's head, she was humming "In the Garden," probably without even being aware of it.

"Baby, when the good Lord takes you on home, thas gone be the sweetest hallelujah."

"No, Mama. The sweetest hallelujah will be when Billie can walk in the front door of any place she pleases, and nobody will tell her she doesn't belong."

Resuming her hymn, Queen smoothed back Betty Jewel's falling-out hair. They stayed that way a long time, both finding solace in the ordinary. Finally, Queen ceased her humming.

"Baby, what you needs is a little perk me up."

"You got any Jack Daniel's, Mama?"

"I might. Just for medismal 'mergencies and such."

"I think this qualifies as a medicinal emergency."

Queen's slippers dragged along the floor, slower than yesterday Betty Jewel was thinking. While her mama was gone, she got off the floor, but it took her a while. By the time she was upright, Queen was back with two glasses full of amber anesthesia.

"I fixed myself a little snort. For my rheumatiz."

Lord, if anybody deserved a little snort, it was her saint of a mama. Betty Jewel tipped her glass. The first swallow went down smoothly, but the next one set everything from her shoe soles to her breastbone in turmoil. She didn't even have the luxury of drowning in her sorrows.

Queen held her head while she heaved over the toilet.

*Lord, this price is too much to pay for loving another woman's husband.*

Cassie didn't know how she got home. She didn't remember driving. She didn't remember the road. She didn't remember anything except the damning words, *Joe is Billie's father.*

Cassie wanted to kill him. She wanted to break him into a million pieces the way Betty Jewel had broken her.

With one arm wrapped around herself to hold the shattered parts together, she picked up her blue stone pitcher and hurled it against the wall. She and Joe had bought it on their first anniversary trip to Mountain City, Tennessee. Got it at Laurel Bloomery. Got a whole set of dishes to match because Joe said the blue reminded him of her eyes.

Cassie plowed through the shards without even cutting herself. That's how mad she was, so furious she was superhuman, made of broken glass and still able to heft a whole stack of pottery plates off the cabinet shelves and smash them onto the floor.

*"Damnyoudamnyoudamnyou!"*

A piece of pottery the size of a baseball flew up and cut Cassie's leg.

*I'm bleeding. I'm perishing.*

"Oh, God." She searched the ceiling for help but all she found was a cobweb that needed raking out of the corner.

With her own blood sticky on her leg, she moved to another cabinet. One sweep sent her wedding glasses airborne. Sun caught the Baccarat crystal as it arced through the air. For a moment there was a rainbow on the wall.

After a rain when the sun was shining just right, Joe used to race inside to get her so they could watch the sky light up together. He would tell her *I want to give you rainbows.*

But he'd given Betty Jewel Hughes a child.

There was an awful sound coming from somewhere far away, the high-pitched wailing of a woman grieving, a woman who had lost everything. Her husband, her memories, her marriage, her trust, her pride.

Cassie cleaned out the cabinets one by one, raking and hurling until there was not a dish left. Not even a salt-and-pepper shaker.

Her kitchen was Berlin, bombed. Her left leg was cut in two places, both arms were scratched, and her linen dress was speckled with blood. She looked like a woman gone crazy. She sank into a kitchen chair and didn't know how long she sat there, paralyzed.

Her legs would hardly hold her as she finally moved through her house, blind, partially deaf. The phone was ringing and ringing, a small annoyance filtering through the swirling red fog of rage.

Cassie focused on the tub, the water taps, the bottle of pink bath beads. She dumped in the whole bottle, then stripped, stepped into the water and vanished in bubbles.

The phone stopped ringing a while, then commenced again. It was probably Fay Dean. She'd promised her sister-in-law they'd see *East of Eden* tonight. "We can salivate over James Dean," Fay Dean had said, and Cassie had laughed at the idea she could salivate over anybody except Joe Malone.

Closing her eyes, she slid under the water and her hair floated out behind her. *I could drown in here. I could stay under and let the water steal my breath, still my beating heart.*

"No!" She scrambled up, sputtering. "Liar! Cheat!" Cassie fought her way out of the tub, slid through the overflowing bubbles, then slammed the bathroom door on the whole mess. Joe's baseball jacket was hanging next to her white linen blazer, polluting her closet, filling it with the stench of betrayal.

Holding it at arm's length, Cassie started to enter her war-zone of a kitchen, then backtracked for shoes and a robe. Back in the kitchen it took her a while to find the lighter fluid, the matches.

When she stepped onto the patio, she was soul-punched by the universe. It was her favorite time of evening, that perfect moment when you can see the faint colors of sunset still bleeding all over the sky while a sliver of moon hangs around on the opposite side waiting for the stars.

It seemed a shame to ruin a perfectly good evening with a bonfire of deceit. Cassie sat in the wrought-iron glider and rocked back and forth, trying to find ease.

There was none. Cassie thought about the sneaky nature of disaster, how it could creep into the room without warning and announce itself in the quiet voice of a dying woman. Shouldn't there have been thunder shaking the ground, sirens screaming, people scattering to take cover? Maybe the quietness itself should have been a warning—the lull before a tornado rips your house apart.

She got up, poured lighter fluid into the bowl of the grill, tossed in a match. She was getting ready to toss in Joe's jacket when grief buckled her knees. She buried her face in the leather and cloth that still retained Joe's scent.

"How could you?" she moaned.

She remained on her knees with the flames licking out of the grill and the sky popping with stars. Finally she smothered the flames with the grill's lid, then went inside and lay down on her bed, clutching Joe's jacket. She cried until exhaustion claimed her.

Her fitful slumber was raided by memories, all bent on inflicting pain. When she awoke, Cassie huddled in a fetal position in the middle of the bed she'd shared with a man she didn't even know, a stranger who'd had a life beyond their marriage.

She'd told Joe everything. She'd kept no secrets. Until today, she'd thought he'd done the same.

Was it still today? It was too dark to tell.

The phone was ringing. Cassie counted twelve rings before it stopped, then started all over again.

Fay Dean was probably upset that she hadn't shown up at the theater, and maybe worried, too.

"I'm sorry," Cassie whispered.

She stumbled to the bathroom and turned on the light. She didn't know the puffy-faced, dead-eyed woman with her feet sunk in wet, bubble-ravaged carpet. She used to find part of her definition as the woman Joe loved, but he'd stolen that from her. He and Betty Jewel.

She wanted to smash something. Hard. She picked up her perfume, gardenia, Joe's favorite fragrance. With her hand raised she was fully intent on hurling the bottle into the mirror.

*What if Betty Jewel's lying?* Her tilted world righted itself. "Of course. That has to be the answer."

Cassie's gut reaction to Betty Jewel's shocking revelation had nothing to do with logic. How could she have let the words of a virtual stranger destroy fifteen years of marriage? How could she have doubted Joe's love?

Powered by restored reason and burgeoning hope, Cassie started jerking on white pedal pushers, a green short-sleeved sweater set. She was planning how she'd race back to Shakerag and force Betty Jewel to admit her lies when she glanced at the clock. It was past ten. She couldn't barge over there and disturb that sweet old lady, Miss Queen.

And what about Billie? She was innocent. No more than a pawn in her mother's cruel game. Cassie couldn't bring the child's world tumbling down as carelessly as Betty Jewel had hers.

Fully clothed, Cassie lay in the dark, waiting for morning.

When Billie woke up to the smell of ham and red-eye gravy, she thought she was in the wrong house. Queen reserved fancy breakfast fixings for Sundays and special occasions. Ordinary days meant biscuit and molasses.

Her mouth watering, she bounded out of bed, slipped into shorts and a halter Queen had made from the printed cotton sacks her Martha White flour came in, then made a beeline for the kitchen.

"Good morning, sleepyhead." The way Mama was smiling almost made Billie think this was just another summer day.

Billie pulled up a chair and helped her plate, as if she'd never heard of cancer. What would it hurt to pretend for five minutes?

"That Miss Cassie Malone is sho' a fine lady." Queen buttered another biscuit and handed it to Billie, though she already had two on her plate. "And smart. Mmm-hmm. I reckon she got mo' sense than any white woman I ever knowed."

There went *pretend* right out the window. Billie couldn't believe her ears. All Queen had talked about last night at supper was that newspaper lady. How smart she was, how pretty, how kind, how nice. Billie didn't know what had got into her. If Miss Cassie Malone told her pigs could fly, Queen would race to the window to see how much pork was in the sky.

"I don't know how you could tell all that with one visit, Queen. I thought she was just a skinny white woman with ugly red hair."

"Young lady, I ain't puttin' up with no sass from you."

Billie figured she was in for a session with Queen's willow switch. She didn't care. She'd go off and spend the day on Gum Pond and maybe the monster who got Alice would get her, and then everybody would be sorry.

"Mama. Go easy on Billie. She's got lots on her plate."

You could say that again. Three biscuits. Two pieces of ham. A pile of backberry jam. It was going to take her practically all morning to eat it.

She wasn't even halfway through when somebody started pounding on the door like Judgment Day was coming and they were about to miss the only train to Heaven.

"It's me. Cassie. Let me in." The door rattled and the banging sounded like that newspaper lady was fixing to break the door down.

Her mama turned the color of Miz Merry Lynn and Tiny Jim's bone china.

"Come on, chile." Queen grabbed Billie's hand and jerked her out of her chair. "You goin' to the park."

"Wait. I'm not through eating."

Queen grabbed a paper sack out of the cabinet and started slinging Billie's breakfast inside while that red-headed newspaper lady was making enough commotion to scare dogs and little children.

"I ain't gone set here all day and argue, Miss Priss. The grown-ups has got bidness to 'ten to, and I ain't gone have no little pitchers with big ears hangin' 'roun."

"You're not *setting,* Queen. You're standing."

"If I gets my switch, you gone change yo tune. Now skedaddle 'fore I whup them smarty-pants you wearin'."

Billie tore out the front door without the paper sack. Her breakfast was probably smashed to pieces in there, and besides, she was no longer hungry.

When Billie popped through the door, the newspaper lady jumped like she'd seen somebody with two heads. Billie had seen a lady with two heads last year at the Mississippi/Alabama Fair and Dairy Show. The tent had a sign that said See the Wonders of the World and Be Amazed. Billie always chose amazement over obedience. But since she didn't a nickel for the privilege, she sneaked around back and crawled under the tent.

The two-headed woman hadn't been amazing. She'd been sad. If Billie could be in charge of things she'd never make a woman with two heads sit on a hard stool and have people point at her. She'd set her up in a little house in Shakerag, tell Queen to make her a sweet potato pie, then tell Miz Quana Belle that the next time her hound dog had puppies, there was a lady with two heads who needed a pet. Everybody needs somebody to love. Even freaks.

Billie wondered if she was a freak. See the Wonder of the World. Be Amazed by the Little Girl Her Mother Left Behind. Maybe she'd join the circus. She'd bet she could make enough money to buy a bus ticket to wherever her daddy was.

First, she had to get away from dead Alice, who was sitting in her porch swing as big as you please. Her eyes were black holes that looked like hiding places for everything in the world you were scared of. Billie let out a scream that brought Mama and Queen both to the front porch.

Even that white woman turned to stare.

"Are you all right?" she asked.

"Leave me alone!"

Billie ran as fast as she could down the steps. Who was going to catch her, anyhow? With a peacemaker she hardly ever plugged in, Queen couldn't catch a cat standing still. Mama could barely breathe when she walked, let alone run, and Billie didn't think any white woman living on the other side of town was going to care where she went.

For that matter, neither did anybody else. She went straight to Lucy's, but she walked backward the last block and kept her fingers crossed behind her back. Everybody knew if you did that, it canceled out bad luck. Billie didn't need any bad luck, like Queen or God finding out she was going someplace she wasn't supposed to.

Lucy was sitting on her front porch, painting her toenails red. Billie plopped down beside her.

"Where'd you get the polish?"

"Sugarbee. My sister hates when I get in her stuff. Don't tell her."

"Cross my heart." Billie made a quick sign over her breastbone. "Where is she?"

"At the park with Bubba and Wash and Doll and Sis. I had to stay home on account of Peanut."

"Can I do mine next?"

"Sure."

Lucy put the last coat on her toenails then handed the polish to Billie. She untied her tennis shoes and slid them off her feet, then bent over her toes. She'd have to be careful to hide her feet from Queen tonight. Queen wouldn't buy nail polish, even if Billie held her breath till her face turned blue. She'd tried it. Queen pinched pennies worse than Ebenezer Scrooge. When Billie found her daddy and brought him home, he'd buy her a dozen colors of nail polish. She bet he spent money like it was water.

"Lucy, I've got a secret."

"What?"

"You can't tell. Cross your heart and hope to die." Lucy made the sign, and Billie knew wild horses couldn't drag it out of her. "Mama's dying, and I'm going to find my daddy."

"When?"

"Soon as I can find out where he is. You gotta help me."

Lucy sat there thinking about it, and Billie didn't blame her. She'd got a whipping the last time she helped Billie. That had been when they'd caught the frog up at Gum Pond to put under old Miz Rupert's chair. A double offense. Going where they'd been told not to and pulling a prank that made the librarian scream bloody murder.

While Billie was waiting, Lucy pointed across the street. "The mailman."

He was delivering the daily newspaper to Miz Merthelene Johnson. She owned the Curl Up 'n Dye where Lucy's mama worked. Miz Merthelene, Miz Quana Belle, Tiny Jim, the three preachers in Shakerag and mean old Miz Rupert were the only people Billie knew who could afford the daily paper.

Lucy and Billie waved at him, and he came across the street, smiling.

"Hello, ladies." Mr. Cotton always called them *ladies*. Billie and Lucy liked that. They couldn't wait to grow up. Lucy was eager to leave home so she wouldn't have to share her room, and Billie thought she might be famous someday like her daddy. Though she reckoned fame was going to have to wait awhile. She had lots to do before she could go off and be a grown woman and end up with her name on the lips of a gazillion fans and her picture in *Modern Screen* magazine.

The mailman reached into his bag and pulled out three Baby Ruths. "A little bird told me somebody was sick and could use some cheering up."

Billie would bet her bottom dollar that little bird was Miz Quana Belle. She minded everybody's business.

The mailman tipped his postal cap and hurried up the street, his mailbag banging his knees. Miz Merry Lynn said he was uglier than sin, but Billie didn't see it that way. He wasn't handsome like Roy Rogers, but he was nice to little kids, and in her book, that's what counted.

He knew practically everybody in town.

"I bet he knows where my daddy is." Billie shot off the porch and took out after the mailman with Lucy running along behind, yelling, "Wait for me."

Mr. Cotton heard them coming and turned around to wait.

"Please, sir, I was wondering if you ever knew my daddy? Saint Hughes?"

"Everybody knew him. He sure could play that horn."

"Mr. Cotton, sir, I've got me a cousin in the Delta who wants to find him." Lucy could tell a lie smoother than anybody Billie ever saw. "Roger wants to join Mr. Hughes's band. You reckon you could help him find the Saint, please, sir?"

"Maybe you can find out where he is." Billie drew circles in the dirt with her toe, acting like she didn't really care. That's the way a Hollywood movie star would do it. Then, just in case Queen's lectures on manners turned out to be true, Billie added, "Please, sir."

"Maybe I can, Miss Billie." He patted her on the head, then walked on down the street, whistling.

They raced back to Lucy's house and plopped down on the porch steps.

"Reckon I can go with you to find your daddy?"

"I guess." Most times Lucy was fun, but sometimes she acted like a prissy girl. "If you won't be a scaredy-cat."

"Hell, no, I won't." Though they were the same age, Lucy was experimenting with being grown-up and said *hell* a lot when her mama wasn't listening. Next she crossed her heart, a sacred sign that neither of them would break. For a while they swung their feet and slapped at mosquitoes. Billie was always the one to think up games, but she had more important things to think about.

A big black-and-white police car cruised by real slow. Probably looking for Miz Quana Belle's daddy again. He was always acting a fool and breaking the law.

The cop waved and they waved back. Suddenly Billie thought he might know more about where she could find her daddy than the mailman. But the police car had already turned at the corner, and it was too late to ask.

"You want to play jump rope?" Lucy said.

"Yeah, but we better give Peanut his Baby Ruth first." Last week Billie would have suggested they eat Peanut's candy and never tell him about it, but this week she was trying to be good. She'd promised God. It might be the only way to save her mama.

# Ten

WITH QUEEN TAKING REFUGE in the kitchen and Cassie standing on the front porch, looking nothing like the woman who'd sat in her living room stoutly proclaiming they were equals, Betty Jewel understood that who we are today might not be who we were yesterday. Yesterday Cassie had been a living, breathing fireball. Today she looked like somebody had snuffed out the light to her soul. Yesterday, Betty Jewel herself had been a proud woman, and today she was not even a woman she recognized. Home wrecker. Adulterer.

Maybe death was not going to be a tragedy for her, but a tender mercy.

"You lied." Cassie's face was so white it looked bloodless, and her voice was little more than a scratchy whisper. "Joe is not Billie's father."

Seeing Cassie this way and knowing she'd catapulted her into hell was another punishment for the great wrong Betty Jewel had visited upon Joe's wife. And Billie and Queen. She'd be gone and they'd be left behind to deal with the consequences. Who would have thought what she and Joe did nearly eleven years ago would come to this: anguish and guilt that ambush you around every corner?

"Come inside." Betty Jewel opened the door, and Cassie slid through like a ghost. All morning she'd known it would come to this. Her coffee had tasted like barbecue, the mocking bird outside her window had refused to sing, and the cherries in her pantry had turned black as the soul of a sinner.

As Cassie hovered near the chair where only yesterday she'd been filled with a crusader's zeal, Betty Jewel thought about the many ways there were to break a human heart. She prayed she had not shattered Cassie's beyond repair.

As she waited for Cassie to speak, she heard the low moan of blues. If your heart wasn't already smashed to pieces, the harmonica was sure to finish it off.

The music sighed through Betty Jewel like a memory, a prayer, a song you didn't want to sing.

"It's not a lie. She's Joe's child."

"No." Cassied covered her ears. "I won't listen to this."

"Then why are you here?"

"I want the truth."

"I'm telling you the truth."

"How do I know that? This could be some sort of petty revenge." As she talked, Cassie gained steam. Betty Jewel could see how much she wanted to believe what she was saying. "You made advances at that horrible juke joint, and he spurned you. Now you want to hurt me the way he hurt you."

"I want to show you something, Cassie. Why don't you sit down?"

"I won't sit on your chair."

That was pride talking. Betty Jewel guessed she'd do the same thing if she were in her shoes—spurn furniture, as ridiculous as it seemed.

"Fine. Suit yourself. I'll be right back."

Betty Jewel left Cassie standing in the middle of Queen's living room while she fetched the secret history of her life.

This took her a while. She'd kept it under lock and key in the top of her closet underneath a stack of old guilts for fear that Billie would find it. Only Queen knew where it was.

Her hands trembled when she took down the album. There was a picture of the Saint with his arm around her, smiling up from page one. A skinny man. The biggest thing about him was his feet. That and his talented lips, those lips that could bring down heaven with a silver trumpet and hell with a bottle of booze.

He had a wide nose and skin that spoke of native drums and Nigerian nights. To say that Billie could have sprung from his loins was as insane as saying a panther could sire a gazelle.

Next were pictures of Betty Jewel and Saint leaning against the bus, posing with his band, strolling down Michigan Avenue, her in a hat with feathers and the Saint in a baseball cap. You couldn't see anything of his face except teeth.

He wasn't the handsomest man on the block, but Lord, did he have charisma. He could light up a pitch-black parking lot with his smile.

And the way he looked at you…as if you were the only person in the room. Lord, Lord…

Had she been wrong to keep the past from Billie? Had she been wrong to let the Saint's name appear as her legal father, then hide him from her? Maybe she should have just gone along with the fable Billie's birth certificate told.

Betty Jewel turned to the page that featured Joe. There he was leaning against the upright piano in the den, crossing boundaries with music, his harmonica to his lips while Queen played the blues.

Betty Jewel had just come back from Chicago expecting to hole up and weep. Instead she'd found Joe Malone hanging out with his blues harp and his laughter that gave a hurting woman wings.

The rest of it simply happened, as natural as two birds migrating toward the same warm place.

Betty Jewel traced his face with a shaking finger. “I didn’t mean to hurt your wife, Joe. I never meant for this to happen.”

She’d thought she could keep her secret forever. She’d thought she could carry it to the grave. Pulling a pain pill from her pocket, she headed back to the den. Cassie was still standing. Betty Jewel didn’t say anything about getting comfortable in a chair. This was not going to be the kind of conversation that would make anybody cozy.

“I have something to show you.” Cassie nodded, giving her permission, and Betty Jewel saw that she’d made some attempt to pull herself together. There was no trace of tears now, only strength and resolve.

“Take a look at these.” Betty Jewel spread three photographs on the coffee table: the Saint, his features flat and his skin as shiny as patent leather, Joe, his cheekbones like knife blades and his dark hair cowlicked in a spot that never would comb down, and Billie.

She didn’t have to point out Joe’s cheekbones rearranged in Billie’s face, his cowlick in her chestnut hair, his green eyes staring out of her face. She didn’t have to say, *There’s no way the Saint could have fathered a girl with Billie’s coffee-cream skin.* She could see in Cassie’s wrecked face that Joe’s wife finally believed her.

“This proves nothing,” Cassie said.

“Billie looks just like Joe. Don’t you see how there’s not a single feature that resembles the Saint?”

“All these pictures tell me is that Saint Hughes is probably not Billie’s father. They don’t tell me who is.”

The truth would slice Cassie in two. Betty Jewel prayed God would forgive her for what she was about to do.

"Billie has a quarter moon birthmark on her left thigh. Just like Joe."

"You're lying." This fresh hell wouldn't let Cassie stand straight. Betty Jewel tried to catch her and they both collapsed onto the sofa. Cassie started crying, and Betty Jewel rubbed her back the way she did Billie's when her daughter had a fever. For a while, Cassie allowed it. For a while Betty Jewel believed they could unravel their tangled-up past and sew a new frock, one that suited them both.

Abruptly, Cassie pushed away from her. "Joe wouldn't have abandoned her. He'd have provided for her."

"Joe never knew."

"He didn't do this. He couldn't have."

"It happened one summer, the summer Saint went to prison."

"Please." Cassie held her hands in front of her face to ward off further hurt, but Betty Jewel couldn't stop now. She'd come too far, and she had a long way left to travel before she could rest.

"Joe was coming to Tiny Jim's, jamming on his blues harp while Queen played piano. One night he came on up to the house, and that's when it happened "

"He didn't love you. He couldn't."

"No, he never loved me, never even pretended to. We just hid our hurt in each other. One blistering summer night. And then it was over, for both of us."

That was a lie, but there was no need to tell Cassie. She'd been a one-night stand, all right, but Betty Jewel had never stopped loving Joe Malone, and that was the truth.

"Joe was the one who broke it off. He told me he loved you, that he'd always loved you. He apologized for what happened and said it would never happen again."

Sometimes, truth is so heavy you can't hold yourself upright. Betty Jewel put out a hand to keep Cassie from falling off the couch, but she jerked away.

"You expect me to believe that?"

Queen's Bible was on the coffee table. You could tell by looking it was not for show. Betty Jewel put her hand on its worn cover.

"I swear, it's the truth."

"You have no proof."

Betty Jewel's only proof was on the coffee table. Nothing else she could say would make a difference. Exhausted, she leaned back against the old couch and watched as Cassie studied Billie's picture, watched as her fierce expression collapsed. Still, her back was stiff with pride when she marched out the door.

Betty Jewel sat in the ruins of her encounter with Cassie, the clock ticking off minutes she didn't have to lose. What was she going to do next?

She heard Queen's shuffling steps, then Queen herself came into the room with a platter of cookies fresh from the oven. Without a word, she set the cookies on the coffee table and Betty Jewel took six. What did it matter?

"I didn't even smell these baking."

Queen patted her hand. "How'd it go, baby?"

"Awful." She ate three cookies before she could say another word. "I don't know how you can stand me."

"You my chile."

*And Billie is mine*, she thought. She'd do anything for Billie.

"Queen, do you think it's possible God can forgive a sinner like me?"

"Oh, baby..." Queen rocked Betty Jewel in her arms and started humming one of her favorite Fats Waller tunes. Betty Jewel didn't point out the tune was "Ain't Misbehavin'."

* * *

Fay Dean's car was in Cassie's driveway. She was waiting on the front porch.

"Cassie! Thank God. I've been calling since last night. I was about ready to call the police." The tragedy on Cassie's face brought Fay Dean to a standstill. "My God...what happened to you?"

Everything was boiling inside her trying to spill out, and yet she couldn't tell anyone. Especially not Fay Dean and Mike. They both thought Joe walked on water.

The whole town did. The man who'd led his baseball team to more championships than any coach in the history of Tupelo High was a hero to the town, a role model for his boys. If Cassie destroyed Joe, she'd hurt a lot of people. Nobody would idolize the man who had a tawdry affair with a woman from the wrong side of town.

Joe had to cross the social divide to find a woman different from her in every way—a rich, dark woman full of warmth and music, a fertile woman who took all the love and tenderness he had to give and then bore his child.

"Cassie?" Fay Dean's voice dragged her back to her front porch where the fragrance of roses combined with the stench of barbecue that still clung to Cassie. She covered her mouth and closed her eyes, but she could still envision the quarter moon birthmark on Billie's left thigh. "Are you all right?"

Fay Dean's hand on her arm jerked Cassie out of hell. Finding her voice, she asked, "What's the worst thing that ever happened to you?"

"That I'm a female lawyer in a Marilyn Monroe world."

"Seriously, Fay Dean."

"What is this, Cassie? What's wrong?"

Cassie moved toward the swing as if she were carrying an

overfilled bowl of soup that was about to spill on the brick floor. A floor Joe laid one summer.

*One blistering summer night.*

Was it the summer after they'd found Alice's body, the summer after Cassie had miscarried for the third time, the summer she'd asked Ben to give her more work at *The Bugle,* the summer Joe had slept on the sofa?

Cassie collapsed onto the swing, then set it in motion.

"Tell me the most awful thing that ever happened in your life, then tell me how you coped. Just talk, Fay Dean. Don't stop."

"I think the worst thing that ever happened to me was the awful fight I had with Daddy about going to law school.... Cassie?" Fay Dean's voice jolted her back to her front porch, her rearranged history. "You're pale. Have you had anything to eat today?" Cassie tried to remember and couldn't. "I thought so."

"The keys." Fay Dean held out her hand, Cassie dug up her keys, and then Fay Dean was inside the house. Cassie heard her on the phone telling her secretary to cancel all her appointments for the afternoon. She heard the refrigerator door slam. Or was it just her heart trying to break free of a body that could no longer contain all its pain?

The front door popped, and Fay Dean settled into the swing and took Cassie's hand. "It looks like a tornado ripped through your kitchen. What in the world happened in there?"

"I can't talk about it."

"Remember our pact? We were eight that summer."

*That summer...*Cassie decided to confront Joe. She didn't know why. There was a vague sense of something awry, a little kernel of fear that drove her out of *The Bugle*'s offices late one night in August.

She'd perfumed herself with gardenia, waited for Joe, told

him she wanted to try for another child. What had he said? Something noble. Something about not putting her through that again. Whatever it was, it had ended his long spell on the couch.

With the past clinging to her like pollen, Cassie leaned her head on the back of the swing and let herself drift to the sound of her best friend's voice.

"We said we'd tell each other everything. Let me help you, Cassie. Tell me what's wrong."

"This is something I have to work through myself, Fay Dean."

"I understand. But if you just want to cry or scream, I'm here for you. Any time, day or night."

Cassie wished she could let herself collapse on Fay Dean's shoulder. Or drive to an overlook on the Natchez Trace Parkway and scream into the silent hills. Just this once she longed to spill her burdens in a healing stream of tears.

But there weren't tears in the world to fix what was wrong.

"Come on, kiddo."

"Where?"

"The least I can do is feed you."

Fay Dean drove them to Dudie's Diner where she bought ten-cent burgers made with a recipe held over from the Depression—fifty percent flour and fifty percent ground beef, the scarcity of meat disguised with plenty of mustard and pickles.

Afterward, she drove back to Cassie's house with her radio blaring Hank Snow's latest hit, the first since 1950, according to the DJ. It took a while for Cassie to realize Hank and his Rainbow Ranch Boys were crooning "I Don't Hurt Anymore." She wished that were true. When she switched the radio off, Fay Dean didn't say a word.

Back home, they washed down their ten-cent burgers with

a Coca-Cola Fay Dean had found in the rubble of the kitchen, then she switched on the TV and found one of the Westerns they'd always loved. Fay Dean popped corn and shared a Hershey bar she found in her purse. Then she made tea, their brew of choice for anything that ailed them. Cassie sipped her drink, but the civilized act of sharing tea did nothing to restore her sense of balance. She was relieved when Fay Dean announced it was time for bed.

Then Cassie remembered.

"There are no sheets in the guest room," Cassie said.

Fay Dean gave Cassie her famous "I'm on to you" look. "That's all right."

Cassie found a gown for Fay Dean, then lay down on top of a quilt called Wedding Ring, a name she was beginning to hate. She hated the quilt called Around the World, too. Joe had promised they'd travel when they retired.

"Where are the sheets?"

"I gave them all to the Salvation Army."

"When?"

"This morning. I'm getting new ones." Nothing that had touched Joe's skin would ever touch hers again.

Fay Dean stood beside the bed, probably searching Cassie for signs of a nervous breakdown. Finally, she said, "Okay," then crowded under the quilts where they lay side by side, not speaking for a long time, measuring their breaths till they were inhaling and exhaling in sync like sisters.

"Cassie, are you awake?"

"Yes."

"Whatever it is, we'll find a way to make it all right."

Cassie wished she could believe her.

# Eleven

THURSDAY WAS ONE OF Queen's pie days. The scent of chocolate cream made Billie's mouth water. It almost made her forget about cancer. But Queen was humming a crying church song, "Abide With Me." The Mt. Zion choir wailed it over everybody who died.

If they planned to sing it over her mama, they might as well forget about it. Billie was planning to light out of Shakerag and bring her daddy home. And he'd make everything all right. Maybe he'd even find a golden palomino and ride to the rescue like the King of the Cowboys on Trigger.

"Billie, you comin' to hep me with these pies?" Queen hollered from the kitchen. She made it sound like a question, but Billie knew better. It was a pure dee order, and she'd better quit lollygagging in bed like some spoiled, rich white girl.

"Yes, ma'am. I'm coming."

Billie put on her nicest flour-sack shorts, the one with purple flowers that reminded her of a meadow somewhere far away. The Alps where it would be so cold cancer couldn't even get a toehold.

"You better shake a leg. I ain't got all day."

Billie scooted down the hall so fast she shimmied. "I'm shaking two legs, Queen."

"Lordy, have mercy. You a natural born sight."

When Queen laughed, all the different parts of her jiggled. It could have gone either way. Just as quick as her tickle box got turned over, Queen could have jerked her willow switch from behind the door and meted out justice for sassing.

The stove was still going, and it was so hot in the kitchen Queen had a sweat mustache and big wet patches under her arms. Pies were cooling all over the table and the countertops, pecan and sweet potato in homemade crusts, lemon and chocolate cream with meringue that looked like angel crowns, all peaked up and golden.

"Can I lick the bowls?"

"You can sop 'em with yo biscuit after you done said grace. And I ain't puttin up with no shirkin', neither."

Billy knew Queen meant business. When she bowed her head to thank the Lord God Almighty for her biscuit, she used a bunch of fancy words she'd learned from Brother Gibson. With her eyes shut tight, she thanked Him for bountiful blessings and bodacious grace. For good measure, she even threw in the Virgin Mary and Baby Jesus.

It worked, too, because when she was finished Queen patted her on the head and called her a *good little chile*.

"After you finishes eatin', you start loadin' them chocolate-cream pies in the basket. And mind not to mash 'em."

"No, ma'am, I won't." What she wanted to do was stick her finger in for a lick, but Queen had eyes in the back of her head.

"I prides myself on my pies."

"Can I go with you to take the pies to Tiny Jim?" Trying to act like her whole life didn't depend on Queen's answer, Billie made a circle on the cracked linoleum with her bare toe.

"What you wantin' to go to that juke joint for? Ain't nothin' there for chil'ren."

"Mama won't let me go to Lucy's on account of Peanut." She crossed her fingers and hoped Queen and God had more important things to do than pay attention to a little girl who wouldn't quit fibbing. "She says I ought to be more help to you, and I can tote the pies."

"Well, now, ain't that nice?"

Just that easy, Billie was heading off to the juke joint in the backseat of Tiny Jim's Bel Air—Queen in the front, holding a basket of chocolate cream pies, and her stuffed in the back with so many pies crammed around her, if she moved she'd end up in the middle of one. Tiny Jim, himself, was driving.

Billie wondered what the preacher would say if he knew she was on the road to Perdition. He was always ranting about how robbing and stealing and lying put you on the dark road to Perdition. She didn't know the whereabouts of Perdition, but she did know where her latest lie was leading her—Tiny Jim's juke joint.

Soon as he stopped the car, she hopped out and started unloading pies without even being asked. Queen and Tiny Jim both patted her on the head and called her a *good little chile.* Then she followed them into the big kitchen at the back of the juke joint, meek as Roy Rogers singing "Happy Trails to You." Nobody would suspect he was fixing to pull out his six-shooter and get the bad guys.

A woman not much taller than Billie stood at the stove stirring a huge pot of soup. Her cornrows were plaited so tight it made her eyes look like a Chinaman's.

"They's plenty'a ham and biscuits you can eat while Miss Queen and I conduct bidness," Tiny Jim said. "If you need anything else, you just ask Ethel."

"Thank you, Mr. Tiny Jim. That's mighty nice."

Queen's eyebrows didn't lift into her hair, which was a sign Billie was staying on her good side. "You stay outta trouble till I gets back, you hear?"

"Yes, ma'am."

Tiny Jim patted Billie on the head, then left her sitting on a stool in front of a platter full of food. But she didn't have time to waste eating, even if it was a breakfast fit for Dale Evans.

"Miss Ethel, I got a powerful urge to go to the toilet."

"Out back. They's a Sears and Roebuck cat'log if you needs it."

"Thank you, ma'am."

Billie scooted out of the kitchen as fast as she could. But not before she'd grabbed a ham and biscuit and crammed it in her pocket.

Behind the kitchen was a short hall with a coatrack on the wall and a spittoon underneath. With the kitchen stove on one side of the wall and the barbecue pits out back, it was so hot Billie thought it might be close to what Hell felt like. She hoped she didn't find out any time soon.

There was a screen door on the left that led to the outhouse. Billie popped it open, but she didn't have any intention of going through. Her mission was down the hall in front of a door marked Office.

Hunkering down till she was no bigger than a butter bean, she flattened her face on the dusty wood floor and peered under the door. Tiny Jim's big shiny shoes were right in front of her nose. Billie put a hand over her mouth to keep from screaming.

When she got through shaking, she noticed they were pointed the other way. She'd write a thank-you letter to God if she knew where to mail it.

"Miss Queen, you and Betty Jewel's askin' for trouble with that white woman."

Tiny Jim's booming voice sounded like it was right in Billie's ear.

"We ain't meanin' no harm."

"Harm's done come, and that's the God's truth." Tiny Jim's shiny shoes stomped across the floor, then back again. "They was another lynchin' last night down in the Delta."

"Who?"

"My cousin, Cleveland. He was passin' out pamp'lets urgin' our folks to sign up for the vote. They strung 'em up on Dark Fear Road."

"Dear Lord Jesus."

Queen began to moan and petition God, the sounds as mournful as the blues that suddenly filled the hot hall. Sweat coated Billie's face and rolled down her dusty legs.

She balled her hands into fists, but she didn't run.

"Miss Queen, you gotta get ahold of yo'self. You and Betty Jewel need somethin', you come to me. Leave Miz Malone out of it."

"We just tryin' to help Billie, thas all."

"We can take care of our own."

"I ain't gone die till I sees her fixed up and outta the clutches of that Saint Hughes."

"He gives you any trouble, let me know. I'll go up to Memphis and see if I can talk some sense into 'em."

The truth burst through Billie bright as Fourth of July fireworks. She unfolded her butter-bean self and tiptoed down the hall. She'd just eased through the screen door when she heard Tiny Jim and Queen coming from his office. Quick as a firefly, she was in the outhouse tearing pages out of the Sears and Roebuck catalog and throwing them down the hole. It never hurt to leave evidence, just in case somebody checked.

She heard the screen door pop open.

"Billie? You out there, chile?"

"Yes, ma'am."

"Time to go."

It sure was. Billie was more than glad to leave the toilet.

When she got to be in charge, she'd make it against the law to have outhouses.

The clock said nine, which was unbelievable to Cassie. She'd slept soundly and long.

That was Fay Dean for you. When she was beside Cassie, she could almost believe that Betty Jewel hadn't rearranged her history, that life would go on as usual.

Cassie squinted toward the bedside table, then picked up the note scrawled on yellow legal paper.

*I had an early appointment I couldn't cancel. I'll be back this evening to take you home with me, and I won't take no for an answer.*

Cassie crawled out of bed, ten years older overnight. Instead of seeing the rose-colored carpet she loved and Joe had tolerated, she was seeing Joe's green eyes in Billie's face. Instead of noticing the blousy English roses blooming outside her window, she was remembering his cheekbones holding up Billie's warm-toned skin, his lanky frame replicated in a ten-year-old girl who was all legs.

Joe's almost-motherless child was locked inside her, and Cassie couldn't seem to get her out. Billie was digging a hole so deep that if Cassie weren't careful, she'd take up permanent residence.

Work, that's what she needed.

On the way to the closet everything inside her splintered. She'd been naive to believe she and Joe were different. She'd been a fool to think they'd somehow escaped the monster that waits behind closed doors to ambush hurting couples.

It wasn't work she needed, but answers. If anyone would know what Joe did the summer Betty Jewel claimed he'd fathered her child, it would be Ben.

Gut-punched with memories, she saw the three of them on Moon Lake, Joe and Ben hooking lures with names like Hula Dancer to their fishing poles, and Cassie sitting in the boat reading aloud from a book of Robert Frost's poems. She used to love the way their conversations mimicked the lazy drift of the currents. She loved the feeling of the sun on her face and listening to the calls of birds. Occasionally she would look up and say, "What's that?" and Ben would say, "Brown thrush."

From her kitchen window, she could see his car in the driveway. That meant Ben was working from home. Without the rigorous demands of a daily paper, he often chose to hole up with his typewriter on his sun porch.

"My muse is a stubborn little sun-worshipping, sweets-loving goddess," he'd tell Cassie. "Sometimes she won't even come out unless I coax her with a plateful of cookies."

If Cassie had cookies in her cabinets, she'd take them over. If she had butter and sugar, time and wits, she'd make Ben a pie. After all he'd done for her, didn't he deserve a pie?

She slipped out of her kitchen and through the hedge to knock on his back door, empty-handed and slightly off-kilter.

"Cassie. What a pleasant surprise." Ben was a square, noble-nosed, sandy-haired man, not much taller than Cassie. She used to glimpse him standing beside her dazzling husband, and Ben would simply vanish, become nothing more than Joe's shadow. Still, when Ben studied you with his laser blue eyes, you'd think he knew things you'd barely even admit to yourself. "Come in. The coffee's hot."

"I hope I'm not interrupting your work."

"You could never be an interruption." He poured her a cup, topped it off with cream, then led her to a wicker rocking chair in his sunroom.

Though she wasn't the kind of woman who needed handling like china, and hardly ever allowed herself the luxury, she was grateful for a friend who knew how she liked her coffee, who understood how she craved sunlight when she was hurting.

"I needed this, Ben."

"I know." He settled into his desk chair, cradling his cup, studying her over the rim.

"How?"

"Fay Dean's car in your driveway last night. Your face. I can always read your face, Cassie." He sipped from his coffee mug, watching without judging, which was Ben's way.

And yet, Cassie wasn't ready to give up the marital history she'd invented. The truth was in her bones, but she couldn't bring herself to talk to Ben about that summer so long ago, the vague sense she'd had that something was amiss. She'd be sitting at her desk at *The Bugle* editing copy when all of a sudden she'd feel as if somebody had stepped on her heart. She'd look up and see a full moon through the window and say, "It must be lunar madness."

Now she understood how you can copyedit your own life in order to delete hurtful truth. She understood how pride wears blinders.

"This is not easy, Ben."

"I'm sorry, Cassie." Ben took a paperweight off his cluttered desk, the Statue of Liberty, forever preserved in a globe of water. He tested its weight as if it were truth and he was judging how much to tell. "I didn't want you to go to Shakerag."

"Obviously the grapevine's alive and well. What are they saying about me now, Ben? Not that I care."

"This is not just some little women's club you've turned upside down. They're saying you're fraternizing with coloreds, and somebody ought to take you down a notch."

Temper boiled her face as red as her hair. "And *they* would be the likes of Rick Monaghan. That's an old grudge, Ben."

"You've stirred up more than the Chief of Police. Cassie, this is the wrong time to be fighting for whatever cause you've chosen up in Shakerag."

Billie rose in Cassie's mind, Betty Jewel's child with eyes that held a tunnel leading back through the years, green eyes you'd never forget.

"How much did Joe tell you, Ben? About that summer?"

Her blunt statement sucked all the air out of Ben, sagged him back in his chair.

"Joe's gone, Cassie. There's no need to dredge up the past."

"I can't ask him what happened. I'm asking you."

"How much do you already know?"

"Did Joe sleep with Betty Jewel Hughes?"

"God, Cassie..."

Ben got up and reached for her, but she jumped out of her chair. All she could see was Betty Jewel, beautiful before cancer ravaged her, spread out underneath her husband, her long brown fingers locked on his back, her fingernails scoring his skin. The skin that tasted like salt and wind after one of his baseball games.

The truth roared through Cassie, a tornado leaving behind a wasteland.

"Why, Ben?"

"He loved you, Cassie. Let that be enough."

"I can't." For a reason she couldn't say, a reason she hoped she'd never have to say, Joe's child dreaming a little girl's dreams, innocent to the ways poverty and prejudice would squeeze her till there was nothing left but hatred and bitterness.

The roller coaster she'd been on since she found out about Joe tilted over and threw her into space where there was nothing to hold on to. Without a word, Ben offered a shoulder, and she soaked his shirt. There was a river running wild in her, and she could no longer construct a dam.

Sudden alarm skittered through her. Was she using Ben? Sending the wrong message?

"I'm sorry, Ben."

"Don't be."

She pulled back from his easy comfort. "I didn't mean to fall apart."

"Nobody does." Ben pulled a handkerchief from his pocket and handed it to her. "He said Betty Jewel was the most hurting woman he'd ever seen. I'm not trying to excuse him, but you know how tender-hearted he was."

It was true. Joe used to catch moths beating themselves to death against lamps and take them outside to turn them loose.

"He said it was a mistake, an impulsive one-night stand. He told me he never stopped loving you, not for one minute. He said he'd give his pitching arm if he could take it back."

That would have been Joe, swearing by baseball, his first love. His second was blues. Until Betty Jewel dropped her bombshell, Cassie had always thought she came third.

Suddenly, the blues lament was so fierce in Ben's house Cassie was stripped of everything except a heart beating too fast. It was a vast relief to realize that the distant music was a Delta bluesman wailing from the radio in Ben's kitchen.

"Does anyone else know?"

When he said, "No," Cassie was nearly washed clean again.

If no one in this town knew, maybe she could pretend it hadn't happened.

Except for Billie.

How could she shut her eyes to Joe's child? Family is family, no matter what.

# Twelve

QUEEN WAS IN THE living room playing that song Billie hated. Her mama sang along, her voice weak and shaky. "I'll Be Seeing You," it was called. It was the theme song to remember the World War II dead. That's how old it was. Billie knew because if there was anything in her house that was sacred, it was the Bible and music.

Billie didn't know why Mama wanted Queen to play such a tearjerker unless she was trying to remind her defiant daughter that she was dying, and afterward when Billie looked at the empty front porch swing she'd see a shadow of her mama sitting here, some kind of ghostly reminder.

It was creepy, plus the piano needed a good tuning. It was a battered old upright that Billie knew good and well wouldn't compare to the rosewood upright Queen had before she was born. She'd sold it to help pay for Billie's mama's college education, but you'd never hear Queen complain.

Billie was trying not to listen to the music. What she was doing was packing what she'd need in a paper sack—a comb, underwear, her nightgown and a change of shorts. A while ago her mama came knocking on her door, and she hid the sack under her bed and grabbed her doll that had one button eye missing.

"What are you doing in here by yourself?" Mama had asked, and Billie told her she was fixing to sew a new eye on Little Ella. The doll was once named Daisy, but Billie had renamed her after she'd overheard her mama telling how she and the Saint were once on the playbill at the Apollo Theater in Harlem with Ella Fitzgerald.

Mama had put her hands on her hips, which was usually a sign she was fixing to get to the bottom of Billie's tall tales, but tonight she just went back to singing that sappy song.

Here was Billie's plan. It was supposed to be clear tonight with a full moon, and she figured it was as good a time as any to go and find her daddy. There was no use sitting around on Maple Street just thinking about it.

Besides, she'd already made plans with Lucy. After she'd found out her daddy's whereabouts, she'd told Queen she was going to the park, then lit out to Lucy's like her coattail was on fire.

Tomorrow she'd be so far away from Shakerag they wouldn't be able to find her with police dogs. Which was another thought. What if they sicced the bloodhounds on her? After dead Alice disappeared, they'd used dogs to find her. Miz Merry Lynn still talked about how she'd wake up in the middle of the night and hear them baying.

In the living room, Queen was still making the piano walk and talk. Ordinarily, Billie would have been right there with them, watching Queen strike her big bass blues chords and hanging over her shoulder, adding a few treble notes.

Shutting her ears to the music that was tugging at her heart and trying to nail her feet to the floor, Billie dragged her sack from under the bed so she could stuff Little Ella inside. She might as well see the world, too.

She'd meant to pack the ham and biscuit she'd snatched from Tiny Jim's that morning, but by afternoon the smell of country-fried ham had knocked her plans a winding. She'd eaten it on the way home from Lucy's.

"Billie?"

She nearly jumped out of her skin. Queen was standing in her doorway, and she hadn't even heard her coming. She wondered if her grandmother had been spying. You couldn't underestimate her. If you did, you'd be in big trouble.

"Playin' with yo doll?"

"Yes, ma'am."

"I'm gone wring the neck of that old Dominecker hen out back. Come hep me pluck the feathers. Yo mama's havin' one a her good days, and she's got a hankerin' for some chicken an' dumplin's."

Wouldn't you know it? Queen was making food you couldn't even pack in plastic containers without the lid popping off and spilling stuff all over yourself.

"Billie, did you hear me?"

"Yes, ma'am. I'm coming."

Billie followed along behind Queen, but she did everything to delay her chore except drag her feet. If she was in charge of things, little girls would never be asked to pull the feathers off a dead chicken, especially one that wasn't even going to end up in the frying pan.

After the longest chicken plucking in the history of the world, Billie had to wash up good then stand in the kitchen while Queen showed her how to make dumplings. She didn't even know if her daddy liked dumplings.

The only good part was when her mama came in to watch.

"You're doing a good job, Billie. I'm proud of you."

"Would my daddy be proud?"

"I'm sure he would."

"Does my daddy love me?"

Mama looked like a balloon that had lost all its air. "If he'd known you, he'd have loved you as much as I do."

"He didn't know me because he was traveling and being famous." She left out the part about prison. The other kids probably made that up, anyway.

"That's right, Billie.... Saint was once the most famous bluesman in the South. And he *was* gone a lot. In fact he was gone when you were born. I never did get a chance to tell him that he had the most wonderful daughter in the world."

All those years of waiting for love through the mail caved in on her chest, and she couldn't breathe. Billie raced out onto the front porch to get some air, but it was so hot outside it felt like bees buzzing around in her head.

Billie swatted the air, trying to bat them away, but her head wouldn't clear no matter what she did. Her mama was standing in the doorway, telling her supper was ready, but she didn't care.

"I'm going to bed."

It would serve her mama right if she never ate again. She raced past her, and Queen hollered, "Billie, you better mine yo mama," but she didn't stop. She wouldn't stop if Queen brought out a gazillion willow switches. She ran, just her and the awful sound of bees.

"Let her go, Mama. She's hurting, too."

Billie stretched out on her bed and tried to replace the bees with the sounds of her life on Maple Street—the clatter of plates and the hum of her mama and Queen talking over their chicken and dumplings, the call of a hoot owl in the pine tree behind old Miz Quana Belle's and the faraway mourn of a blues harp. She lay there till the moon shone through her window, till there was no sound in the house except her own breathing.

And when the moon was laying a path through Shakerag that looked like you could follow it to someplace faraway, someplace better, Billie grabbed her paper sack and lit out. But the bees were still buzzing in her head to beat the band.

Cassie and Fay Dean were lying side by side on the woven hammock she and Joe had bought the summer they'd gone to Pawleys Island, just lying there with candy wrappers on their stomachs and their eyes fixed on the stars.

Joe had swung the hammock between two ancient cedars, and she had planted hostas, ginger lilies and a gardenia bush because she loved the fragrance. She called this place her angel garden because this was where she came when she needed to listen to the wisdom of the universe, when she needed to hear the whisper of angels.

The gardenia bush had grown so big she and Fay Dean had to wait for the moon to rise over the top before they could appreciate its full splendor.

"I'm glad you said no about going to my place." Fay Dean pushed her foot against the cedar tree and set the hammock into motion. "Your house is so much more beautiful and peaceful than my efficiency apartment."

Cassie didn't know if Fay Dean was right about the peacefulness. Since Betty Jewel's bombshell, there had been none, no matter where she turned.

"Look." Fay Dean pointed to the night sky. "There's Venus rising just beneath the moon. And Saturn."

Watching the spectacular threesome, Cassie listened for whispers and listened hard.

"A friend once told me he could never look at the nighttime sky and think unkind thoughts," Cassie said.

"He must have been a saint."

Fay Dean was right. Only a saint could look at the stars

and forget what Joe had done. Cassie had never come close to sainthood. Didn't even aspire to it.

Suddenly she was seeing Betty Jewel with her sticking-out bones and Billie with Joe's eyes, and she was thinking about betrayal: she was thinking about her husband with another woman for one prodigal summer evening. She was thinking how something ugly, something ripping her heart out, had produced an innocent human being, a little girl who had nothing to do with a marriage plunging over a cliff, a memory now tainted beyond repair.

The universe was whispering, and Cassie was listening. You can't go through life with a shut-down heart, is what she was hearing. You can't crab walk backward and crawl into a hole. To live abundantly, you have to race toward the future with arms and heart wide open. You have to risk everything and let the universe take care of the details.

And you have to pay attention.

Fay Dean shoved her foot against the trunk of the cedar tree and set the hammock in motion once more. Cassie closed her eyes, lay very still and imagined the universe rocking her in tender and loving arms.

Betty Jewel couldn't have said what woke her—the awful feeling that she'd entered her own nightmare and couldn't find her way back or the wail of sirens. They sounded like somebody crying. They really did.

She lay on her bed covered with sweat, unable to find the strength to push back her tangled covers and get up to pee.

"Betty Jewel? Baby?"

Queen was standing in her doorway looking like a rumpled pile of laundry. She was always perfectly groomed, even before daylight, her lisle cotton stockings rolled around her knees and her starched apron in place. As if her appearance weren't enough to set off alarms, she was so pale she looked as if she'd been dusted with Evening in Paris bath talc.

"Mama, are you sick?"

"It ain't me. It's Billie."

They say that when your child is in danger, you can pick up the end of an automobile. Betty Jewel jumped out of bed and raced down the hall, her legs suddenly strong enough to run to Hell and back if she had to.

Billie's room had that empty feeling a house gets after somebody dies, all her earthly possessions still in place but looking as if nobody had touched them for years. Her bed was made without a wrinkle, her teddy bear propped against the pillows. Her Sunday dress was in her closet along with her winter coat and her Sunday shoes. But her everyday shoes were gone, as well as the little pair of flower-sack shorts she'd have pulled off and laid by the side of the bed last night when she put on her gown.

"She's probably outside on top of that old bus, Mama."

"I done looked. She ain't there."

Queen crumpled onto Billie's bed and commenced assailing the Gates of Heaven to keep her child safe.

"Stop it, Mama. She's at the park."

"She wouldn' go off without tellin'. 'Specially not 'fore daylight."

"She has to be at Lucy's."

Billie would never tell that she was going someplace she wasn't supposed to be. Charged with a new hope, Betty Jewel was halfway down the hall to phone Sudie when she remembered that people like Wayne and Sudie didn't have telephones, barely-hanging-on people with fear in one pocket and despair in the other.

She leaned against the wall to catch her breath. Behind

her, Queen shuffled up, her bedroom slippers dragging more than usual.

"Set down, baby, 'fore you fall."

Suddenly weak-kneed, she let her mama lead her to the couch. Billie was gone. She knew that as surely as she knew she was dying. Had someone taken her? Saint Hughes sneaking through the night? Had her nightmares been brought on by the specter of her own death or by the stealthy sounds of a devil-man hidden by shadows as he climbed through Billie's window and snatched her out of her bed?

"Mama, we've got to check Billie's room again."

Her window was open, as were the windows in all the stifling hotboxes in Shakerag during the summertime. Undisturbed, the screen held a collection of moths that had beat themselves to death trying to follow the light. But it held no slits or tears, no signs of forced entry.

Still, with the faint echoes of a blues harp stripping her skin off inch by inch and the smell of barbecue so strong in the house the air she breathed tasted of pork, Betty Jewel felt no relief.

"Do you see anything missing, Mama?"

"Little Ella's done gone. And them checkedy shorts I made last summer."

"Oh, my God." She couldn't go traipsing all over Shakerag looking for Billie. These days she could barely even get from the bedroom to the kitchen. And Queen's hip wouldn't last two blocks.

"We needs to call Tiny Jim, baby. He'll know what to do."

It was Merry Lynn who answered, not Tiny Jim. Volatile, childless Merry Lynn with her gaping wound that would never heal. How could Betty Jewel tell her that Billie was missing?

She dredged up old acting skills she'd used when she'd

enter the spotlight after Saint had turned into the devil on hard drugs, enter with a smile on her face and a song on her lips. Watching her from the audience you'd never know she was a glass woman just waiting for the hammer blow that would break her apart.

She apologized for calling so early, made some excuse about not being able to sleep and needing to talk. She endured Merry Lynn's lecture about not letting her and Sudie take Betty Jewel to a Memphis doctor, about not allowing Merry Lynn to take her to Curl Up 'n Dye for a new hairdo.

"With what, pray tell? The three hairs I have left on my head?"

"You could get a wig. They've got some in Memphis that would make you look like Ava Gardner."

"Good Lord, why would I want to look like Ava Gardner?"

"I ought to come up there and whip your butt, Betty Jewel."

"About my hair?"

"About letting that white woman come to our neighborhood. Everybody's scared to death. No telling what she'll accuse you of. For God's sake, Betty Jewel, look what happened to Hilliard Brooks."

The man who had been shot to death over in Montgomery, Alabama, for trying to board the bus from the front. That Merry Lynn would grab a hold of one of the worst incidents from three years back just showed the state of her mind.

"I'm not trying to get on a bus, Merry Lynn. Just get through what's left of the rest of my life."

With her head and heart both about to split, Betty Jewel inquired about Tiny Jim.

"He's gone."

"Gone? Where?"

"To the Delta. To his cousin's funeral. Didn't Miss Queen tell you?"

Of course not. Her mama kept all talk of death and dying from Betty Jewel. She even turned off the radio when there was news of another arrest, another KKK burning, another lynching.

The knowledge that Billie had vanished into a world gone crazy was bad enough. That she'd vanished under her mother's care made her disappearance unbearable. After she hung up, Betty Jewel toppled sideways. Wrapped in her mama's arms she cried the river Jordan. And when there were no more tears, she picked up the phone and called the parsonage. The preacher's wife answered.

"Is Brother Joshua there?"

"He's over in Arkansas to conduct his best friend's weddin'. Anything I can do, hon?"

Betty Jewel imagined timid Martha Sue beating the bushes of Shakerag in the dark, looking for a lost child.

She said, "No, thank you," and hung up, despair pouring over her like dirty dishwater. "He's not there, Mama."

"Ain't no sense callin' the cops. No bunch a white men is gone set out 'fore daylight lookin' for a little colored girl." Queen heaved herself off the couch. "I'm gone get on my stockin's and fetch Wayne."

"Good Lord. You can't walk to Sudie's in the dark. You'd kill yourself."

"Ain't but one thing to do, then."

"I can't just sit here waiting. But if I start out to Sudie's, I wouldn't make it halfway."

"Who said anythin' 'bout waitin'? I'm thinkin' it'd be bes' to call Cassie."

"For God's sake, Mama!"

"God's sake is right. He done put a kine bone in that woman's body. I seen it plain as day."

Betty Jewel hated being beholden to anybody, especially the woman she had betrayed. But still, she picked up the phone and dialed. Because her back was to the wall. Because she was a mother who would do anything for her child, even grovel.

# Thirteen

THE PHONE JARRED CASSIE out of sleep. "Hello," she said, and a shaky voice on the other end of the line said, "You've got to come."

"Come where? Who is this?"

"It's Betty Jewel. Billie's gone."

Beside her, Fay Dean sat upright, instantly alert in that cat-like way of hers, and snapped on the bedside light. "What's wrong, Cassie? Give me that phone."

She held up her hand, holding off the sister-in-law who wanted to fix everything, and could do it, too, if she got half a chance. Then, covering the receiver, she said to Fay Dean, "It's business. That's all."

She was becoming a woman she didn't even know, a woman with easy lies on her lips.

Still, how could she leap out of bed at the crack of dawn and race off to Shakerag to help the woman who had betrayed her when she could barely even help herself?

Something approaching forgiveness comes easy in the company of your best friend and a moon so beautiful it makes you cry. It comes harder in the cold light of reality.

In a gown and mussed hair that allowed for no self-delusions, she saw herself for what she was—a drowning woman clinging to every little ragged plank of hope that floated by, clinging by her fingernails and trying to hold on.

And wasn't Betty Jewel doing the same thing? Calling a white woman she barely even knew to join forces with her in the middle of a dark storm that was sweeping through the South with such force it was bound to blow them both away.

"Please," Betty Jewel said. "I have nowhere else to turn."

"I'll be right there."

Cassie looked at Fay Dean, who guarded every one of her secrets as if they were Fort Knox and she was entrusted with the only key. But how could she say, *I'm off to help find your brother's little café-au-lait child?* Instead she said, "Don't even ask."

It was still early, even for Shakerag. The men who worked the cotton fields and slaughtered hogs at the packing house were long gone, but the maids heading to the Jefferson Davis Hotel and the dishwashers walking toward Dudie's Diner and Johnny's Drive-In filled the air with their chatter. Some of the lucky ones were going to the fancier restaurants like the Gaslight and to the big houses in Highland Circle and on Church and Jefferson Streets in downtown Tupelo.

The minute Cassie's red Ford Coupe convertible came into sight, their chatter ceased. They'd have been hardly more than dark shadows moving along the cracked dirt pathways except for the sullen stares they cast her way.

She wished she'd taken a cab. She wished she'd swapped cars with Fay Dean. She wished to be anywhere except driving through this hostile crowd, her milky skin covered with freckles and her hair blowing in the wind like a red flag waved at a bull. Riding in a nearly new convertible with the top down, to boot.

If she made a quick turn into Tiny Jim's Blues and Barbecue, she could head back toward Highland Circle. Obviously these people thought that's where she belonged. And so did everybody else. Ben wasn't happy with her bullheaded ways, and her father-in-law would be mortified if he knew what she was up to. Fay Dean had told her she was the latest hot topic of gossip at Tupelo's garden and book clubs. Even Fay Dean, herself, would have tried to talk her out of today's errand, which was probably useless and might well prove to be dangerous.

But then there was Billie, vanished. Not just Joe's illegitimate child or Betty Jewel's soon-to-be orphaned daughter, but a little girl who reminded Cassie of herself at that age, a fierce, independent ten-year-old Cassie was beginning to think of as separate from what Joe had done.

She white-knuckled the steering wheel and stayed her course, being careful to keep her eyes straight ahead. When Betty Jewel's house came into view, she'd have felt relieved if there hadn't been a car parked out front, an ancient Studebaker with both taillights missing, a dented front fender and so much of the paint gone you couldn't even tell what color it had been.

Now what?

She got out of her car and smoothed down her pants. This was not the kind of day to wear a skirt. Who knew where the search for Joe's child would take her?

Miss Queen appeared in the doorway, every line in her face holding her heartbreak. Blues and the scent of barbecue swirled around her so thick she reminded Cassie of one of the pictures she'd seen on the wall inside, the Ascension of Jesus Christ, almost invisible behind the clouds.

"Come on in. Betty Jewel's waitin' on you."

If there was ever anybody who needed a hug, it was this

proud old woman. But Cassie didn't dare. Push the boundaries too far and no telling who would get hurt.

She followed Miss Queen into the same shabby living room where life as she knew it had ceased. Betty Jewel sat in the corner of the sofa hugging a threadbare pink chenille bathrobe around herself, and opposite, her posture as straight as the back of the chair on which she sat, was a woman Cassie didn't know, a hard-working woman with cracked knuckles and a mended skirt, tight cornrowed hair and weary eyes.

"Cassie, this is my best friend, Sudie Jenkins. Her little girl, Lucy, is missing, too."

"I'm sorry, Sudie."

Sudie studied Cassie with the thoroughness of somebody looking for every flea on a hound dog. She'd didn't know when she'd felt so out of place and out of her element.

Finally Sudie said, "Betty Jewel, you have plumb lost your mind."

"I asked Cassie to come. To help me find Billie."

"We don't need a white woman telling us what to do. I've had my bait of it, and I'd think you would, too."

Torn between leaving and staying, Cassie was just deciding on the former when Miss Queen stood up, her thick eyebrows drawn down so low she looked like she was glaring at Sudie through a blackberry bush.

"Sudie, I ain't never allowed no back talk to guests in my house, and I ain't fixin' to start now."

"I'm sorry, Miss Queen." Sudie left her chair and headed toward the door. "Betty Jewel, are you coming with me or not?"

For a heartbeat, it looked as if Betty Jewel would follow Sudie. And then Cassie would be off the hook. She could go back to Highland Circle and start piecing together a life that didn't include good memories of a philandering husband. But

Betty Jewel just shook her head *no,* a gesture both hopeless and filled with a stubborn belief in her own decisions.

Sudie rushed out of the house, slamming the front screen door behind her.

Her departure left a silence so big nothing could get through, not even the sound of the blues. Sweat inched down Cassie's face in this little shack slowly baking in the sun. By noon, the heat would be brutal. Spying a fan from Mt. Zion Baptist Church that featured a picture of Jesus wearing a crown of thorns, Cassie jerked it up and started to cool herself.

"I guess I have just plumb lost my mind." Betty's Jewel's voice was so faint, at first Cassie wasn't sure of what she'd heard. Then she knew. She and this woman were just alike.

"I have, too," Cassie said. "People have been telling me that all my life."

"Thank God."

"Amen." Queen tacked on her benediction. "I'm gone perk us some strong black coffee and make plenty a biscuits. We gone need it."

"Thank you, Miss Queen, but I've already eaten." Cassie hadn't, but she wasn't about to consume food in the house of people who looked as if they could barely afford to feed themselves.

After Queen left, there was no sound in the room except the echo of faltering footsteps. When the silence between them had stretched to the breaking point, Betty Jewel asked, "Are you scared to eat Negro food?"

"No. I'm just not hungry."

Surprised at the sudden hostility coming from the woman who had called for help, Cassie struggled to remain calm. What in the world was she doing on this godforsaken side of town? Everybody was right about her. She ought to turn around, go home and mind her own business.

She was halfway out of her chair when she thought of Billie, an innocent child whose best chance for being found just might be with Cassie.

Sinking back, she said, "How long has Billie been missing?"

Betty Jewel bent over, coughing, her breath stolen by cancer and fear. Remorse, too?

"She went to bed early last night, and she was gone when Mama got up. Before sunrise. I'm hoping she's off someplace playing. I thought if we could ride around in your car, we might find her."

"Not till I put the top up." Remembering the sullen shadows gliding silently through Shakerag, Cassie cringed at the thought of what might happen next. "And do you have a head scarf I could borrow?"

"Yes. As long as you're not scared of Negro germs."

Heat colored Cassie's skin, but shared heartache held her still, hers and Betty Jewel's, and a past they'd shared whether they'd meant to or not.

"Betty Jewel, let's get something straight. I'm here because I choose to be. But I'm no saint. I have my limits. If we're going to find Billie, we have to be united."

"When I get to thinking too much about everything, I lash out at everybody, even my saint of a mama."

"I do, too. I broke every dish in my kitchen."

"I'm sorry, Cassie."

"Me, too." She held out her hand because it felt like the right thing to do. For a while it looked like a pale fish waiting there between them, but finally Betty Jewel took it. And holding on to her didn't feel a bit different than holding on to Fay Dean.

"Biscuits is ready," Queen hollered from the kitchen, and Betty Jewel said, "Let me get you that head rag."

★ ★ ★

Betty Jewel had died and gone to hell. That was the only way to make any sense of Billie fleeing in the middle of the night and her sitting in a rich, white woman's car, driving through Shakerag in plain sight. If a coughing fit didn't kill her, then a rock hurled by somebody whose cousin had been lynched, torched or dragged behind a pickup truck would do the job. The best she could hope for was that folks would think Cassie had come to pick up her maid.

Miz Quana Belle looked up from sweeping her front porch and glared at them as they drove away from the blue house; her daddy, leaning sideways and losing his liquor in front of Tiny Jim's, straightened up enough to shake his fist. The only friendly face Betty Jewel saw was J. D. Cotton loping along the dusty path to deliver the *Daily Sentinel* to the pitiful few customers in that part of town.

Cassie pulled alongside him and rolled down her window. "Good morning, J.D. We're looking for two little girls, Billie Hughes and Lucy Jenkins." Cassie handed him the little black-and-white Kodak picture Betty Jewel had given her. "Have you seen either of them?"

"There were some little ladies playing at Carver park when I passed by. I didn't notice who was there. Is something wrong, Cassie?"

"We hope not. But if you see Billie and Lucy, please tell them to go home. Their mamas are worried."

"I sure will." He tipped his hat and walked on down the path, his mailbag banging against his knees.

Cassie headed the car toward the park, but Betty Jewel's instincts told her what they'd find—a ragtag group of kids too young to work the fields, too young to be in charge of their siblings but babysitting nonetheless because there was nobody else at home to do the job.

Cassie parked her car at the entrance to Carver Park, and Betty Jewel barely had enough breath to say, "You go while I sit here and rest a bit. Besides, it'll be quicker without me."

As Cassie raced off, Betty Jewel was no longer thinking of her as the white woman she'd betrayed but as a fierce, compassionate woman who had risked her life coming to Shakerag to rescue her own dead husband's mulatto child.

If Betty Jewel were her sainted mama, she'd bow her head in gratitude. But she didn't have time to close her eyes. She couldn't shut her eyes till Billie was safe.

A black-and-white police car with homely Charlie Monaghan at the wheel slowed to a crawl when he saw Betty Jewel sitting in a fancy white folks' car. A different place, a different time, she'd have asked him for help, but with the specter of Jim Crow towering over them, Betty Jewel averted her gaze and waited for him to go on by.

By the time Cassie slammed the door and slid behind the wheel, the police cruiser was out of sight.

"I'm sorry, Betty Jewel. They're not in the park." Cassie adjusted the old blue cotton head rag. Under different circumstances, she probably wouldn't have been caught dead in it. "Where to next?"

"Mt. Zion. Sometimes Billie and Lucy go up there to play jacks in the church parking lot or dolls on the back steps."

When they pulled up at the church, Sudie's car was already there, and Sudie, herself, was heading their way. She saw them and shook her head. *No.*

Betty Jewel rolled down the window. "Sudie," she called, but her best friend just kept on walking.

"Maybe it's best this way," Cassie said. "Search teams often split up."

This was not about a split-up search team; it was about a friendship coming apart at the seams, a lifeline Betty Jewel had expected to hold on to till the end, slowly coming unraveled. Still, she suspected Cassie already knew that. She was too smart not to. And maybe it was best to pretend she didn't. Maybe the only way either of them could survive this strange alliance was to pretend that the rest of the world didn't even exist, to focus only on a lost little girl.

They combed the neighborhood. They searched A.M. Strange Library inside and out, and Glenwood Cemetery where Billie and Lucy loved to play among the tombstones.

Standing there among the granite markers with a woman she'd barely known until today, Betty Jewel felt pieces of herself fly off and hover over them like blackbirds. Until today she'd been sure of her own color and of her own place. Now, with her heart opened wide by the kindness and unexpected possibilities of Cassie Malone, she saw herself in a different light, a woman with mercy and grace pouring over her like water, and hope spreading through her as fast as kudzu on a ditch bank. In spite of the fact that her daughter was still missing, Betty Jewel sat down on a pink marble tombstone, her lips moving as she silently gave thanks.

Cassie glanced at her watch, a beautiful gold band with a diamond-studded face that had surely cost more than Betty Jewel's house. Yesterday she'd have seen the watch as a symbol of all that separated them. Today she saw it merely as a way of keeping time.

"Betty Jewel, my house is right down the block. Let's ride down there so we can get you inside to rest and have a bite to eat." Cassie reached down to help Betty Jewel up, then held on as they made their way to the car.

Even in her current state, Betty Jewel still had mind enough not to go marching through the front door of a house in Highland Circle. And she had too much pride to go scuttling to the back door. She already knew Cassie would never let her, anyway.

"Your neighbors would probably say I was in there robbing you blind. Let's go report to Mama. She'll be worried sick."

To Betty Jewel's relief, Cassie turned the car back to Shakerag. "You remind me of Fay Dean. She's the one who usually saves me from my own rash actions. Or picks up the pieces afterward."

"Who is Fay Dean?"

"My sister-in-law and my friend."

Betty Jewel thought about the limitless capacity of the human heart, and how friendship blooms without regard to the things society deems important. But she left these things unsaid, and a veil settled between them like smoke.

Though it was already three o'clock when they arrived at the house on Maple Street, Queen said, "I been waitin' dinner on ya'll."

It came as no surprise to Betty Jewel that Cassie sat down at the kitchen table and bowed her head over turnip greens and corn bread while Queen said the blessing, the old blue cotton head rag still tied under her chin.

Following the sound of bloodhounds baying through the dark woods and the wavering path of a hundred lights, Cassie held on to her own flashlight and tried not to tangle her feet in the shadowy underbrush. Who knew what lurked there? Cottonmouth moccasins as big as a grown man's leg had been reported lying in wait to sink their fangs into anybody foolish enough to disturb their territory around Gum Pond.

Owls took flight from their night perches, and scurrying sounds in the underbrush told of night creatures, cotton rats and rabbits and opossums, hurrying to get out of the way of the three bloodhounds following the scent of two little lost girls.

Trailing along right behind the dogs, moving fast for a man his size, was Tiny Jim, who had called in the dogs and organized the hunt the minute he got back from paying respects to his slain cousin in the Delta. Sudie and Wayne trotted beside him, hands joined as they searched for their daughter. Neighbors from Shakerag and relatives from as far away as Verona and Guntown had joined the search. Betty Jewel and her mama were waiting at home, Queen praying every breath and Betty Jewel too weak to hold her head up. Cassie was taking their place, braving the shuttered stares of trodden-down people who didn't want her there but were afraid to say anything about it.

She was wearing an old baseball cap with her press card in the band. It helped tame the suspicion, but not much.

Through the darkness a voice shouted, "Up ahead," and another, "What you see?" The silence was broken only by footfalls padding on the mossy forest floor and the long howl of dogs. Then out of the darkness came the answer, "Ain't nothin' but a possum."

Cassie hadn't realized she was holding her breath until the disappointment punched it out of her. What would she find at the end of this horrible day? Billie cut into six pieces and stuffed into a cotton sack? She didn't think she could bear it.

After her sparse lunch of turnip greens and corn bread, she'd insisted on taking Betty Jewel to file a missing-child report at the Tupelo Police Department. As she'd feared, Police Chief Rick Monaghan treated the woman he considered a troublemaker with coolness.

"You're jumping the gun here, Cassie," he'd said. "As usual."

Cassie had let his remark slide. No use resurrecting the outright hostility that had come on the heels of her article in which she railed against his department when they stopped searching for Alice Watkins's killer.

"Rick, we'd appreciate any help you can give us in finding these two little girls."

"I'm short-handed and strapped for cash besides. You know as well as I do I can't pull my men off the streets to hunt for two young'uns who are probably hiding under the front porch somewhere, scared to come home and take a whupping. They don't come home tomorrow, you come back down here with your friend and let me know."

The way Rick Monaghan said *friend* told Cassie everything she needed to know. When the time came to search, he'd make a cursory effort, at best. Not only that, but the next time she called for help, she'd be kept waiting as long as the law allowed.

Now, briars grabbed at her pants and latched on to her right foot. Trying to keep her balance, she flailed her arms and dropped her flashlight. A black hand the size of a Virginia ham reached out to grab her, and she found herself being hauled upright by Tiny Jim Watkins.

"Thank you."

"You always been nice to me and Merry Lynn," he said, then hurried on through the darkness.

Cassie picked up her flashlight and raced to catch up. Ahead of her, the bugling of the dogs had taken on a new note, a sound you might make if you were in deep sorrow and had found one single hope you could cling to.

"I got something," a man shouted, and another yelled, "Over here. By the pond."

A hundred flashlights swung toward the sound and converged on a tall, skinny man in overalls standing at the edge of the water, clutching a rag doll.

"It's Billie's." Sudie's voice broke, and she fell to her knees, keening, the sound so sharp and fearful it caused birds to leave their nests.

Wayne plunged into the pond, and a dozen dark hands reached to pull him back while the bloodhounds circled in ever-widening circles, sniffing the ground for the secrets only they could discover.

"Lemme go. I gotta find my baby."

"It's too dark to see." Tiny Jim towered on the banks of the pond, holding Walter back. "We'll start seining first thing tomorrow."

Sometimes when you think the worst that can happen is already behind you, a new horror grabs you by the throat and won't let go. The thought of Billie in Gum Pond almost knocked Cassie to her knees. She'd come this far held upright by sheer willpower and hope, and now she had nothing left to hang on to and no idea how she'd get back.

The lights began to move back through the forest, flickering like fireflies among the oaks and loblolly pines, but the sudden baying of the hounds brought them to a halt. Lights followed the sound. Two of the bloodhounds were at a point beside a thicket of blackberries, and the third lay curled next to the figure of a little girl.

"It's Lucy," Tiny Jim called.

Surging forward, Wayne grabbed his daughter up while Sudie started crying.

Cassie strained her eyes toward the pool of light, but there was only one little nest in the brambles, one little girl in her daddy's arms, unmoving.

"Is she dead?" When Wayne didn't respond, Sudie started punching him with her fists. "Tell me my baby's not dead! You tell me!"

Suddenly Lucy hiccupped, and Sudie fell into her husband and child, crying.

"Hallelujah," Tiny Jim said, and shouts of "Amen" echoed through the woods.

It was Tiny Jim who asked the question burning through Cassie. "Where's Billie?" Lucy just shook her head. "Is she with you?" She shook her head again *no,* and wailed so hard you could hear the night creatures scampering away from her terror.

The bloodhounds were quiet now, lying on the ground near the briar patch where they'd found Lucy, their tongues hanging out and dripping saliva onto the blackberries. There would be no more discoveries in the woods. Billie was not there. Only Lucy knew where she was, and she wasn't talking.

The search party turned back toward Shakerag, their circle of lights flashing around Sudie and Wayne and Lucy like a fractured star. Somebody in the group started singing, a male with a voice so powerful you'd imagine him lifting cotton bales and slaughtered hogs and hope. The rest of the search party joined in.

"Gonna lay down my burden, down by the riverside, down by the riverside…"

Out of the darkness, a big hand reached for her elbow. "Here, Miss Cassie. Let me help you home."

Tiny Jim. Offering mercy when she'd least expected it.

# Fourteen

Billie didn't know which was worse, the awful smell or the way she bounced around in the bed of the old truck every time they hit a bump. Which just so happened to be every time she found a spot that was halfway comfortable. If it was up to her, there wouldn't be any potholes in roads, and if you happened to come upon a little girl standing alongside the highway with her thumb stuck out, you'd find a place for her in the front with the cabbages and tomatoes instead of sticking her in the back with the pigs.

She guessed she didn't have any right to complain. Riding was better than walking. But she'd sure feel better about everything if Lucy hadn't chickened out.

They'd barely gotten out of Shakerag when she started whining that her mama was going to tear her up, and she was scared to go walking to Memphis in the dark.

"It's not that far," Billie had told her.

"How do you know?"

"Because my mama used to sing in nightclubs up there."

"That don't mean it's not far."

"Does, too. She could leave home and get back the same day. She said so."

"Riding not walking. I want to go home."

When Billie had said, "I'm not going back," Lucy started to cry. Nobody could cry like Lucy. When she got really cranked up, she sounded like a pack of wild coyotes. Nothing could shut her up except handing over Little Ella.

"Here. Little Ella's the bravest doll I know. Take care of her. When I get back with my daddy, you have to give her back. Promise?"

Lucy had made the pinkie promise, which she wouldn't break if you whipped her twice, then made her stand in the corner all day. Still, Billie wished she at least had her doll. It was hard to be brave all by yourself, especially since the farmer she'd hitched a ride with was only going as far as the farmers market in New Albany.

Billie didn't know how far that was from Memphis, but she sure hoped she didn't have to walk the rest of the way. She already had blisters on her heels from the long walk she'd made all by herself till she caught her ride. She'd bet she had walked at least five hundred miles.

Of course, it was due to her talent as an actress that she'd gotten the ride in the first place. The farmer was a stooped-over old man with his overalls so loose they looked as though a big sneeze would knock them right off. And he asked more questions than Queen. Billie reckoned when you got to be older than God, it was considered a mortal sin not to dig around in a little girl's business till she didn't have a single secret left.

"What you doin' out here on the road in the dark all by yo'self?" That's the first thing the old man had asked after he'd stopped his jalopy.

It didn't take much effort for Billie to start to cry.

"There now. I ain't gone hurt you. Tell me yo name and where you live, and I'll take you on home."

"I don't have a home. Except up in Memphis with my daddy. My mama's dead, and I've gotta find my daddy."

He'd introduced himself as Troy Stroup, then called her a *poor little motherless chile.* And now here she was, wondering how God was going to make her pay for telling such a lie. Maybe riding with pigs was her punishment.

She was so glad when they finally got to the New Albany farmers market she danced a jig. Mr. Stroup gave her a ripe tomato to eat, then commenced setting up his produce.

"They's a couple come down from Olive Branch with they pickles and pies and such. When market's over, I'll see if they can take you far as they goin'."

Billie was so hungry she'd already bit into her tomato before she remembered to say thank you. And then because Mr. Stroup was still looking at her, she bowed her head and said grace. Queen would be proud.

After she ate, she found a patch of grass to wipe her hands because she didn't want to show up in Memphis with tomato juice all over her shorts. She wanted to make a good impression on her daddy.

Next, she went to the outhouse, then sidled around the produce stalls till she saw her opportunity to dart under a table full of pies. It was as far away from Mr. Stroup's pigs as she could get, and it would be a fine place to take a nap till she set out to Olive Branch.

The name sounded like a place full of houses all painted pretty colors and shaded by trees where white doves could grab the nearest branch if the Lord God ever decided to send another flood. She'd bet the couple she'd be riding with had a white fence around their yard and maybe even a swing without a rusty seat. It would be a nice place to visit till her blisters healed.

Except she had to get on to Memphis.

She pictured how the Saint would look, all shiny and polished like patent leather, a smile so big it showed sixteen gold teeth, and every bit of it because his little girl had come home.

When she hitched her next ride, she'd say, "My daddy's a famous trumpet player, and he's richer than President Eisenhower. He might even hand out a reward for me."

Billie went to sleep dreaming about being a little girl worth a big reward.

By the time the farmers began to pack up their leftover produce from the New Albany market, it was nearly dark. Billie scrambled from under the table and searched the crowd for Mr. Troy Stroup.

She hopped up and down trying not to wet her pants, but she wasn't about to run off to the outhouse and miss her ride to Olive Branch. Just when she was about to pop, she saw Mr. Stroup heading her way with a nice young couple who didn't look much older than Lucy's sister Sugarbee. The man walked all cocky, like he had a pocketful of money, and the woman was pregnant. Billie knew because she looked like she'd swallowed a watermelon, and she wore a blouse that ballooned out around her big belly. Queen called it *bein' in the fam'ly way*, but Lucy had told her the real word for it. Billie didn't know why grown-ups told lies all the time, then called it *sugarcoating*.

"Jim and Ida Mae Hurt, this here is Billie. The poor little motherless chile I tole you 'bout."

The couple looked at her with such pity that for the first time since Billie had left home she really did feel like a poor little motherless chile. Her stomach was growling, and she wanted to pee and she wanted her mama. But most of all, she wanted to get to Memphis so her daddy could make everything all right.

And so she told them about her daddy being famous and

playing a silver trumpet. The only thing she left off was the part about the reward. Her daddy might not have a gazillion bucks.

"Why, ain't you just the sweetest little thing?" The woman took Billie's hand. "You come on with Ida Mae, sugah. We gonna take you far as the service station in Olive Branch where my brother is the night janitor. He'll take you on to Memphis."

"Reckon he knows my daddy?"

Jim Hurt's laughter was as cocky as his walk. "Won't be no trouble finding a trumpet player on Beale Street. Y'all ready?"

"Can I use the outhouse first? I'm about to bust."

"Come on, sugah. You and me is in the same boat."

"Thank you, ma'am."

As Ida Mae led her toward the outhouse, Billie figured that if she minded her manners like Queen told her, she might not have to ride in the back of the truck.

As it turned out, she got to sit up front—squeezed between Ida Mae and her husband. The truck was the best one on the lot. Mostly green without any scraped fenders, and it smelled like it had never hauled a single pig.

"I bet you hungry." Ida Mae opened up a greasy paper sack.

Billie didn't tell her yes, which wouldn't have been polite, but Ida Mae handed her a molasses and biscuit just the same. She ate it in small bites to make it last, then took a long swig from the jug of water Ida Mae passed around. She thought it was the best supper she'd ever had. When she got grown she was going to make sure to have plenty of molasses to go with her little children's biscuits.

After they had gone about a gazillion miles, it started to rain, the sound so soothing Billie leaned her head on Ida Mae's shoulder and imagined being all grown up and doing exactly what she wanted to. She'd wear silk stockings and use plenty of lipstick.

They pulled into a service station, a little white stucco building set so close to Highway 78 you could hear the whine of tires on the pavement. There was a meadow on one side of the building and on the other side a vacant lot with nothing but a pile of bricks and old tires. The rain had stopped, but dark clouds hid the moon.

There was a gray-headed white man inside at the cash register and a younger man in blue coveralls with a red patch on the breast pocket. Beyond them was a tall man pushing a broom. Billie thought he was so handsome he looked like Roy Rogers.

"There's my brother, Clete." Ida Mae smoothed the front of her blouse. "Billie, you wait right here with Jim."

Billie sat up straight and tried to forget about how bad the blisters on her feet burned. She tried not to think about her mama and Queen. Mama was probably grieving herself to death and Queen was singing her old hurting songs. She pictured how happy they'd be when she got back with the Saint and he made her mama well. She might not even get a whipping for running away.

Ida Mae ambled back out of the service station, one hand holding her back like it hurt. When she opened the truck door and said, "Come on, sugah," Billie was glad to get out and stretch her legs.

"Now, Billie, you wait right here where they's plenty a light. Soon as the service station's shut down and Clete's finished mopping, he's gonna take you up to Memphis and help you find your daddy. Can you be a good little girl?"

"Yes, ma'am. Thank you, ma'am."

"Anybody ask you what you doin', just say you waitin' on Clete. You hear?"

"Yes, ma'am. How long will I have to wait?"

"It won't be long." Ida Mae kissed her on the top of her head, then squeezed her in a smothering hug. Billie guessed it might be something women in her condition did for practice. "Bye, sugah."

When the green truck disappeared down the road, she felt like part of her hide had been peeled off. It was one thing to be in the dark with people she'd barely met when she was safe inside a pickup truck, heading somewhere. It was something else to be sitting on a stack of Coca-Cola cases in the dark outside a place far from home, waiting on a man she didn't even know. Something too scary for a tired little girl to think about.

Instead, Billie thought about Lucy, how she'd already be in bed holding on to Little Ella, her mama in the next room talking to her daddy about who came into Curl Up 'n Dye and what kind of hairdo they wanted. She hoped Lucy didn't let her little sister rip Ella's other eye out.

Finally, everybody left the service station except Clete, who turned the radio up so high Billie was nearly blasted off the stack of Coke cartons. She twisted around to see him hanging on to his mop with one hand as he did the shuck and jive.

She wished she could go in there with him, but the gray-headed man had locked the door behind him, and she'd been told to wait outside. Trying to forget how hungry she was, and how lonely, Billie decided it wouldn't hurt to stretch her legs. Especially since nobody was looking.

It was the firefly that caused her to leave the safety of the Coke cases, that and her natural-born habit of disobedience. The firefly was practically under her nose. If she could catch it, it would be a nice surprise for her daddy. The thought perked her up, and she raced after the prize.

In the sweet smell of meadow grasses and the glow of the

lightning bug, Billie forgot that she was a runaway in the dark alone. She was just another little girl chasing a firefly on a summer's night.

"Little Missy? Are you ready to go?" Clete was calling from the doorway, and she hurried so she wouldn't miss her ride.

Up close, he was bigger than he'd looked through the window. Catching hold of his hand, she felt almost as safe as she did when Queen tucked the quilt under her chin and read her a Bible bedtime story.

Clete's truck was not fancy as his sister's, but Billie didn't care, just as long it got her to her daddy. She climbed in and found a spot on the seat where the sticking-up springs wouldn't pinch.

"How long till we get to Memphis?"

"Ain't far. You jus' rest. I bet you tired, a little bitty girl like you, up all hours."

"I'm not a bit sleepy."

The next thing she knew, a loud laugh jerked her awake. It took her a minute to remember she was in Clete's truck. But where was he?

Moonlight flashed through the window, and so did a green-and-yellow neon sign that said Horn Lake Juke 'n Jive. She didn't know where Horn Lake was. The only thing she knew is that it wasn't Memphis.

That big laughter sounded again, like somebody having a party Queen would call the law to. She looked out the window and saw three women her grandmother would call *hoes,* though Billie didn't think a single one of them could cut a weed out of the turnip patch. She'd bet they couldn't even bend over without splitting their tight skirts.

Billie sat there trying to think what to do next. She could get out and commence walking, but her feet hurt and she might be a hundred miles from Memphis, and even if she found it, she didn't know where Beale Street was. Queen always said, *Bein' patient builds charc'ter,* but Billie had about all the character she wanted. Now, she just wanted her daddy.

Her mama, too, but she couldn't think about Betty Jewel without crying, so she didn't. Sitting there in the dark with the green-and-yellow lights striping her skin and the hoes' big mouths filling part of the night and her fear filling the rest, Billie pictured herself meeting her daddy. He'd be coming down a gold staircase, and she'd smile at him like Dale Evans smiling at Roy Rogers, then they'd join hands and go off together someplace high up like the top of his touring bus, singing "Happy Trails to You."

That's how it would be. Then she could tell Lucy all about it.

The door of the Horn Lake Juke 'n Jive burst open, and out popped big Clete, waving a bottle and walking sideways, which Queen said was three sheets in the wind.

She waited patiently, building her character, while he opened the driver's door and crawled behind the wheel. He left the joint fast, like somebody glad to go, gravel spewing up behind him to beat the band. Billie looked out the back window to see if they were being chased. Seeing nothing coming behind them, she scrunched down as small as she could get because being three sheets to the wind had turned Clete into somebody who couldn't half see. He was weaving all over the road like he was trying to find it, and he probably wouldn't even remember who she was if he saw her.

About a gazillion hours later, he pulled up in front of a house smaller than hers and without a speck of paint, best she could tell in the dark. Next thing she knew, Clete had bailed out and left her sitting in the truck.

She rolled down the window to let the smell of corn whiskey out, then waited. Finally, she decided Clete had forgot about her entirely, and the best thing she could do was get some sleep so she could start fresh in the morning.

The good thing was that she had the whole seat to herself. She stretched out and put her sack under her head, but it didn't compare to her feather pillow back home.

"Lord God Almighty, what's that man gone and done now?"

The sound of the woman's voice jerked Billie upright so fast she banged her elbow on the steering wheel. A skinny woman, with hair chopped off and greased up so it looked like porcupine quills, was peering in the window at her, using words that sounded like Queen except the *holy shit* part. You could bet your bottom dollar this woman wasn't praying. The only good thing Billie could see about the situation was the sunrise beyond the woman's head.

"Hi, I'm Billie. I'm trying to find my famous daddy."

"Famous daddy, my ass. You git outta that truck and skedaddle 'fore I calls the law on yo high-yeller-strumpet self." The woman jerked the door open, muttering, "See if I don't kill that Clete."

She grabbed Billie's legs and commenced pulling and hollering. For a while, Billie tried to hang on to the steering wheel, but it was no use. Like Queen always said, *They ain't nothin' a woman with sand in her craw can't do.* And this woman's craw was just full of it.

She popped from the truck like a ripe plum and found herself almost eye to eye with a funny-haired short woman.

"Lord God Almighty. You ain't nothing but a tall young'un."

Standing there in the middle of a street she didn't know

in a place she couldn't name, just standing there in front of a house with nothing but a bunch of old tires piled up in the yard, Billie started to cry.

# Fifteen

Cassie looked out her bedroom window where it had started to rain. "Where are you, Billie?" she whispered, then said a silent prayer that wherever she was, she was someplace safe and dry.

She grabbed a cup of coffee and the two articles she'd written after she got back from the search party—"Bloodhounds find Lucy Jenkins" and "Who Will Fight for Billie?"—then went outside to her car.

A deep scratch ran the length of her right front fender, the clean straight line as painful as if a blade had sliced into her.

Were those footsteps running down her sidewalk? The backs of two teenage boys disappearing around the corner?

"Come back here, you cowards." She sprinted in that direction and then stopped—just stood there on her own sidewalk, wondering what was happening to her safe, sane world.

She went back to the car and ran her hand over the scratch. It hadn't been there when she'd parked it. Who would do such a thing? Was it kids pulling a prank or something more sinister, a warning meant to scare Cassie?

Trying not to worry about the deeper significance of the small scratch, Cassie pulled herself together and drove to work. She went straight to Ben's office. His desk at *The Bugle* was bigger than the one on his sunporch, but just as cluttered. Seated behind it, bent over copy with a blue pencil in his hand, he looked as if he'd had as little sleep last night as she.

"Cassie? Are you okay?"

"I'm not the one to worry about." She plopped the stories onto his desk. "Take a look at these."

She sank into a burgundy wing chair in front of him, too tired to do anything more than rest her head against the leather. It had been late when she'd returned from the search for Billie, and then she'd had to spend an hour on the phone, convincing Fay Dean that she was okay.

As if that weren't enough, she couldn't sleep until she'd crawled out of bed and turned Joe's photograph facedown on the bedside table. There had been a time she couldn't sleep until Joe came to bed, wrapped his arms around her, whispered, *You'll always be my girl, Cass.* She hardly knew who she was anymore, let alone what she wanted.

"What's this?" Ben picked up "Who Will Fight for Billie?" and started to read. She knew the minute he came to the part about unequal justice for children, about a Chief of Police who combed Tupelo for a lost white child but turned his head the other way when a colored child went missing.

He dropped the article onto his desk. "I'm not going to print this."

"Why not?"

"You know why."

She was surprised by how painful it was to see the worry that creased Ben's brow. "Cass, I'm afraid for you."

"I'm afraid for us all, Ben. When are we going to come to our senses and stop pretending white is the only color that matters?"

"White's not a color."

"Exactly. Neither is black."

His mouth turned up in that quirky way of his, and Cassie relaxed.

"You can wipe that victory smile off your face, Cassie. I'm not going to toss your torch onto gasoline, and neither should you."

"Don't think I didn't consider the *Chicago Tribune*."

"Of course you would. And they're both good enough. But Cassie, I don't see how printing these articles in *The Bugle* will help find this little girl. All they will do is stir this town up and set it against you."

The phone on his desk jangled, and Ben picked it up. "Bugle." His brow puckered as he listened, then he handed the phone to Cassie.

The caller was Betty Jewel, saying that Lucy had started talking this morning, that she'd left Billie on the side of the road trying to catch a ride to Memphis.

"I'll be right there." Cassie replaced the receiver and flew out of Ben's office with him right behind her.

"Cassie? What's wrong?"

"It's Billie." She grabbed her purse from off her desk.

Ben said something else, but Cassie didn't hear. She was already streaking toward the front door, picturing a ten-year-old alone on the side of a dark two-lane highway filled with truckers in Peterbilt rigs on a long haul from Birmingham to Memphis. Billie with her thumb stuck out, looking for trouble.

No sooner had Betty Jewel hung up from talking to Cassie than Queen puffed into the room swinging her iron skillet.

"Mama, what in the world do you think you're doing?"

"I'm gone fine whoever done this and beat some sense into 'em with my fryin' pan." She held up two clothespin dolls, one black with a noose around her neck, and the other painted white with red hair, a red grin on her face.

"Oh, my God! Where'd you get that?"

"In the backyard, hangin' on the line with my dishrags."

Betty Jewel felt her blood drain out. Whoever had placed the dolls had meant them as a clear warning for her and Cassie.

"Mama, I can't leave you by yourself. Not with those threatening effigies. I'm going to call Merry Lynn to stay with you." Queen didn't say a word, just started putting on her bonnet. "Mama, did you hear me?"

"I heard. I'm goin' with you."

"You can't." Betty Jewel clenched her teeth on the pain that wanted to buckle her knees. Last night standing in front of her mirror she'd said, "Death, show your face before I find Billie and I'll spit in your eye." Nearly two days of not knowing what had become of her daughter had turned her into a wild woman it wouldn't do to mess with.

She led Queen to the couch and untied her bonnet. "Mama, I need you to stay home in case Billie turns up."

"She ain't gone turn up. She be lookin' for that Saint Hughes."

"I think you're right, Mama, which is going to make her easy to find." Defying death and lying to her own mama. What would she do next?

The sound of Cassie's car was a blessed relief. She reached for the phone to call Merry Lynn.

"Don' call nobody. I ain't scared a no voodoo dolls. If somebody come messin' roun' here agin, I'll give 'em what for. You go on, now, baby."

Jewel gathered her blanket and pillow, her purse and her pills, a water jug and the little paper sack stuffed with plenty of Queen's biscuits.

"Bye, Mama. You be careful, now." She bent over to kiss Queen's cheek. "I don't know when we'll be back."

"I'll be prayin' for you ever' breath, baby."

Queen would, too. It was her way.

When Betty Jewel left the little house on Maple Street and stepped out into the rain, she knew she wasn't alone. Echoes of her mama's prayers followed her, swirling in the rain like smoke from a smoldering fire.

Cassie's fine red car looked as out of place—sitting there spattered with mud—as Betty Jewel felt when she climbed into the front seat.

"I hope you're not stuck. Shakerag in the rain is not for the fainthearted."

"I don't fit that bill." Cassie handed Betty Jewel a handful of tissues to wipe the dampness off herself, then turned the car around, her wheels spinning so that Betty Jewel expected any minute they'd be mired axle-deep. Finally the powerful engine pulled them out of the ruts, and they were heading out of Shakerag, spewing up mud as they went. "I know it's hotter than the devil in the car, but the rain will cool things off."

Wet and trying not to shake from a chill and fear, Betty Jewel thought if it got colder, they could kill hogs in the car. She wrapped the blanket around her shoulders and kept her mouth shut about freezing to death.

"She'll be on Beale Street with Saint Hughes," she said.

"If she got that far." Cassie swiped her hair back from a face shiny with sweat. "It's hard to believe a ten-year-old could hitchhike a hundred miles."

"You don't know Billie."

"I'm beginning to."

Cassie's smile was confident, the kind you'd see in a woman who wouldn't back down from anything, including getting a child away from the man she idolized. Or Maybe Betty Jewel was looking for the least little thing that would give her hope.

"We'll stop at truck stops along the highway and ask if anybody has seen her," Cassie was saying, and Betty Jewel just nodded. How many white truckers would be paying attention to a little colored girl?

What neither of them said was that Billie might not be on the road to Memphis. She might not even be alive. While Betty Jewel was sleeping, somebody could have snatched her child off the road and done no telling what-all. Pain threatened to tear her apart. She tasted blood trying to hold it back.

"Are you all right, Betty Jewel?"

No use lying. She and Cassie had come so far past lying they were now traveling in the same shaky boat. "Just trying to keep myself from falling apart."

"Me, too." With her eyes still on the road, Cassie reached over and squeezed her hand. "What else did Lucy say this morning?"

"Sudie asked her how far she and Billie got, but Lucy didn't know. All she remembers is coming back in the dark by herself with Billie's doll, then hiding at Gum Pond because she was too scared to come home."

"She didn't have Billie's doll when we found her. It was in the edge of the pond. Did she say what happened up there?"

"She was sitting by the edge of the pond, playing, when she heard something that scared her. I guess she dropped the doll when she ran and hid."

"Did she say what she heard?"

"A haint."

Cassie's laughter was a beautiful thing to hear, uninhibited and glorious, coming as it did in the midst of a day where Betty Jewel had thought she'd find nothing to smile about.

The Belden Truck Stop was up ahead, and Cassie pulled into the lot beside a Peterbilt rig.

"You wait here while I go inside to ask about Billie."

Betty Jewel watched out the window, anxious sweat gathering under her arms. The minute she saw Cassie coming back, she knew something was wrong. She looked as if somebody had a cattle prod after her.

She got into the car, not even looking at Betty Jewel.

"They said *no.* They haven't seen her."

"What else did they say?"

"What do you mean?" Cassie turned in her direction, her pale face still mottled with angry red patches.

"There's no way a redhead can hide her fury. What'd they say to you?"

"You sure you want to know?"

"I asked, didn't I?"

"They said, 'White bitches who go around looking for their nigger kids will get what's coming to them if they don't watch out.'"

"And you said?"

"I'd rather be me than you, you Dark Ages Neanderthal."

"Reckon he knew what Neanderthal meant?"

"He probably thought it was a new kind of beer."

Queen said laughing through your troubles was just another way of showing your faith. Betty Jewel said a silent prayer for Cassie, who didn't back down at anything, and for her mama, waiting in Shakerag with Jesus in her heart and a cast-iron skillet/weapon in her hand

"Cassie, you don't have to go on with this. I should have known better than to put you through it."

"Just try to stop me."

Cassie cranked the car and headed north, braving every

wayside station, truck stop, service station and hamburger joint along the way. But no one had seen Billie.

When Cassie climbed into the car from the latest 7-Eleven, her hair was plastered to her head with rain and her skin looked as if somebody had struck a match and lit a fire.

"I don't think I've ever met a woman with such grit, except my mama."

"That's the nicest thing anybody's ever said to me, Betty Jewel. I mean that."

"I do, too. You and Queen are quite a pair."

By mid-afternoon they were only halfway to Memphis, and every mile of it futile. So far, the only good news was that the rain had stopped.

"Tell me about Saint Hughes," Cassie said. "What kind of man is he?"

"Until the drugs got a hold of him, he was a good man. But after all he's done, I can't let him have Billie. If she's still alive."

"She's alive." Cassie's statement, made with such conviction, lifted Betty Jewel.

"Thank you, Cassie."

"You're welcome, Betty Jewel. And I mean that, too." Cassie glanced at her watch. "It's after two. You can't keep going without food and a bathroom break, and neither can I."

"I've got biscuits and I can pee behind a tree on the side of the road."

"We'll stop at the next restaurant. You can go in with me."

Betty Jewel didn't have any high hopes of how that would turn out. Still, watching the miles click by, she decided that if Cassie wanted to test the goodness of mankind, she'd be right alongside, leading with her chin and her pride. When you've lost everything, you can walk through hell and not even feel the heat.

★ ★ ★

Only the optimist would call the place Cassie stopped at a restaurant. A clapboard hut painted a hopeful yellow, a neon sign on a pole proclaiming Joe's Eats, it was little more than a tiny diner with a drive-thru window. The window would have been a smart choice, but Cassie's most pressing need was not food.

As she parked in a slot between a black Ford pickup and a green Chevrolet Bel Air, she wondered what had drawn her to stop at a place bearing her husband's name. Betty Jewel would surely have noticed. Did she think Cassie was rubbing salt in the wound? Showing that the past was behind them?

If she'd asked, Cassie might have said a little of both. What she *did* say was, "Stick close by me."

As she bailed out of her car and helped Betty Jewel out, she put on what Joe always called her *fighting face,* chin out, eyes shooting sparks and an attitude as big as Texas. "Are you ready for this, Betty Jewel?"

"Ready as you are."

Cassie took Betty Jewel's arm, telling herself she was supporting her so she wouldn't fall. But in the end, it felt just like going arm in arm with Fay Dean. It was strange how trouble could bring women together in a way that no amount of conversation could.

Joe's Eats buzzed with chatter. A middle-aged man wearing a Memphis State baseball cap laughed at something his companion said—a cheerleader type with pouty pink lips and cheekbones painted to match. A worn-looking young woman with a child in a booster seat and three more fighting over the French fries tried to restore order. Three pimply-faced teenaged boys flirted with a pretty blonde at the lunch counter. A burly man behind the lunch counter was tossing hamburgers on a grill.

Cassie, with Betty Jewel in tow, headed straight for the sign that said Women, Whites Only.

"Where in the Sam hill do you think you're going?"

It was a male voice, coming from behind the lunch counter. The roadside diner was suddenly as quiet as Tupelo's Lee County Library.

"Keep walking," she told Betty Jewel.

"I'm talking to you, nigger. I guess you can't read that sign."

Cassie whirled on him, her red hair flying every which way from humidity and fury. She figured she looked like a madwoman. She hoped she did.

"We're both perfectly capable of reading." She started to add *jackass,* but thought better of it. "This is the famous jazz singer, Betty Jewel Hughes. I'm her agent, and we're in need of a bathroom break and food, in that order."

She marched back toward the toilet, with Betty Jewel stumbling along beside her.

"Betty Jewel, if you fall down now, I'm going to kill you."

"Stand in line," Betty Jewel said.

She delivered her comeback between scary-sounding panting that had Cassie wishing she was somebody different, a woman who didn't pick up every gauntlet thrown in her path.

Footsteps hammered behind them, and Cassie could almost feel the man's angry breath on the back of her neck.

"I don't care if she's the Queen of England," he yelled.

"Keep walking, Betty Jewel."

Cassie made it to the bathroom door, but Betty Jewel wasn't fast enough. The man caught her arm and pinned her against the wall.

"Around here, this is the colored bathroom." He thrust a Dixie cup toward her.

"If you don't take your hands off her, I'm going to have you arrested for assault."

"Cassie, don't." Betty Jewel took the paper cup. "If using a Dixie cup will help me find Billie, I'll pee in a hundred."

"So will I." Cassie held out her hand. "Where's my Dixie cup?" When the man handed her the cup, he was red-faced with rage. Cassie looked him straight in the eye. "What's your name?"

"Claude Harkins, bitch. What's yours?"

"Cassie Malone. Remember it."

Elbowing him aside, Cassie walked out of the diner, her teeth gritted to keep from buckling under Betty Jewel's sagging weight. Back in the car, Betty Jewel fell against the seat, her skin so pale they looked almost the same color.

Cassie reached for the water jug and held it to her lips. What if she'd killed Betty Jewel with her stubbornness?

"I should have known better than to subject you to that. I am so sorry."

"I'd do it again if I weren't sick."

"You're not mad?"

"No. But I am wondering about something."

"What?"

"Are you really going to pee in that Dixie cup?"

"Just watch me."

They didn't actually pee in the Dixie cups. Cassie found a secluded farm road that had a thicket of blackberry bushes big enough to hide two women too stubborn to bow to Jim Crow.

Back in the car, Betty Jewel leaned against the seat. "I need to rest a bit."

"We'll sit here awhile."

Cassie needed a break herself. Battle-weary and uncertain, she studied the sick woman beside her. They had to be about the same age. What would it be like to lose a child at thirty-eight? To be dying of cancer, far too young? To wonder if your child would have a future that didn't include lynchings and bombings and peeing in a Dixie cup?

"Do I need to take you to a doctor?"

"I think I'm okay now," Betty Jewel said. "How about you?"

"Don't you worry about me. Just hang on to whatever makes you strong."

"If I were my mama, I'd say a prayer. But lately all I'm doing is hanging on for Billie. What makes you strong, Cassie?"

"A stubborn streak that won't let me quit. But I'll have to say that if I keep stopping to ask about Billie at every wayside spot, we won't get to Memphis tonight."

"There's no use stopping anymore to ask."

"Why?"

"Nobody is going to notice Billie. People like us are invisible."

Feeling a collective shame and guilt, Cassie backed out of the farm road, then turned her car toward Memphis.

"Wait! Stop the car, Cassie." Betty Jewel reached for the door handle.

"Do you see something?" Cassie braked and eased her car off the road. "Is it Billie?"

Betty Jewel didn't answer, just barreled out of the car, bent over double.

Watching for the break in traffic so she could get out of the car on the driver's side without having her legs clipped off, Cassie finally saw her chance and took it. When she rounded the corner and saw Betty Jewel heaving, she wrapped her arms around her to keep her from toppling.

"I can't go on, Cassie."

"I'll get you to a hospital." And what about Queen? The

idea of making a phone call that would destroy that poor old woman had Cassie wishing for help.

Fay Dean. She always knew what to do.

"No. If I can just rest till tomorrow, I'll be all right."

They were only thirty-five miles from Memphis. The idea of driving back to Tupelo, then starting from scratch tomorrow made Cassie want to hit something.

"All right, then. You're not going to die on me. I'm not going to let you."

"I'm too pissed-off to kick the bucket."

"Good. We'll stop at the first motel we see."

"You've lost your mind."

"Not yet." But she was close.

Sometimes, the only thing you can do is forget about your problems and just keep moving forward. And so, Cassie pushed on, hoping Billie would be at the end of the journey.

# Sixteen

THE SHORT WOMAN'S NAME was Ernestine, and she was Clete's wife.

"You help me and I help you," Ernestine had said once she'd figured out Billie was no high-yeller strumpet. "Thas the way it works roun' here."

She thrust a mop into Billie's hand. "Soon's we finish, if Clete ain't up, I'll help you find this famous daddy you blabbin' about. Unless he's somethin' you trumped up."

Billie was so tired of mopping and washing dishes and hanging sheets on the line, she was thinking of how she could just run off and find him herself. Besides she didn't want to be in the truck with Ernestine, who had the longest stinger of any woman she had ever met. There was no telling where that mean little woman would take her.

Billie reached into the basket for a pillowcase, her stomach complaining. Ernestine had fed her nothing all day but a biscuit and a soggy mess of turnip greens. Billie was never going to eat another turnip green. She'd outlaw them if she could.

In the house behind her, Ernestine started a ruckus, using her stinger on Clete. Billie commenced humming, but not one of Queen's old hurting songs. It was "Don't Mess With Me," Li'l

Rosie advising *Get outta my way, don't you mess with me; the last one did is hangin' from a tree. Take your lies outta here, I don't give a damn; if you mess with me, you'll find out who I am.*

Billie was the daughter of a famous jazzman, and she was liable to slap the next person who said any different.

"Little Miss Billie." Big Clete was standing in the yard, looking hangdog. "I didn't mean to do what I done las' night. It jus' come over me."

"That's all right." Billie reached into the clothes basket and brought out another limp pillowcase that Queen would have starched and ironed.

"If you ready, we gone see 'bout finding yo daddy."

Billie was so happy she didn't even care that she was wearing wrinkled shorts. She did want her hair to look nice, though. She didn't want her daddy to think her mama and grandmother hadn't raised her right.

"Can I go comb my hair first?"

He nodded *yes,* probably too beat up by his wife's stinger to do anything else, and before you could say *jack rabbit,* Billie was sitting crossways in his truck to avoid the busted-out seat spring, her hair all nice and soft with curls falling around her face, riding right down the middle of Beale Street. It was lit up like a Christmas parade, even in broad daylight. A gazillion people tromped up and down the street, their laughter drifting through the window so sweet Billie nearly cried.

She knew her daddy would live in a place where folks laughed all the time. No switch behind the door. No cancer.

But in that crowd, how would she ever find him? She didn't even know what he looked like.

All of a sudden she saw the sign, Saint Hughes in lights, blazing like the moon and a hundred feet tall. She'd bet it was prettier than Queen's Pearly Gates. She was always saying, *Billie, when I get to them Pearly Gates, they gone be lit up like stars, and I'm gone dance with a bran'-new hip 'cause Jesus done laid His hands me.*

Wait till Queen heard how He'd laid His hands on Billie. She'd pass under that shining sign and there would be her daddy, waiting to make up for ten years of lost love.

"Wait!" When Clete drove on by, she'd have jumped out if the truck hadn't been moving. "Did you see that sign?"

"Ain't it purty?" he said, and Billie realized Clete couldn't read.

"You've got to turn around. That's my daddy's name in lights, right back there."

"I'll jus' go park and we can walk back. You can show me the way."

It took about fifteen years to park, and another ten before Clete could convince a man even bigger than he was that they had serious business going upstairs to the apartment where Saint Hughes didn't like to be disturbed in the afternoon.

When Billie said, "Please, mister, he's really my daddy," the bouncer led them to a set of dark stairs that would have scared Lucy. Billie thought the stairs were mysterious and just what her daddy needed. Celebrities had to keep everything on the q.t. so they wouldn't get mobbed by fans.

The hall at the top of the stairs was dark, too, with high ceilings and no windows, and walls Queen would have tackled with a rag and a bucket of lye soap. But Billie thought it was the most beautiful hall she'd ever seen because the sound of a trumpet drifted from the door at the end—long, slow notes that slid across your skin like sunshine on a summer day, followed by a blues riff that made you want to crumple at the Saint's feet and just lie there, boneless and content.

The music was so amazing that both Billie and Clete tiptoed the rest of the way. The Saint's door was cracked open, but she didn't dare peer around. Famous people with golden lips needed warning when their lives were about to turn upside down.

Clete knocked, and the music halted. "Who's there?"

Her daddy's voice was like his music, dark and mysterious and so wonderful Billie wanted to cry.

"It's Clete Lefeert, Mr. Saint Hughes. I brought yo daughter."

"Billie?"

She wanted to read a million kinds of joy in her daddy's inquiry, but all she heard was a question and the sound of his footsteps.

And suddenly he was there, her daddy. He was shorter than she'd imagined, and darker. And he didn't look a thing like Roy Rogers. But, oh, when he saw her, his eyes lit up with a fire she couldn't even imagine, and his smile stretched a gazillion miles.

She waited, polite like she'd been taught. Then he dropped to his knees and folded her in his arms, crying. She dropped her paper sack of belongings and started crying, too.

Finally, he said, "Does your mama know you're here?" and she said, "Yes, sir," starting off her new life telling a lie. She hoped being polite made up for it.

The next thing she knew her daddy was pulling a dollar out of his pocket, handing it to Clete, which said loud and clear that he was a man with money. Just wait till she told Lucy.

As Clete left, the Saint took her little paper sack and shoved it into the room behind him, which Billie was dying to see; but he shut the door and she wasn't about to start off on the wrong foot by asking to go inside before she was invited. Her daddy wiped her face with a handkerchief that smelled like cigarette smoke and blues, then tucked her hand in his and said, "I'm fixing to show my daughter the town."

Billie skipped along beside him, down the dark stairs and

into the bright street, a little girl of such value her daddy wouldn't even let go of her hand.

Driving along Highway 78, Cassie searched the roadside for motels. Betty Jewel, huddling into a blanket in the passenger seat, still looked pale and clammy.

"Betty Jewel, are you sure I shouldn't get you to a doctor?"

"Cancer's more a roller coaster than a downhill slide. If I can just stretch out, I'll be fine."

"God, please find me a motel." Cassie whizzed past a gas station, a mom-and-pop restaurant, a used-car lot...everything except what she needed.

"Just up ahead."

"Wouldn't you know it's Dwayne's Motor Hotel?"

"The next time, ask God to send you the Plaza." Grinning, Betty Jewel pulled the blanket up like a hood. "Lord, if Queen heard me say that, she'd whip my butt with her willow switch."

"There might not be enough of you left to whip after the rats get through. I'll bet this place has rodents bigger than that Persian cat across the street from me."

Cassie hoped Dwayne's Motor Hotel wouldn't be nosey about who stayed there.

When she pulled into the parking lot, Betty Jewel said, "I hope this won't be another Dixie cup event."

"Not this time. I'm taking the coward's way out."

"And that would be?"

"I'm going inside to register for two, which includes my sister Maude, who is waiting in the car wrapped in a blanket, too sick to uncover her head."

"If you call me Maude, I'll have to kill you. Call me Janice." Betty Jewel hunkered down inside the blanket, making sure her face was covered, and Cassie headed toward the dingy office to spin her tale.

Fortunately, the man behind the registration desk asked only one question, "One key or two?"

"One. My sister is too sick to leave the room by herself."

Once inside the room, Betty Jewel collapsed on the bed. While she was sleeping, Cassie drove around gathering supplies—toothbrushes and toiletries, a change of underwear and gowns for both of them. Hot, disgruntled and anxious, she couldn't stand the thought of another day in her sweat-soaked blouse. As she picked out a white shirt for herself, she thought of Betty Jewel curled under a threadbare blanket in a crumpled, too-big dress.

Cassie hurried to the dress racks. Pink would look good with Betty Jewel's dark skin, a dress with a belt that could be cinched tighter as the weight peeled away. She took her time, searching for the perfect color, the perfect style. She added a scarf to match, silk so it would be soft against Betty Jewel's ravaged hair and pink to put some color into her face.

After a stop for food, Cassie headed back. It was dark by the time she got to the motel, her own color high and her arms full. Betty Jewel was awake, hanging over the toilet, being sick.

"Oh, my God." Cassie set her purchases on the desk and grabbed a wet washcloth to swab Betty Jewel's face.

What would happen if she couldn't go on, if she died? If Billie was with Saint Hughes, Cassie had no doubt she could find her, but would she be able to bring her home?

Cassie led Betty Jewel back to the bed, where she perched on the edge of the mattress.

"I'm sorry, Cassie."

"7UP might settle your stomach. Let me get some ice." She raced outside and found the ice maker in a dingy hall between units, then had to kick it twice before it dispensed ice. Betty Jewel was still sitting on the bed when she got back, fragile as a dandelion. Drink sloshed over Cassie's hand as she poured it. "Here. I've got some soup, too. Eating might help. I found a nice little deli where everything was homemade."

"When I get where I'm going, I'll nominate you for sainthood. If I don't end up in the other direction."

"If you do, there's no hope for me." Trying to keep her anxiety from showing, she watched Betty Jewel sip her drink. "Your color's coming back. Do you feel better?"

"I do. The 7UP helps." Betty Jewel took another sip. "You remind me of Sudie."

"How's that?"

"She tries to control everything and act like she's not."

"Joe said the same thing about me."

His name conjured him up, and suddenly he was there between them. Now Cassie could only think of him with Betty Jewel. Her hurt finally spilled over.

"How did it happen?" Betty Jewel got very still. "Did my husband initiate it, or did you?"

"It was not what you're thinking, Cassie."

"Then what was it, Betty Jewel? This is eating me up inside. There's not room in me for anything except you and Joe."

"All right, then." Betty Jewel stacked the pillows against the headboard and leaned back. "Looking back, I feel a kind of awe that steals the breath and hushes the heart."

*It's the pure truth,* is what Cassie was thinking. Joe had a way of enchanting everyone he met.

"Joe was up at Tiny Jim's all the time that summer, sitting over in that corner all by himself, sometimes taking out his blues harp and hitting a few licks. One night, he asked Tiny Jim if Saint had ever played there. Tiny Jim got to telling him about the old days when Saint and I were America's jazz sweethearts. All of us talked till the place closed, and Joe ended up at Queen's house to look at Saint's old touring bus."

"He never mentioned it." But then, why would he, especially after he'd slept with Betty Jewel?

"Joe told me, 'I have the only three records Saint Hughes ever made. He was a genius,' and I said, 'Would you like to see his traveling bus?'"

"Wait." Cassie didn't want to picture it, to hear it. And yet she had to.

"Cassie, I don't know why you want to torture yourself like this. What happened was nothing but the impulsive action of two vulnerable people. If I could change the past, I would. But I can't. Just let it go."

"Don't." Cassie held up her hands as if she were warding off blows. "I want the truth, Betty Jewel. I *need* the whole truth."

"All right, then." For a moment, Betty Jewel folded her hands as though she was praying. "We were in that old bus just talking about Saint, and what happened next took us both by surprise. Afterward when Joe said, 'I'm sorry,' I put my hand over his mouth and said, 'Don't you ever say that to me again.'"

"Did he?"

"No. He left that night and never came back."

"I won't let you off that easy. A one-night stand doesn't make it right."

"Don't you think I know that?"

"Did he give you the harmonica? The one with painted roses?"

"I found it the next day on the piano stool in the living room. I didn't think he'd want me calling up to return it."

Cassie felt as if she'd burst out of her skin. When Betty Jewel reached for her, she just shook her head.

"Cassie, I didn't deny my feelings then, and I won't deny

them now. That man fixed my soul. The Saint had flattened it out and stomped on it, and Joe Malone picked it up out of the dirt and washed it clean with tenderness."

The tenderness of Joe's hands and his heart swept over Cassie in memories so vivid she felt as if her husband had entered the room and now stood watching them.

*What, Joe? What you do want of me now?* Cassie thought.

Cassie didn't know if she had anything left to give. Not to Joe. Not to Betty Jewel. Not to Billie.

Betty Jewel had a child, while Cassie had a roomful of memories she was trying to suffocate. Some heartaches are simply too big for words.

They sat on separate beds simply looking at each other. If Betty Jewel said anything else, even *I'm sorry,* Cassie didn't know what she'd do. Shatter and break. Turn tail and run. Scream.

"I got a few things." Cassie rose from the bed and rummaged in the shopping bags, pulling out toiletries and toothbrushes. Finally she found what she wanted and handed Betty Jewel one of the gowns and the pink dress. "These are for you."

"No. Thank you. You've done more than enough."

"This is not charity, Betty Jewel, and don't you poke that stubborn pride in my face and pretend it is. Dammit, I almost peed in a Dixie cup for you!"

Betty Jewel started laughing first, and soon they were hanging on to each other while tears rolled down their cheeks. Through it all Cassie noticed Betty Jewel's shoulder blades stuck out like wings, as if she were a sparrow set to take flight.

Suddenly Cassie saw a change in Betty Jewel, like she was standing in the ocean tides responding to the pull of the moon. Cassie stepped back to look into her face.

"Betty Jewel, what's wrong?"

"Sometimes I get so mad at this cancer I want to scream and hit something."

Betty Jewel reached for her 7UP, her hands trembling. Then she lifted her shoulders and squared her chin.

"Scream if you want to, Betty Jewel. I'll stuff a pillow against the doorjamb. And if anybody comes to tell you to shut up, I'll punch him in the face."

Betty Jewel's guffaw caught 7UP in her throat and sent her into a coughing spell. Cassie patted her back, wondering just how hard you could pound the back of someone who looked as if the slightest little thing would break her in half.

"Cassie, if you'll help me up from this bed, I'd like to brush my teeth and take a bath."

"You're sure? I don't want you to fall and hurt yourself."

"Just sit down, Cassie. Breathe. Watch some TV. I'm fine." As Betty Jewel made her way to the bathroom, her patchy hair gave her the look of a frightened baby bird, but her eyes told another story, the story of a warrior woman.

Cassie turned on the TV, not caring that the only channel she could get was showing the news. As the black-and-white images of the reporter flashed across the screen, Cassie thought about the journey she was on, one that had called into question everything she knew about Joe. She and her husband had started in the same place, never dreaming of the sharp curves in the roads, the treacherous detours. And yet, though they'd taken different paths, they'd come full circle, and ended up with Joe resting in the family plot and Cassie on the road searching for his child.

"I'm all done." Betty Jewel emerged in a swirl of steam in the new pink gown that camouflaged her sharp bones. If you didn't know better, you'd think she was an ordinary woman getting ready for bed, instead of one drowning in a thousand different ways. She paused in front of the TV, her sagging shoulders giving away her despair.

"Betty Jewel, are you all right?"

"I was just thinking about my baby."

"We'll find her," Cassie said. "I'll never give up."

Betty Jewel crawled into bed and smiled at her.

Sometimes reward comes in the quiet smile of a dying woman. Cassie turned to rummage in the shopping bag for her toothbrush and gown so Betty Jewel wouldn't see her cry.

"Do you want me to turn off the TV?"

On the bed, Betty Jewel had already fallen asleep. Still, Cassie checked for the rise and fall of her chest. Then she turned the TV volume down to give Betty Jewel the rest she so desperately needed.

As the silent images flickered across the screen, a little missing girl raced through Cassie's mind, a child whose mother had placed her hope in Cassie.

Finally she lay on the bed opposite Betty Jewel, and kicked down her sheets so the only thing covered was her feet. Somewhere in the room a cricket started his night song, and Cassie smiled in the dark. Wasn't a cricket in the house good luck?

# Seventeen

IT WAS LATE WHEN Cassie woke up, a new day. She felt a sense of lightness, as if she'd been carrying a suitcase full of rocks that had suddenly flown off and landed somewhere on the road behind her.

Betty Jewel slept even later, then woke up shivering, her teeth chattering so hard she sounded like a woodpecker at the door.

Cassie jerked the covers off her bed, the thin blanket, the cheap bedspread, and tucked them around Betty Jewel. But her shivers continued.

"What can I do? Tell me what to do, Betty Jewel."

"Turn the air conditioner off."

Cassie fumbled with the knobs, saying words under her breath that would probably cause Queen to get her willow switch. Finally she figured it out, and the unit clattered to a stop.

Cassie sank onto the edge of the bed and pressed her hand to Betty Jewel's forehead. "I don't think you have a fever, but I'm no expert. Are you in pain?"

"Some. My pills are in my purse."

Cassie got a glass of tepid water from the bathroom to wash

down the pills, then rummaged in the closet for more covers. All she could find was a threadbare blanket that looked as if it wouldn't keep a flea warm, let alone a woman with cancer slowly freezing her blood. Still, she tucked that around Betty Jewel, then sat awhile rubbing her cold hands.

"Do you need a doctor, Betty Jewel?"

"No."

"If you lie there and die trying to be brave, I'm going to be mad as the devil."

"I'm not dying, just freezing. Since the cancer, stress does that to me."

"You just rest, then. I'm going to get some more blankets and something for us to eat. Wait right here." Good Lord, where did she think Betty Jewel would go?

She tucked the thin blanket around Betty Jewel, then hurried off. By the time Cassie returned to the room with blankets and food, it was raining again and she hadn't even thought to get an umbrella. She dashed inside and was immediately struck by what felt like a solid wall of heat.

The room was a sauna, but Betty Jewel was still shivering. With sweat turning Cassie to a puddle, she pulled the new blankets out of the shopping bag and began layering them onto Betty Jewel.

"How many'd you get?"

"Six." Sweat dripped off Cassie's nose and onto the white blanket that covered Betty Jewel like a snowdrift.

"I'm sorry, Cassie."

"Hush up. I can handle it."

Cassie sat on the end of the bed and wrapped her hands around Betty Jewel's blanketed feet. She wished she'd bought socks, too, warm fuzzy socks that would make Betty Jewel feel cozy no matter how cold she was.

What if this was more than the chill of stress? Cassie's chest felt flushed, and she couldn't have said whether it was from worry or fear or the torturous heat in this mean little motel room. She couldn't even raise a window for fear of sending Betty Jewel into another teeth-knocking chill.

Cassie went outside to fill the ice bucket. When she got back, she began taking off her clothes.

"Cassie? Good Lord Almighty, what are you doing?"

"I'm about to melt. Am I embarrassing you?"

"If I wasn't colder than a hog on ice, I'd be laughing my head off." Betty Jewel's sputter became full-fledged laughter, and it was the most hopeful thing Cassie had heard all day. "Carry on, Cassie. Just don't expect me to throw any dollar bills."

"Shoot, I was expecting twenties."

Cassie stripped down to her panties and bra, the kind of sensible white cotton she wore now that Joe was gone. Grabbing a handful of ice cubes, she ran them over her throat, across her chest and down her arms. Then she sat down with an ice cold Pepsi and a tepid sausage and biscuit.

"I bought some food. Do you feel like eating?"

"Not yet." The sudden yearning that came into Betty Jewel's face made Cassie think of the way sunflowers always search for the sun. "I wonder what Billie's doing now."

"Maybe you shouldn't talk."

"Sometimes it helps. It pulls me back to this earth."

"I have to believe that if she found your husband, he'll be good to her."

"That's what I keep telling myself. And then I get to thinking about all the bad things he did. What if he's high on cocaine?"

"What if he's not? Let's not borrow trouble, Betty Jewel."

"Trouble has set up housekeeping with me, and I can't get rid of it."

Nothing Cassie could say seemed adequate. She sat on the edge of the bed and chafed Betty Jewel's cold hands.

"These days, I don't have the energy to do anything with Billie. We used to go down to the park and play ball, and to the Tombigbee River to swim." Betty Jewel took a shaky breath. "And what about her future? I want so much for her, Cassie, *so much.*"

"Oh, I know you do, but you're getting all worked up. I can feel your pulse racing. That can't be good for you."

"What's going to happen to her after I'm gone? Tell me that, Cassie. Can you tell me?"

"Hang on to me. And try not to worry." Betty Jewel's hand felt fragile as a soap bubble. "Let's take first things first. You're going to get better, and we're going to find her."

"Then what? I don't know if Sudie can take care of Billie when I'm gone."

"Why? She seems like a good woman."

"She is. But Wayne's lost his job and Sudie's got seven children pulling her in a million different directions. Billie'd have plenty of love, but if something happened to Queen, she'd be mostly raising herself."

"I'm sure it will all work out, Betty Jewel."

"You and Mama." Betty Jewel gradually stopped shivering. "I think I might eat something now."

"Good. These biscuits are nearly as good as homemade, and the sausage has plenty of grease." Cassie chuckled, thinking of Joe's rigorous fitness schedule and Fay Dean's eagle-eyed obsession with keeping her sister-in-law well. "Fay Dean would have a fit."

"As Billie likes to say, what she doesn't know won't hurt her."

Betty Jewel set her half-eaten biscuit on the bedside table and turned onto her side, finally warm and quiet.

Watching until her breathing became even, Cassie thought of all the things Fay Dean didn't know that *would* hurt her—her brother's affair, his secret child, even her best friend hiding the truth.

The ice rattled as Cassie reached for another piece to cool her face. She tiptoed to the bed and watched Betty Jewel, breathing normally, peaceful in her sleep. Wishing she was more like Fay Dean, who could work out her problems with a good, hard run, Cassie went into the bathroom and had a good, hard cry.

Cassie marveled at Betty Jewel's spirit, trampled every day, and yet she continued to remain strong.

With the hours ticking by and the ice melting on her hot skin, Cassie kept watch until Betty Jewel opened her eyes.

"I feel better now." Still weak, she pushed back the blankets and sat up, resting a moment against the headboard. "Will you help me dress?"

"I don't think you ought to get out of bed. I can get us something for supper at a drive-by, and maybe tomorrow you'll feel like traveling."

"Cassie, if we wait for me to feel like traveling, we'll be here till Gabriel toots his horn. I have more ups and downs than a seesaw. Besides, I can't stand to not be searching for Billie." She swung her legs over the bed and stood up, determination written all over her. "Where's that pink dress you got so all-fired mad at me about?"

"You called it charity." Cassie found the dress and the pink silk scarf.

"Now, I know better."

"Don't you forget it, either." She unbuttoned the dress and slipped it over Betty Jewel's shoulders. "Let's get you prettied up and head to Memphis. The faster we get there, the sooner we can bring Billie home."

★ ★ ★

It had been so long since Betty Jewel sang on Beale Street, she'd forgotten how it lit up at night, the flashing neon signs promising paradise in a glass of two-bit booze and blues so sweet you'd forget everything except the man on the stage with his horn.

The three-foot-high sign in front of the Blue Note announced Saint Hughes in flashing orange lights. Out front, a sandwich board held a poster of him in a white suit with his talented lips pressed against a trumpet. Prison had grayed his hair and peeled off fifteen pounds, but other than that, he still looked like a man who could thrill you with his music and steal your heart with one look.

She imagined how Billie would have felt, arriving on Beale Street, seeing the poster of the man she thought was her daddy. She pictured the Saint laying eyes on her, the daughter he thought was his own, the little girl who could melt you with a smile and charm you with a look, even when she was being disobedient.

"Betty Jewel, I'm going to have to park down the block in a paid parking lot. If you don't feel like facing Saint Hughes, you don't have to. I can do it."

"He'll tell you a pack of lies and make you believe every one of them. Just pull over at the curb and let me out at the front door."

"Okay." Cassie eased the car to the curb and helped Betty Jewel out of the car. "You wait right here for me. I don't want you to face him alone."

Neither did she. Betty Jewel nodded *yes,* then swiped her mouth with Tangee lipstick so old she didn't even recall when she'd gotten it. Tying her new pink silk scarf over her thinning hair, she willed herself to stand tall and proud. She might not look like much, even in her brand-new pink dress, but when she confronted the Saint, she planned to act as if she ruled the world.

As Cassie's car rolled away from the Blue Note, Betty Jewel stole apart from the jostling crowd, trying to blend in with the shadows. She hadn't even thought about what she'd say to the Saint. Her only hope of winning a confrontation with that charismatic man was divine intervention. She had no doubt that Queen had battered so hard at the Heavenly Gates, God would be waiting inside the Blue Note to give her a helping hand.

"Are you ready?" She startled at Cassie coming out of nowhere, moving fast and strong, a determined set to her jaw that was now as familiar to Betty Jewel as her own pride-tilted chin.

"Yes."

They went in discreetly, Cassie buying two tickets, then going through the front while Betty Jewel went through a side door. The colored section of the club was rank with sweat and Evening in Paris perfume. She almost lost the hamburger she'd had for supper.

Finding a seat in the corner, she leaned back, grateful to the wall for catching her, grateful to the dark for hiding her shaking hands. She was even grateful to the Saint for being on the stage, casting a spell with his trumpet.

*Gotta walk this road all by myself.*
*Gotta walk this road, me and nobody else.*

The refrain got in Betty Jewel's head and wouldn't go away. She'd sung it a million times, Li'l Rosie's lament, back when she had money in her pocket and hope in her heart.

*If I had a dime for ever' lonesome mile,*
*I'd be waltzin' 'round this town in highfalutin style.*

*If I had a nickel for ever' tear I've cried,*
*I'd be shootin' craps at Jim's and eatin' Kentucky fried.*

The lyrics clogged Betty Jewel's throat. Death was the lonesomest road she knew. Even the thought of gaining Queen's *eternal reward* couldn't stop the tears she'd cried, always in secret, deep in the night when no one could hear. But she would go on, by God's grace or without. She couldn't die now. She had too much to do.

Turning from the scattered applause, Saint strode backstage, the spotlight following along like an adoring fan. From a distance he was mesmerizing; up close he was lethal.

Standing backstage, Betty Jewel steeled herself against him. What astonished her was that in spite of the years, she was not immune. Cassie's quick intake of breath, the way she stood taller, told Betty Jewel that even she was moved by the legendary Saint.

The best thing would be to get this over as quickly as possible. Else, who knew who would fall victim?

Before he had the chance to start spreading his charm like snake oil, she said, "I've come to take Billie home."

"Betty Jewel! You changed your mind about singing with the band." With a smile that lit up the dim and dusty backstage, he started toward her. "It's good to see you, sugah."

She sidestepped his embrace. "Don't you try to sweet-talk me, Saint Hughes. I know my daughter's here, and I'm not leaving without her."

Cassie stepped forward. "And I'm here to see that we do."

"Two against one?" He turned his spellbinding smile toward Cassie. "And who is this beautiful lady?"

"I'm Betty Jewel's friend, Cassie Malone." Bold as in-your-face-blues, Cassie stepped forward and offered her hand.

"You're a great musician, and it's a pleasure to meet you. Under other circumstances I'd do a newspaper article about you for *The Bugle*. But tonight my concern is finding Billie. She's missing."

The Saint barely touched Cassie's hand. Even in the dark without witnesses, there were lines that couldn't be crossed.

"You said my daughter's missing?"

"Yes, and her family is sick with worry. Is there someplace we can talk in private?"

Glad to let Cassie take the lead, Betty Jewel pulled in big gulps of air and tried not to show how close she was to sinking to her knees.

"My dressing room. Follow me."

He whizzed past, and Betty Jewel was dragged along in his wake. He stopped in front of a plain wooden door. In their heyday, they'd had the best dressing rooms at the club, side by side, with big gold stars on the doors.

She and Cassie followed him into a cramped-up room with a kidney-shaped dressing table, an old pair of blue jeans and wrinkled chambray shirt hanging on a hook, one straight-backed chair, a pair of well-worn brogans underneath. Size eleven. She knew. There was a time when she'd bought black patent leather shoes for him at the best store in Chicago.

"I'm sorry I have only one chair. Do sit down." He turned to see her in the full light, and the moment Betty Jewel had been dreading was suddenly upon her.

"I don't want your pity." She could see it in his face. Her knees wouldn't hold her, and she sank into the chair, bent over to catch a breath.

"Betty Jewel." He dropped to his knees in front of her. "Why didn't you tell about being sick?"

She hadn't wanted him to know. She hadn't wanted to show the least bit of weakness in front of the man who would seize every advantage. Still, there was something different about this post-prison Saint, something softer.

"I just want to take my daughter and go home." Betty Jewel reached toward him. "For the love of God, Saint, if you know where she is, tell me."

He just knelt there, the knees of his white pants on that dusty floor, and looked at her as if he were trying to remember who she was.

Let him look. She no longer cared. She'd pull her fine silk head scarf off and beg if she had to. The only thing she wouldn't do is tell him that Billie was not his child. That would destroy Billie and tear Cassie's family apart; the gossip would turn the entire town against them. A dying woman had enough to worry about without turning a Southern town upside down.

"Please," she whispered, and the Saint bowed his head. Was he praying? Thinking up a pack of lies?

"I don't know."

He didn't know what? Billie's whereabouts? What he was going to do?

Cassie started forward with that look on her face she'd had when that shameful man thrust the Dixie cup at Betty Jewel. She shook her head. Cross Saint and there was no telling what he'd do. He could tell a lie so smooth it tasted like strawberry ice cream, then take Billie and run so far they'd never know where she was.

Saint got up from his knees and walked as far away as he could get. It wasn't much. The dressing room couldn't be more than six feet wide.

Betty Jewel took a good look around the little room. The second-class nightclub wouldn't have had a prayer of booking the Saint in his heyday. The top of the table held Saint's hair cream and the fine-toothed comb he liked to use. Saint had always been proud of his hair.

There was an old faded green cotton skirt tacked around the table, sagging in the center where the thumbtacks had worked loose, a reminder that the man in front of her no longer had the power of his youth.

"What have you done with my baby?" She didn't know where she found the strength to get out of her chair, let alone get right in his face.

"You're wasting your time here, Betty Jewel."

"She's here. I know it."

"Why would she come here?"

Betty Jewel called on every reserve of strength to call his bluff.

"If you don't get my baby, I'll send you back to prison."

"Come on now, sugah. This is me you're talking to."

"Just try me. I'll send you back so fast your head will spin. Don't think I won't."

"We'll get a search warrant," Cassie said.

"Hold on now. No need for the law."

"Then, Mr. Saint Hughes, I suggest you start telling the truth."

Betty Jewel nearly applauded. If she hadn't already decided Cassie was one of the spunkiest women she knew, she'd be singing her tune now. Still, the Saint just hovered there, his black-eyed stare as mesmerizing as a cobra's. Get too close and you'd find yourself entangled, with Saint squeezing the life out of you.

"I can sit here till Kingdom Come, Saint. You might as well start talking."

"She's here." Saint's confession took all the bluster out. "Upstairs in my room." Betty Jewel didn't try to hold back her tears, and neither did Cassie. They caught hands and held on. "She got here last night with a man named Clete. Hitchhiked ninety miles all by herself. That Billie, she's something else. You've raised her good, Betty Jewel."

"I couldn't have done it without Queen. Where's your room?"

"Now, hold on. I didn't say I was giving her back. I just said she was here. Safe."

Lord Jesus, she didn't have any more persuasion left, and she didn't have time for courtesy and fairness.

"If you don't get her now I'm going to start screaming. I'd hate to see you trying to explain that to a white security guard when you've got a white woman stashed in your dressing room. They're lynching Negroes for less."

"Good God, Betty Jewel."

"I mean it, Saint."

He turned the color of brown sugar. "All right. I just wanted some time with my daughter, that's all."

He'd taken Billie in. He'd wanted her, probably loved her in his own way. Still, she could never forget who he was. Underneath the white suit, the slicked-down hair, the wide smile, was a powder keg of a man who could explode any minute and blow your life apart.

"I'll go upstairs and get her. But don't think I'm done. When the time comes, I'll be there to claim my daughter."

When he left, Cassie said, "Don't worry, Betty Jewel. I think he's bluffing, but if he's not, my sister-in-law is a lawyer. He wouldn't stand a chance against her with Sudie and Queen and me on Billie's side."

Sometimes mercy takes you by surprise, and all you can do is breathe. Cassie's pledge to keep Billie safe, spoken in the back of a night club that reminded Betty Jewel of a past gone wrong, was a map out of despair. For the first time since she'd found out she was dying, she was ready to face whatever came next.

# Eighteen

Her Betty Grable paper doll had on a red paper dress, and Billie was pretending she had gone to visit Betty while the Saint and Betty's husband, Harry James, played a trumpet duet.

"My daddy said he would teach me to play the trumpet," she told Betty, who smiled and twirled around the rug in her red dress.

The rug was faded and full of holes, but Billie didn't mind. It was better than cracked linoleum. Though her daddy's apartment had only one room with a kitchenette at the end, she thought it was the most glamorous place in the world. Her daddy's bed was real brass and the couch where she'd slept had a big purple fringed shawl that covered the places where the stuffing was coming out. In case she didn't want to go down the hall to the toilet, her daddy had rigged a curtain in the corner to hide the chamber pot.

From the second-story window she could see Beale Street and beyond, signs flashing every color and buildings so tall she couldn't see over. She'd bet even Hollywood houses didn't have her daddy's view.

Thumbtacked to the wall were two pictures of the Saint,

one with B.B. King and one with Elvis Presley. Billie waltzed Betty Grable over to ask Elvis if her daddy could borrow the pink Cadillac that Queen had said he'd bought for his mama.

Yesterday, she didn't have time to tell her daddy about her sick mama. They were too busy seeing the city. Her daddy had bought her a hot dog from a red cart and a ten-cent book of paper dolls from the dry-goods store across the street. A. Schwabs, he'd called it, and Billie told him, "This is a grand store."

"Sure is." He'd patted her head, which he did a lot. Billie took it as a sign that he loved her and was really, really sorry he'd never sent her a birthday card. "I get Sundays off. If I had a car, I'd take you to the zoo."

Driving back to Maple Street in style went right out the window.

"That's all right, Daddy." He patted her head again and called her a *sweet chile.* "I bet you know some famous Memphis doctors."

He'd laughed and told her the only doctor he knew was a toothless old veterinarian on the cotton farm in Greenville where he grew up.

Now, standing in front of Elvis with Betty Grable clutched in her hand, Billie was practicing what she would say when the singer with the hips that wouldn't stay still came to Beale Street to pose for another picture with her daddy.

"Please, sir, I sure would be grateful if you'd let the Saint borrow your pink car. He'll be real careful driving. And while you're at it, maybe you know a Memphis doctor who can make my mama well."

Anybody who had a smile that nice was bound to say *yes.*

As Billie waltzed around the room with Betty Grable, she wondered what her mama was doing. And Queen. Even

Lucy. Her eyes welled up, but she wasn't about to act like a sissy crybaby.

She heard the key turning and rubbed her fists into her eyes. A great jazzman like Saint wouldn't want to come back to his apartment to find a little girl who had everything she'd ever wanted crying her eyes out.

"Billie, it's me," the Saint called, then walked through the door, so shining in that white suit he looked like Christmas. "Come over here."

He squatted by the door with bad news written all over his face. Billie ambled over and leaned against his knee. He smelled like hair oil and smoke from the Blue Note. She wrapped her arms around him and wanted to hold on forever.

"Your Mama's downstairs, and she's in a bad way."

"Am I going to get a whipping for not telling?" She hadn't seen a willow switch, but that didn't mean her daddy didn't have one.

"No, sugah, but you got to go home with her."

Billie hid her face and started crying then, fat tears that ran into her mouth and wet the sleeve of his suit.

"Can't you get a doctor to make Mama well?"

"I wish I could. I sure do." He mopped her face with a big white handkerchief. "You hush crying now. You're a big girl." The tears started fresh, and she couldn't get them to stop. "Why, you're so smart and fine, someday you're gonna be singing center stage and I'm gonna be in the front row listening."

"For real?"

"For real, Billie. There now, that's a good girl."

He took a hold of her hand, then, and led her down the stairs.

She knew her mama was waiting, but going back felt like walking barefoot on nails, every step bloody evidence that nothing was going to turn out the way Billie imagined. She would have dragged her feet, but she didn't want her daddy's last impression to be of a stubborn little girl without any manners.

"You remember what I said now, Billie?"

"Yessir." Her daddy's promise felt like a star in her pocket. She clenched her fist and held on.

When Saint handed her over, Billie shut her eyes. She might not open them again. Cancer and death are so scary it's hard to look it in the face.

"Billie, look at me." The Saint pulled a harmonica out of his pocket and dropped it into hers. "Now, be a big girl, and go with your mama. As soon as I get back on my feet, I'll come get you and teach you to play that harmonica."

"Cross your heart?" She wasn't about to add the *hope to die* part. There was already too much dying in her family.

"Cross my heart."

If Billie had a car like this redheaded white lady's, she could go anywhere, including back to Beale Street and her daddy. But she was just a little girl who got shuffled off wherever anybody wanted to send her, including back to Shakerag.

"Billie, are you all right?" Her mama sat in the backseat, hanging on to Billie's hand and sounding like she was holding back a scream as big as Africa.

Billie didn't answer. She didn't plan on talking ever again. If anybody wanted to know what she was thinking, they'd better try to get on her good side. No matter what grown-ups thought, little kids had them, too.

"I was worried sick about you, baby."

Now would be a good time to say *I'm sorry.* But Billie wasn't sorry. She'd found her daddy, even though he didn't know a doctor who could make her mama well. Her daddy's smile when he saw her had made her long journey worthwhile, in spite of the fact that she was being dragged back like a thief. The only difference between an ordinary thief and Billie was that her jail wouldn't have bars on the windows.

"Saint said a man named Clete brought you to Memphis. I'm glad he did. Really, I am, Billie. But, baby, you know how dangerous it is to ride with strangers."

Wait till she told Lucy. She might skip over the part about the pigs in the truck, but she would describe her daddy's sign in living Technicolor. It lit up the sky. Lucy would be sorry she got scared and missed their big adventure.

Billie wondered if Lucy still had her doll. She'd ask, but she didn't want to give her mama and that Cassie Malone the satisfaction. Cassie was up front, putting in her two cents. "I'm so glad we found you, Billie. I'm looking forward to getting to know you better."

"You can come for dinner tomorrow," her mama said. "Mama will want to thank you with one of her feasts. You and Billie can talk."

Like Billie was going to hang around for that. Grown-ups didn't talk to little kids. They asked questions, every one of them none of their beeswax.

"I'll bet Queen will fry a chicken. Would you like that, Billie?"

Not if she had to pluck the feathers. Why would Queen fry a chicken anyway? Fried chicken was for Sundays and birthdays and funerals. Was her mama fixing to die because Billie ran away? Was that why she was wearing a new dress? When the Grim Reaper came for old Miz Quana Belle's mama, she got her a pink dress for the casket.

Billie shut her eyes so she wouldn't see her mama's funeral dress, then scrunched into the corner of the seat. She took a deep breath so she wouldn't start crying. The seat was leather and smelled like something the Lord God Almighty might use to pad His throne so He could sit in comfort after walking His golden streets. When Billie got famous, she was going to get Queen a car like this.

"I think she's asleep," her mama said, and that Cassie said, "Poor child."

Billie would double-dog dare anybody else to call her *poor.* Someday she was going to be richer than God.

Billie had meant to be on Gum Pond looking for angels before the day got too far along. Or at least take her harmonica and her paper dolls up on top of her daddy's bus where grown-ups didn't ever set foot. But hitchhiking all the way to Memphis and finding out her daddy couldn't do a thing to help her mama had Billie tuckered out. She was putting on her shorts when somebody came knocking at the door. Probably that Cassie Malone. It sounded like her knock. Sharp and quicklike.

She tried lollygagging, but Queen hollered, "Billie, if you ain't dressed and out here 'fore I counts to ten, I'm comin' in with my switch."

If you didn't know better, you'd think life was back to normal on Maple Street. But her world was so far from normal and her dreams flushed so far down the toilet, she might as well be in China.

"Billie? You hear me?"

She thought about sticking to her plan of silence, but when Queen called her again, Billie gave up swift-and-sure punishment in favor of fried chicken.

"Yes, ma'am. I'm coming."

Her mama was already at the table, skinnier than when Billie had left home, but except for that she looked normal, which was a big relief. That Cassie was sitting at Queen's table in the kitchen as big and nosey as you please. But she smelled nice. When Queen asked where she got her perfume, she said it came from Paris. A place Billie planned to go someday.

Other than the way she smelled, the only other good thing about having her for company was that Queen said a short blessing that wouldn't make anybody fidget, and Billie got to start eating fried drumsticks.

That Miss Cassie asked her silly questions, like, did she enjoy school and did she have lots of friends—things she could answer with two words: *Yes, ma'am.* Queen couldn't accuse her of not minding her manners, and Miss Cassie probably thought she was too dumb to talk in complete sentences.

When Billie figured she'd stayed at the table long enough to avoid Queen's wrath, she pushed back her plate and said, "I'm finished, and I want to go to Lucy's."

Her mama said, "I guess it's all right."

"I better not hear of no runnin' away, or I'll bust them britches wide open," Queen said. She'd speak her mind if Cassie Malone was Mamie Eisenhower. Which was another thing Billie could say in the woman's favor. She was a whole lot prettier than the President's wife. She'd seen Miz Mamie in a newsreel before a Tarzan movie, and thought she would benefit from a trip to Curl Up 'n Dye.

Billie scooted out of her chair and was almost to the door when Queen hollered, "Miss Billie Big Britches, you get back here. Where's yo manners?"

"It was nice to have you here, ma'am." When you tell lies, your mouth puckers up like you've been eating persimmons. Billie ought to know. She'd told plenty.

Behind her, she heard that Malone woman saying, "It really was a lovely meal, Miss Queen. Thank you." Then, quicker than a lightning strike, she was in the hall telling Billie, "I'll take you to Lucy's if you'd like."

Billie's blistered heels hurt like all get-out, and she'd like to sit on the leather seats again, but she wasn't about to ride through Shakerag like some rich little white girl. She'd have to whip half the kids in the neighborhood. She could just hear the names they'd call her.

"No, thank you, ma'am." Billie streaked past her and out the screen door so fast it was a wonder the tailwind didn't knock her down.

There was dead Alice, floating over Queen's Canadians, but ever since she'd appeared when Billie found out where her daddy was, she seemed more like a friend than something to scare you half to death. Still, Billie wished she'd go away. She was a sure sign disaster wasn't through with Billie yet.

She set in to running and didn't stop till she got to the yellow house. Lucy was on the front porch, playing with Little Ella, her face and arms and legs covered with so many scratches she looked like she'd been fighting a cat.

"I've come for my doll."

Lucy handed over Little Ella, saying, "I didn't do it."

Poor Little Ella was as dirty as Peanut after spending the day making mud pies. Billie tried to smooth the hair, but it was so stiff it stuck out like somebody had stuck Ella into an electrical socket.

"What happened?"

"Me and Ella was hiding in the briar bushes by the pond."

"Did you see any angels?"

"One. Had wings this big." Lucy stretched her arms out as far as they would go. "But something scared me so bad I hid in the blackberries till Mama and them found me."

Lucy was always getting scared about something. When she plopped onto the porch steps, Billie sat down beside her and handed over Little Ella.

"Here. You can hold her awhile. What scared you?"

"Don't know. It might'a been a bear."

"We don't have bears."

"Do, too. It was ten feet tall."

Billie was not in an arguing mood. She would take her doll and go home if there was anything in her house except grown-ups with their mouths full of questions. Leaning back on her elbows, she listened to Sugarbee fighting with Peanut about going outside.

"Was your daddy handsome?"

"Naw, but he's real famous. His name was in lights a hundred feet high. I'll be going to live with him someday."

"Can I come visit?"

"I reckon. Soon as he gets his feet going good."

"What's wrong with his feet?"

"No car and all that walking." Billie lifted up a dusty foot to show Lucy her blisters. That was about all she had to show for her five-hundred-mile trip, that and a promise from her daddy.

# Nineteen

When Betty Jewel got up from the table and followed Cassie into the hall, all that bright hair and her shining face, she thought of the lighthouse beacon in Biloxi, how she'd watched it the year she and Saint played the Gulf Coast, watched it from the hotel window because coloreds weren't allowed on the beach. The very sight of that beacon had made her feel safe.

"Can't you stay a little longer? Mama's fixing us all another glass of sweet tea."

"If you don't mind talk from the neighbors."

"Let 'em gossip. I've got bigger things on my mind."

It felt natural to link her arm through Cassie's, just right to sit beside her on the front porch swing where she wrapped herself in her mama's quilt called Around the World. She didn't have enough time to see much more of this world, but she sure wasn't anxious to see the next.

"Are you all right, Betty Jewel? You look like you've lost five pounds since yesterday."

She was glad Cassie didn't mention the cane. It galled her to think she was so weak today she couldn't even get around without something to hold her up. "Seems like I'm on a cliff now, trying not to fall over the edge. And Mama's not much better. She tries to hide her sinking spells, but I see her bent over, trying to be brave."

"I'm so sorry, Betty Jewel. Is there anything I can do?"

Next door, Quana Belle came onto her porch and shook her dust mop over the side so the dust drifted toward Cassie. *Deliberately,* Betty Jewel decided.

"Yes. Stick out your tongue at that old witch next door."

Cassie turned around and glared toward the mop-wielding curmudgeon, and Betty Jewel actually found herself giggling. Lord, it felt good. Quana Belle scooted back into her house and banged the door shut.

"It's so good to hear you laugh." Cassie reached for her hand. "Seriously, though. What can I do to help you? Anything. Just name it."

"Sometimes I wake up in the middle of the night so worried I feel like an elephant's on my chest."

"Call me."

"At 3:00 a.m.?"

"Anytime. Day or night. You told me it helps to talk. So call me and talk till that elephant leaves."

"Lord have mercy, Cassie. You don't know what you're in for."

"Does anybody ever know?" Cassie set the swing in motion. "Tell me about Billie. She seems fine since that ordeal in Memphis, but how is she, really?"

"She likes to pretend nothing bothers her, but don't let her facade fool you. Her passions run deep. And she's got so many ideas and emotions it would take you all your life to figure her out."

"Joe was like that. I always dreamed I'd have a little girl just like him. If I'd carried my third child to term, she might have been very much like Billie."

Betty Jewel saw her longing, and the effort it took to pull herself back from the painful past.

"I'm sorry, Cassie. I wish you could have had children."

"The past is over and done with."

Cassie was still hurting over her empty womb, and maybe Betty Jewel was partly to blame. A woman facing the end of her days shouldn't have to add regret to the load of fear she was carrying, but there it was, settling into Betty Jewel's bones.

"It's you I worry about, Betty Jewel. After I leave, promise you won't just sit here and fret."

"I'd read if I had something good. The only magazine in the house is a last year's *Modern Screen* Sudie brought from the beauty shop. Merry Lynn tried to find *The Healer* for me at the library, but A.M. Strange is as likely to have the latest bestseller as I am to jog to Memphis and back."

"I'll check it out for you at the library downtown and bring it over tomorrow." Cassie stood up and smoothed her slacks. "I'm going inside to help Miss Queen. There's no use in her waiting on me hand and foot."

As Betty Jewel watched Cassie go inside, she understood why Joe had talked about her with a hushed sort of awe. Lord, look what she'd done for Betty Jewel, sitting in that mean, airless motel room in her underwear, icing herself down to keep cool so Betty Jewel wouldn't freeze to death under the air conditioner.

A sound made Betty Jewel shade her eyes and search the street. Sudie was striding toward the porch in that forceful way she had when she'd made up her mind that she had a bone to pick with somebody.

"Sudie! I'm glad to see you!"

Sudie stood in the yard, her face a study in fierceness and sorrow. "I see Cassie's car is here."

"She's inside with Mama."

"Betty Jewel, you're playing with fire. A white woman in this neighborhood could bring all kinds of trouble."

"If you came to warn me off Cassie, I won't listen."

Sudie had the good sense to look chagrinned. "Actually I came to apologize. I acted a fool the day the girls ran away. The only excuse I have is that I'm scared to death of losing you. I'm sorry."

"Sudie, get your butt up on this porch instead of standing out there in the dirt like some stranger." Betty Jewel smiled and held out her arms.

"I don't have long. It's my lunch break." Sudie climbed the steps, then sat down and hugged Betty Jewel. "Somebody ought to pin a medal on me. I wouldn't walk two steps in this heat for anybody except my family and you and Merry Lynn."

"How's Merry Lynn? I tried to call her last night and she didn't answer."

"She's been in bed ever since Tiny Jim went to the Delta to his cousin's funeral. You know how she gets when she's depressed."

When she got like that, nothing could get her going again except Tiny Jim or an act of God.

"How's Wayne?"

"Still out of work, and it's a long time till the crops come in. I guess I ought to count my blessings that Sugarbee's big enough this year to haul a sack and pick a right smart of cotton."

Agony rocked Betty Jewel so hard she had to wrap her arms around herself to hold it in. Billie's future spread before her, an endless road of toil with a cotton sack over her shoulder, her lively mind withering until there was nothing left but weary resignation.

"Anybody want some sweet tea?" Queen called as she and Cassie came through the screen door.

Sudie got up from the swing. For a while, it looked as if she and Cassie would just stand there, facing off like two cats on a fence.

Finally Sudie said, "I'm sorry for being such a pissant the day Billie and Lucy ran away."

"No harm done. You had every right to be upset."

Cassie held out her hand, and when Sudie took it, something clawing inside Betty Jewel settled down.

"Let me git another glass a sweet tea," Queen said. "Ain't nothin' like settin' on the front porch with frien's drinkin' somethin' cool on a hot day."

The library downtown was located in one of Cassie's favorite buildings, the former home of U.S. Congressman Private John Allen, who famously won a fish hatchery for the town by telling congress that catfish would walk miles overland to get to the water in Tupelo. Cassie walked through the beveled glass doors into the high-ceilinged front room and took in the smell of books.

"May I help you?" The polite inquiry came from a young woman at the front desk, a new employee Cassie guessed, or one of the many volunteers Cassie didn't know.

"Thank you, but no." She went straight to the *S*'s in the fiction section and had her hand on a copy of *The Healer* when she heard voices filtering through the stacks.

"A white woman has no business up in Shakerag. I don't care if she does call herself a reporter."

Cassie would know that nasal whine anywhere. It was Myrtle Tubb, of all people. They were in the book club together, and she'd always been nice to Cassie's face, telling her how grateful she was for the feature Cassie had done on her husband when he announced his political campaign. She even dropped by every Christmas with homemade gingerbread.

Cassie felt as if she'd been slapped.

"Joe Malone would be rolling in his grave." Myrtle Tubb was talking to Rick Monaghan's wife, Priscilla. She was a known gossip, and it was no secret in town that she'd been gunning for Cassie since her scorching article about the Chief of Police during the Alice Watkins case.

"Just because this town named a baseball field after her husband doesn't mean Cassie can go around doing whatever she wants," Myrtle said. "She ought to be ashamed. Consorting with Negroes! If you ask me, that father-in-law of hers ought to lay down the law."

Gathering her composure and her purse, Cassie marched around the stacks.

"Both of you are wrong. My father-in-law never lays down the law, and my husband would be applauding me. And *those Negroes* I'm consorting with have more class in their little fingers than you have in your whole self-righteous bodies."

"Cassie!" Myrtle blanched. "I didn't know you were here."

"Obviously."

If Priscilla had a comeback, Cassie didn't hear. She turned and steamed toward the desk to check out the book for Betty Jewel.

It was a relief to burst through the library's front door and breathe air not tainted by the hurtful judgment of people Cassie had socialized with all her married life. She'd even considered Myrtle a friend. But friends don't talk about you behind your back. They don't spread gossip that could have dangerous consequences.

As she climbed into her car, Cassie added Myrtle and Priscilla to the long list of people who had turned on her.

Driving home, Cassie knew she was doing the right thing for her friends in Shakerag, but she kept feeling as if the ground were shifting beneath her feet, that at any moment it would split apart and swallow her. When she saw Fay Dean waiting for her on the front porch, she breathed easier.

She'd barely had time to park before Fay Dean swooped from the porch and folded her close.

"My Lord, Cassie! Daddy and I have been worried sick about you. You're the talk of the town."

"You can say that again." As Cassie and Fay Dean linked arms and went into the kitchen to put on a pot of tea, she told Fay Dean about the library gossips.

"Forget those old biddies. It's the radicals I worry about." Fay Dean rummaged in the cabinets till she found cups and saucers. "Daddy wants you to come and stay on the farm till the gossip dies down."

"It won't die down unless I back down, and I'm not going to abandon my friends just because they're on the wrong side of town."

"I knew you'd say that. That's why I brought my pajamas."

"I'm always glad for your company, Fay Dean, but you know I can take care of myself."

"Joe would rise up from the grave and haunt me if I didn't watch out for you."

It was times like this that made Cassie question whether keeping her secret was right or wrong. Would her sister-in-law's pain at Joe's infidelity be tempered with the knowledge that Billie was his flesh and blood?

Still lost in her thoughts, Cassie poured the tea, then kicked off her shoes and sat at the table. Fay Dean lifted her cup and smiled over the rim.

"Cass, just so you know, I gave up a dinner invitation from Sean O'Hanlon for this."

"He's perfect for you. Call him back, Fay Dean. Tell him yes."

"And leave you? Not a chance."

They laughed together and sipped their tea and talked about things more ordinary—Fay Dean's legal cases and the sewing projects Cassie hadn't started. Sometimes the only way to remain strong is to hole up with your best friend and try to forget you are standing on a stick of dynamite with enemies lined up, itching to light the fuse.

# Twenty

FAY DEAN LEFT AFTER breakfast the next morning, and Cassie gathered the library book and drove to Shakerag.

Billie was in the front yard playing with the raggedy old doll that was all too vivid a reminder of the awful night she ran away and the frantic search on Gum Tree Pond. The minute she caught sight of Cassie, she lit out, her coltish legs pumping as she raced around the house toward the backyard.

"Billie? Where's yo manners?" Miss Queen called after her. She was in a rocking chair on the front porch with a pile of quilt scraps in her lap, smiling a wide welcome.

"That's okay." Cassie mounted the porch steps. "I just dropped by to bring this book for Betty Jewel."

"Ain't that nice?" Miss Queen took the book, then picked up her quilting again. "She's inside feelin' poorly, and I'm jus' settin' out here quiltin' and prayin'."

"Oh, Miss Queen, you must be so scared for Betty Jewel."

"Why, honey chile, death ain't nothin' but goin' on home."

If Queen could bottle her faith and sell it, Cassie would buy a dozen containers. Feeling a bit chastened, she sat down on the swing. "Can I do anything to help?"

"Why don' you go inside an' talk to her, baby? Seems like you got a way a soothin' her saggin' spirits."

The image of the brave old woman bent over her quilting scraps, her lips moving in prayer, stayed with Cassie as she went inside.

She found Betty Jewel lying down on the couch under two quilts, her face pale and covered with perspiration. Cassie took a lace-edged handkerchief from her purse, then knelt and wiped her friend's face.

"I'm having a really bad day, Cassie."

"I wish I could make it all go away." Cassie sat cross-legged on the floor, then took a firm grip on Betty Jewel's hand, willing her own strength to flow into her friend.

"You've done more than enough, Cassie." Betty Jewel tucked her straggling hair under the pink silk scarf. "Shouldn't you be at work?"

"I don't have to be at *The Bugle* for a while yet. Tell me what I can do."

"There's a little locket in my room, folded up in a pair of socks in my top dresser drawer." Betty Jewel paused for a shaky breath. "I don't have much to leave Billie, but when the time comes, after I'm gone, I want you to give it to her."

"You know I will. But shouldn't Miss Queen be the one to do that?"

"Mama will be too upset to remember it, and so will Sudie and Merry Lynn. But I want to know it won't be forgotten." Betty Jewel tried to lift herself, then fell back against the pillows. "Help me up. I'm tired of being flat on my back, helpless."

"You're far from helpless, my friend. You've got the spirit of a lion." Cassie stood up and leaned close. "Put your arms around my shoulders."

Betty Jewel was no more substantial than a dandelion. Any minute she might disintergrate and blow away on the wind.

"Take this, Cassie."

Betty Jewel reached into her pocket and pulled out a picture of a young and beautiful woman with clear eyes and a wide smile.

"My gosh, Betty Jewel. Is that you?"

"Yes. I want Billie to remember me strong. I'd put the picture in the locket myself, but my hands shake too bad. Will you do it, Cassie? When the time comes?"

"I promise you, I will." Cassie closed her fist around the little photo, and it felt like a star, brilliant and burning.

"She'll need something to hang on to, the story of me. Help Billie remember who I am. Sudie can help you with that."

"I will make sure she never forgets you, Betty Jewel. I *know* you. And my memory is long."

"I'm counting on it."

Betty Jewel lay back down and closed her eyes, her breathing finally slow and even. Cassie held on to her hand until she fell asleep.

Queen tiptoed in, then she and Cassie sat side by side, watching over Betty Jewel. Every now and then Queen whispered, "Yes, Jesus," and "Thank you, Lord."

"Amen." It was the only prayer Cassie could say, and she hoped it was enough.

The elephant that had sat on Betty Jewel's chest all morning, even after she'd given Cassie the picture for the locket, was still there in the middle of the night. The silence in the house was so complete Betty Jewel could hear Death coming.

Bundling herself in the blanket and one of Queen's quilts, she tiptoed through the quiet house, careful not to trip over furniture and wake her mama and Billie. Lord knows, she didn't want either of them getting up in the middle of the night worrying over her.

Leftover ham and biscuits were wrapped in waxed paper in the refrigerator, and the small light from the interior was enough to see the kitchen clock on the wall. Two o'clock in the morning. The hour of worry.

Betty Jewel set in to eating, hoping the simple act of filling her growling stomach would be enough to stop the feeling that she was going to be snatched up and carried off into the dark. Was death a dark void or was it the shining light of Glory Land, as Queen believed? Was it eternal damnation for being bad or a crown of gold for being good?

Lord, her own past was so checkered Betty Jewel couldn't be sure which way she was headed until she arrived. And once she was there, would she remember those she'd left behind? Maybe that was the meaning of God's mercy, that death wiped out your memories and gave you a fresh start.

The idea of forgetting Billie, even after death, shot Betty Jewel from her chair and set her prowling the house. She tried to calm herself by sinking onto the couch in the den and taking deep breaths. The telephone was within easy reach. Cassie had said *call,* but was there any use in two people losing sleep?

When Cassie said, "Hello," Betty Jewel looked at the receiver in her hand as if it had jumped off the phone cradle all by itself. "Hello? Is anybody there?"

"Cassie, it's me. Betty Jewel. I didn't mean to call. I'm sorry. Go back to sleep."

"No, wait!" There was the sound of rustling—Cassie getting comfortable against her headboard? "Now, talk to me."

"I'm scared."

"You have every right. In your shoes, I'd be a blubbering mess."

"I'm afraid I'll die before I've done everything I need to do.

I want to wake up Billie and say 'I love you' and not stop until the Angel of Death comes to take me away." She felt like a madwoman. "Good Lord, listen to me. Being selfish to the core."

"You're not selfish, Betty Jewel. Keep talking. I'm listening."

"Oh, God, I want to tell Billie about growing up, about how to follow her dreams, how to choose the right man, but who am I to talk? Look what a horrible mistake I made with Saint."

"Maybe it wasn't a mistake. Maybe it was just part of your life's journey."

"I don't want Billie to have that kind of journey. I want to run out the door right now and slap every boy in Shakerag who might even look at her twice and then pick up a whiskey habit. I don't want her enduring the kind of hell I had with Saint."

"Is he bothering you again?"

"No. I haven't heard from him since we got back from Memphis. But I keep thinking that he's going to come traipsing down here, stirring Billie up again."

"If he tries to start anything about Billie, I'll come over and put the fear of God into him."

"Thank you, Cassie." Relief flooded Betty Jewel, and she settled back against the cushions, as limp as a pricked balloon. "I didn't mean to bother you about any of this, but I'm just feeling so torn up tonight, I actually want to march next door and slap Quana Belle."

"Quana Belle? That old lady with the broom?"

"That's the one."

"I'd like to take a whack at her, myself. The way she acts, she ought to be riding that broom."

Cassie started chuckling, and Betty Jewel laughed so hard tears rolled down her face.

"Oh, Lordy, I'm going to wet my pants." She dabbed her face with the sleeve of her chenille robe. "Cassie, you've rescued me from the dark."

"That's what friends are for."

After Betty Jewel said goodbye, she lay down on the couch and pulled the covers up to her chin. In spite of her cathartic laughter with Cassie, she didn't drift off until daylight tinted the windowpane.

And when she woke, it was to the sound of angel voices. Betty Jewel thought she had died and gone to Heaven. Then she realized it was Queen humming "Amazing Grace."

Betty Jewel wasn't in Glory Land at all but in her own living room with her mama. She sat upright to see Queen with one hand over her heart and one holding a mirror.

"Mama, what in the world?"

"Glory be. My baby's done come back to me. My prayers is answered."

"Good Lord." Betty Jewel swung her feet over the side of the sofa and discovered that she was not only alive, but having one of her good days. "What are you doing with that mirror?"

"When I seen you wadn't in yo bed and I foun' you out here crumpled up, I fetched my mirror to see if you was breathin'."

"Where's Billie?"

"I sent her out the back door to play with Lucy."

"You did the right thing." She hugged her mama. "I'm sorry I scared you."

There was a sudden commotion at the front door, and Sudie's and Merry Lynn's voices drifted through the screen. Betty Jewel went into the hall with Queen right behind her, still clutching the mirror.

"Ya'll come on in and set down in the livin' room," Queen said. "I got pies to 'ten to, and I don' need no distractions."

"Yes, ma'am, Miss Queen." Merry Lynn hugged Betty Jewel, then followed her back to the living room. "What'd I do this time to get on her bad side?"

"It's not you. It's me." Betty Jewel told them about waking up to find Queen checking her breath with a mirror. "I reckon I got my poor old mama's day off to a wrong start."

"We've got something to put it right." Beaming, Merry Lynn turned to Sudie. "Go ahead. Show her the wig."

Her lips twitching, Sudie held out something that looked like a dead possum.

"That's a wig?" Betty Jewel didn't know whether to laugh or cry.

"You're too stubborn to go to that wig shop in Memphis. This is the best they had at the Curl Up 'n Dye." Merry Lynn snatched the wig from Sudie and arranged it on Betty Jewel's head. "What do you think, Sudie?"

"It looks like a cow paddy."

"You don't have to be so critical," Merry Lynn said.

"If you don't want the truth, don't ask."

Merry Lynn stuck out her tongue at Sudie, then made spit curls and pulled them toward Betty Jewel's face. "Oh, my God, you're right, Sudie."

"Let me see," Betty Jewel said. The mirror above the mantle reflected a scrawny face underneath a too-small wad of tight brown curls. "I look like Topsy from *Uncle Tom's Cabin*. Good Lord, Merry Lynn, what did you expect me to do with this thing?"

"Wear it for your funeral?" Merry Lynn looked sheepish, then started guffawing, and soon the three of them were hanging on to each other, laughing till tears rolled down their cheeks.

"Oh, my God, I needed that." Betty Jewel sank onto the couch, with her friends on either side. "Merry Lynn, if you put a wig on me when I die, I'm rising up and slapping you silly." Betty Jewel took off the wig. "Can you return it and get your money back?"

"It's nonrefundable," Merry Lynn said.

"In that case, you might as well get your money's worth." Betty Jewel crammed the wig back on her head. "Let's see if Queen's got coffee."

The pot was still on the stove, and the kitchen smelled like sugar and vanilla, coffee and the bacon grease Queen kept in a Mason jar by the stove. Seeing them in the doorway, Queen dusted her hands on her apron and pursed her lips.

"Baby, that looks like a ugly cat on yo head. If you don' git it off, I'm fixin' to take my rollin' pin an' kill it."

The three of them got tickled all over again, and when Queen joined in, they shook the rafters with laughter.

The sounded drifted through the little house, already heating up under a merciless sun, and onto the front porch where Cassie stood knocking, her hair caught up in a straggling ponytail and her heart full of worry.

Betty Jewel had sounded desperate when she'd called last night, and Cassie had hurried through breakfast so she could get to Shakerag and see about her friend.

"Hello? Anyone here?"

An old rattletrap of a car drove by, and the driver, a sullen-looking, middle-aged colored man in a raggedy cap, glared at her. Shivering, Cassie pushed open the door, never mind the niceties, and walked toward the sounds coming from the kitchen.

"Miss Queen?" she called.

"Honey chile!" Queen stepped into the hallway, bringing with her the scent of good home cooking, dignified in spite of the dusting of flour on her apron. "Come on in the kitchen and set down. We was jes gone have some coffee."

Cassie followed her into the kitchen where Betty Jewel and her friends were seated around the table. Sudie looked nervous and Merry Lynn's face was closed as a fist. There would be no warm welcome from those two.

Still, Cassie called out a cheerful, "Good morning!" then bent to hug Betty Jewel, holding on a bit longer than usual.

"Are you all right?" Cassie said.

"Fine," Betty Jewel replied, and then smiled. "It's been quite a morning."

"Ain't that the truth?" Queen said, and Sudie added, "Amen."

Merry Lynn's conspicuous silence would have screamed around the room but for Queen bustling about, saying, "Mmm-hmm," and rattling cups and saucers.

"Miss Queen, let me help you with that coffee." Cassie was only too glad to leave Merry Lynn's unrelenting stare. Arranging Queen's heavy stoneware cups and their chipped saucers, Cassie relaxed into the feeling of Queen's solid presence and the love that wafted off her like the flour dust from her apron.

As she leaned on the counter, Queen poured rich dark coffee into the cups and whispered, "Don' pay her no nevermine," then winked.

Cassie winked back, and the two of them carried the coffee cups back to the table.

"Cassie," Betty Jewel said. "I was going to call you anyhow to say thank-you for making me feel better last night."

"What'd she do?" Sudie asked, and Betty Jewel told about the late-night phone call.

"You could have called me, Betty Jewel." Merry Lynn's face looked sharp as needles.

"I know I could have, Merry Lynn. I *know*."

"Well, next time, call *me!*" She gave Betty Jewel another

aggrieved look, then stormed toward the door. "Are you coming, Sudie?"

"I'm sorry, Betty Jewel." Sudie hopped out of her chair, looking apologetic. "I have to get to work."

It was suddenly quiet except for angry footsteps in the hall and the loud pop of the screen door.

"Don't think bad of them," Betty Jewel told Cassie.

"I don't."

"Sudie is salt of the earth, and Merry Lynn's really a good person."

"It's okay, Betty Jewel. I understand."

Cassie reached for her hand, all the while struggling to keep from staring at Betty Jewel's hideous wig. What had she been thinking?

The oven door opened, and Queen took out two pies, the meringue so thick it looked like a summer cloud. As the rich scents of coffee and chocolate and coconut cream wafted around the room, a sense of peace settled over the women and they drifted into a conversation as meandering as a brook.

The telephone shrilled, interrupting their talk.

"I'll get it," Betty Jewel said, then hurried toward the den and picked up the phone. "Hello?"

"Betty Jewel, how're you doing, sugah?"

Lord God, it was the Saint with his honey-dripping tongue and his devil's intent.

"What are you doing, calling here?"

"Can't a man check on his wife and daughter?"

"I'm not your wife." Betty Jewel almost yelled, *and Billie's not your daughter.* Then Saint would come to Shakerag demanding to know who the father was. The scandal would blow Billie and Cassie apart and inflame a town already smoldering. "If you call here again, or come messing around my family, I'm going to make you sorry you were ever born."

Betty Jewel slammed the receiver down and turned to find Queen and Cassie in the doorway.

"Good grief, Betty Jewel," Cassie said. "What's wrong?"

"It was Saint." Obviously bent on stealing Betty Jewel's last peaceful moments on earth and making Billie's life a living hell. "I just want to scream."

"Don't let him get to you," Cassie said, linking arms with Betty Jewel. "Come on, why don't we get out for a while. Clear our heads."

"Where to?"

"You'll see. I know exactly the place."

Betty Jewel gathered the quilt and the coconut cream pie her mama insisted they take, then climbed into Cassie's car, so grateful to get out of the hot little house and away from the threat of another call from Saint, she didn't care where they went.

They ended up on a beautiful farm owned by Cassie's father-in-law, Mike Malone. The lake where they parked was tucked among tall pines and sweet gum trees and oaks so old Cassie said some of them had been there since before the Civil War. Weeping willows dipped their branches into the shallow end on the east side where the sun sparkled on the water.

She led Betty Jewel up a small incline where suddenly the trees opened and they could see for miles, a sweeping vista of soybean fields and green pasture and grazing cattle and the stream that wound through it all.

Betty Jewel felt the urge to scream bubbling up inside her, so many forces pulling at her battered heart. Death topped the list. She'd imagined her journey would be like a boat trip, with her drifting away on the currents while her family and friends stood behind on the shore, waving and calling good-bye. Queen's faith would see her through, and Cassie's stout heart. Staunch Sudie would endure and even Merry Lynn would find her way through the loss with a lot of support from Tiny Jim. But what of Billie? What of the child who would grow up without a mother's guidance and a father to provide for her? What if the Saint got his clutches on her?

She started screaming then, the sound building until it echoed across the fields. Cassie took a deep breath and joined in, pain and loss and rage pouring out of them, catching up in the wind that carried it away.

And when Betty Jewel could scream no more, when her throat was raw and she was as empty of everything except gratitude, she leaned into Cassie's hug.

"I used to come here when life became unbearable. When I lost the babies, when I lost Joe," Cassie said. "I'd yell till I thought I'd collapse. My friend Sean O'Hanlon calls it the primal scream. It's like loosening a valve to let out the pressure before the cooker explodes."

"If it weren't for you and Sudie and Merry Lynn, my cooker would have exploded a long time ago. It wouldn't be a pretty sight."

"Thank God I don't believe a woman always has to be a pretty sight," Cassie said. "I'll take my friends with a little garden dirt under their fingernails and a lot of sass on their tongues."

"Amen to that, sister." Betty Jewel braced against Cassie while she leaned down to kick off her shoes. When she noticed the direction of Cassie's gaze, she snatched the wig off her head and flung it as far as she could. "Oh, my Lord, I didn't realize I was still wearing that tacky thing. Why didn't you say something, Cassie?"

"I thought you liked it."

"Do I look like I've lost my mind? Get me down from this hill before I have to slap you."

As they descended the hill, Betty Jewel reveled in the feel

of sweet summer grass under her feet. When they got back to the lake, Cassie spread the quilt underneath the willow trees, close enough so Betty Jewel could reach out and trail her hand in the water, and then she unwrapped the pie.

There it sat in the middle of the quilt, a tempting confection, just the pie and two forks. No knife to cut it and no plates.

"Who needs plates?" Betty Jewel forked out a gob of sweet coconut cream filling and gooey meringue and tender crust. "Dig in, Cassie. Mama will have her feelings hurt if we don't eat it."

"The whole thing?"

"Why not? We deserve it."

Cassie stuck her fork in and came out with a bite so big she could hardly cram it into her mouth. They both started giggling at the same time, and soon they were laughing so hard they startled a blue jay in the willow tree. They ate until there was nothing left in the pie tin except flaky crumbs, then they collapsed onto the quilts, holding their stomachs and laughing.

"If they don't have pies like that in Heaven, I'm not going," Betty Jewel said.

"I'll see if the postal service delivers to the Pearly Gates."

"Knowing you, you'll try."

Content, they stretched on opposite sides of the quilt, friends against all odds, their faces dappled by sunlight and the soles of their feet pressed together.

# Twenty-One

When Billie got up this morning and saw Dead Alice sitting on the front porch, she should have known something awful was going to happen. Sure enough, the day wasn't half over before Lucy's mama came streaking home from the Curl Up 'n Dye yelling, "We gotta go to the hospital, Billie. It's your mama."

Billie jerked up her doll and got in the car so fast she barely had time to tell Lucy bye.

Just the other night at the supper table, her mama had been laughing when she'd said she wasn't hungry because she and Cassie had eaten a whole pie. Now here Billie was scrunched in the front seat of Sudie's old Studebaker with her on one side and Merry Lynn on the other, squalling.

Why would Billie's mama take such a bad turn unless it was punishment for Billie running away? She hung on to her doll and tried to think up a prayer promising to be good if God would let her mama leave the hospital alive, but she was too scared to think.

Sudie reached over to pat Billie's knee, and the car swerved toward the ditch. Any minute now, Billie expected to get killed.

She squeezed her eyes shut and tried to keep prayerful, like Queen was always telling her to do. *Please, God, if you won't let my mama die, I'll be good.*

"What's the prognosis, Sudie, do you know?"

Merry Lynn craned her neck to look over the top of Billie's head. She might as well quit acting like Billie was dumb. She knew *prognosis* meant somebody was making progress toward the grave but nobody wanted to tell how far they had to go.

"I don't know, Merry Lynn. Miss Queen was upset, and so was I. The ambulance was coming, and I was at the beauty shop and couldn't leave till I swept up the hair and folded a load of towels."

"Billie, your mama's a saint and you're a lucky little girl," Merry Lynn said, then set in to bawling again.

Billie thought that was the dumbest thing she'd ever heard anybody say to a girl with a dying mama. If that was luck, she pitied the little kid who was unlucky.

"Merry Lynn," Sudie said, "just shut up. You act like you're the one dying."

The car careened to the other side of the road, and Billie closed her eyes.

She never thought she'd be relieved to arrive at the hospital, but she was. By the time they got to Mama's room, Merry Lynn had commenced falling apart again, and Billie was just plain scared.

Sudie wrapped her arm around Merry Lynn. "Billie, you go on in to see your mama. I'll take care of Merry Lynn and be down there directly." They walked off down the hall in the direction of a sign that said Colored Waiting Room. Billie guessed white folks didn't have to wait.

The hall smelled like medicine and chamber pots and was painted a slimy green color that made Billie think of the scum on Gum Pond. A laundry cart with spilling-over dirty sheets was parked in front of a pair of big double doors.

The place was spooky, and Billie was glad she had Little Ella. Holding her doll tighter, she pushed open the door to the room when her mama's voice stopped her cold.

She darted back behind the laundry cart and hunkered down—the awful truth in her dying mama's room shrinking her till she was no bigger than a black-eyed pea.

Death didn't come on angel wings and white chariots to carry you home. It came on waves of nausea while fluids pumped into your veins and your mama hovered over you praying.

If it hadn't been for Queen and Cassie standing by Betty Jewel's bed, she might have shut her eyes and said, *Lord, just come on and get me. I can't do this anymore.*

"Now, you listen to me, Betty Jewel," Cassie said. "You're strong and you're going to get through this. The doctor's said so." Betty Jewel held on to Cassie's hand, and tried to focus. Forget that she was sandwiched in a ward with nothing to separate her from three other beds except a circle of ugly beige curtains. Forget the smell of bedpans and sickness and defeat. Her time was running out.

"Cassie, you have to promise me something."

"Anything, Betty Jewel. Just name it."

"I want you to take care of Billie."

"Of course. I'll keep a close watch on her. And Miss Queen and Sudie and Merry Lynn, too."

"Please." Betty Jewel struggled for breath, her left fist balled, nails biting into palms so she wouldn't pass out. She'd thought about this decision all night, prayed about it, agonized over it. And when daylight came she felt the peace that comes from knowing she was right. "I don't have time to beat around the bush. Mama can't do this by herself. I want you to adopt Billie." Cassie turned two shades whiter. "I want you to love her. Educate her and give her a chance to be the woman she's destined to be."

Cassie still didn't say anything and Betty Jewel felt her own confidence faltering.

"I thought Sudie could do it, but she can barely take care of the ones she's got. Cassie, I'm asking you to be a mother to Billie. I want you to make her your child, legally."

Cassie's face became a river, awash in tears. She leaned over Betty Jewel, pressed her mouth against her cheek, whispered, "Hush, Betty Jewel. You're going to be all right. The doctor said so."

"For how long, Cassie? I'm not going to live forever. But I can't go till you say yes."

"You don't know what you're asking, Betty Jewel."

Betty Jewel closed her eyes against the fresh onslaught of nausea and fear. Lord God, was she strong enough to beat back this cancer till she convinced Cassie?

"I know exactly what I'm asking. Good Lord, Cassie, the only good thing that came out of my ridiculous little newspaper ad was *you*. Your friendship means the world to me."

"I love you, too, Betty Jewel. You're as dear to me as if I'd known you all my life."

"I know you can love Billie, too." Betty Jewel fought against a strong fading sensation. "Think about it, Cassie. You have to promise me."

"Don't talk like that, Betty Jewel. Just hang on."

"*Promise me,* Cassie!"

"I promise."

Betty Jewel closed her eyes, grateful at last to drift. Cassie's promise wasn't all she wanted, but for now, it was enough.

★★★

Hunkered behind the hospital cart, Billie's world turned upside down. She'd been eavesdropping long enough to hear her mama's shocking request. And that wasn't Queen's dark molasses voice Billie heard making an equally awful promise. It was Cassie Malone.

Billie's mama and Cassie were still talking, but the buzzing in her head was so loud she could hear nothing but a humming sound and the sharp tattoo of footsteps heading her way.

She layered her arms around herself till she was the size of a pearl onion. Around the edge of the cart she saw Sudie, pinch-faced and weary, coming back down the hall with Merry Lynn barely holding herself together.

Cassie stepped out into the hall just as the women were approaching the room.

"How's Betty Jewel?" asked Sudie.

"The doctors are going to draw off some fluid." Cassie looked as if she'd been crying. "Betty Jewel's going to be all right."

"Who made you God?" Merry Lynn said and strutted past Cassie as if she'd been sent by the President of the United States. Billie wanted to shout *Amen.* Instead she stayed crouched with Little Ella.

"I'm sorry," Sudie said, then hurried in behind Merry Lynn. Embarassed, it looked like. Cassie stood for a moment, stunned, tears pooling in her eyes. Then she headed on down the hall.

Billie was glad to see all of them go. This awful day felt heavy as an elephant. The Angel of Death was fixing to carry her mama off, and she was going to have to live with a white woman.

She scooted from behind the cart and was about to duck

through the double doors when she turned back to risk a peek into her mama's room. It might be her last.

Tubes stuck out from her every which way. It looked like a scene from a horror movie.

Billie tiptoed backward, then turned and raced toward the double doors as hard as she could. Behind her, Cassie called out, "Billie? Wait."

Billie felt her sadness expanding to the bursting point. The only hope she had was that her mama wasn't really dying.

She raced down the hall without having any idea where it would take her. Away. That's all Billie knew. If she wished hard enough, maybe she'd be transported out of this awful place like Dorothy and end up someplace else. Not Kansas but her daddy's bus. Right this very minute she'd be sitting in the lawn chair looking up at the stars.

Cassie's footsteps began to sound fainter. No way could anybody catch Billie. She was invisible.

She burst from the hospital and kept on running, never looking back to see if Cassie was still chasing her.

When Billie was eight, she had a dream that she was no bigger than a pinhead. When she woke up, she couldn't feel her feet and legs, her arms and hands. She barely felt her heartbeat. All she could feel was the rise and fall of her chest, and so she knew she was breathing.

That's what it felt like now.

Winded, Billie stopped on a curb in front of a repair shop, then started shaking and couldn't quit. It hurt to look up. She'd never seen a bigger moon, and there must have been a million stars in the sky. She'd always loved this view, but suddenly the world was too big and she was too small. It was going to swallow her up if she didn't find something to hang on to.

In the distance the hospital blazed with so many artificial lights it looked like a giant ship of the sick and dying. You get on board and sail away to ports unknown. If Billie went back, she could hide in there just about forever and watch from afar while her mother sailed away.

But she didn't want to go back. She couldn't stand to see her mama dying.

Out of the corner of her eye she saw flashing lights. A police car cruising by. She wondered if they were looking for her.

She darted into the alley between the repair shop and Weiner's Dress Shop till she could get her bearings. The picture show was not far, and she knew the bus station was within easy walking distance. Suddenly indecisive and feeling very small, Billie leaned against the wall. What would happen if she got on the first bus out of town and went as far away as it would take her?

She didn't even have to feel to know there was nothing in her pockets. Except the harmonica her daddy had given her on Beale Street. Closing her hand over the cool silver, Billie checked to see if the coast was clear, then started walking toward Shakerag.

Clouds had gathered, and it was like a veil had dropped over the world. Still, Billie could make out a red car heading her way, going by real slow. When it passed under the street lights, she saw Cassie Malone's red hair. Billie ducked behind a hydrangea bush and waited till Cassie's car was out of sight.

If she was old enough, she'd hang out in an alley somewhere, then go off in the morning and get herself a job. Then she'd be her own boss and nobody could tell her where she had to live. But she's not the right age, and you can't just live off the streets. Not if you have a lick of sense.

Billie tried to think, but it's hard when you're upside down and wrong-side out in a world you don't even know anymore.

There was only one place she knew, one place that never changed for her.

★★★

It started to sprinkle, and soon the sprinkle turned to a downpour that sent water rushing through the gutters and slashing against the windows of the few cars on the streets.

Caught in the sudden summer storm, Cassie felt her car start to skid. She got it back under control and squinted through her window, but the rain made it impossible to see anything, let alone a little girl who knows how to hide.

Would Billie go home to get out of the rain? Trying not to despair, Cassie turned her car toward Shakerag. She drove slowly, glancing toward Tiny Jim's and Mt. Zion Baptist where it sounded as if there was a rally of some kind. Since the brutal killing of Reverend Lee for his voter registration activities down in Belzoni, violence had escalated all over the South and beyond. The Negro churches were rapidly becoming leaders in the resistance.

Now was not the time for Cassie to be alone at night in a place where she was clearly considered the enemy. Her car and her good intentions would be no protection.

Promising to think about adopting Billie now seemed rash. Even if she wanted to, it would be impossible. Cassie pushed forward, staying focused on finding Billie.

Sudie's Studebaker was parked in front of Betty Jewel's house. Cassie hoped that meant Billie was home, safe in bed.

The rain slanted in sheets now, and Cassie searched for something to cover her head. Finding nothing but a copy of *The Bugle,* she grabbed the newspaper. As she dashed toward the shelter of the front porch, the sound of blues and the smell of barbecue followed along behind.

"Hello. Is anybody home?"

Her only answer was the moaning of the wind and the savage sound of raindrops on the tin roof of Betty Jewel's house.

"Sudie? Billie?" Her voice was drowned out by rain.

Cassie knocked, but no one came to the door. Could they even hear her? She twisted the knob, and the door cracked open. Cassie stuck her head inside the house and called them again. There was no response, no sound, not even the creak of a footstep on the worn linoleum.

When she left the shelter of the porch, the rain drenched every inch of her, including the newspaper, which sagged and glued itself to her head. Fighting panic, fighting for footing on the slick ground, she worked her way around Queen's pitiful flower beds toward the back of the house.

A clothesline came into view, then a shed with only half a roof and what looked like a school bus parked inside. Cassie forged through the driving rain.

There was a faint outline of someone on top of the bus.

"Billie? Is that you?"

"She won't come down." Sudie materialized, standing beside the bus with her arms wrapped around her soaked self, shivering.

Cassie tromped through the mud, peeling the soggy newspaper off her head as she joined Sudie.

"Where's Merry Lynn?"

"She's home, trying to pull herself together."

"Does Betty Jewel know Billie ran?"

"No. After I searched all over the hospital, I told her we didn't bring Billie with us. And I told Merry Lynn that if she opened her mouth and said any different, I'd kill her."

"I'd have done the same thing."

They both stared at the small figure on top of the bus. Soaked through, Billie huddled with her arms wrapped around herself as if she were trying to keep her heart from flying right out of her chest.

"Billie, please come down out of the rain. Sudie and I will help you get through this."

"Go away." Billie's voice was small, a broken thing. "I don't need you. I don't need anybody."

"I'm coming up."

"No," Billie said.

"You'll fall and break your neck," Sudie told Cassie. "The ladder's slick."

She almost lost her footing on the slippery third rung. At the top, she struggled to transition from the ladder to the slick slope of the bus. No wonder Sudie had not attempted the climb.

Casting all dignity aside, Cassie spread out her arms and clawed her way onto the top. By the time she was upright, she was panting.

Billie stared straight ahead as if Cassie were not even there. Cassie wanted to wrap her arms around the child, say something to open up her heart. But all she could do was stand in the rain, shivering.

And waiting. For what, she didn't know. Inspiration, maybe. Maybe she was waiting for Joe to appear and tell her some great cosmic truth that would set things right.

All she could think of was how you can go through your whole life living only on the surface. You build a little fortress around your job and marriage and friends, and think *This is everything.* You never consider throwing yourself in front of a train.

Scared and feeling inadequate, Cassie moved toward the old lawn chair and squatted directly in front of Billie. She waited silently until the child turned to face her.

"Billie, whatever is bothering you, we will work it out. Together. I promise."

Billie was silent, and then slowly her face crumpled and she leaned toward Cassie, a willow yearning in the wind, bending and bending. But not broken.

She held out her arms, and Billie buried her face on her shoulder. The little girl felt light as a moonbeam and heavy as a star.

"It's all right, Billie. Go ahead and cry. Let it all out."

From below, Sudie called softly, "Everything all right up there?"

In the hospital, the idea of raising Billie had seemed as formidable as the peaks of Everest, but on top of a rusted old touring bus, it seemed as natural as breathing. Billie needed her, and she needed Billie. It was that simple, that perfect.

"Everything's all right," Cassie said. She tightened her hold and Billie curved closer.

Billie sobbed, and Cassie's heart broke, the two of them raw as an open wound.

Billie lifted her face and wiped her nose on her arm. "Is Mama dead?"

"No. Your mother's going to be all right."

"Don't lie to me." She jumped up and overturned her chair. "I'm tired of people lying to me."

Cassie tried to stand but was so close to the edge of the bus, she was afraid any movement would topple her over the side.

"I didn't mean that your mama is going to get well. I wish that were true, but it's not. The doctors can't make her well, but they can do things to make her feel better, and she will come home again."

"For how long?"

"I wish I knew." Finally Cassie inched away from the edge and got upright.

She held out her hand. "Let's go inside, Billie. I'll make hot chocolate."

It was a truce Cassie offered, and Billie said, "Okay."

Cassie claimed the moment as a small victory.

Sudie reached out to steady Cassie as she descended from

the top of the bus. It was more than an offer to help; it was a gesture of acceptance.

"Can you handle it from here, Cassie?" Sudie's soft-spoken question was full of genuine concern.

"I can handle it," Cassie said and smiled. "Go on home to your children, Sudie."

Mud sucked at Sudie's shoes, and Cassie was left alone with a little girl she wanted desperately to help—if only she knew how.

# Twenty-Two

IT WAS HARD TO make hot chocolate in someone else's kitchen. Cassie focused on locating the cocoa and a pot to warm the milk.

Billie hadn't spoken a word since they came down off the bus, and Cassie didn't know what to say to her. She was slumped in the kitchen chair, her hair hanging in wet ropes around her face.

Aching for this beautiful, miserable child she couldn't reach, Cassie brought the chocolate to the perfect temperature, poured it into two cups, then sat down at the table.

Billie said, "Thank you." Distant. Polite. They were two strangers caught in the middle of a storm.

"I'm here to help you." Cassie reached out to pat Billie's arm, but she jerked it out of reach. "I'm not going to leave until your family gets home."

The look Billie gave her was full of suspicion, full of hurt. Cassie tried to turn the situation.

"I always find a warm drink soothing on a rainy night, don't you?"

Billie just stared at her, saying nothing. She'd hardly touched her chocolate.

Cassie pushed her mug aside. "It's been a long day. Why don't we go to bed?"

Billie ran out of the kitchen, and Cassie heard a door slam from the back of the house. Good Lord, was she running away again?

Racing after her, Cassie tried to figure out which would be Billie's bedroom. The first door she pushed open led to a tiny room barely big enough for a twin bed and a nightstand that held a big Bible. Queen's room, she guessed.

Behind the next door, in a room smelling of barbecue and cherries, she discovered the pink chenille robe she'd seen Betty Jewel wearing thrown across the bed.

Cassie eased open a third door and found Billie curled up in the middle of her bed. The rain had finally stopped and a streak of moonlight illuminated the patchwork quilt covering her. Queen's handiwork, no doubt. Beautiful, simple and heartbreaking.

"Sleep well," Cassie said. If Billie heard, she didn't let on.

Cassie backed from the room, then went out to the front porch to catch her breath. Leaves rustled in the maple tree, the night wind passing through. In the distance, a dog barked.

Back inside, she made sure to lock the door, and then she found her way to the old sofa. It was even more uncomfortable than it looked. She tried several different positions before she was satisfied.

She was chilled to the bone. Her hair was wet, her clothes were still soaked, her skin felt clammy. She wished she'd at least grabbed a blanket from Betty Jewel's bed.

No way was she going to go back down the hall and disturb Billie. That poor child had enough trouble heaped on her head to bow a full-grown oak. How could Cassie get past the child's hurt to a place where Billie would start to heal and be happy again? How could she ever win her love?

Questions tossed in Cassie's mind until she was finally so exhausted she felt herself drifting toward the blessed peace of sleep.

A small movement roused her, and she squinted toward the window, disoriented. Through her fog she became aware of a shadow, a blanket falling over her.

"I thought you might need this."

Billie, stood beside her in a little blue gown, smelling of rain and dreams. The moon made a bright path between them, and when Cassie reached up, Billie came into her arms. In that shining moment, Cassie knew she'd made the right decision. She knew she could love this child, that she *already* loved her.

She held on as long as Billie allowed, and then the child vanished as quietly as she had come, leaving Cassie with her blanket.

Sometimes, suddenly, there was mercy.

The smell of coffee woke Cassie. She followed her nose, stopping to ease open Billie's door to ensure that she was still there. She was sleeping, curled into a ball around her raggedy old doll.

In the kitchen, Queen stood by the stove, and it looked as if every pot she owned was stewing or frying with something that smelled good.

"Miss Queen, how's Betty Jewel?"

"Doin' better, praise the Lord. The doctors done put up a No Visitors sign so's she can rest up."

"That's probably best." She sat down at the table, hoping to do what she could to ease this dear old woman's mind. "Miss Queen, I want you to know that what she asked of me is the greatest honor one friend can bestow on another. I'm going to tell her yes."

"Oh, honey lam." Queen wrapped Cassie in a deep hug that felt like falling into a feather bed. She could stay there all day if she'd let herself. "What you doin' is the miracle I been prayin' 'bout."

"I don't think I'm anybody's miracle, Miss Queen. I don't know a thing about children."

"You smart and kine and got a heart fierce as a lion. That's all it takes, chile. That and a little help from me and the Good Lord."

Cassie wished it would be that simple. Forget the fact that she knew nothing about how to raise a child. But a colored child? What school would Billie go to? Could she take Billie to the movies? To a restaurant? To the public swimming pool? Good Lord, whites were pouring acid in pools where Negroes tried to swim.

"Here, baby. Drink this." Queen set a cup of coffee in front of her and smoothed back her hair. "You a strong woman. You done proved it. Me and you, we got lots to do. Tellin' that chile 'bout her daddy, for one."

Shock rippled through Cassie, and she had to set her coffee cup down for fear of spilling it.

"You know?" If anybody knew about Joe, it would be Queen. Somehow it was a relief that after Betty Jewel was gone there would be one other person in the world who shared the burden of her secret.

"I been knowin' all these years." Queen wiped her eyes with the corner of her apron. "Le's eat breakfast now. We gone get through this."

Cassie believed it for the first time. She finished her coffee, then stood up to leave. "Miss Queen, I can't stay for breakfast. I need to get home and clean up so I can get back to the hospital and talk to Betty Jewel."

"Lemme walk you out then, baby."

Miss Queen fixed a heaping plate of chicken and they headed through the house. They got to the front porch and Cassie was stunned to see her car, sitting low on one side.

"What the heck?" Cassie barreled forward with Queen trailing after her.

"Somebody done slit yo tire."

"If I could get my hands on the person who did this, I'd strangle him." On top of everything else, this was the last straw. "Who would do such a thing?"

"Cowards, chile. This world's full of 'em. They ain't got the sense God give a billy goat."

"Why don't they show their faces? How can I possibly know who my enemies are if they hide in the dark?" She stalked back into the house with Queen huffing along behind. Still steaming, Cassie went to the kitchen sink and splashed water on her hot face. "I could just scream. I don't have a clue how to fix a flat tire."

"Don' you worry none, baby. I'm gone call Tiny Jim. Just 'cause the rest a the world gone crazy, don' mean he gone put up with that kine a meanness in Shakerag. We got our pride."

What would they do next? As Queen made the call, the enormity of Cassie's promise to Betty Jewel crushed the air out of her lungs.

"This is just the beginning, Miss Queen." Queen came back to the kitchen, and Cassie tried to regain her composure.

"I s'pec you right, baby. But jus' set back an' eat yo breakfast now. Ain't no sense gettin' worked up over a tire."

Cassie picked up a biscuit and tried to eat, but all she could do was listen for Billie to wake up, listen for the big man who was, once more, willing to reach out and lend a helping hand.

When Tiny Jim finally arrived and set in to changing the tire, he looked so huge hunkered by her car, Cassie wondered how he'd ever get back up.

"I hope helping me won't cause any trouble for you."

"They's folks actin' fools on both sides of the fence, Miss Cassie. I aim to find out who done this. Violence ain't no way to solve problems."

The tire iron clanked to the dirt, causing Cassie to jump. If she didn't pull herself together she would be of no use to anybody.

By the time Tiny Jim got the spare tire on and she'd thanked him, Queen was standing on the front porch with the plate piled with chicken.

"Just a little somethin' to git you by. When the soul's hurtin', I feed it."

Cassie hugged Queen, then got into her car with the full intention of going home to bathe and change. But as she pulled out of Shakerag, she found herself heading in a different direction.

Fay Dean's bright turquoise law office was in a row of Victorian houses downtown, most used for business, all painted pastel except hers. Fay Dean herself was wearing a purple blouse that matched her eye shadow, and Cassie was still in the wrinkled, barely dry clothes she'd had on last night.

"Good God, Cassie. You look like a mess. What's wrong?"

Fay Dean wet a paper towel to press against her forehead, then hurried off to the break room and returned with a cup of water.

The simple gestures—water when you're faint, blankets when you're cold, a hand when you're falling—told of friendships so strong they could withstand anything, even long-held secrets and a promise that would inflame a town. Still, Cassie dreaded that moment when she told her sister-in-law the real purpose of her visit.

"Fay Dean, talk to me. Did you ever have dinner with Sean?"

"I did. He's smart and funny. I like him."

"Coming from you, that's high praise. Sean just won the Date of the Year award."

"Forget about all that," Fay Dean said. "Let's talk about you."

"I don't even know where to start."

"You can start by telling me why you look like hell and sound like you're about to cry."

Fay Dean was right. One little word might reduce Cassie to tears, and if she ever started crying, she didn't know how she'd stop.

"I've made a huge decision, Fay Dean. One that will affect all of us."

"You know I hate suspense. What's the bottom line, Cass?"

Cassie couldn't continue stalling, not with Fay Dean, of all people. She sucked up her courage and looked her best friend straight in the eye.

"I'm going to adopt Billie Hughes."

"That little colored girl from the ad in *The Bugle?*"

"I know what you're thinking, Fay Dean, but she's a wonderful little girl, full of spunk and sass. And she's very bright. You're going to love her."

"Wait a minute." Fay Dean perched on the edge of the desk, crossed her legs, then lit a cigarette—her way of throwing up a smoke screen to cover emotions she didn't trust herself to speak.

"Forget the obvious for a moment. Why would you take on a child at your age?"

"I've always wanted a little girl. And I'm not that old."

"You're not that young, either." Fay Dean blew another smoke ring.

How could she look into Fay Dean's eyes and tell her the truth: that Joe cheated on her and Billie was his child?

Cassie removed the white cloth and offered the plate of fried chicken. She thought Queen's advice to feed a hurting soul might be the wisest words she'd ever heard.

"Queen Dupree made this. Have some."

For a while there were no sounds except the whirr of the ceiling fan and the crunch as they bit into chicken crust.

Finally Fay Dean said, "I suppose you want me to do the legal work?"

"Yes, if you will." Cassie could feel sweat collecting on her scalp. She hated being afraid, hated that her own body betrayed her. "Or I can get somebody else."

"Cassie, I think this is a terrible mistake, and I'm not going to aid and abet you. I'm sorry."

Cassie stood up and moved to collect her purse.

"Shit," Fay Dean said as Cassie reached for the door. "Have you thought this through, Cassie? She's a *Negro,* for God's sake."

"I know."

"Have you thought what that means? I'm your best friend and even I'm shocked. Can you imagine how the rest of the town will react? Jesus, Cassie! How do you plan to raise a little colored girl in a place called the *lynching state?*"

Cassie knew Fay Dean was right, but she'd gone so far past logic there was no turning back. Billie and Betty Jewel were firmly entrenched in her heart. Even Miss Queen. Besides, how could Cassie ignore the fact that Joe's blood coursed through Billie? No matter what anybody said or thought, that child was family.

"My mind is made up."

"What would Joe say about this?"

Cassie's blood drained from her head, and she clung to the doorknob to keep from sinking.

Fay Dean pulled a cigarette case from her pocket. "I'm not going to help you with this, Cassie. It's a grievous mistake."

Cassie wanted to walk out the door, but it was hard to walk out on a lifetime of friendship and, worse, to sever a family tie.

"I'm sorry, Fay Dean."

"I wish you'd never seen that ad."

"You know me better than that. It was more than the ad."

"Then, for God's sake, *tell* me. How can I understand if you don't talk about it?"

"I can't," Cassie said, and it was tearing her up inside.

"You're the most stubborn person I've ever met."

"Joe used to call me bullheaded."

"He was right."

Joe was dead, and now she was losing Fay Dean, too. The finality of it shot through Cassie.

Holding back the sting of tears, she left Fay Dean's office and stumbled to her car. It was a full minute before she could turn the key in the ignition and head home. Her tires on the still-wet pavement made that low, humming sound Joe used to make on his blues harp.

As she showered and dressed, she was still thinking how she'd lost Joe and now Fay Dean. Trying to buck up, she caught her still-damp hair in a ponytail, then went outside and cut roses from her garden. After finding a vase for them in the kitchen, she climbed into her car and drove to the hospital.

The head nurse wasn't about to let her into a room marked No Visitors, and Cassie wasn't about to back down. After a heated standoff which Cassie finally won, she pushed open the door and tiptoed to the bed. Watching Betty Jewel as she slept, Cassie silently prayed for her friend, prayed for Billie, prayed for them all.

"Cassie?" Betty Jewel opened her eyes. "I didn't hear you come in."

"How are you?" Cassie leaned down to kiss her forehead.

"Better, now that you're here." Betty Jewel reached for the roses, buried her face in them and took a deep breath. "Heavenly."

Cassie set the vase on the bedside table close enough for the fragrance to reach the bed. "I had to badger the head nurse to let me in."

"I've no doubt you were magnificent."

"Just stubborn."

"Like Billie," Betty Jewel said.

"Yes, like Billie." Cassie pulled a chair close to the bed and held Betty Jewel's hand. "I want you to know that I'm pigheaded and opinionated and don't know the first thing about children. I do things that make people mad and don't promise to change and I'll probably make a very bad substitute mother. But if you haven't changed your mind, I'm willing to try."

There is a kind of quiet that makes you both scared and hopeful, the kind where you hold your breath waiting to see how it will all end. When Betty Jewel smiled through her tears, Cassie finally let out the breath she'd been holding.

"Cassie, you don't how grateful I am, and how relieved."

"I want to be a good mother to her, and I'll try so hard. I really will, Betty Jewel. I love Billie."

"That's all it takes. A whole lot of love, a good dose of common sense, and that big, fierce heart of yours." Betty Jewel looked her straight in the eye. "I'm counting on you, Cassie."

"I won't let you down. I promise," Cassie said, and they tightened their hold on each other and didn't let go.

# Twenty-Three

THE SMELL OF HOME cooking woke Billie, but she just hunkered down in her bed with Little Ella. She didn't care how much chicken Queen fried. She didn't care if she'd wrung the neck of every hen in Shakerag. Nothing was going to make her live with Cassie Malone.

Billie knew a bribe when she smelled it. Queen always sided with Billie's mama.

She liked Cassie, but that didn't mean she was fixing to go live with her. Besides, she'd bet her bottom dollar, if she had one, that Cassie would die before she'd park the Saint's old bus in her backyard.

Billie hugged her doll closer. She wished her mama would walk into her bedroom like she used to. She could make the hurt go away with one hug.

Billie lay there listening to Queen and Cassie and hanging on to her doll. When the commotion in the house finally died down, she and Little Ella went into the kitchen.

"Good morning, sleepyhead." Queen put a plate heaping with fried chicken and biscuits in front of her.

After running across town last night in the rain, she ought

to be starving, but she just stared at her plate while Queen turned back to the stove, humming "Bringing in the Sheaves."

"Can I see my mama?"

"Ain't nobody 'lowed to see yo mama."

"Cassie said she was going today."

Any other day Queen would have talked about *little pitchers with big ears* and threatened swift justice with her willow switch, but today she just smiled at Billie the way grown-ups do when they don't have a thing to smile about.

"She need some peace and quiet, and that don't include little girls that ain't eatin they fried chicken." Queen shuffled over to pat her on the head. "Eat yo chicken, baby."

How could she eat when she kept seeing her mama hooked up to tubes and a bunch of other stuff that sounded like something in a scary movie? But Queen was the one with the willow switch, and she might change her mind about using it. If Billie didn't want to spend the rest of the day sitting at the kitchen table staring at a drumstick, she'd best get on her grandmother's good side.

She forced herself to take a bite and discovered she was hungry, after all. Still, the house didn't feel the same without her mama. All she wanted to do was get out as fast as she could. After she'd had enough to satisfy even Queen with her eagle eye, she pushed back her chair and put her plate in the sink of soapy water.

"I'm going to see Lucy."

"Hold yo horses, young lady. You ain't goin' nowhere till you dry these dishes. They ain't no Queens a Sheba 'roun here."

"Yes, ma'am." The dishcloth was thin in the middle, but Billie knew better than to use that as an excuse for doing a sloppy job. Queen didn't like shirkers any better than she liked liars.

By the time she set out to Lucy's, it was so late she figured they'd barely have time for a good game of hopscotch. It was hot, too, so hot that nobody much was out but Billie.

She skipped over the dirt path, careful not to step on a crack. *Step on a crack, break yo mama's back* is what the other kids said. She didn't believe in stuff like that, but she'd be willing to do anything that might change her luck.

Lucy was in her house cutting paper dolls out of her mama's Sears and Roebuck summer sales catalog.

"You can play with one," Lucy said.

"I'll take the blonde." Someday Billie might dye her hair blonde so she could be like Marilyn Monroe and wear shorts Queen didn't have to sew from flour sacks. Or maybe she'd get a cowboy hat, too, and then she could be like Dale Evans.

Lucy cut out a dining room table with six chairs, and for a while they pretended they were at a fancy dinner party where every dish was served from a silver platter. When they put their paper dolls to bed, Lucy's got scared by a haint.

"There's worse things than a haint," Billie told her.

"Is not."

"Is, too." Billie gathered her paper dolls into a stack. "I got a secret that's even scarier than a haint." Billie tried to act like the secret wasn't burning a hole through her.

"What is it?" When it came to secrets, Lucy was all ears.

"You have to swear on the thing you love best you won't tell."

Lucy grabbed an old stuffed rabbit she'd had since before Billie could remember. Henry was his name. He used to be pink, but now he was brownish with most of his hair rubbed off.

She set Henry down between them and put her hand on his overstuffed belly. "Ready."

The secret she'd been bursting to tell Lucy suddenly felt

like a lump in Billie's throat. She drew circles on the floor with the toe of her sneaker and tried not to be a sissy crybaby.

"Well, are you going to tell, or not?"

Billie took a breath like she did when she was up a tree and fixing to jump off a limb so high she might break her neck. "My mama is trying to give me away to a white woman. Swear you won't tell."

"I swear on Henry." For good measure, Lucy made the pinkie promise. "Who is she?"

"I'm not telling that, because I'm not going."

"I won't get to play with you anymore."

"Will, too."

"How?"

"My daddy's rich and famous. He won't let anybody else have me."

Cassie was nice, and she'd been good to Billie and her mama and Queen. But how could her mama think Billie would ever want to live with anybody except her daddy? Saint had said he'd come and he would. He'd made the pinkie promise.

For Betty Jewel, everything suddenly took on a great urgency, and yet time seemed to move like a slow motion film.

Tiny Jim had brought her home yesterday, and she'd been grateful to wake up in her own bed. She sat on the front porch with Queen, just sipping coffee and not saying a thing.

As she raced toward crossing the Jordan, Betty Jewel noticed every little detail—the soothing smell of lavender and the old rusty spot by the faucet, the crusty tops of Queen's biscuits and the way she held her coffee cup, the wasp nest clinging to the naked lightbulb over the front door, and the warped graying boards on the porch floor worn smooth by the passage of feet and time. She noticed every blade of grass, the colors of the sky. She heard the wings of hummingbirds and knew the secrets of the stars. She reveled in the sun-drenched smell of sheets fresh off the line and ached over the beauty and vulnerability of Billie's slender neck as she bent over her paper dolls.

"Mama?" Billie looked up from her paper dolls, more grown up it seemed than just a few days ago. "Will you have to go to the hospital again?"

"I hope not." She held out her arms. "Come here." She held her daughter closer and longer than usual, but Billie didn't squirm, anxious to race off for a little girl's play. That, more than anything, broke Betty Jewel's heart. "How would you like to go for some ice cream?"

Billie's eyes lit up. "In a cone?"

"Yes. If you'll fetch my purse, maybe Queen will take you."

Billie raced inside, and Queen got out of her rocker, slower than Betty Jewel remembered.

"Mama, are you sure you're up to it? Maybe I ought to call Merry Lynn to take her?"

"I gotta git some bologna and bread, anyhow, an the walk might loosen up these old bones and do me some good."

Queen left with Billie skipping along, a feisty little girl once more, already lobbying for a picnic in the park.

"If you don' slow down, I ain't gone make it out of the front yard," Queen told her. "Ain't gone be no ice cream, let alone no bologna sam'wiches in the park."

"Yes, ma'am." Billie tucked her hand into Queen's and slowed to a walk, but every now and then she took a little hop that made Betty Jewel smile.

She watched until they were out of sight, then gathered the coffee cups. In the kitchen, a chill came over her, and she dragged a quilt off her bed and stretched out on the couch. It seemed she'd barely closed her eyes, when somebody knocked on the door.

"Anybody home?" Sudie called.

Betty Jewel dragged herself to the door and saw her on the front porch with Merry Lynn, looking anxious. They hadn't expected Betty Jewel to come home. Betty Jewel knew that as surely as she knew their names.

"I guess I should have called ahead to tell Miss Queen not to cook." Merry Lynn held up a covered dish. "We brought lunch, peppermint tea and a salad."

"Queen's gone to the park with Billie." Betty Jewel went onto the porch and sank into the swing, still hugging the quilt around her. "Lord, is it lunchtime already?"

"It is." Sudie poured the tea into paper cups while Merry Lynn served up the salad in paper bowls. "The peppermint tea is supposed to be soothing."

Betty Jewel took a sip, but the tea didn't soothe a thing, and the salad tasted like nothing she'd ever eaten. "What is this stuff?"

"Mystery salad," Merry Lynn said. "It's supposed to cure cancer."

"Don't be ridiculous," Sudie said.

"Don't *you* be ridiculous, Sudie. Look how good Betty Jewel's getting around now. There might be a miracle."

The fact was, Betty Jewel believed in miracles but not for herself, not anymore, not since the cancer had reached out and grabbed hold so tight it was hard to breathe. For Betty Jewel, the miracle would be death.

"I want both of you to listen to me. I love you like sisters and would never do anything to hurt you, but I need you to face the truth."

Sudie bucked up, the way she always did under pressure, but Merry Lynn looked as if somebody had punched her in the stomach.

"Don't say it, Betty Jewel."

"I have to, Merry Lynn. I'm going to be leaving. Soon, I think."

"Remember when you told us you had cancer?" Sudie said. "We were sitting in the car outside the doctor's office, all of us crying, and Merry Lynn said, 'You're not going to die,' and I said, 'Nobody but God knows that, so let's just eat some chocolate milk shakes and shut up about it.'" Sudie wiped her eyes on the back of her arm. "I guess you didn't need us to just keep on denying the truth."

"Oh, Betty Jewel." Merry Lynn got into the swing and put her head on Betty Jewel's shoulder. "I thought we'd be eating chocolate milk shakes together forever."

"You wouldn't like that, Merry Lynn. You'd be yapping at Sudie and me about all that milk and sugar making us fat." Her friends smiled through tears, and Betty Jewel steeled herself. "I know this is hard, but I need you to listen. I want both of you to help raise Billie after I'm gone."

For a moment, they just stared, still unwilling to accept the truth. Finally, Sudie lifted her chin.

"You know we will. She'll be just like one of mine and Wayne's."

"Tiny Jim thinks the world of Billie." Merry Lynn struggled hard not to break down. "We'll treat her like our own."

"I know you will." Betty Jewel reached out and squeezed their hands, her gratitude so big it brimmed over. "And I'm counting on you to help Cassie, too."

"Betty Jewel!" Sudie stared at her. "What are you saying?"

"Sudie, Merry Lynn, I'd die before I'd hurt you. You know that, don't you?" They nodded, but they didn't understand, and who could blame them?

"I've prayed over this and agonized over it. Cassie is a wonderful person, and nothing daunts her. She's as smart and determined and loyal as you, Sudie. As fierce and witty and unconventional as you, Merry Lynn." The truth was beginning to dawn. Betty Jewel could see it in their faces. "She has the heart and the will and the resources to give Billie the kind of future I want for her. I've asked Cassie to adopt my daughter."

"For the love of God, Betty Jewel!" Merry Lynn jumped off the swing. "Do you even know what you're saying?"

"I can't believe this," Sudie said. "My Lord, how do you think Billie's going to feel when Cassie's friends turn up their noses at her?"

"Don't you think I haven't agonized over that? But I've seen Cassie stand strong against that kind of prejudice. It'll be hard, and she'll need both of you. So will Billie."

"Why on earth did you pick her?" Merry Lynn grabbed a cigarette out of her holder and tamped it so hard against the porch railing, tobacco and tissue paper scattered every which way. "She's nothing but an overprivileged, white troublemaker. I don't like her."

"Merry Lynn, you watch your mouth," Sudie said. "I took the time to get to know Cassie. She's a good woman."

"I don't care if she's God. I'm as good as she is."

"Of course you are," Betty Jewel said. "But I want you to see Cassie the way I do. You should have seen her fighting for me when we went to find Billie. She even looked a man straight in the eye and said if I was going to have to pee in a Dixie cup, so would she."

"She didn't!" Sudie smiled, but Merry Lynn clamped her mouth in a tight line.

"She did. And when I got the chills, she shut off the air conditioner and spent all afternoon talking me through my misery. It must have been a hundred degrees in that room, but I never once heard her complain about the heat." Just the memory of it made Betty Jewel smile. "You know what she did, instead?"

"I don't care to know," Merry Lynn replied.

"I do," Sudie said. "Tell it, Betty Jewel."

"She stripped off her clothes and iced herself down."

"Good Lord," Sudie said.

Betty Jewel cast aside her quilt. "Cassie will be a good mother, and I'm counting on you to change your mind and support her."

"I'd walk on nails for you," Merry Lynn said, "but I can't do this. It's not right."

Sudie didn't say a word. In spite of her approval of Cassie, she obviously agreed with Merry Lynn on the question of who should take care of Billie. They sipped their peppermint tea in heavy silence and poked at the mystery salad, which Merry Lynn finally carried to the kitchen and dumped in the garbage can. She was coming back onto the front porch when an unmistakable red car came down the rutted road, kicking up dust.

"What's she doing here?"

"Don't start something, Merry Lynn," Sudie said, trying to keep the peace.

Cassie got out of her car, a green silk scarf covering her bright hair, and sunglasses over her eyes. Downtown nobody would have looked twice at her.

She stopped just short of the porch and took off her sunglasses, her smile warm and friendly. "Hello, Sudie, Merry Lynn. It's so nice to see you here."

"We don't need your approval." Merry Lynn's hostility hung over them like a shadow. "And we certainly don't need you. We can take care of Billie."

"Merry Lynn, there's no need to make things worse," Sudie said.

"I'm not the one meddling. It's her." Merry Lynn wouldn't stop. She never did. "Do you plan on moving to Shakerag? How about switching your church to Mt. Zion? Do you plan to raise Billie colored or white?"

Merry Lynn's questions froze them.

"I plan to raise her with love," Cassie said.

"You have all the answers, don't you?"

"I wish I did have all the answers, Merry Lynn. All I know is that I'm not going to uproot Billie from Shakerag. As long as she has her grandmother and Miss Queen is able, this is where she'll be. I hope all of Betty Jewel's community will help me. Especially both of you."

Merry Lynn stood up and dusted off the seat of her skirt. "I've got to go before I say something I can't take back. You coming, Sudie?"

"Just a minute." Sudie hugged Betty Jewel with a quick, "We'll talk later," then followed Merry Lynn to Tiny Jim's big Bel Air.

Next door, old Miss Quana Belle was watching, leaning so far over the rail it's a wonder she didn't topple over.

"This is just the beginning, Cassie," Betty Jewel said.

"I'm not afraid of the future, my friend." Cassie wrapped her arms around Betty Jewel and half lifted her off the swing. "This world's got to change. What if it could start with four women?"

# Twenty-Four

INSIDE, CASSIE HELPED Betty Jewel to the sofa, then made tea, but it didn't help. Trouble was raining like pea soup, and Cassie was standing there with nothing but a fork.

"I'm glad you came, Cassie." Betty Jewel was so frail the sight of her broke Cassie's heart.

"I wouldn't be anywhere else. How are you? Really?"

"I'm on a freight train that's lost its brakes." The teacup trembled in Betty Jewel's hands. Cassie reached over and held it steady.

"I'm here, Betty Jewel. And Queen's talking to the conductor." Betty Jewel's smile was weak.

"Mama's praying about you, too, Cassie. You haven't changed your mind about Billie?"

"I promised you. I will *never* change my mind."

"You don't know how relieved I am to hear that." Betty Jewel reached into a drawer and drew out some papers. "I wrote this and signed it, Cassie—my intent for you to adopt Billie."

The papers lay on the table between them like a parachute, one they'd stitched together hoping it would be strong enough for Billie to fly.

"Make it legal, Cassie. First thing. In case that fool in Memphis turns over a new leaf and keeps his promise to Billie."

"I will. And when the time comes, I won't be this kind of mess."

Cassie pulled two wrinkled tissues out of her purse, handed one to Betty Jewel. She thought of the cycle of life and how plants, dead throughout the winter, sprang to life in the spring. She thought about love, and how you have to open your hand and let it go, let it fly free before it can come back to you. But she didn't want to open her hand. She wanted to hang on to Betty Jewel and not let go.

"I've seen your courage under fire, Cassie. Why do you think I picked you?"

"Oh, God, I don't want to lose you."

"Hush up, now, or I'll start bawling. I've got to get this said… I want Billie to know her roots. I don't know how long Queen will be around after I go, but I'd like to think of Billie still playing with Lucy and going to the movies with Merry Lynn after my mama's gone."

"She will. I promise you that."

"If you can get past Merry Lynn's stinger."

"I got past yours, didn't I?" Suddenly Cassie's confidence waned. "But how will I ever get past Billie's?"

"Children blow hot and cold. Billie can love me and hate me all in the same day. She just needs to know you better, Cassie. Tomorrow, let's take her on a picnic. To my favorite spot."

"Let's invite Sudie and Merry Lynn." Cassie stuffed the papers in her purse, her heart hurting that she could no longer invite Fay Dean. How would she ever repair their friendship?

The screen door popped. "Betty Jewel? Cassie?" It was Sudie.

"In here," Betty Jewel called.

Sudie walked in holding a pie. "Coconut cream. One of Queen's from Tiny Jim's place. Merry Lynn sent it as an apology. To both of you."

It was a pure relief to think about pie. Cassie went into the kitchen for plates and forks, a knife to cut the pie. When she got back, Sudie and Betty Jewel were cracking up.

"What's so funny?"

"We're planning Betty Jewel's funeral."

They grinned at Cassie, sheepish, then looked at each other and started laughing all over again.

"Her *funeral? My, Lord!*"

"Yes. The undertaker puts these awful grins on everybody," Sudie said to Cassie. "And then he uses this hideous orange lipstick."

"I don't want to look like a clown at my own funeral. And I don't want any sad dirges, either. Lord, Sudie, if you let Mabelene Crumpett sing 'Rock of Ages' I'm going to come back and haunt you."

It amazed Cassie how women could find laughter in times of trouble. She didn't know where they got this kind of courage.

"I want all my friends wearing red, and I don't want any long faces. You hear me, now? I want a party with fried chicken, Kentucky fried. I don't want Queen cooking. And I want the Saint's record played."

"I wouldn't let that rascal play for my dog," Sudie said.

"He won't be there. Just his music. I think it will help Billie. Besides, I like the idea of being wheeled out to 'When the Saints Go Marchin' In.' It'll make everybody think I'm heading in the right direction."

"Which reminds me, if I don't head home, Wayne and the kids will put out a search warrant."

"I want to go to the river tomorrow, Sudie. Can you come?"

"I wish I could. But that old barracuda I work for is not about to let me off work on the day everybody's coming in for their church hairdos."

Sudie said goodbye, then her footsteps echoed in the hall, and the screen door popped behind her.

"I have to be going, too."

"Take the rest of the pie home with you, Cassie. You'll need all the strength you can get."

Cassie stood to leave, but something was burning up inside her. If she didn't get it out, she might go up in flames.

"Betty Jewel, someday I want to tell Billie about Joe. When she's old enough to understand. And to forgive."

"Have you?"

"Do you think I'd spend all day in a bucket of ice cubes if I didn't forgive?"

Their laughter felt just right, like a glass of warm milk before bedtime.

Cassie carried the plates and cutlery back to the kitchen, washed them in a dishpan with the strong soap she found. Afterward, she hugged Betty Jewel for a long time, afraid if she let go, her friend would vanish.

When she got home, Cassie put Miss Queen's pie with the golden meringue in her kitchen, then leaned her head on the table and gave full vent to her heartache.

After Cassie left, Betty Jewel went out to the front porch to nap so the walls wouldn't close in. A car pulling up in front of the house woke her, a faded brown Chevrolet with a rusty-looking beige top. It heaved to a shuddering stop and out stepped the last man on earth she wanted to see.

"Saint," she whispered. "My God." He stopped in the

weeds she called her front yard. "I told you not to come. What are you doing here?"

"I borrowed a car to come down. Don't send me away. Please. I had to see you again."

He was seeing her all right, the pink silk scarf sliding sideways, uncovering her ravaged hair, her stick-thin body even skinnier than when he'd last seen her on Beale Street, her eyes sunk into her face.

"You can't have Billie."

"This visit is not about Billie. It's about you and me." He was still standing in the yard, waiting for her invitation, it seemed, to come onto the front porch. "It's about all the winter nights you spent without heat while I drank up our last dollar."

He started advancing then, and she no longer had the strength to run.

"Please..." She held up her hand, but he just kept coming.

"It's about taking you away from a great career and giving you nothing in return. It's about booze and cocaine and broken promises. I never meant to hurt you."

"It's over and done with, Saint. Forgotten."

He was on the steps now, coming up on the porch, his eyes asking her for something more, begging, his soul exposed, tattered and weary as her own. A great need rose in her, an urgency to finish her business in this life before she moved on to the next.

"Forgiven," she said. "The past is forgiven."

The words weighed him down, and he collapsed at her feet, buried his head in her lap.

"I'm sorry," he said. "I'm sorry."

Betty Jewel's hand hovered over his head, but she couldn't make herself do this one last thing, for while his apology was easy to bear, his presence was not. The Saint on her front porch in Maple Street threatened Billie's future.

"I said I forgive you. You can go now. And don't come back."

He snapped upright, the old fire showing in him. "I can't. I have a daughter here."

It took the last bit of her strength to stand up, but Betty Jewel was not fixing to fight this battle sitting down. She drew herself up tall and proud, willing to forgive but unwilling to show defeat.

"Saint, you had nothing to do with Billie for ten years, and I don't want you ruining her future now. If you have one ounce of decency you'll leave us alone."

"I love Billie."

"You've got the kind of love that can kill." Saint lost his dazzle right before her eyes. "Promise me, Saint. You'll walk out of our lives and leave us alone."

The Saint remained silent while Betty Jewel stifled on humidity and pain. There was a large shadow at the door. Queen. Listening and waiting.

Betty Jewel hoped to God Billie was off playing somewhere far away.

"Promise me."

She didn't know why she was wasting her breath. Saint's promises were as worthless as a ticket to the moon. When he was sober he could make you think he was going to set the world on fire, and the next minute he'd be roaring drunk and everything around you would be up in flames.

She watched him wage a battle between doing what was right and doing what he wanted. The Saint never could keep his emotions from showing.

"Betty Jewel, I can't promise you a thing except to do the best I can."

She should have known better than to expect a miracle from him. She held herself upright while he walked away, watched until his old car rattled down the road and out of sight.

Betty Jewel sank back into the swing. "Mama, you heard?"

"I did. Don' you worry, baby." The screen door popped, and Queen stepped onto the porch. "I been prayin' the whole time. We got God on our side."

It was good to see her mama smile. "Where's Billie?"

"Merry Lynn done took her and Lucy to see the movin'-pichure show, that Mar'lyn Monroe woman with seven years a itchin'."

Merry Lynn, trying to make amends. Thank God. It was not the kind of movie she'd have chosen, but maybe the glitz and glamour of Marilyn Monroe was just what Billie needed—her little girl with the big dreams and the grit to achieve them.

# Twenty-Five

When Cassie woke, the papers lying on her bedside table looked like something she'd dreamed. Beauty and terror buffeted her, and she leaned on the windowsill to collect her thoughts.

The phone rang, startling her, and she fumbled with the receiver.

"Cassie, come over for breakfast? I've made muffins." It was Ben.

"I can't. I'm going on a picnic with Betty Jewel and Billie."

"Good God, Cassie! You need to stay away from Shakerag. The night riders are out in force. This thing's going to blow wide open."

Cassie knew about the latest incident, and it made her fighting mad. Cowards hiding behind hoods and the dark of night had planted a burning cross in the front yard of the Methodist parsonage near Tulip Creek. And all because the preacher had stood up in his pulpit calling for level heads and open minds.

"My *Lord,* Ben, when will this madness ever stop? Can't we do something about it?"

"We're all hog-tied by the law, and it's not going to change anytime soon."

"Law or no law, I refuse to stop going to Shakerag. My friend is dying up there."

"I don't want you to die, too, Cassie. At least let me go with you."

"I won't involve you, Ben." She glanced at the clock. If she didn't hurry, she'd be late picking up Betty Jewel and Billie. "I've got to go, but I promise I'll be careful."

How would she be careful? A scarf and sunglasses? Who was that going to fool?

She said goodbye to Ben, then threw on her slacks and a blouse and her wide-brimmed garden hat. After packing drinks and the sandwiches she'd picked up at TKE the day before, she stepped outside. Though it was only eight-thirty, it was already ninety degrees. Mississippi in the summertime was not for the fainthearted. Climbing into her car, she headed toward Shakerag.

Betty Jewel and Billie were waiting for her on the front porch, Betty Jewel a ghost of herself, leaning heavily on a cane, and Billie in a little pair of homemade shorts, hanging on to that old rag doll.

"Where are Queen and Merry Lynn?"

"Queen's on the couch with another sinking spell, and Merry Lynn said no."

"I'll bet that's not all she said."

"You don't want to know." Betty Jewel put her arm around Billie, as watchful as a brown field mouse. "Billie, say *hi* to Cassie."

"Hi," Billie said, her voice small. She drifted past and climbed into the backseat of the car, a little girl hiding her hurt behind a solid wall of silence.

Cassie turned east out of Shakerag, heading to Highway 78 and the Tombigbee River, Betty Jewel with her head leaned against the seat and Billie in the back singing to her doll—an old camp song Cassie remembered from her own childhood, "Kumbaya." *Come by here, Lord.*

Beyond the city limits they passed through Skyline, a nondescript suburb. Its most prominent feature a two-story Victorian house with a huge sign across the front—Knights of the Green Forest. The home of the local chapter of the Ku Klux Klan.

Betty Jewel roused and stared at the sign, despair written in every line of her face and body.

"Don't look," Cassie told her. "Don't even think about it. I don't want anything to ruin our day."

From the backseat, Billie's clear child's voice rang out. "Kumbaya."

"Amen," Betty Jewel whispered, and Cassie reached out a hand, then held on.

The river waited for them, deep, cooling waters surrounded by a green cathedral that left no room for anything except peace. Billie went straight to the edge and started skipping rocks across the water.

Supported by Cassie and a cane, Betty Jewel took an eternity to walk to the shade of a blackjack oak. By the time she settled onto the quilt Cassie spread, her face was drenched with sweat.

Cassie wet a dishcloth from the thermos, then ran the cool cloth over Betty Jewel's face and down her bare arms.

"We shouldn't have come. It's too much for you."

"I'd walk through fire for Billie." Betty Jewel took the cloth from Cassie. "Go to her. I want her to know you."

A breeze had come up, lifting Billie's soft wavy hair off her neck and making little eddies in the water. She didn't even look when Cassie sat on the riverbank, took off her hat and rolled up her sleeves.

"I wish I could skip rocks like that."

Billie glanced at her, wavering, and then reached into her pocket and dropped a handful of rocks onto the ground. "I'm tired of this game."

Cassie knew that was the child's confusion speaking. Undeterred, she cast about for another way to engage her.

"Would you like to swim?"

"Mama said I can't go into the water without a grown-up."

"I'm a grown-up." Cassie tried to coax her with a smile, but all she got from Billie was the hint of a smile and a green-eyed stare that seemed to see straight to her soul.

"I don't want to swim." Billie was still holding on to a child's fierce pride.

"That's okay." Cassie, who didn't have a patient bone in her body, made herself sit quietly. There had to be a way to get through to Billie. "The water looks so cool. It would feel mighty good in this heat."

"Maybe."

"I used to do water ballet at Belhaven College."

"You did?" Though Billie tried hard to appear nonchalant, she was practically bursting with excitement.

"I *did*. I wish you could have seen us, eight women doing synchronized strokes all over the pool."

"Did you do backflips?"

"Backflips, front flips, dolphin rolls. You name it, I did it." Cassie stood up and dusted the back of her pants. "Come on. I'll teach you."

When Billie glanced back at her mother, hesitant, Cassie came up with the perfect argument to tip the scale: bragging rights.

"I'll show you some tricks today, and the next time, we'll bring your little friend Lucy and you can show her."

"She'll just about die!" Billie plunged into the water, and Cassie hustled to strip down to the swimsuit she wore underneath her clothes. "Hurry up, Cassie. I want to learn the backflip first."

It was as natural as breathing to step into the water and slide her arms around Billie. Soon they were laughing and splashing like two children, and the day seemed filled with endless possibilities.

Watching from the riverbank, as her child cavorted with Cassie, Betty Jewel thought about hope, and how you can find it when you've come to the end of your road and think you can't go on. She thought about grace, and how it can flood down when you least expect it, how it can wash over you like water, like a river that just might overflow its banks and wash the whole world clean.

When they finally came out of the river, Billie picked up the rocks she'd dropped and started skipping them on the water. Cassie knotted a towel around her hips and joined Betty Jewel.

"I think she's beginning to like me."

"I *know* she is. I haven't seen her laugh like that since we got back from Memphis. You did good, Cassie."

"I made progress." Cassie nabbed a drink from the picnic basket. "Maybe you and Queen and Billie could come to my house tomorrow for lunch. I believe we need to talk to her about the adoption."

"You're right." Betty Jewel shifted to get more comfortable. "But are you sure you're ready for what your neighbors will say about us?"

She watched Cassie closely for any sign of hesitation, any second thoughts about the course they were on. But not a flicker of doubt crossed her face.

"I'm ready. What about you?"

Betty Jewel smiled. "We've come this far, Cassie. If it will help ease Billie's mind about the future, nobody's going to stop me from flaunting myself in Highland Circle."

"Oh, Lord, I can just picture it." Cassie grinned, and then she began to crack up. Soon they were laughing so hard they had to hold their sides.

When Cassie got hold of herself, she said, "I want so much for her, for all of us."

"I do, too, Cassie, and I can leave this earth easier because of you."

Billie had big plans to go to Lucy's after breakfast and tell her about learning water ballet, but Queen blew that all to pieces. She said, "My rheumatiz is killin' me," then went off down the hall to watch the Dodge Dancing Party, leaving Billie in the kitchen to help her mama shell the bucket of peas Tiny Jim had brought over. Queen had the TV so loud, Billie could barely hear what her mama was saying.

"Billie you know I love you and I'm going to hang on as long as I can." Her mama looked all bones. Her color was gone, too, not like it had been at the river yesterday.

"Yes, ma'am." Billie didn't want to talk about dying.

"But as much as I want to, I can't be here forever, baby." Her mama set her bowl of peas aside, then came around the table to hold Billie close. "Queen will take good care of you after I'm gone. Sudie and Merry Lynn will help, too."

"I'll be all right, Mama. I can wash and Queen's teaching me to cook."

"Oh, baby, I know how smart you are. But you're going to need someone to take care of you like I would." Her mama's hold tightened, which scared Billie more than anything. "I've asked Cassie."

Billie hated cancer, and she hated secret conversations where nobody asked her opinion and she hated that her daddy was off in Memphis instead of in Shakerag putting in his two cents' worth. But mostly, she just wanted to cry.

"You like her, don't you, honey?"

"She's nice and fun, but I've got a daddy."

"Oh, honey." Her mama got that long-suffering look, like she was peering inside herself at something so scary it wouldn't do to tell. "Go and put on something pretty. We're going to Cassie's for lunch."

"Do I have to?"

"I'm not going to make you, but I think you'll miss a lot of fun if you don't come."

"Okay," Billie said, and her mama smiled like everything was hunky-dory. "Is Queen coming, too?"

"She's not up to it today, honey. Now hurry up and change."

"Okay." Billie raced out of the kitchen, but when she got to the hall, she slowed down in case Queen could hear over the TV. She hated running in the house, and she had radar ears, a trait Billie was trying to develop.

Cassie's house was probably fancy. Billie got her best shorts with the lavender flowers out of her closet. She'd barely got changed when Queen called her.

"Miss Cassie done come to get you."

"Yes, ma'am. I'm coming."

Cassie was standing in her hallway with Queen, wearing a yellow sundress with her red hair tamed by a headband. She looked like one of the women *Modern Screen* magazine photographed at a rich and famous party. She was nice, too, but she wasn't Billie's mama, and she'd double-dog dare anybody to make her live with Cassie. She had a daddy.

"Good morning, Billie." When Cassie smiled she was nearly as pretty as Merry Lynn.

Billie's mama came out of her room in her pink dress, and

Queen leaned down to hug Billie. "Have fun. Mine Miss Cassie, now, an' be sweet."

"Yes, ma'am," Billie said politely. Like she'd been taught. Then she followed her mama and Cassie to the front porch.

Suddenly, blues swarmed around her like hummingbirds on honeysuckle, and the smell of barbecue was so overpowering it was like you could reach out and pull pork right out of the sky.

Did liking Cassie make her disloyal to her mama? And what about her daddy? Still, it was just lunch, and besides, Cassie had taught her to swim like a genuine water ballerina.

Billie and her mama climbed into the car on seats as soft as a bed, and they headed out of Shakerag.

Cassie had this old-lady music playing, but Billie wasn't about to get on anybody's bad side by complaining. She just looked out the window and let her mama and Cassie do all the talking.

Cassie pulled up in front of a house that looked like a Hollywood mansion out of *Modern Screen* magazine—big front porch with a real brick floor, white wicker furniture with cushions so deep you could disappear, ceiling fans making a breeze, roses tumbling over a white railing that didn't need a speck of paint. Wait till she told Lucy.

When they got out of the car, a yellow-haired lady watering petunias on her porch across the street gawked as bad as old Miz Quana Belle. Billie would have made a face at her except her mama took her by the hand and hustled her through Cassie's front door.

They stepped into a great big room, and the first thing Billie spotted was the baby grand piano. Wouldn't Queen like to get her hands on that? On top of the piano, a man with movie-star looks and green eyes smiled up at them from a frame Billie would bet was real silver.

"That's my husband, Joe. You would have loved him. He coached baseball and played the harmonica." Cassie picked up another frame that showed a beautiful woman in a fancy dress with a tiara on her head. "And this is my mother, Gwendolyn Baker. She was a singer."

"Like me," Billie's mama said.

"Did she sing with Ella Fitzgerald?" Billie said. Maybe this Gwendolyn Baker had even sung with Billie Holiday and Cassie could tell her all about it. But it turned out Cassie's mama had performed opera, which was sung in funny languages and nothing even close to the blues. Billie knew the difference because Queen made sure she did.

The next room had a dining table big enough for President Eisenhower and two dozen important men. The room had a real crystal chandelier and so much silver in the china cabinets she wished Queen was here to see. Wouldn't she like to serve her pie with that?

"I thought we'd eat in the kitchen where it's cozier." Billie thought this great big house was anything but cozy. She was more likely to get lost here, but she didn't want to say so and hurt Cassie's feelings.

Then because her mama was looking at Billie with that bright, expectant smile, she said, "Your house is pretty. And it smells nice. Sometimes Lucy's house smells like chit'lins, which I hate." Cassie's smile was as big as the moon. Queen always said, *Ever'body loves to hear nice things 'bout theyselves,* and here was just another case of her being right.

In the kitchen there was a platter of fried chicken on the table, but Billie would bet her harmonica that Cassie didn't have a flock of chickens in her backyard that she'd have to catch and wring their necks. Still, she was hungry, and there was a bowlful of mashed potatoes, besides. Plus gravy and two gelatin salads and two kinds of pies, chocolate and lemon ice box, Billie's favorites.

They all sat down at the table, and Billie set in to eating, letting Cassie and her mama do all the talking. They were laughing up a storm. Still, when they suddenly turned all serious, Billie got a sinking feeling.

"Billie, I know this is hard, but your mother and I need to talk to you." She poured milk in a glass with a silver rim. "At the river, we discussed some things we both want you to know."

Why couldn't grown-ups be like little kids and just play with rag dolls and share fingernail polish and secrets?

"I love your mother very much, and I love you and Miss Queen." Billie could spot the truth from a lie quicker than any kid in Shakerag. Either Cassie was a real good liar, or she was telling Billie the God honest truth. "Please believe that, honey."

"Yes, ma'am." Billie's whisper was small enough to fit into a teacup. She'd rather pluck feathers off a dead chicken than talk about this.

"Cassie is one of the best women I've ever known, Billie," her mama said. "That's why I asked her to legally adopt you after I'm gone."

"Billie." Cassie leaned forward to take her hand. "I promise you I will take good care of you and keep you safe."

"My daddy will do that." Billie didn't care how many pies Cassie had on the table and how many warning looks her mama sent; they might as well listen to her for a change.

"Now, Billie…" her mama said, but Cassie burst in with, "It's okay, Betty Jewel."

Then Billie had an awful thought. What if her daddy didn't come, and Queen went on to her Glory Land?

"Do I have to live here?" she asked softly.

"Oh, honey." Cassie's hands felt like butterflies as they stroked her hair, soft and pretty. "I'm not going to take you away from Queen and your friends."

Something that had been clinched inside Billie unfolded. Cassie was nice as anybody in Shakerag, and some of the stories Billie had heard about white people were just a big fat lie.

"You'll have two homes," Cassie added. "One with Queen and one here with your very own room, anytime you want to stay."

"Queen, too?"

"Yes, I'll have a special room for her, too. I'm going to have both rooms repainted, and you can decide the color."

All this grown-up talk was like bees buzzing in her head. Billie wanted to go home. But her mama liked being with Cassie, and Queen had said *Be sweet…*

"Can I please be excused now?"

"Of course." Cassie and her mama exchanged a look which was probably some kind of grown-up secret message that Billie didn't even want to know. "There's a basketball hoop in the backyard. How about if you and I play ball?"

Billie didn't want to play with Cassie right now. She just wanted to be by herself. But it was Cassie's house and her ball.

"Okay," she said. "You can shoot first."

Cassie's back porch had enough chairs to fill Tiny Jim's juke joint. Billie guessed white folks got tired and had to sit a lot. Her mama sat in one of the chairs under the ceiling fan, coaching from the sideline while Cassie hit the basket like a Harlem Globetrotter. Billie would bet even the Saint couldn't do better.

Cassie's basketball court was nothing like the one in Carver Park. Instead of a tromped-down patch of cracked dirt, this one had real concrete, and the post didn't lean. Instead of rusty swing sets and a sand pile growing over with grass, Cassie's yard beyond had flower beds filled with petunias and Canadians that didn't need weeding. There were flowers everywhere, most with names Billie didn't even know, some in trimmed beds and some in pots without a single crack.

She didn't get much chance to shoot baskets at Carver Park because the bigger kids always hogged the ball. Soon she was playing so hard and having so much fun she wasn't even thinking about the conversation in the kitchen.

Cassie played ball better than Lucy, but she was sweating a lot, and her hair was sticking out every which way. Billie wasn't going to ever get so old she sweated like that.

On the porch, her mama was sweating, too. Cassie noticed and made the time-out sign.

"How about some lemonade?" Cassie said.

"That sounds like a good idea, Billie," her mama said. "I'm getting so hot I can barely coach this game."

"Can I stay outside and play?"

"Of course," Billie's mama told her.

"Just come inside if you get too hot," Cassie said, "and I'll have a big glass of lemonade waiting."

Billie laughed. Didn't Cassie know that little girls and summertime went together like biscuits and gravy?

Billie dribbled the ball, but it wasn't as much fun playing by herself. Besides, she could use some lemonade.

She had her hand on the doorknob when she heard Cassie say, "She has his eyes, Betty Jewel."

Who was *she?* Billie got a feeling like she'd just walked into church naked. She scrunched down behind the wicker chair to listen.

"Yes, she does," her mama said.

"Billie's green eyes always make me think of Joe," Cassie said, and suddenly all the air was gone from the back porch, and Billie couldn't breathe.

"Her hair is what reminds me of him," her mama said.

What about her hair? Filled with fresh alarm, Billie touched her head. The silkiness she'd always been proud of was suddenly something that set her apart.

"I wish Joe could see her," Cassie said. "I think he would have loved knowing he had a child."

Billie put her hands over her ears, but as much as she willed herself to be home in her little blue house with Queen listening to *Ma Perkins* on the Philco, it wasn't enough to drown out the conversation inside.

"She idolizes the Saint, and she's obsessed with the idea that he's going to come and get her after I'm gone." Her mama's voice seemed to be coming from the moon while Billie hunkered down with no place left to hide. "I wish she could know he's not her daddy."

Billie squatted behind her chair, shipwrecked. If the Saint wasn't her daddy, then who was she?

*I'm nobody.* Motherless and now fatherless. A little girl suddenly stripped of everything.

Footsteps heading her way shot Billie from her hiding place. She climbed into a chair and scrunched down till she felt no bigger than a watermelon seed. Closing her eyes, she tried to be invisible.

Inside, her mama had moved on to the subject of Billie's church and her school, and Cassie started talking about school clothes, but their voices were growing faint. Were they moving to another part of the house?

Suddenly Billie heard the door pop, smelled Cassie's perfume.

"We thought you might want some lemonade," she said cheerfully, the glasses clattering as she set them on the wicker table. "Billie? Are you all right?"

Cassie squatted beside her and Billie's mama leaned over and put a hand on her forehead. "Honey, what's wrong?"

"I have a stomachache."

For once, Billie didn't have to lie. She felt like a seashell tossed under the ocean currents, at the mercy of waves.

"Can I get something for her, Betty Jewel? A wet washcloth?"

"I think we'd better just take her back home, Cassie."

Shakerag. A place Billie no longer belonged.

She uncurled herself, but she didn't say a word, just let Cassie carry her to the red car while her mama followed along behind.

When the little blue house on Maple Street came into view, Cassie parked the car, then got out and leaned in to pick Billie up.

"I can walk," she said, but still, Cassie held on to her hand.

The words *Joe's child* were screaming so loudly through Billie's head, she clamped her mouth shut to hold it inside. When they got in the house, her mama talked to Queen about stomachaches and Pepto-Bismol.

Let them turn their own insides pink, Billie thought, and then rushed to the bus and climbed on top. Sitting in the lawn chair she waited, hoping God would bend down and whisper to His hurting child, like Queen always said, but all she found was a breeze coming off the oak tree and the sound of old Miz Quana Bell next door calling her dog.

Still, Billie didn't leave. With her whole history rearranged, the bus was now the only home she could count on.

# Twenty-Six

BETTY JEWEL WAS WORRIED sick about Billie. She hadn't come off that old bus till Queen went out and made her come in before dark. Then she didn't even eat supper, though she loved black-eyed peas and corn bread almost as much as fried chicken.

Betty Jewel glanced at a jar of cherries open on her bedside table and the rose-gold locket on the sheets. She'd tried everything she could to ease her mind before slipping down the hall to check on Billie. Her sheet was kicked back, and she was sprawled out with her doll, but she was sleeping, thank God.

Betty Jewel went on down the hall and picked up the telephone. When Cassie said, "Hello," it tethered her to a world that was quietly drifting away.

"Is Billie okay?" Cassie asked.

"She's fine now. She's so strong I keep forgetting that she's just a little girl with too much to handle."

"Maybe I ought to back off for a while," Cassie said. "Give the two of you some breathing room."

"No. You're doing good. I think the more time you spend with Billie, the easier her transition will be. I want you to come to church with us on Sunday." Cassie said *yes,* and a beam of moonlight fell on the little rose-gold locket. "Cassie, there's one more thing I need you to do."

"Anything."

"If you come over tomorrow, bring a picture of yourself. I want to put it across from mine in the locket."

"Oh, Betty Jewel." Tears sprang to Cassie's eyes. "Next to being asked to take care of Billie, that's the most beautiful thing I've ever heard. I'll be glad to accept that honor."

The weight she'd felt before the call eased into something Betty Jewel could bear. Before she said goodbye, she told Cassie what her friendship meant, what the locket meant, and then she picked up the little necklace and lay down under the covers, clutching hope in her hand.

Across town, Cassie cradled the receiver and thought about the shopping trip she'd planned. She didn't know the first thing about buying school clothes for a little girl, but she was excited at the prospect. It was just the kind of adventure Fay Dean would have loved, and Cassie's heart broke all over again that she and Fay Dean hadn't seen each other or even talked since their split over Billie.

Setting the alarm clock so she could get an early start, Cassie lay down and tried to put anything except the positive out of her mind. She was going to be adopting a little girl, and wasn't that a wonderful thing?

Bright and early the next morning she drove downtown to JCPenney's and walked into the children's department, a wilderness of denim and ruffles.

"May I help you?" The saleswoman was gray-haired and efficient looking, her hair in a bun, her shoes built for comfort, and her shirtwaist dress conservative and subtle.

"Yes. I'm looking for a dress." Cassie's dreams of shopping

for a child had died with Joe. Now Cassie was filled with excitement about watching Billie try on her new school clothes.

"What size?"

Cassie flushed with embarrassment.

"She's growing so," she said, and smiled uncomfortably. "She's ten, but all legs and arms. You know how that goes." She smiled as if she and the sales clerk had just shared a secret.

"I know just how that is." The woman pulled a pretty little dress with ruffles off the rack. "Does this look about right?"

"I think that's perfect." What little girl didn't love ruffles? "Do you have anything with lace on the collar?"

Cassie left JCPenney's with an armload of packages and was soon in Shakerag hurrying into the house for Billie and Betty Jewel to see.

Her excitement was short-lived. When she arrived, Betty Jewel was in bed having one of her bad days, and Billie picked through the pile of frilly pastel dresses spread across the couch—horror, disdain and stubborn pride playing across her face. With the innocence of a ten-year-old, she hadn't learned the value of hiding her feelings.

"Ain't they fine?" Queen said with a smile, fingering the blue satin with lace ruffles.

Regret sliced through Cassie. She should have asked Betty Jewel what Billie liked. She should have asked Billie. She should have been more observant. A little girl who would set out on a 100 mile odyssey by herself was the kind who would want blue jeans and cowboy boots, plaid shirts and denim skirts with pockets—not frilly dresses.

"I can take them back." She sounded anxious to please, something she'd always considered a character flaw. *There will be days you'll want to crawl in a hole and pull the dirt in behind you,* Betty Jewel had warned her. "Better yet, you and Miss

Queen can take the receipt to Penney's and swap them for something you'll like."

"It ain't polite to return gifts." Queen lowered a look onto her granddaughter that would make any little girl think twice before she spoke. "Billie, what you gone say?"

"Thank you, ma'am."

Cassie wanted to cradle the little girl, but the set of Billie's shoulders stopped her. "You're welcome, honey."

Moving in the way of a little girl who's had to grow up too fast, a willowy grace just beginning to show through her childhood awkwardness, Billie went to the sofa and picked up the green dress. It was the plainest of the lot, soft cotton with no ornamentation except a bit of embroidery at the collar.

"I like this one."

"It's my favorite, too, Billie," said Cassie. "It matches your pretty eyes."

Billie stared quietly at the dress. She looked so much like Joe it was almost disturbing. Cassie was waiting for the other shoe to drop when suddenly Billie stood up and bolted from the room.

"Billie," Queen hollered, but Cassie said, "Please. Just let her go. She's been through too much."

"You soun' just like Betty Jewel." Queen sat down heavily in the rocking chair, her ankles swelling over the tops of her rolled-down stockings.

"How is she? Really?"

"Getting weaker ever day, chile."

"I hope I can learn to be half the mother she is, Miss Queen." Cassie pushed aside the dresses and sank beside them. "I'm going to miss her."

"She's gone be with the angels, up there singin' them sweet hallelujahs." She dabbed her eyes with the edge of her apron. "Set a spell, Miss Cassie. You look like you need it."

Cassie's own eyes welled up with tears. She searched her purse for a handkerchief but couldn't find one.

"Just cry it out. When the troubles collect so deep a body can't handle 'em, it's bes' to let yo tears roll down like the Jordan. It's the Good Lord's way a givin' you some relief."

Queen started humming, the bluesy sound soft at first but then rising into something fearsome and powerful. And with it came the haunting notes of a harmonica. Alice, warning of things to come? Or Joe sending a message from beyond the grave? *The devil done dealt these cards, ain't a single ace in sight. Ain't leavin' this game till I wins, even if I has to stay all night.*

"That was one of Joe's favorite songs," Cassie said, remembering the lyrics as if she'd heard them only yesterday.

Queen smiled knowingly and kept right on humming.

"Miss Queen, I don't know why Betty Jewel thinks I can raise Billie."

"Why don' you start by takin' them frilly dresses back and gettin' Billie some sturdy jeans an' a checkedy shirt? All 'ceptin' the green one."

"Miss Queen, you're the wisest woman I know."

"It's the Good Lord done showed me the light. No use tryin' to make Billie somethin' she ain't. Jus' let her be, thas all."

# Twenty-Seven

IT WAS SUNDAY MORNING, the day Queen would be watching out to make double sure Billie minded her p's and q's, and that included thanking the Lord God for all His blessings. Her mama was still alive and Billie had a closet full of new clothes. That ought to be enough to make her feel grateful. But after learning about her real daddy, all she was feeling was scared.

"Miss Cassie's gone be here soon." Queen marched into Billie's bedroom wearing her church dress. She'd plaited her hair into a crown on top of her head and even combed down her woolly-worm eyebrows. "Why don you wear that nice new green dress?"

She liked the blue jeans and shirt Cassie had swapped for better, but she wasn't going to argue. Queen would have a conniption fit if she asked to go to church in blue jeans.

She pulled her green dress out of the closet, and Queen came in and sat on the bed. "I got a surpise fo' you, chile." The only surprises she'd had lately were the kind that made her sick at her stomach, but she knew better than to back talk Queen. "These here is yo Mama's. She wants you to have 'em now."

Queen was scaring her. If her mama was already giving away her stuff, that meant she was fixing to die.

Queen opened her fist and there lay her mother's pearl necklace, glowing in her grandmother's dark palm like angel tears. Billie turned around and lifted her hair off her neck so Queen could fasten them.

When she put her hand over the pearls, she could picture her mama someday leaning down from heaven, proud to see Billie wearing her necklace. She'd be wearing a golden crown and big wings, and she wouldn't have a single sign of cancer.

"There now." Queen turned her around. "You look nice, chile."

"So do you, Queen."

"Miss Cassie's gone be here in 'bout five minnits."

That gave Billie time to tiptoe into her mama's room to show her the pearls. She pushed open the door, and Betty Jewel smiled.

"Come here, baby. Let me see." Billie twirled around, then climbed into bed for her mama's bony hug. "You look mighty pretty, and I'm mighty proud of you."

Her mama sounded weak.

"Can I stay here with you, Mama? I don't think I feel so good."

"Let me see." She pressed her lips to Billie's face. "Why, you feel better than good. You feel perfect."

She shut her eyes, and Billie thought she'd gone to sleep. She was getting set to climb under the covers and tell Queen she was too sick to go to church when there was a knock on the front door.

"Billie?" Her mama's eyes popped open. "You need to hurry, baby. I want you to introduce Cassie to everybody. Can you do that?"

"Yes, ma'am."

"And when you get home, I want you to help Queen set

the table. Smells like we're having peas and corn bread and apple pie."

Billie hoped Queen had some ice cream for the pie. In the hall, she saw Cassie standing on the front porch.

"I hope I'm dressed right." She had on gloves and a little veiled hat that perched sideways on her red hair. She looked like Rita Hayworth, only her lips weren't as red.

"You looks fine, chile," Queen told Cassie. "The Lord don' care what you wear in His house." Queen adjusted her own hat, black straw with a large brim covered in a jillion fake flowers. "Ever'body at church is gone want yo hat."

Billie thought so, too. They all climbed into Cassie's car and headed toward Mt. Zion.

Cassie helped Queen climb the steps, with Billie lagging along behind. She didn't want to make introductions, but she sure wanted to hear everything that was said.

Billie wasn't a bit surprised when everybody in the church turned to gawk at them. There was a stunned silence and then a buzz of whispers. Merry Lynn just stared, and the preacher's wife opened and closed her mouth like a catfish. She had stiff brown hair that looked like plastic and a pale mustache she tried to cover with pancake makeup. Billie thought Curl Up 'n Dye had something to pull the hairs out by the roots. Painless, of course. Somebody ought to tell her.

Billie reached for Cassie's hand and squeezed. "You look nice." For once Queen didn't lower her eyebrows and lecture Billie about whispering in God's house.

"Thank you, Billie." Cassie squeezed back. The three of them lingered in the foyer trying to make up their minds whether to sit in the main hall or upstairs in the balcony. Billie was just getting ready to suggest the balcony when Sudie suddenly bolted from the choir loft and came running toward them so fast her robe flew out behind her.

"Cassie, I didn't know you were coming." She put her hand over her heart to catch her breath. "There's something I've got to tell you."

Before she could finish, the heavy oak doors to the robing room popped open.

"Oh, my Lord," Cassie said. "It's the Saint."

"Ain't nothing saintly 'bout that man," Queen mumbled.

"That's what I was trying to tell you," Sudie said. "Today he's playing trumpet with the choir."

Suddenly the Saint was staring right at Billie, and she felt as if she'd been struck by lightning.

The Saint was both dangerous and dazzling standing there in a white suit, his trumpet dangling from his hand. Whispers rippled across the church crowd.

Cassie's insides shattered like plate glass shot with a deer rifle. Any minute she could fall completely apart.

Miss Queen saved her. With a look that could wilt bitterweeds, she said, "I ain't stayin' here with no trash." Then she grabbed Billie's arm and marched out of the church.

Cassie wished she'd thought of that. Billie was the one hurting. She was the one who needed protecting. The Saint was making his way toward them.

"Do you need me to go with you, Cassie?" Sudie asked.

"You stay here and sing. And Sudie, thank you for trying to warn me."

"God, forgive me for saying this in church." Sudie rolled her eyes. "What I'd like to do is knock Saint over the head with his trumpet. Then you'd have reason to thank me."

"Give him a lick for me," Cassie said and then hurried to catch up with Queen and Billie.

Cassie spotted them by her car. If you didn't know Billie you'd never know anything was amiss, but Cassie could see tragedy and turmoil in the droop of her shoulders, the way she held her mouth.

Silent, they all climbed into the car, Miss Queen up front like a storm cloud and Billie in the back with her mouth clamped shut, holding back God knows what kind of emotion.

Cassie searched the radio for a station that played blues, a language all of them spoke fluently, a language that might give voice to their pain.

"Ain't no use tellin' Betty Jewel 'bout this," Queen said. "Billie, you hear?"

"Yes, ma'am."

In the rearview mirror, Cassie saw Billie put her hands over her ears. She wished it were that easy to shut out the world.

The little blue house came into view, and when Cassie pulled the car to a stop, Billie jumped out of the backseat and bolted.

"I should go after her."

"Leave her be awhile, baby. The Good Lord done put magic in chil'ren. They got ways a workin' thangs out we won't never learn."

"We can't let the Saint have her, Miss Queen."

"Ain't no way he's gone get his hands on Billie."

Cassie thought about grief and how it could eat you alive. She thought about injustice and promises and the way a life could veer so far off course you could lose your way and never find it again if you weren't careful.

"I got confidence in you, baby. An' I got a powerful big talk I'm gone have with God."

Cassie and Queen entered the house and quietly slipped into the kitchen, the murmur of their voices carrying down the hall to Billie's room.

She was huddled in the middle of her bed, hugging Little Ella.

She wanted to be excited about seeing the Saint in church today, but all Billie could think about were the words, *Joe's daughter.*

Neither one of her so-called daddies had seen Billie play the fairy in her second-grade play. They hadn't known she was the only child in the room to get the wings and the crown because she could sing. They hadn't patted her on the head like her mama and said, "That's my good girl."

Billie felt like a big walking, breathing lie.

From the direction of the kitchen came the low hum of voices. Billie listened but couldn't hear what Cassie and Queen were saying. She was about to get off the bed to eavesdrop when she heard footsteps in the hall, then the front door open.

"You take care now, chile," Queen said, then shuffled back to Billie's door. "Billie? Billie, let me in, honey chile."

Sometimes Queen could make her voice sound just like raindrops coming down from the sky. But it's not rain; it's sugar that melts all over you and makes you feel like nothing in this world can harm you because you are her honey chile.

Billie opened the door, and her grandmother folded her close. "You jus' go on and cry, baby. Queen ain't gone let nothin' harm you."

They sat on Billie's bed till she emptied all her tears, and evening shadows collected in the corners of her room.

"Queen, do you have any pictures of Mama with the Saint?"

Queen sat awhile trying to think up a reason to refuse. "Yo mama ain't gone like this," she said, but Billie didn't say a word. Queen mumbled to herself awhile, then finally got up and left, her slippers flapping against the floor in a rhythm that made Billie think of a sad, sad song.

When she came back, she was holding on to a wide brown album like the kind Billie used to paste valentines in. It was scruffy around the edges, and the string that bound it was loose. Billie pictured her mama taking it out late at night so she could run her hands over the pages and feel her memories.

The bed creaked under Queen's weight. "This here was made when your mama and the Saint lived up in Chicago." Billie was looking at a picture of a mother she didn't remember, a young beautiful woman who was smiling as if she was fixing to climb to the top of the world and never come down. The Saint looked very much the way he did today, not the handsomest man in the room but the shining kind who would make you sit up and take notice.

Billie tried to see the least little feature that looked like her, but the Saint didn't even come close. She thought about the time Lucy had said Billie had ocean eyes, and the time she'd said her hair was too soft to plait in cornrows.

Still, Saint was the daddy she'd fantasized about all her life, the only daddy she knew. And now he was back to take care of her. Just like he'd promised.

"Can I keep this picture by my bed?"

Queen pulled it out of its little black paper corners and handed the photo to Billie. Then she heaved herself off the bed.

Launching herself at Queen, she sank into the comfort of a hug that felt like a feather pillow and smelled like lilac talcum.

"Billie, how 'bout me and you makin' some sugar cookies? Go out to the henhouse and get some eggs."

Gathering eggs was better than plucking feathers. Mostly the hens didn't mind, and Billie liked the surprise of reaching into a nest and coming back with a treasure. She skipped through the door, mindful not to let it pop behind her, then sashayed across the yard with Little Ella, pretending she was a famous musician on the way to the Blue Note to sing with Ella Fitzgerald.

When they got back to the kitchen, Billie holding on to

Little Ella and the two eggs they'd found, Queen wrapped her in an apron that went around her twice. Before she knew what was happening, Billie was lost in her grandmother's world of flour and sugar and spices. She could see why Queen always lit into baking when she was upset.

The way Billie figured, it was going to take a powerful lot of cooking to get through their latest trouble.

Monday morning Cassie didn't even want to get out of bed. Seeing the Saint at Mt. Zion had robbed her of a good night's sleep, and she didn't want to face another day that meant she'd have to figure out why he was in Shakerag and what she could do about it. But sounds on her front porch woke her. Grabbing her robe, she hurried to her front door and pushed it open.

Ben stood on her porch with his morning paper tucked under his arm, his hair mussed like he'd been running.

"Ben, what a nice surprise!" Belting her robe tighter, she started through the door.

"Cassie, wait." He caught her arm. "Don't come out here."

"Good Lord, what's all the mystery?" She stepped outside, smiling. "Can't a girl give her friend a proper welcome?"

Cassie turned to hug him, and her smile froze. There, on her front door, someone had scrawled the words *Nigger lover.*

The hateful racial slur hit her with the force of a two-by-four.

"Oh, my God. Ben, who would do this?"

"I don't know." He steered her inside. "When I was getting my paper, I saw two men on your front porch. I chased them, but they drove off before I could get a look."

"I'd have shot them dead."

"Thank God you don't have a gun, Cass."

"Maybe I ought to get one."

"God forbid." Ben ran his hands through his rumpled hair. "I'll make coffee."

Ben was thoughtful, but Cassie didn't think coffee was going to help.

"This is about me going to church with Queen and Billie." She followed him into the kitchen. "I want to find out who did this, Ben. I want to put a stop to it."

"It's going to take more than us to hold back the avalanche." Ben put the coffee on, then leaned against the counter. "I think you ought to get away awhile. Go to Mike's farm."

"I'm not going to let anybody drive me from my home."

"Then I'll come over at night and bunk on your couch."

"I won't impose on your friendship. And you might as well not insist."

Instead of arguing, he waited while the coffee perked, then brought two cups to the table. For a while Cassie let the pleasure of hot coffee and Ben's company lull her into thinking her life would go on, just as it always had. She'd continue visiting Queen and Billie and Betty Jewel. She'd mend fences with Fay Dean and celebrate holidays with the Malones, and Ben would occasionally bring over her morning paper, then sit at her kitchen table and talk.

The sign on the door had changed everything.

# Twenty-Eight

BILLIE WAS NOBODY'S FOOL. Ever since the Saint had shown up in church, Queen was watching her as if she was a prisoner. Yesterday Merry Lynn had come over with a coloring book and Queen had made her stay home all day. Billie didn't even like to color. She was about to pop when somebody banged on the door.

"Billie?" Queen hollered. "See who's knockin'. I'm up to my elbows in lye soap."

Billie was in no hurry to answer the door. Lately, there had been nothing coming through but trouble. She dragged her feet, pretending she was Tarzan's Jane, fighting her way through the jungle, till Queen hollered, "Billie, I mean bidness!"

"Yes, ma'am." When she opened the door, Merry Lynn whizzed past her toward the kitchen, madder than a hornet.

Trouble was brewing as sure as her name was Billie Hughes.

"I'm going to kill that man," Merry Lynn yelled.

Billie rushed into the kitchen and found her tearing around, with Queen shuffling along behind, saying, "Now, hush, Merry Lynn. Set down and les talk sensible."

Billie knew opportunity when it knocked.

"Queen, can I go play with Lucy?"

Queen puffed to a halt, her eyebrows knitted. "I don' reckon yo mama ain't gone mine. But don' get in no trouble, you hear? An' be back 'fore dark."

"Can I sleep over?" Queen got purse-lipped, which meant she was thinking up a gazillion reasons to say no. "Please, ma'am," she pleaded.

Merry Lynn started banging through cabinet doors, which distracted Queen.

"Well, then, I reckon. But mine yo manners. Don' let me hear tell you acted like you ain't got no raisin'. And if I hears of any runnin' off, I'll tear them britches up."

"Yes, ma'am," Billie said, and took off running so hard she left every one of Queen's rules lying in the dust.

Lucy wasn't home, but Sugarbee said she was at Carver Park. Billie preferred Lucy's front porch steps to the rusty old swings in the park, but she was glad for a chance to run. When she was running she didn't feel a thing except the wind in her face and her heart pumping so fast she knew she was alive.

At the park, mean old Miz Rupert's nieces were hogging the swings, but Billie found Lucy under a cedar tree near the fence, searching the ground.

"What're you looking for?"

"Angel feathers. I saw Alice up yonder in the cedar tree a while ago."

Billie knelt down to help her look. "I got something better than that."

"What?"

"I saw my daddy at church." The lure of having a living daddy instead of one she'd never know tugged at her. Saint was more real to her than Joe Malone, richer and clearer in her mind because of all the years she'd spent imagining her made-up version of him. Besides, she wanted Lucy to think of Saint as her real daddy. Billie would die if word got around Shakerag that she was the daughter of a white man. No telling what the other kids would say.

"Merry Lynn's sleeping on our couch on account of your daddy."

So that was why she was at Billie's house, storming around her kitchen. "What's my daddy got to do with it?"

"She's mad at Tiny Jim for giving him a job." Lucy squatted down and continued looking for angel feathers, but Billie had lost interest in the search. Now that her daddy was in town to stay, she pictured herself waiting in the wings till the Saint finished his last set, then eating Tiny Jim's barbecue while they talked about Billie joining his show.

She didn't know if Saint could ever make up for ten years of watching out her window for a daddy who never came. But in the sort of grace that is granted to the child of a broken-to-pieces parent, she'd ended up loving him anyhow. Forgiveness was a fountain that flowed continuously from Billie's heart to his.

"What else did Merry Lynn and your mama say about my daddy?"

"I don't know." Lucy tucked the feather she'd found into her pocket. "I'm tired of the park. Let's go to my house and play."

"Queen said I could spend the night." Billie fell into step beside Lucy, who was chattering about paper dolls.

But Billie was thinking about the Saint. She imagined the two of them sitting on a front porch somewhere, playing duets that were so sweet the neighbors gathered to listen—father and daughter lost in the music and the pleasure of being together at last.

Cassie had bought red paint for her front door. As she watched the hateful slur vanish under her paintbrush, rage threatened to overwhelm her. She forced herself to take deep breaths and finish the job.

Inside, she cleaned up and was just coming out of the shower when the phone rang. It was Betty Jewel, and she sounded anxious.

"What's wrong?" Cassie asked. "Are you feeling okay?"

"It's not the cancer," Betty Jewel said. "It's the Saint. Merry Lynn said he's performing up at Tiny Jim's juke joint."

"Oh, my Lord." If he was here to stay, he would cause all kinds of trouble.

"Merry Lynn's threatening to run him off with Tiny Jim's shotgun, and I can't say I'd care if she did." Cassie could hear Betty Jewel's labored breathing through the phone. "Billie's confused enough without Saint hanging around, making it worse."

"Maybe I should go to Tiny Jim's and talk some sense into him."

"I'd worry about you up at that juke joint, Cassie. Everybody in Shakerag's stirred up over what happened to that Chicago teenager down in the Delta."

It was all over the news. Emmett Till had been dragged from his uncle's house in the middle of the night and beaten to death, his body later found in the river, weighted down with a forty pound cotton gin fan. And all for supposedly whistling at a white woman.

"Anger's running so high I don't even know if Tiny Jim could protect you," Betty Jewel added.

She was right. Cassie had the horrible feeling that both of them were mired in hot taffy with no way out.

"Don't worry," she told Betty Jewel. "I'll think of something."

After Cassie said goodbye, she laced up her sneakers and tucked her hair under one of Joe's baseball caps. The truth used to be a map for her, each path simple and straightforward. Now, it felt like a dangerous, twisting road full of land mines that could blow up at any moment. If she told Saint about Joe, she might back him off Billie but she would surely destroy Fay Dean and Mike.

Cassie raced off down the street, hoping a long jog would help clear her head. The cemetery was not her intended destination, but she ended up there anyway.

Sitting on Joe's headstone, she rubbed her hand across marble that still held the heat of the afternoon sun.

"Joe, I don't know what to do anymore." Sitting quietly with her hand against the tombstone, Cassie watched the pattern of shadows, the infinite shades of evening in grass and bush and tree, the play of light from the high-swinging moon. "I almost wish I hadn't fallen in love with your fierce child."

The silence in the cemetery was complete. Cassie lifted her face to the night sky, looking for signs, but all she saw was a perfect burning evening star that took her breath away.

In the distance, the haunting mixture of harp and horn drifted out of Shakerag, weaving a spell that felt like heartache. Was it Joe, telling her to love his child? Telling her to keep Billie safe?

Or was it Saint, weaving a plot as seductive as his music. With her hand still on Joe's tomb, she had a sudden inspiration. What if she could appeal to the Saint's better side?

The blues riff hung in the still air, and suddenly Cassie recognized it. Before every ball game, Joe would pull his harmonica out of his pocket and play that same riff. Then he'd lean down to kiss her and say, "I'm off to fight the good fight, Cass."

"Thank you, Joe." Filled with gratitude for what they'd had and for the unexpected gift he'd given her—a child when she'd lost all hope of one—she pressed her palm into the stone that was still as warm as a hand over your heart.

Cassie hurried home to shower again and change. By the time she got to Shakerag to fight the good fight, Tiny Jim's neon sign was flashing through the darkness. Mouth-watering smells of barbecue wafted through Cassie's car windows, along with the bending, moaning notes of the blues. She could almost believe it was just an ordinary, lazy summer night, when really she was a match about to walk into a keg of dynamite.

Only a fool would be so naive. All over the South, racial violence was escalating as fast as the rising heat of August. The Till murder had added the sharp focus of the national spotlight to the turmoil.

Two huge Negro men lounged outside the front door of the juke joint. Given the current racial climate, her best bet would be to avoid them.

From the reporting she'd done when Alice had gone missing, she remembered a side door in the alley, a private entrance for Tiny Jim and whoever was on stage that night. She found a parking spot far from the entrance, then picked her away through the dark.

In the alley, Cassie found Billie standing near the stage door with a little paper sack in her hand. She knelt in the dirt and gathered the little girl close. "Billie, oh my God! What in the world are you doing out here in the dark by yourself?"

"I want to live with my daddy," she said softly.

"Oh, honey. I know you do."

Cassie's heart broke at the thought of the ten-year-old sneaking through Shakerag after dark, trying to belong to somebody.

"Billie, let me drive you back to your mama and we'll talk about this in the morning."

"I can't."

"She'll be worried, Billie."

Billie's lower lip trembled, and Cassie held her close.

"Tell me what's wrong, honey."

The weight of Billie's silence was almost too much for Cassie to bear.

"I can't go home." Billie sniffled, then wiped the back of her arm across her face. "I'm supposed to be staying with Lucy."

"All right, then." Cassie stood up, keeping a firm grip on the child's hand. "We'll go to Lucy's."

"They'll be mad about the juke joint."

"We don't have to mention it."

She longed to put her hand over the child's heart and tell Billie it would be all right, that she wouldn't let anything happen to her. But how could she make that promise with the Saint in Shakerag? With Billie's fierce loyalty to a man who was not even her father?

Back in her car, Cassie breathed a silent prayer that she'd found Billie before anything awful happened, and the child settled in beside her, miserable and uncertain.

When Billie had hatched the plan to go to the Saint, she hadn't counted on walking along the dark dirt road that was scary no matter how brave you were. She had hoped that when she got to the juke joint the sight of her daddy would make her feel better, but the window in the alley was so dirty she could barely see him. Still, she could tell he was lighting up the stage like a summer storm, his audience stomping and clapping every time he put that horn to his lips.

She scrunched lower in the front seat of Cassie's car, confused and scared. Cassie reached for her hand and Billie hung on.

"You're not mad at me?" Billie said.

"Oh, honey. Why would I be mad?" Cassie squeezed her hand, smiling. "You're a little girl with a big imagination and a fierce heart, that's all."

In the lights from the dashboard, her red hair looked like a halo. Queen said God sent guardian angels when you needed them, and maybe Cassie was hers. Maybe that's why she showed up every time Billie started running toward a daddy she didn't even know.

A star bigger than she'd ever seen shone through the window. Was it God, trying to tell Billie it was all right to love this woman who had been so good to her family?

"Cassie, do you think God sends signs?"

"I believe He does, Billie, if we'll only open our eyes to see."

Billie scooted across the seat and leaned against Cassie.

When Lucy's house came into view, Billie could see something was glowing on the front porch like a devil's eye. As she got closer, she realized it was Merry Lynn smoking a cigarette. She didn't say a word when Cassie led Billie to the door.

"Be real quiet, Billie," Cassie whispered, "and I think you can slip inside without anybody ever knowing you were gone." She leaned down to kiss the top of Billie's head.

Dead Alice couldn't have been quieter. Billie stood in the doorway of Lucy's room till she could make out which side of the bed was hers. Finally she slid in beside her friend and pulled the sheet up to her chin. Then she lay there with her eyes wide open, wondering if she'd ever live long enough to feel her oats. And where she'd be if she did.

Nothing stirred inside the house, and on the front porch, it was dark except for the glow of Merry Lynn's cigarette.

"I've misjudged you." Merry Lynn was barely visible behind the tip of her cigarette, her voice so soft it was little more than a whisper on the night wind.

"You don't know how much that means to me, Merry Lynn." Cassie leaned against the porch railing, listening for any sounds in the house, but Billie seemed to have gotten inside without waking anyone. "I'm scared to death. I'm going to need you and Sudie every step of the way."

"I'm not much to count on, but Sudie's a rock."

"Don't be so hard on yourself," Cassie said. "If it weren't for you, I would never have known Saint Hughes was playing at the juke joint."

"That low-down, yellow-bellied cur. I know stuff that would send him back to the devil."

"I'm going back to the club to talk him into leaving."

"If you can't, I might have to shoot him." Merry Lynn took another draw on her cigarette. "Good luck with that, Cassie."

"That means a lot, coming from you."

"When you see the Saint, tell him I said this—" Merry Lynn made a rude gesture with her finger, and they covered their mouths to stifle their giggles.

"Maybe I will." Cassie tried to see the dial of her watch, but it was too dark. Still, it was time to face the music. "Will you make sure Billie gets home safe tomorrow?"

"Yes. I was going to see Betty Jewel anyway."

"And, Merry Lynn, I hope you didn't see any of this tonight."

"Who, me? I'm blind as bat shit."

# Twenty-Nine

As Cassie headed back toward Tiny Jim's juke joint, she almost wished she'd asked Merry Lynn to come with her. She didn't know what she'd find in the middle of the night in a place she didn't belong.

Cassie slipped through the alley door into the juke joint and stood awhile to get her bearings. The place had changed since she'd last been there, after Alice's death. She made her way toward the sound of a trumpet, then hovered in the shadows of a packed, smoky room. Onstage, the Saint was playing such seductive blues it would have been easy to slip into a chair and forget everything except the beauty of his music.

"Miss Cassie?" Tiny Jim walked out of a shadow and stood before her, his bulk blocking her view of the stage, his forehead wrinkled with worry. "You ain't got no bidness here. Let me escort you to yo car."

"I need to talk to the Saint," Cassie said. "Please."

"He ain't hurtin' nobody, Miss Cassie. He's jus' tryin' to get back on his feet."

"I just need to talk. It's important to Betty Jewel and Billie."

"I don't know," said Tiny Jim, shaking his head. A large man at a corner table suddenly spotted them and began heading their way. "Follow me, Miss Cassie. I don't want no trouble." Moving fast for such a big man, Tiny Jim ducked into a darkened hallway.

Glad to be shielded from a crowd restless with a white woman in their midst, Cassie followed Tiny Jim through a kitchen and into a small back office dimly lit with a naked bulb hanging from the ceiling.

"You can wait here. I'll send the Saint back soon's he finishes the show." Cassie flashed Tiny Jim a smile of gratitude. "Soon's you finish, wait here and I'll take you to yo car. It's hard times."

"I'd appreciate that."

"Miss Cassie, I ain't one to offer advice to white folks, but maybe you ought'n be comin' up here no more. That Chicago boy's murder done stirred up a hornet's nest."

"I know. I'll be careful."

Tiny Jim closed the door behind him while Cassie, unable to sit still, circled the room. The desk and the chair behind it were dark oak and massive, exactly what you'd expect from a man the size of Tiny Jim. Opposite was a straight-backed chair with a ruffled cushion made from a printed flour sack. There was not much else in the room except the photograph of a Negro soldier on a wall-hanging shelf.

Cassie stood in the middle of the room holding on to her purse as she waited for Saint Hughes.

When he finally entered the room, he was sweating profusely. Out of the spotlight he seemed shrunken and tired.

"Mrs. Malone. Won't you sit down?"

His manners were beyond reproach, his gallantry a hook that could lure her into complacency. Still, she dared not forget how Betty Jewel had suffered under his hands. Cassie decided she'd best do her talking standing on her own two feet.

"What kind of man are you, inviting Billie to a place like this?"

"Billie was here?"

"Yes, with her clothes in a little paper sack"

"Jesus. I didn't ask her to come here."

*Nothing is ever black and white,* Joe used to say, *only shades of gray that blend so we can't find the edges.*

The Saint had no edges now, and neither did Cassie; neither did Joe and Betty Jewel. They were all merely trying to find their way through the fog, filled with longing and trying to cope. The poignancy caught Cassie high up under the breastbone, and she sat in the chair, after all.

"Mrs. Malone, are you all right?"

"I'm fine, thank you. It's been a long day."

"For me, too," Saint said. "I don't know if this talent is a blessing or a curse. Depends on which day it is, I guess."

If the circumstances were different, Cassie would be pulling out her notebook to interview this jazz legend for *The Bugle.* But the irrevocable past had cast them as enemies, and the present left no room for negotiation.

"Billie is hurting and confused, and you're making it worse for her. I'm here to ask you to give Betty Jewel some peace in her last days. Please, just leave Billie alone."

"I can't do that. She's my daughter."

Cassie could end everything right here. *She's Joe's,* she could say, and he'd say, *I don't plan on raising a white man's child.* Then he'd pack and go, leaving behind a wreckage Cassie could never repair.

"Betty Jewel's dying wish is for me to adopt Billie. A courtroom battle would be very hard on her. If you love Betty Jewel, if you love Billie, I beg you to go back to Memphis."

"I've done things in my time, bad things, but I swear I'll be good to Billie." He mopped his face with a once-white handkerchief, the heat in the close little room getting to him. Or was it Cassie's presence? "She's my daughter and I can't walk away."

"Please reconsider. For love of Billie."

"Why should I reconsider a future with my own daughter?"

The Saint's dignity and sincerity were probably nothing more than the performance of a man who knew how to play to his audience. Cassie could talk until dawn and never appeal to his good side. She was beginning to doubt he even had one. A sense of defeat crept over her. There was only one argument that would change the Saint's mind, and she'd rather parade down the middle of Main Street naked than use it. Still, there was no other way.

"I didn't want to tell you this." Cassie gripped her purse so hard her knuckles turned white. "If this story gets out, a lot of people will be hurt, especially Billie."

"What story?"

"Billie was not even conceived until after you'd gone to prison."

"That's a lie."

Cassie thought the walls might close in on her. She'd rather be anywhere than in this sweatbox of an office, facing Saint.

"It's the truth. You're not Billie's father. Can't you tell by looking at her?"

"She's the spit image of her mama. And she's got her French grandaddy's blood."

"She's got Malone blood. My husband is Billy's father."

Saint took the news with such infuriating calm, Cassie wanted to scream.

"Then why is he not the one up here trying to claim her?" Saint asked.

"He never knew about Billie. He died before she was born."

"That's very convenient, Mrs. Malone."

"It's true."

The Saint started laughing, and Cassie wanted to jump out of her chair and claw his face. If Tiny Jim hadn't called through the door, she probably would have.

"Saint, time for the second set," Tiny Jim said, slicing through the tension in the room.

"Mrs. Malone," Saint said, "I guess I'll see you in court."

Saint walked out the door, leaving Cassie to stumble through the juke joint behind him and Tiny Jim.

Thankful for the cover of smoke, she stole one last glance at the stage. With his sequined coat and his shiny horn, Saint was electrifying, bigger than life. Looking at him underneath the spotlight you'd never notice the frayed cuffs on his white shirt and the deep lines etched into his face by wrong living and bad choices.

He put his horn to his lips and started playing a little-known blues lament that Cassie wouldn't have recognized except for the fact that Joe used to play it when he was down and out. The song was called "Mercy On Me," and she wondered if the Saint was playing it just for himself or for all of them.

Tiny Jim hustled Cassie out the side door and into her car where she sat in the dark, limp with conflicting emotions—fear for Billie's future, relief that she no longer had to carry the secret, fury that the Saint was making Betty Jewel's last days harder, and absolute certainty about what she had to do next. She turned her car onto the rutted dirt road that led out of Shakerag, past the turnoff to Highland Circle and all the way to Fay Dean's apartment.

Though it was past midnight, light poured from the window. Fay Dean, ever the night owl, would be up watching television or working on a brief.

Before their split over Billie, Cassie wouldn't have hesitated to knock, to walk right in and pick up in the middle of a conversation they'd started the day before. Now, she stood in the hall with her hand poised over the buzzer, uncertain for the first time since they'd met.

Suddenly the door opened. Fay Dean, her feet bare and her reading glasses perched on her nose, stepped into the hall and pulled Cassie close.

"Now, get your butt in here." Fay Dean led Cassie into a cozy sitting area with all the lamps burning, the radio playing blues, and legal papers spread all over the coffee table. "I'll make popcorn."

And it was that easy to pick their friendship. No torturous discussions of why they'd disagreed in the first place, who'd been wrong and who was right. Cassie just walked into the kitchen and sat at the table while Fay Dean poured oil into the corn popper, then stood at the stove turning the handle.

"You're out late, Cass."

"I know." She propped her elbows on the table, not yet ready to tell why she'd barreled through the night to Fay Dean's apartment. "What are you working on?"

"Nothing exciting. Just a property settlement." They fell into their old, comfortable silence while the corn popped, then Fay Dean poured it into a huge stoneware bowl and sat beside Cassie. "What have you been up to lately?"

Where do you start when the truth you are about to tell will change your friend's life?

"Promise you won't ask any questions until I've finished," Cassie told her.

"Quit beating around the bush and just talk to me."

"Promise me, Fay Dean."

"Shit." Fay Dean went to the refrigerator, poured two glasses of wine, then sat back down. "I promise."

Cassie told of the awful summer when she and Joe had drifted apart, his love of blues and his trips to Shakerag, the night he and Betty Jewel had come together in Saint's old touring bus, and finally of Billie.

"Joe's child?" Fay Dean pulled out a cigarette, lit it and took two deep draws. "My God, Cassie, what is this shit?"

"It's the truth."

"The truth? Are you trying to tell me, my brother had a child with Betty Jewel Hughes? Good Lord! Joe was not capable of that."

"That's what I thought at first. But Ben confirmed the affair, and Betty Jewel has pictures of her and Joe." Fay Dean stood from her chair and began to pace around the kitchen. "Billie has his cheekbones, his eyes, his talent. She even has his half-moon birthmark on her left thigh.... She's his, Fay Dean."

"Why didn't you tell me earlier, Cass? Me, of all people?"

"I didn't want to hurt you and Mike. I didn't want to hurt anybody."

Cassie fumbled in her purse and pulled out the little school picture Betty Jewel had given her the first time Billie ran away. Fay Dean studied it closely.

"That's Billie," Cassie said.

"My God," Fay Dean said, pressing her fingers over her mouth.

The soft strains of a harmonica echoed through the kitchen, and Cassie wondered if it was merely Fay Dean's radio or Joe sending a message.

"She's exquisite, Cassie."

"She's family, and we could lose her."

"Not while I have breath in my body." Fay Dean sank into the chair beside Cassie, still studying the little photograph in her hand. "I can't believe my brother's child was living so close by all these years and I didn't know."

"I know. It seems impossible, doesn't it?" Cassie took a sip of her wine. "I have to tell Mike, too, but I don't even know how to begin."

"Let me handle Daddy, Cass. He'll be a bear at first, but once he realizes she's Joe's child, he'll come around." Fay Dean set Billie's picture on the table. "My God, just look at her. Don't you think she has the Malone eyes?"

"I think she has your eyes, and I think you're going to love her."

They sat there smiling at each other while the barely touched popcorn cooled and the moon tracked across the sky.

Later, lying in the daybed in Fay Dean's guest room, Cassie said a prayer of thanks that the secret she'd kept for so long had not ripped her sister-in-law apart. She gave thanks for the grace that pours down when you least expect it—and wasn't that just another name for love?

# Thirty

WHEN CASSIE WOKE UP, she found a note from Fay Dean on the bedside table.

*I have to be in court this morning. I can't wait to meet Billie. We'll talk later. Hugs.*

As she drove home to change out of clothes that still reeked of smoke from the juke joint, a sense of urgency clawed through Cassie. She had to get to Betty Jewel before the Saint could.

When she finally got to the little blue house on Maple Street, Queen met her at the door.

"That Saint Hughes devil done called here sayin' he was comin' and wadn't nobody gone stop 'em."

"Oh, my Lord." Cassie followed Queen into the kitchen where Merry Lynn, Sudie and Betty Jewel were seated around the table, looking grim.

"Where's Billie?" Cassie sat down beside Betty Jewel and took her hand.

"When Saint called, I took her back to Lucy's, then grabbed

Sudie," Merry Lynn said. "I'm sorry, Cassie, I told Betty Jewel you went to the club last night to talk some sense into him."

"You ast me," Queen said, "that man ain't got no sense."

"I'd have to agree, Miss Queen," Cassie said. With Saint likely to show up any minute, Merry Lynn and Sudie had to know the truth. Cassie felt as if she might be sick, but still she took the biscuits and gravy Queen was passing around. She knew better than to refuse Queen's cooking. "Betty Jewel, last night I told him the truth. Fay Dean, too."

"The truth? What truth?" Merry Lynn said, confused.

In a voice as quiet as water, Betty Jewel told Merry Lynn and Sudie the secret she and Queen had carried since Billie's birth.

"My Lord, Betty Jewel! Coach Malone's child!" Merry Lynn glanced from Cassie to Betty Jewel, stunned. "How could you keep something like that from Sudie and me?"

"Because of Billie." Sudie spoke with the authority of someone who knew the courage it took to be a mother. "Now hush up, Merry Lynn. If Cassie can handle it, so can we. Besides, it doesn't change one hair on Betty Jewel's head."

"What hair?" Betty Jewel adjusted her scarf, and they all laughed. "Now, let's figure out what to do about the Saint."

"Merry Lynn and Sudie's got them letters you wrote, baby. We gone sen' that pole cat back to Memphis with his stripedy tail 'tween his legs." Queen gathered up the plates and carried them to the sink. "Ya'll go on to the livin' room, an I'll be there direc'ly. I ain't entertainin' no trash in my kitchen."

The women grew solemn as they trooped into the living room, but they were filled with a steely resolution. They settled Betty Jewel onto the couch and formed a protective circle around her. Then they waited.

★ ★ ★

In the sweltering living room a fly buzzed against the window screen, trying to escape the heat, while out on the dusty road Billie never even broke a sweat as she hurried home.

Merry Lynn had snatched her out of there so fast, she hadn't even had time to protest, let alone get Little Ella. She and Lucy were going to play grown-up, and what good was that without her doll? If she sneaked in the back way, she could be in and out so fast she might avoid a lecture from Queen.

The coast was clear in the kitchen and the hall, too. Where was everybody? Cassie's red car was out front, and so was Tiny Jim's. What was he doing here?

As Billie tiptoed toward her bedroom, it wasn't Tiny Jim's voice she heard but the Saint's. Something was cooking in the den, and it was probably her goose. If her mama and Queen found out she'd been at the juke joint last night, she might as well wait for the willow switch.

Flattening herself against the wall, she scooted to the den and peered through the keyhole. The Saint, dressed in a suit that looked brand-new, stood by the mantel ramrod straight.

Sudie was in the rocking chair frowning like she did when Lucy and Billie didn't mind her, and Queen was on the couch with her mouth set like she was fixing to lay down the law. Cassie and Billie's mama sat beside her, and they didn't look happy, either

Merry Lynn pranced around the room like she always did, spitting words like bullets.

"You're not Billie's daddy. You're nothing but a boozing, drug-addicted, skirt-chasing scoundrel."

Saint lowered his head, and Billie wished she could disappear.

"You need to leave town, Saint," Billie's mama said. "We've all told you the truth. You have no legal claim to my child."

"I can't," he said. "I promised Billie."

"Yo promises ain't worth a hill a beans." Queen glared at him. "Sudie, Merry Lynn, read them letters."

"What letters?" Big beads of sweat rolled down Saint's face, and he wiped them with a dingy handkerchief.

"The ones I'll use in court if you try to get Billie," Cassie said.

Merry Lynn opened the pack of letters and started reading. A chill mist swept over Billie. The contents were awful, beyond her worst imaginings.

Listening with a wrecked heart, she pictured her mama waiting at home in the worst winter Chicago ever had in nothing but an old sweater while the Saint got arrested for back-alley brawls, so high on cocaine he never remembered whether he was the one who had first pulled a knife.

It was all there in the letters, every word a sledgehammer that made the Saint sag against the mantel. He was shrinking before Billie's eyes.

Mercifully, Merry Lynn finally stopped reading. Billie wanted to snatch her doll and run back to Lucy's where all she had to think about was hopscotch and jacks and make-believe.

Queen hefted herself off the couch and shook her finger in Saint's face.

"You was a rattlesnake when you brought my baby home, an' you still a ratttlesnake… Inconsiderate, that's what you is. I ain't never wished no harm on no man, but you is pure dee trash and I ain't got no use fo' trash."

"You tell him, Miss Queen," Merry Lynn yelled.

"I tol' Betty Jewel the first time I ever caught her cryin', I said 'Baby, ain't no human bein' meant to live in no such condition.' Ain't nothin' but pigs lives like that."

"Miss Queen, I'm afraid you're getting too upset." Cassie got up to take her arm. "Why don't you sit back down?"

Queen clamped her mouth in a tight line and glared at the Saint like she was fixing to beat the snot out of him. Rile Queen and you couldn't unrile her in a hurry.

Billie wanted desperately to be back at Lucy's playing dolls, but she couldn't move. It was like watching a horror movie where you know the monster is going to jump out from behind a dark door and scare you to death, but you keep watching anyhow.

Sudie opened another pack of letters, and they were horrible, too, like bees buzzing in Billie's head, taking up every bit of the space. They told of her mama eating nothing but oatmeal for two weeks, her mama stranded at a Texaco station in Texas because the Saint was so doped up he went off and left her, her mama finally coming home with nothing but the Saint's bus.

Billie closed her eyes, felt her breath moving in and out, counted the beats of her heart. Her whole life was going up in smoke.

The sound of Sudie's voice mixed with the bees in Billie's head until she felt as if she was about to explode. Through the keyhole, she saw the Saint shriveling.

*I'm destroying him,* was all Billie could think. *I'm reducing him to nothing but a shadow.*

"Stop!" Billie burst through the door screaming. "Please, stop."

Her feet were moving and she was running, but she couldn't feel a thing.

"He's not my daddy! He's not my daddy!"

And then the world went black.

Betty Jewel sat on one side of Billie's bed and Cassie on the other. The only thing holding Betty Jewel together was pure grit. She leaned over her child and ran a wet washcloth over her face.

Queen's and Merry Lynn's and Sudie's voices drifted from the kitchen.

"God done run that skunk off," Queen said.

"God didn't run that skunk off, Miss Queen. It was five women who wouldn't take no for an answer," Merry Lynn told her.

"The way he lit out of here," Sudie added, "I'll bet he won't stop till he's clear out of the country."

Cassie quietly got up and shut the door.

"It must have been awful for her." Cassie leaned over Billie and smoothed back her hair. "I'm so sorry she had to hear all of that. How do you think she knew about Joe?"

"Eavesdropping. It's her specialty." In spite of the circumstances, Betty Jewel smiled. Her child was tough and smart and resourceful. She was going to be all right. "I can't say I'm sorry she knows, Cassie. Now she can get to know her real family."

Billie's eyelids fluttered open. "Where's Saint?"

"He's gone." Wrapping her arms around Billie, Betty Jewel felt the steady beat of her daughter's heart, the wiry strength of childhood. "Oh, honey, what you loved was the idea of Saint, not the real man."

The way Billie sat there, so still, broke Betty Jewel's heart.

"Billie, I love you." Cassie scooted close. "We're going to get through this. Together."

"Honey, maybe I made a mistake all those years ago letting you believe the Saint was your daddy. I don't know. But what I *do* know is that you are surrounded by people who adore you."

"That's right," Cassie said. "You have all your friends in Shakerag and now you have Joe's family, too. A grandfather with a farm full of animals and an aunt who looks an awful lot like you."

Billie regarded them in one of those wise stares Betty Jewel had noticed lately. Was it God's way of showing her a glimpse of the woman her child would one day become? And then she smiled, the most blessed sight Betty Jewel could imagine.

"Does he have a horse?" Billie said.

"Does he have a horse!" Cassie's face was lit up. "He has four, and I'll bet he'll teach you to ride."

Billie considered that awhile, and then Betty Jewel's child, her lovely, resilient child, hugged Cassie and whispered, "I'd like that."

Betty Jewel's heart was full of thanks. *I can leave this world now,* she thought. *I can leave this world and everything will be all right.*

# Thirty-One

Tiny Jim had closed the juke joint for their private party where Billie was supposed to meet her new relatives. The whole place smelled like barbecue and made Billie's mouth water. Merry Lynn had moved back in with Tiny Jim after the Saint left for good, and Lucy was there with her ball and jacks and her jump rope, and everybody was in a smiling mood.

Still, Billie didn't feel much like celebrating. Ever since that awful day with the Saint, her mama had been going downhill. She now looked like a skinny little songbird set to fly out the window and leave them all behind.

*Goin' on to Glory Land,* the preacher had called it last Sunday, but Billie called it scary. Still, she didn't want to make things worse for her mama by acting like a scaredy-cat, so she just went on pretending everything was hunky-dory.

She'd acted hunky-dory yesterday when Cassie had come over. She'd brought over a doll, and it was the prettiest thing Billie had ever seen, blond curls and painted red lips in a porcelain face, a frilly yellow dress that looked like it was made with fairy dust. Billie really loved it and told Cassie so, but she wasn't about to hurt Little Ella's feelings by taking up with another doll just because it had both eyes and a fancy dress.

The minute she was back in her room, she'd shoved that new doll under the bed, snatched up Little Ella and held her tight. Her old doll had been with her through the worst summer of her life, and she wasn't about to replace her with something shiny and new.

Now, she held Little Ella tight, watching the door, waiting for her first look at the the family she'd never known.

"Hey, Billie." Lucy came up beside her. "We could play jacks on the stage while Mama and Merry Lynn set the table."

The stage was strung with red and green lights that made the juke joint look like Christmas year round. Any other day Billie would have jumped at the chance to play there, but today she didn't want to go off and leave her watch post. And she didn't want Lucy to know about her secret family, either. Not yet. She'd told her mama so, and Queen and Cassie, too. For once, she didn't have to argue.

"Ain't nobody's bidness till we make it they bidness," Queen had said, and that was that.

Now Billie told Lucy, "I don't want to play." She felt so bad about saying no, she handed Lucy her doll. "Here, you take Little Ella to the stage. I'll come in a minute."

Lucy skipped off, and the door opened. There stood Cassie with the sun shining in her halo of hair. But all Billie could see was the two people with her, a beautiful dark-haired woman and a tall, older man Billie was pretty sure was her grandfather. He had laugh wrinkles around his eyes and was wearing a cowboy hat that made her think of Roy Rogers.

Billie's mama approached her and said, "Honey, are you ready?"

Billie nodded, then drifted toward the door in her wake, barely aware of the floor under her feet, the Christmas lights shining on Lucy and Little Ella, the smell of Tiny Jim's barbecue.

At the door, Cassie smiled at her, but it didn't do one thing to ease the butterflies in Billie's stomach. "Billie, I want you to meet Fay Dean and Mike, Joe's sister and his father."

The tall man stood back like Billie did when she was sizing up a situation, but Fay Dean just squatted down right by her, bold as you please. Billie found herself staring into green eyes exactly like her own. "Oh, Billie. I'm so happy I could cry."

Billie had had enough of crying, and apparently so had Queen. She rolled forward in the black hat with a gazillion flowers she usually reserved for Sunday.

"Ain't no long faces and cryin' allowed roun' here today. This here is a celebration."

"You must be Miss Queen." The woman who was Billie's aunt, which might turn out to be a good thing but could just as easily go the other way, stood up and reached for Queen's hand. "At last I can thank you for that delicious fried chicken you sent home with Cassie."

"There's more where that come from and plenty a barbecue, too. Tiny Jim done killed a whole hog." Queen motioned to Merry Lynn and Sudie standing over by the table arranging an assortment of pies. "Ya'll git over here and introduce yo'selves so we can git this party started."

Her mama's friends hurried forward, even Tiny Jim and Wayne, and soon everybody was laughing and talking. Everybody except Mike Malone and Lucy, still on the stage with Little Ella, staring wide-eyed.

Billie meandered toward the stage, glancing back over her shoulder every now and then at the tall, quiet man.

"You want to play jacks?" Lucy asked, and Billie squatted beside her and picked up the ball, glad to be let off the hook.

Mike Malone's approach was quiet and easy without being sneaky.

"My son used to play jacks when he was a little boy," he said. "Do you mind if I watch?"

"Okay," Billie said.

Most grown-ups would have started asking nosey questions that were none of their beeswax, but Mike Malone just watched like he was really interested in the game. She liked that about him. For a while all you could hear was the rubber ball hitting the hardwood stage.

"Want some gum?" He pulled two sticks out of his shirt pocket. Juicy Fruit, her favorite.

When Billie said, "Thank you," she grabbed the chance to study him close up. He was as creased and tan as Peanut's baseball glove. There was a pair of reading glasses in his pocket and a stubby pencil, too. From the looks of it, he spent a lot of time outdoors and he liked to be prepared, both big pluses in Billie's book.

Trying to act like her heart wasn't tripping with excitement, she grabbed up the ball and got back to the game.

Mama and all her friends were still chattering and carrying on like it was Christmas, but it was quiet on the stage, just Billie and her best friend and her new living, breathing granddaddy who really did have a horse and might turn out to be better than the King of the Cowboys.

He watched awhile and then said, "My son's name was Joe." He had that faraway sad look in his eyes that made her want to say something nice to make him feel better.

"That's my middle name, but most people just call me Billie."

He thought about it awhile, his head tilted slightly to one side the way Billie did when she had a powerful lot to think about.

"Do you mind if I call you Billie Joe?" Mike Malone smiled right at her, and Billie felt about ten feet tall.

★★★

When they got home from Tiny Jim's party, Billie's mama said, "It's been a good day, hasn't it?"

"Yes, baby, it sho has." Queen sat down at the piano and started playing the familiar notes of "I'll Be Seeing You."

"Come sit by me awhile, Billie."

Her mama patted the couch, and Billie went over and sat down. But Queen's sad song didn't match the day. Billie didn't want to think about her mama being all bones and sounding like every breath she took was a struggle. She wanted to remember how her new granddaddy had made her think of her favorite cowboy hero and how everybody had talked and laughed together.

"Mama, can we go outside on the porch and watch the stars?" If her mama and Queen could climb, she'd have suggested the rooftop patio on the bus where they could all be on top of the world.

Outside, the stars were big as baseballs and so close she could nearly touch them. Billie leaned against her mama, who set the porch swing into motion.

"Mama, when you die will you be turned to a star?"

"I don't know, Billie. I might."

The idea that her mama might be up in the sky shining down on her every night made Billie feel better. She'd bet God would make her mama the brightest star in the sky.

They watched until the entire sky was a blanket of twinkling lights. Finally, the moon tracked behind the trees, and Queen got up from her rocker. She shuffled over and kissed them both on the cheek.

"I'll see my babies in the mornin'," she said.

"Good night, Mama," Betty Jewel called after her. "See you in the morning."

Lulled by the rocking motion of the swing and the stillness of the stars, Billie tried not to drift off.

"Did you like Fay Dean and Mike?" her mama asked.

"He's really a nice man, and I like her, too." Billie didn't want to burst her mama's bubble, but she was going to wait and see about Fay Dean. She was as colorful as Merry Lynn, which could be fun or might turn out to be a big fat headache.

"Oh, honey, I'm glad. It makes me happy to know you'll have so many wonderful women watching after you."

Billie was relieved her mama didn't say *when I'm gone.* She wanted to stay in the swing with her mama forever.

"We'd better get you inside before the sandman comes," Betty Jewel said, noticing Billie starting to nod off.

Billie didn't have the heart to tell her she was too big to believe in the sandman. They went back inside where Queen's snores rattled the windowpanes. Billie put on her blue gown and got into bed with Little Ella.

Sometime in the middle of the night, Billie sat straight up, like somebody'd rung a bell in her ear. The house was quiet, not a sound. Billie glided down the hall, something pulling her toward her mama's room.

She was lying on her side, and Billie could hear the sound of her breathing from the door.

"Mama?" Billie waited for the answer, and when it didn't come, she went over to the bed and slid under the covers. "Mama, it's me."

At first Billie thought her mama didn't hear, but slowly she rolled over, reached for her hand. "Honey, what're you doing up?"

"I couldn't sleep. Can I sleep with you?"

"Of course."

Billie climbed in and tried to get comfortable, but there wasn't much left of her mama, just sharp angles and bony hands. "Mama?" Her breathing took up all the space in the room. Billie could suffocate in here. "When you found out about me, did you want me?"

"Oh, Billie…" Her mama struggled to hug her. Billie lifted herself off the mattress, then settled back against her mama's shoulder.

"I wanted you more than anything in the world. I love you, baby. I've always loved you."

"Mama, I don't want you to leave me."

"I don't want to leave you, either, baby."

The moon laid a silvery path along the covers, and Billie wondered if they had a moon in heaven, if she might look up some night and see her mama sitting on a heavenly front porch watching the same moon shine. She scooted closer to her mama, feeling very small.

"Where will you go?"

"I will always be right here, Billie." Her hand settled over Billie's heart.

Something inside Billie settled down. She watched the moon for a while, then closed her eyes.

When she opened them again, it was the sun she saw, sending a pale pink light over the windowsill. Billie didn't want to wake her mama up. She tried to inch away but something was holding her back, her mama's hand still across her heart. She lifted the hand that always touched her with the softness of butterfly wings, but it was stiff and cold, so cold Billie felt her panic rising.

"Mama?"

Billie jerked upright, still calling her mama's name, but all she saw was an empty shell. All she heard was silence. Billie filled it up with screams.

★★★

Cassie's phone woke her up. As she reached for the receiver, the deafening sound of Queen's sobbing filled the room.

Sometimes something as simple as a phone call can snap you like a twig, break you into sharp halves so that you can't even feel your own heartbeat. Cassie searched the room, looking for something, *anything* to let her know she was still alive.

Her eyes fell on the clock. Five o'clock on a Tuesday morning. The exact moment her life changed.

And Billie's. Billie, who needed her, who was now in her keeping.

"You just hang on, Miss Queen. I'm coming."

How Cassie got dressed and into her car, she'd never know. Maybe Queen had sent angels to give her strength.

It was too early for the maids. What Cassie encountered at half past dawn in Shakerag were men of all sizes, burly and big, bony and shrunken, young and old, heads down, walking toward their jobs, unaware that Shakerag had lost its brightest star.

*I'm counting on you, Cassie.*

She could almost hear Betty Jewel's voice. Cassie swiped at her face, bucked up her courage. Finally the little blue house on Maple Street came into view.

"Miss Queen?" Cassie pounded on the door.

Queen came to the door in a worn yellow chenille robe, her hair wrapped around pink foam curlers, her face ravaged with tears.

"Oh, honey..." Queen reached for Cassie and they stood in the doorway with arms wrapped around each other, rocking.

"I'm so sorry. I'm so sorry."

"She died real quietlike in her sleep. It would'a been a blessin' if Billie hadn't a been in there with her."

"Dear God…" Stepping back, Cassie rummaged for tissues in her purse and handed one to Queen.

"She said she ain't never comin' out." Queen honked her nose. "And when that chile make up her mine, ain't no use tryin' to change it."

The hallway was quiet, a sacred peace that reminded Cassie of what it felt like after Joe had died, as if the whole world had stopped to take a deep breath.

Cassie tapped on Betty Jewel's door. "Billie? It's Cassie."

"Go away," Billie called from inside the room.

"Let me in, honey." Cassie rattled the knob.

"Billie done locked it and they ain't no key 'cept inside."

Cassie imagined the child's terror, waking up to find her mother dead, her world falling apart, not knowing which way to turn.

Cassie turned back to Queen. "Do you have a hairpin?" she asked, and Queen shuffled off to fetch one. On her knees in front of Betty Jewel's bedroom door, Cassie thought of the time she'd accidentally locked herself out of the house and Joe had come home to find her trying to squeeze through the tiny laundry room window. *I'm going to teach you to pick locks,* he'd said.

Was he on some great cosmic plain now, watching her try to get to his daughter? Was Betty Jewel standing beside him?

Queen handed her the pin, and after a moment she felt the lock give and the door open. It took a while for Cassie's eyes to adjust to the dimness. The curtains were closed and Billie was kneeling beside the bed, clutching a hand gone slack. The room smelled of death and grief.

Holding in her own grief for the child's sake, Cassie knelt beside Billie, slid an arm around her waist. Death had wiped the pain from Betty Jewel's face, made her beautiful again, given her the look of a woman keeping a truth so amazing that the mere telling would change you forever.

"Goodbye, my dear friend," Cassie whispered.

Even if she could have thought of something wise and wonderful to say, words were inadequate. All she could think of was a line from an old blues song Joe used to play: *Gotta walk this road all by myself. Gotta walk this road, me and nobody else.* Cassie could hear the haunting riffs of a blues harp, feel Joe's presence hovering in the room, just out of view.

"She knew the name of every wildflower in the woods." Billie's soft voice bloomed like a winter bulb shooting up toward the sun.

"I don't know how to bury my mama."

A silence full of hurt sucked all the air out of the room.

"I do. Sudie does, too. Your mother told us exactly what to do." Billie's shoulders felt too narrow to carry this burden. "We're going to get through this together.... Okay?"

"Okay," Billie whispered, and she started to cry. A small river of sorrow poured into Cassie's waiting arms.

Cassie thought she murmured words of comfort, *There, there now, precious. I'm here, we're all here...*but she couldn't be sure. Betty Jewel filled her heart. She was close, but already growing cold, gone to a better place. Cassie hoped her friend, so dear, so unexpected, was now in a beautiful, green place, not unlike their picnic spot by the river. Cassie hoped she was running barefoot in deep, cool grass, arms wide open, laughing.

When Billie had cried herself out, Cassie led her to Miss Queen, waiting in the hall, fully dressed and holding two glasses filled to the brim with a dark liquid she could guess by the smell.

"For medismal purposes," she said with a sympathetic smile.

Cassie lifted her glass. "For one of the best women I've ever known. My friend, Betty Jewel."

"To my baby," Queen said.

They clinked glasses, then waited in the deep stillness of the house, sipping their drinks and trying to take it all in.

"Miss Queen, I need to spend some time alone with her."

"You go right ahead, honey lam. Me an' Billie's gone go into the kitchen an' make some biscuits."

After they vanished into the kitchen, Cassie eased back into Betty Jewel's bedroom and shut the door.

"I won't let you down, Betty Jewel," Cassie said, and suddenly she could feel her friend in the room with her, so real she almost expected to see her rise up from the bed, her pink scarf tied elegantly around her hair.

"I promise."

Cassie sat beside Betty Jewel awhile, holding her cold hand, wishing she were made of steel instead of bone and sinew and blood, every ounce of it calling out for the friend she'd lost.

Cassie held on awhile longer, her heartache translated into prayer. "God, watch over my dear friend. Over us all."

Finally she wiped her eyes and gently tucked the sheet around Betty Jewel's chin. Their goodbyes had been said by the river.

In the den, she settled on the couch to finish the drink Queen had concocted. By the time the glass was empty, Cassie was thinking all drinks should be called medicinal.

The screen door opened, and footsteps came down the hall. Without a word, Merry Lynn and Sudie linked arms with Cassie, and they all started to cry, a circle of three now, mourning the one who had been taken away.

"There'll be things to take care of," Sudie said, and as hard as it was to think about, Cassie knew she was right.

"Sudie," she said, "are you wearing red to the funeral?"

"I'm doing everything Betty Jewel wanted, including pitching a party after it's all over."

"Count me in," Merry Lynn said.

"Me, too," Cassie said. "And if anybody tries to stop me, I can't be responsible for what I do." She stood up, the effect of grief and Jack Daniel's making her lean on Sudie and Merry Lynn. "Come. Betty Jewel is in the bedroom. I think she'd like it if all of us went in together to tell her goodbye."

When they tiptoed into the darkened room and gathered around Betty Jewel's bed, Cassie could swear she saw her friend smile.

# Thirty-Two

None of this was real. Billie felt like she'd been split in a million pieces and put back together with baling wire and chewing gum.

Mt. Zion was an old brick building built in 1890, with a set of double steps that led to the front door on both sides.

The church had blue walls, pale blue like a summer sky. It had eight ceiling fans and a pulpit big as Noah's ark, and behind that was a mural of the last supper.

Billie wondered why the disciples were all looking so pleasant if they knew what was going to happen next. The pianist was Buford Watson, who was even bigger than his cousin Tiny Jim. Spread all over the piano stool like dark sorghum molasses, he was making the ivories talk, hitting big blues licks in "The Solid Rock" and "Amazing Grace" and "Thank you, Lord," while the choir hummed and swayed and sang in such close harmony Billie thought the angels must be bending down to listen.

She hoped her mama could hear. She hoped she was bending down, too.

The choir started singing, "I'll Meet You in the Morning." If it was left up to Queen, that's the way it would be.

She had a radiant look like she was seeing right through the Pearly Gates.

Merry Lynn was the one carrying on, acting just the way Billie felt, sobbing and moaning and swooning so hard it took four church ladies to tend to her, two to hold her up and two to wield the fans. They were dressed like nurses, all in white, wearing little name tags that said Mabel and Earshalene and Juanita and Glennell. Up front in their black robes, Brother Gibson and five visiting preachers sat in carved chairs as big as thrones. Billie felt like she was in the middle of a Beale Street show instead of her mama's funeral. She sat quietlike, not doing anything that would embarrass Queen or even her mama, in case she was looking down from heaven.

Billie stole a glance at Cassie, sitting on the other side of Queen, wearing a dress with shoes that matched and sporting little white gloves with a bunch of bangle bracelets on the top.

Billie felt empty and dusty as the Sahara, not a drop of water anywhere. She'd used up her tears the day her mama died.

Queen's arm slid around her, and Billie leaned into the comfort of a soft lap and the smell of lilac talcum powder. If she looked at her mama up front in the fancy casket with pink roses on the side and a pink silk lining, she'd start crying, so she looked all around. The church was packed. Mama had lots of friends.

Billie tried to keep her mind off the fact that her mother was gone. Queen said she was still there in spirit. Only this morning she'd told Billie, "My baby's up in Heaven right now, chile, sportin' angel wings an' watchin' from on high, lovin' us still."

Now, Billie put her hand over her heart, feeling her mother's love so strong it was like she was sitting there beside her. Up in the choir loft, Sudie was singing first soprano in a voice that could be heard clear to the courthouse. She had a strong voice Queen always said could wake the dead.

Billie wished she could wake her mama up. Even if it was only for a little while. First she'd tell her it was all right about Saint Hughes not being there to watch Billie grow up, that the daddy she'd invented had been as real to her as the one she'd found in Memphis. Then she'd tell her mama that she was the best mama in the world, and Billie was glad she was Joe Malone's child because that gave her Cassie.

When the music stopped, there was a hush so perfect Billie could hear angels' wings.

"Yea, though I walk through the valley of the shadow of death, I shall fear no evil," one of the visiting preachers bellowed. As he read the twenty-third psalm, Billie saw her mama walking beside still waters, her new white wings so wide they covered her when she lay down in green pastures.

Her mama wouldn't have to be scared of anything anymore.

Merry Lynn was wailing again. Loudly. Billie pressed her cheek closer to Queen to shut out the awful sound. Mama thought funerals were supposed to be celebrations and Queen did, too. She was wearing a bright yellow dress with poppies all over it and a brand-new red hat with so many flowers on top Billie wondered how Queen could hold her head up under the weight. Queen could lift the world if she took a notion.

When the visiting preacher sat down, Brother Gibson stood up, and his shout took up all the space in the church. There wasn't room for anything else, not even Billie's fear.

"I'm gonna preach it to you today, children. Betty Jewel's on that gospel train headin' to Heaven." From all over the church came the response. "Mmm-hmm… You tell it, brother. Preach it." Billie fell under the spell of worship, so like the cadence of the blues it felt like being rocked in a cradle.

As long as she was sitting in church, swaying under a spell

of Jesus blues, Billie didn't have to think about the future. She didn't have to think about anything.

Ceiling fans and church fans depicting Jesus praying on the Mount of Olives stirred up a small breeze, but they were no match for the August heat inside a church without air-conditioning.

Except for the heat, the packed church reminded Cassie of Joe's funeral, standing room only. Betty Jewel, the once famous singer and wife of legendary Saint Hughes, was as iconic in Shakerag as Joe had been in Tupelo. While the rhetoric of six preachers carried her through the Pearly Gates, Cassie thought of two stars colliding, Betty Jewel and Joe. She thought of their untimely deaths and the void both had left in her heart. She even imagined them meeting on the other side to comfort each other.

As Brother Gibson said the last *Amen,* Cassie whispered, "Go with God, my friend."

She wrapped her arm around Billie and followed the casket to the recorded sounds of Saint Hughes wailing "When the Saints Go Marching In" on his silver trumpet. It was the first time that day she'd seen Billie show any emotion.

But even now, her tears were silent.

Joe had been like that, self-contained and private with a dignity that demanded respect. She guessed he'd saved all his hurt for the harmonica. The only time she'd ever seen him cry was when he'd played the blues.

Near the back of the church, Fay Dean, Mike and Ben joined the long line of mourners making their way to the gravesite.

When they entered the colored cemetery, Cassie thought about Joe's tombstone over at Glenwood, everything carved in marble as permanent as death. Though there was a tent erected over Betty Jewel's open grave and the sun was sinking in a spectacular show of gold and red, it was still so hot Cassie could hardly breathe. The temperature had to be hovering near ninety-five. Add the humidity, and it felt like a 110. Two church ladies fanned Miss Queen while another held an umbrella over her head.

It seemed like only yesterday she and Betty Jewel had been laughing together on the riverbank.

In the stillness, a hummingbird darted toward the flowers beside the fresh grave, its wings stirring the air like a blues riff.

*Joe,* Cassie thought. Or was it Betty Jewel, free at last to fly?

Fay Dean laced hands with her, and Cassie felt as if a cool breeze had stirred across her cheek, though the boughs of the cedar tree were as still as Betty Jewel's grave.

With the soaring prayers of six preachers carrying her on home, Betty Jewel was finally laid to rest. The church ladies led Billie and Miss Queen away, with Merry Lynn and Sudie right behind. Sudie separated herself and walked over to where Mike had joined Cassie and Fay Dean.

"Ya'll are coming back to Queen's, aren't you?" Sudie said.

"Ben had to leave, but I'll be there in a little while." Cassie glanced at her in-laws. "Are you coming?"

"Daddy and I wouldn't be anywhere else, Cass. We'll follow you."

They headed out, but Cassie stood awhile longer, watching the pattern of sun and shadow on the grave. *Betty Jewel would like that,* she thought. Sadness coursed through her, but Cassie refused to let grief strip her of strength. Back in Shakerag, Betty Jewel's mourners would be gathering. Queen would be looking for her and Billie.

As she turned to leave she was surprised to see Saint Hughes, hovering in the shadow of a low-hanging cedar tree.

They stared for a moment, then he put on his sunglasses, gave a little nod and walked off.

Cassie had to get the starch back in her legs before she could climb into her car and pull off her gloves. Then she sat awhile, breathing in relief, before she headed to the little blue house, Fay Dean and Mike following

Queen was on the front porch swing, still wearing her hat, a yellow plastic glass in her hand and her friends crowded around her on the porch. When they saw Cassie and her in-laws, they grew quiet.

Queen rose from her chair, as majestic as she was determined.

"This here is Cassie Malone an' her fam'ly. Cassie was a good frien' to Betty Jewel an' a good frien' to me. Y'all make them welcome, now."

Sudie was the first to emerge from the crowd and introduce them to the mourners on the porch. Slowly the atmosphere relaxed.

Queen's guests murmured pleasant greetings and Cassie moved among Betty Jewel's neighbors with a grateful heart. Tiny Jim took Mike under his wing, and Fay Dean joined Queen on the porch swing. Those two would be a pair.

"I bet you didn't eat a thing today." Sudie took Cassie's arm "Come on. There's enough food in the kitchen for Noah's Ark." Merry Lynn joined them, holding on to her iced tea and crying. "Buck up, Merry Lynn. Betty Jewel wanted a party."

"Y'all are going to have to buck me up, then, because I can't do it by myself."

"That's what we're here for," Cassie said, and the three of them sat down at the table. Overflowing with stories of Betty Jewel, they began to reminisce.

Lucy wafted through the kitchen, eyeing a blackberry cobbler, and Cassie scanned the room for Billie.

"Lucy?" She knelt by the child. "Where's Billie?"

"On top of that ole bus. I'm scared to play up there in the dark."

Cassie raced through the back door, relieved to see the tiny figure on top of the bus. She kicked off her high heels, hiked up her skirt, and made her clumsy, unladylike way up the old ladder.

Billie giggled, and it was the sweetest sound Cassie had ever heard.

"Looks like you're going to have to teach me how to climb."

"Didn't you ever climb trees?"

"Not in about a million years." As Cassie got herself into a sitting position, she spotted Billie's old doll. It was probably a comfort to her. Something her mama had given her.

A star popped out, the first of the evening. *Betty Jewel, watching over Billie,* Cassie thought. She slid her arms around Billie, and they both lifted their faces to the sky.

"Cassie, Queen says Mama's in Glory Land." The child's voice was a small, broken thing. "I wish she was that star."

"Oh, honey," Cassie said, leaning her cheek against Billie's soft hair. "I think that star is your mama, looking down to say she loves you, to say she loves us all."

# Thirty-Three

TODAY WAS THE DAY Billie officially became somebody else's child. She thought she'd wake up feeling different, changed somehow. But all she felt was the scary kind of excitement you got when you were at the top of the Ferris wheel, wondering if you were going to land safely.

Billie pulled her fancy porcelain-faced doll out from under her bed in gratitude to Cassie. She'd named her Mamie on account of the satin dress. Only uppity-ups wore satin. Fortunately, Little Ella didn't get her feelings hurt, especially when Mamie let her try on that pretty satin dress.

A commotion drew Billie into the hall to see Merry Lynn and Sudie and Lucy coming through the front door.

"You go on and play awhile," Sudie said, and Lucy skipped toward Billie.

"Can I play with your new doll?" Lucy asked.

Billie handed Mamie to her, and they skipped outside and climbed to the top of the bus.

"Billie, how come Mama made me wear a dress today?"

Billie put down Little Ella and smoothed her dress.

"Lucy, if I tell you a secret, will you promise not to tell?"

"Cross my heart." Lucy ran her finger across her chest.

"My daddy was a white man and Cassie's going to be my new mama." Billie paused, but Lucy didn't say a single word, which was not like her. "Do you still want to play with me?"

"Even if you have to move, Billie, you'll still be my best friend forever."

Billie smiled with relief.

"I don't have to move," she finally told her, but Lucy wasn't convinced. She wasn't strong like Billie. She needed some bucking up. "You can have Mamie."

"For keeps?" Lucy hugged the doll so hard Billie thought she might crack its head off.

"For keeps," Billie told her. "Just don't let Peanut get a hold of her and shave her head."

"If he comes near her I'll knock the snot out of 'em." Lucy smoothed Mamie's dress, happy-looking till her tears started spilling over. "Billie?"

"What?"

"If you leave, who will I talk to?"

"I told you," Billy said, trying to be patient, something Queen called a virtue and said Billie needed plenty of. "I'm not leaving. I got two homes now. One with a new pink room. You can come visit."

"Promise?"

"Pinkie promise."

They linked fingers, and Billie looked up to see the sun shining through the oak trees. She reckoned it was God's smile. Queen said it was.

"Billie," Queen hollered. "You an Lucy git down off that ole bus. Cassie's here."

"Coming," she said, then started climbing down to her brand-new life.

★★★

Outside, the house had the same faded blue paint that made it look worn out, but inside it had a holiday feel, bursting with excitement and people.

Standing in the midst of the crowd, Cassie felt gratitude so deep it brought her to tears. Queen was there, wearing her hair in a coronet of braids and a dress with a lacy collar. Merry Lynn and Sudie were both wearing the red dresses Betty Jewel had wanted for the funeral she'd called her going-away party.

Behind them was Billie, hanging on to Lucy with one hand and her little doll with the other. Billie's dress was disheveled and her doll looked as if it need resuscitation, but Cassie thought she'd never seen a more beautiful sight.

The child of her heart.

Cassie squatted beside her and looked into eyes so like Joe's. "Are you ready, Billie?" She nodded, and Cassie took the little rose-gold locket out of her pocket. "Your mother wanted you to have this. It was very special to her. She told me once that anytime she felt scared or lonely, she held this little locket and it gave her hope."

"It's so pretty." Billie ran her hands over the rose-gold heart, loss and dreams and hope all reflected in her wistful face.

"Look." Cassie opened the locket where she and Betty Jewel smiled up at Billie from the photos, their hearts shining right from their eyes. "I know I'll never be the same as your mama, Billie. But I promise you I'll always love you with all my heart."

"Can I wear it today?"

"Oh, honey, nothing would please me more," Cassie said, hugging Billie. When she fastened the locket around her neck, she heard a blues riff and laughter as clear as tinkling of silver bells. Was it Joe and Betty Jewel, smiling down on their child?

"This is going to be a very special day," she told Billie.

"It sho is." Queen began to bustle about, herding them all into cars. "God done smiled on us today."

Fay Dean and Mike were waiting for them at the courthouse, looking almost as excited as Cassie felt. Ben was there, too, a dear friend whose approval of her plan had been hard won. In the end, though, his loyalty to Joe and Cassie never wavered. They all crowded into the judge's chambers for the brief ceremony, and then cheered when the judge announced that Billie was now officially Cassie's daughter.

*Her daughter.*

She signed the papers with a flourish. It was that simple, that miraculous.

When she first saw the little newspaper ad that led her to Betty Jewel, she'd never have believed she was heading toward the beginning of a remarkable friendship that would have an even more amazing ending. Cassie thought about the journey she'd made, the audacity, the heartbreak, the bravery—all for love of Billie.

Sometimes life can surprise you in ways you least expect.

# Epilogue

THAT SUMMER DAY IN Shakerag when Billie had run all the way home with Alice's ghost breathing down her neck, she'd have double-dog dared you to tell her that she'd have a pink canopied bed in her own room in Highland Circle by fall. She'd have beat the snot out of you and called you a liar.

Now, here she was with Lucy, sitting cross-legged under the frilly canopy in a room a gazillion times bigger than her bedroom in the little blue house on Maple Street, talking about their new fifth-grade teacher and cutting out paper dolls from the Sears and Roebuck catalogue. Just an ordinary day. Two best friends playing together after school like they always did.

Laughter and mouth-watering smells drifted up from the kitchen. Cassie and Queen were downstairs cooking up a storm, with a whole lot of bossing around from Sudie and Merry Lynn and Aunt Fay Dean, it sounded like.

"What's going on down there?" Lucy asked.

"Nothing special. They're always like that."

There was lots of laughter in Billie's house in Highland Circle, and not a single willow switch in sight. She reckoned Queen liked it, too. She stayed in her pretty blue room here as much as she did in her house in Shakerag. She had plenty of blue pillows and a big fat recliner that she said helped her rheumatiz.

Queen had even been with Billie and Cassie to Mike's farm, which had lots of stables. If Cassie would let her have a horse, she'd name him Trigger. She'd asked, but Cassie had just said, "We'll see."

Mike had winked at Billie behind Cassie's back, which probably meant she'd have her own horse by Christmas. He talked a lot about Billie's real daddy and said she should call him Granddaddy. Maybe she would someday. She liked the idea of having a granddaddy.

Things had changed a lot since that day at the courthouse. Billie still got her best information from listening at keyholes, but she reckoned Cassie had caught on. Now she was careful about what she said behind closed doors. Still, if Billie had to have a mama besides her own, she was glad it was Cassie, who would just as soon be in the little blue house with Queen teaching her how to make biscuits as downstairs in her own kitchen.

Billie and Cassie sat on the second-floor balcony a lot, and she talked about anything Billie wanted to. She liked to talk about Billie's real mama and her real daddy, but in spite of everything, Saint was still the daddy of Billie's heart. Someday that might change. She really hoped it did because it would make Cassie so happy.

Billie heard footsteps on the stairs, and it was Cassie, smiling as she walked into the room and asked if they wanted tea and cookies. Was she kidding? Little girls and cookies go together like gravy and biscuits.

They followed Cassie to the balcony. She didn't serve her tea in a Mason jar with ice, which Billie personally preferred, but she always had plenty of homemade cookies. Sometimes she served little sandwiches she let Billie cut into hearts.

But the best part was that they were all there gathered around the table laughing and talking—Queen and Aunt Fay Dean and Sudie and Merry Lynn. When Cassie joined them, the circle was complete, all the women who were Billie's true home. It felt like being on top of the world.

Billie hoped her mama and Joe were bending down to listen. She hoped they were smiling.

★★★★★

# Acknowledgments

THIS BOOK WOULD NOT have been possible without my amazing agent, Stephanie Kip Rostan at Levine Greenberg, and my remarkable editor, Erika Imranyi at Harlequin MIRA. Stephanie encouraged me to finish a story I had started more than ten years earlier, and Erika loved it enough to give it a good home. They guided me throughout the process, and I am forever grateful for their generosity and support.

The journey of my characters in this story is entirely fictional, but I would like to acknowledge the nonfiction books that gave me a better understanding of the obstacles they faced: *Black Like Me,* John Howard Griffin; *Simeon's Story: An Eyewitness Account of the Kidnapping of Emmett Till,* Simeon Wright with Herb Boyd; *Free at Last: A History of the Civil Rights Movement and Those Who Died In The Struggle,* Sara Bullard; *Civil Rights: Yesterday and Today,* Herb Boyd, Todd Burroughs; *I Have A Dream: Writings & Speeches That Changed The World,* edited by James M. Washington.

My deepest gratitude also goes to The Honorable Judge Jacqueline Estes and David Sparks, Attorney at Law, for invaluable advice about adoption and for research into the amended law of 1955 that made Billie's adoption possible.

To Jane Talbert, dear friend and former colleague at Mississippi State Univerisy, hugs and a steak dinner for helping me recall the rules that match the writing constructions.

Kudos to my research assistant, the incredible Susan E. Griffith.

The Deep South with its riches of music and food, and eccentric, outrageous, courageous people shaped this story as surely as it shaped me. I have an abiding love for my home, and I hope that shines through.

Thank you for reading. I hope you will laugh and cry at my quirky, redemption-infused story, and I promise to write more of the same.

1. Discuss how the themes of sin and redemption play out in the lives of Betty Jewel and Cassie. In what ways does Cassie save Betty Jewel and vice versa?

2. What do you think of Cassie's decision to adopt Billie? Is it dangerous? Selfless? What does it say about Cassie's character, about her friendship with Betty Jewel, and about her marriage to Joe? Would you have made the same choice? Why or why not?

3. Discuss the role of family in the book. In what ways does familial responsibility drive the actions of the characters? Do you agree or disagree with the line "Family is family no matter what"? Why or why not?

4. *The Sweetest Hallelujah* features a cast of strong female characters: Betty Jewel, Cassie, Billie, Queen, Fay Dean, Sudie and Merry Lynn. Discuss each of

their roles in the story and how they drive the narrative forward. Which of the characters do you relate to the most and why? Do you have a favorite?

5. The novel is told in alternating perspectives between Cassie, Betty Jewel and Billie. How does this affect how you read/understand the book? What are the advantages and disadvantages of multi-perspective storytelling?

6. History plays a particularly important role in *The Sweetest Hallelujah*. In what ways does the setting and period (Mississippi in the summer of 1955) impact the story? How would the story have been different if it had been set in the present?

7. Discuss Billie's journey in the story and her relationship to Betty Jewel, Queen, Saint, Cassie and Mike Malone. How does each of these characters impact Billie's life? How do you think her life will play out after the last page of the book has been turned?

8. Discuss the role of Dead Alice in the story. What does her presence signify, and how does it change throughout the book?

9. Betty Jewel, the Saint and Joe are all musicians. There are song lyrics referenced throughout the book, and the gentle sound of the blues is present at every turn. Discuss the significance of blues and music in the story?

*The Sweetest Hallelujah* is a beautiful novel of friendship set during a difficult period in American history. What was your inspiration for the story and characters in the book?

*More than ten years ago I read a news story that captured my imagination—a bedridden African-American woman in a section of my hometown known historically as Shakerag was looking for someone to take her daughter to the mall and the movies. I began to extrapolate. What if she were dying? What if she had no one to take her daughter? What if her only hope was a woman she had every reason to hate?*

Why did you set this story during the Civil Rights era in the South? What drew you to this period and setting? What kind of research did you do, and what were the challenges you faced writing a historical novel?

*When I set the story in 1955, the stakes became very high. My characters were suddenly thrust into a climate that made crossing color lines not only dangerous but almost impossible. With the murder of Emmett Till that summer and other equally terrible events, Mississippi was known as the lynching state. I did enormous amounts of research, which included reading numerous books (listed in the Acknowledgments). My biggest challenge was to tell the brutal truth and still convey the deep love I have for my native South and its people.*

As a white woman, did you find it challenging to write about the African-American experience? What sort of research did you do to ensure the authenticity of the characters and life in 1950s Mississippi?

*When I write, I vanish completely and inhabit the hearts of my characters, no matter the color. One of the most important women in my childhood was Lynn, the dear African-American woman who worked for my mother. I have a musician's ear, and can still hear her voice as she shelled peas in the kitchen and told stories in rich, honeyed tones. After I started writing this story, I spent lots of time in African-American churches, soaking up the music and the blues cadences of the sermons. I also witnessed the amazing pageantry, heartbreak and hope of a funeral of a black friend. I hope my characters and my scenes ring true and sure.*

When you started the book, did you have Betty Jewel and Cassie's journey already mapped out? How did they surprise you along the way? Were there any interesting surprises from other characters?

*I knew the bare bones of the story, but I always love to see where my characters will take me. Betty Jewel not only surprised me, but also educated me: Facing death strips you of all pretense. I expected Cassie's compassion, but totally underestimated her capacity to love. Of all the characters, Sudie surprised me most.*

*She was simply a background character until she blew onto the page. I simply fell in love with her sass and surety. What can I say about Billie and Queen except that I want to grab them off the pages, sit on my front porch swing and listen to them talk?*

What was the greatest challenge of writing *The Sweetest Hallelujah*? Your greatest pleasure?

*With a story of this scope, written in multiple points of view, the greatest challenge was in knowing which scenes to keep and which to cut. Still, cutting scenes was excruciatingly painful. I wanted Queen to hand me a glass of Jack Daniels for "medismal purposes." My greatest pleasure was in watching the characters and the story come alive. I almost felt like a spectator in a movie theater.*

You like to describe yourself as "Southern to the bone," and your passion for the South comes through on the page. What are some of your favorite things about the South, and why do you think it makes such a rich backdrop for fiction?

*Here's what I like about the South: Blues, fried chicken, barbecue, front porch swings, courageous women, emphasis on family, iced tea on hot summer days, Sunday mornings singing gospel in the church choir, the slow sweet cadences of the language, and the great love of storytelling. And that's just the start. I love Southern ostentation, too, big gaudy jewelry and pink lipstick and high-heeled shoes—nothing sensible, just over-the-top fun.*

*With a history that is both tragic and noble, the Deep South has endless stories to tell. It has been romanticized and demonized in books and movies and song. I wanted to strip away the extremes and present my home with honesty and love.*

Can you describe your writing process? Do you outline first or dive right in? Do you write scenes consecutively or jump around? Do you have a writing schedule or routine? A lucky charm?

*I am a disciplined writer with an office and a writing schedule. My stories begin with character sketches and a loose idea of the plot then progress sequentially. I never make outlines, but work from a synopsis that runs about ten pages long and leaves plenty of room for invention. My routine starts with opening the curtains so I can watch the birds in my gardens while I write. I always have a cup of hot green chai tea on my desk, a CD of Native American flutes on the player, and my two dogs on the rug at my feet. I don't have a lucky charm, but I surround myself with whimsy—a blue dragon in a musical water globe that plays the theme from "Camelot," a smudging bowl given to me by a Mohawk friend, a blue dolphin lamp, a tin box for stamps that features Marilyn Monroe's photo and quote: "I just want to be wonderful."*

Can you tell us about your next novel?

*I can tell you what I know. The story is set in 1969, the summer Neil Armstrong landed on the moon and Hurricane Camille blew away the Mississippi Gulf Coast. Against that backdrop of enormous hope and impending doom, Sis Blake and a cast of feisty, formidable women discover just how far they will go to save one of their own.*